MISS PRIM AND THE MAVERICK MILLIONAIRE

BY

NINA SINGH

All rights reserved including the right of reproduction in whole or in part in any form. This edition is published by arrangement with Harlequin Books S.A.

This is a work of fiction. Names, characters, places, locations and incidents are purely fictional and bear no relationship to any real life individuals, living or dead, or to any actual places, business establishments, locations, events or incidents. Any resemblance is entirely coincidental.

This book is sold subject to the condition that it shall not, by way of trade or otherwise, be lent, resold, hired out or otherwise circulated without the prior consent of the publisher in any form of binding or cover other than that in which it is published and without a similar condition including this condition being imposed on the subsequent purchaser.

® and ™ are trademarks owned and used by the trademark owner and/or its licensee. Trademarks marked with ® are registered with the United Kingdom Patent Office and/or the Office for Harmonisation in the Internal Market and in other countries.

First Published in Great Britain 2017
By Mills & Boon, an imprint of HarperCollins*Publishers*
1 London Bridge Street, London, SE1 9GF

© 2017 Nilay Nina Singh

ISBN: 978-0-263-92290-5

23-0417

Our polic
products a ... nd
manufactu ... of
the countr

Printed ar
by CPI, B

LANCASHIRE COUNTY LIBRARY	
3011813458360 2	
Askews & Holts	30-Mar-2017
AF ROM	£5.99
NAN	

Nina Singh lives outside of Boston with her husband, children and a very rambunctious Yorkie. After several years in the corporate world, she finally followed the advice of family and friends to "give the writing a go already." She's oh so happy she did. When not at her keyboard, she likes to spend time on the tennis court or golf course. Or immersed in a good read.

This is Nina Singh's first book.

For my wonderful husband and children.
Thank you for all the patience, faith and support.
Not to mention the many very-needed nudges.
And for the best group of fellow writer friends
I could have ever hoped for.

CHAPTER ONE

THIS DEFINITELY WASN'T in her job description.

Jenna Townsend glanced at her watch, not actually noting the time. Then glanced at it again. A car should be picking him up from the airport right at this moment. Which meant he would be here at her office within the hour. She took a too-large swig of coffee and gasped as it burned her tongue and throat. Why was she so nervous? Babysitting the CEO of Jordan's Fine Jewelry for the next several days shouldn't warrant this much anxiety.

Cabe Jordan, CEO extraordinaire, was on his way back to Boston. The man who'd taken the small business his parents started in the historic North End and made it one of the most profitable national corporations of the last decade.

Hard to believe they'd grown up together in the same small town just outside Boston. Two years ahead of her in school, Cabe had been her older brother's bane of existence, besting Sam at everything. Her brother had not been happy when she'd taken the position of regional manager and started working for his nemesis. But opportunities like this weren't ones to be passed up, not for someone like her.

The job had been everything she could have hoped for and more. Until the email in her inbox the other day "requesting" her assistance in escorting Mr. Jordan as he revisited the flagship Boston site. For some reason, he'd specifically requested that she be his local liaison on this trip. Jenna shook her head.

Why did he need one anyway?

She'd felt like she'd been sent to the principal's office, unable to shake the feeling that he was really here to check up on *her*. Had she done something wrong? Let something crucial slip through the cracks? Or had he woken up one day and realized he'd hired a small-town hick with no real-world experience. Maybe he was looking to replace her with some hotshot MBA from a real business school and he wanted to tell her in person. Maybe Sam had been right all these years and Cabe Jordan really was an elitist who had always looked down his nose at people like her.

Heavens, she had to get a grip. And try to stay positive. There could very well be a good reason for Cabe's visit. Hadn't she just come across an internal email regarding an opening in upper-level management? Perhaps he was here to tell her she was being promoted. It was possible. After all, her numbers spoke for themselves.

Did she dare to hope? Her job here meant so much for both her future and everyone who depended on her.

A quick knock on the door preceded the abrupt entrance of her assistant carrying a gleaming silver tray laden with pastries, a coffeepot and two brand-new porcelain mugs. Nothing but the best for Mr. Jordan.

"Thanks, Nora," Jenna said as she set the tray down on a side bureau.

"You got it. Do we know his ETA yet?"

"Won't be much longer now."

Nora put her hand over her heart, a dreamy, faraway expression on her face. "I wonder if he'll have Carmen with him."

"Carmen?"

"You know, that Spanish model he was photographed with recently."

Jenna shrugged. "I wouldn't know."

"Oh, come on. You have to be as curious as the rest of us. He's been spotted out and about with at least three different beauties in the last month alone."

Jenna merely smiled. If she was curious about anything, it was the reason for this whole trip to begin with. "Mr. Jordan's personal affairs are none of my concern. I simply work for the man."

"And what a dreamy man he is." Despite being a happily married grandmother of a newly born infant, Nora was unabashed in her appreciation of handsome men.

"Be that as it may…" Jenna brushed an imaginary piece of lint off her right shoulder. This conversation was making her uncomfortable. Cabe had always been an endless source of gossip around here. She understood the curiosity—of course she did. Handsome, successful, mysterious. Cabe had really made a name for himself in the retail jewelry business. But endless speculation about the man wouldn't get her a regular paycheck.

"I should probably get back to work on this presentation I set up for him." She glanced at the graphic on her screen. She'd worked all night on it, taking the initiative to put together a slide presentation for Cabe's review. Even though she didn't know the exact reason for his visit, she figured presenting him with some specifics on the current business numbers wouldn't hurt.

"I'm sure you'll impress him, dear. Please don't fret."

Nora, of all people, knew how much Jenna needed this job. Her school loans alone were enough to keep her in debt for a good portion of her adult life. But as far as assurances went, Jenna wasn't convinced.

"It can't hurt to be prepared."

"Of course, dear." Taking the hint, Nora walked out of the office, gently shutting the door behind her. As much as she wanted to relax about all this, Jenna couldn't seem to heed Nora's advice not to "fret."

She had to face it. Whatever his reasons, for the next several days, she would have to be Cabe Jordan's glorified and overqualified chaperone. If only she could figure out why he needed one.

The only thing draped on Cabe's arm when he walked in was his suit jacket. Not that she'd really thought he'd have a date with him when he came into the office. Though if the gossip websites were to be believed, he didn't travel far without female companionship. Jenna stood as she eyed him in the reception area, chatting with Nora.

She watched as he walked over to the doorway of her office. Dressed in a well-tailored suit that fit him like a glove, he looked impeccable. Tall, still fit. Jenna drew in a deep breath. Those websites hadn't done him justice. She'd refused to acknowledge it since receiving that email, but the truth was absolutely impossible to ignore now. The silly schoolgirl crush she'd had on him as a kid hadn't abated one iota.

Well, if he was out of reach then, he was downright

unattainable now. Still, like Nora, she could certainly appreciate his…pure masculinity.

Snap out of it.

He was waiting for her to invite him in as she stood there with her mouth gaping open. Staring at him. How utterly unprofessional. So much for coming across as the dynamic, invaluable employee Cabe's company couldn't do without.

"Mr. Jordan. So nice to see you here. Come in. Please."

Wow, now she was positively dazzling him with her talent for witty conversation. He strode into the room and gave her a warm smile that sent electric volts down to her toes.

"Jenna. We've known each other a long time. Please call me Cabe."

He spoke the words cordially enough, but she couldn't shake the feeling that she sensed some subtle undertone, some kind of underlying message. Or maybe that was just her silly attraction to him that she'd thought she had gotten over eons ago. She'd been so wrong about that.

Definitely not the time to realize it.

She gave her head a brisk shake to clear it. She could not blow this initial meeting. She had the distinct impression the future of her livelihood depended on it.

"Would you like a cup of coffee? Cabe."

His smile grew wider. "That's more like it. And I'd love some coffee. But only if you'll join me."

She nodded and moved to the serving tray. Cabe held up a hand to stop her. "Please, let me."

Really? *He* was going to serve *her*?

"How do you take it?"

"Just cream, please."

He poured with a steady hand, doctored it with the small pitcher of creamer and handed her the cup. He poured a cup straight black for himself before sitting down across from her desk. In the smaller chair.

Was it her or was Cabe going out of his way to make her feel less of his employee and more of his equal?

Jenna cleared her throat. "So, what brings you here?"

He shrugged. "Just figured it's about time I visit the flagship Boston site. Now that the Manhattan store is thriving, I can devote some attention to other areas. This is where it all began, after all. Feel I may have been neglecting it over the years."

Did he mean it would have fared better if he'd been more involved? But the regional New England stores were doing fine with her at the helm. Sales had grown progressively over the years. Not at an astronomical pace but pretty steady, despite the slow economy. Heavens, why such paranoia?

"I see."

"Just for a few days."

"Well, I think you'll be pleased with the overall numbers. Here, let me show you." She walked over to the other side of the desk to face her laptop and motioned for him to follow.

Mistake. She hadn't thought to pull over another chair facing the computer. They had no choice but to stand side by side. He smelled of pine and sandalwood.

She pushed herself to go through each slide, hardly aware of content. She stammered on every other sentence. Hopefully, she was at least coherent.

Cabe nodded at all the right points, so that was at least encouraging. He also asked some pertinent questions that Jenna was blessedly prepared for. Still, when she finished with her presentation, she felt as if she'd just trekked the full length of the Freedom Trail. And felt just as out of breath.

If Cabe noticed, he was too much of a gentleman to let on. "Very impressive," he said, still staring at the upward slope of the graph on the last slide.

"Thank you."

"Both the performance numbers and your presentation."

"Thank you." Again with the witty conversation.

"I'm not surprised. You're a very capable regional manager."

Don't you dare say "thank you" again. She simply nodded, tried not to duck her head at the praise. The burning in her cheeks crept clear up to her scalp. She resisted the urge to fan herself like an old-fashioned Southern belle.

He did seem genuinely impressed. Maybe she'd been wrong to be so nervous. Perhaps he really was here to talk to her about a promotion. Stranger things had happened.

She decided to take a chance. "Oh. Well, then. Excuse me, Mr. Jordan—"

He interrupted her. "Cabe."

She smiled politely. "I mean Cabe. If you don't mind my asking… Why are you really here? After all this time. What aren't you telling me?"

Cabe's response died on his lips as the older secretary entered Jenna's office. "Excuse me, Mr. Jordan. There's a call on the office phone for you, from Corporate."

He fished his cell out of his pocket, realizing he'd left it in airplane mode after his flight. "Thanks, Nora." Sure enough, the phone started buzzing as soon as he changed the setting. A naughty text from Carmen popped up. He tried not to groan out loud. The woman could be draining. He would have to do something about that pretty soon. She had her sights on something that wasn't going to happen. He'd have to find a way to let her down gently. No doubt it would cost him a pretty penny.

Then there were numerous messages from his assistant in New York, no doubt about the Caribbean expansion deal. Nothing about the project so far had run smoothly.

And so it began.

The interruption was just as well. He wasn't sure how much he could share with Jenna Townsend just yet. Sharp as she was, she'd surmised that something else had prompted his visit.

He wanted to believe there'd been some kind of mistake, that she had no involvement. But it wouldn't be the first time he'd misjudged someone.

"Would you mind if I take this, Jenna?"

She shook her head. "Of course not." She walked toward the door. "I'll give you some privacy."

"There's no need for that." But she'd already left by the time he reached for her desk phone.

Cabe hung up the phone several minutes later and tried not to curse in frustration. He'd been right. There were indeed yet more complications on the resort island where he planned to open a new high-end retail jewelry store, this time to do with zoning issues.

He would have to fly down there. The sooner the better. Which meant he had to wrap up here in Boston as quickly as he could. He had to address the real purpose of this visit. Of all the reasons to have to come back, a thieving employee. He shook his head at the utter surprise of it. There was absolutely no reason for an employee to steal from him. The company paid well and provided numerous benefits. The only reason had to be greed.

His head of security assured Cabe that such thefts were usually inside jobs, almost always involving the store manager, who in this case was Jenna Townsend. The timing couldn't have been worse—Jenna had been on track for a major promotion before the theft came to light.

As soon as he'd heard the name, he'd wanted to deal with the matter himself. He'd hired Jenna personally. His parents had always been quite fond of her. They'd asked him to give Jenna a chance when she'd graduated top of her class from business school two years ago. Despite what the town had thought about the Townsend family and its troubled history over the years, his parents had insisted that Jenna was cut from a different cloth and that she just needed a chance to prove it. His mom and dad were all about giving people a chance. He liked to think that had served them well, at least as far as their son was concerned.

Cabe's original plan was to spend a few days with her. Maybe even find some evidence. So he'd asked for her specifically to be his assistant on this trip. But now he had forty-eight hours at the most before he had to fly to the Caribbean to deal with the other pressing matter. That left him with only one choice. He had to come right out and ask her what, if anything, she knew about the missing jewelry.

He could be quite persuasive when he had to be. Besides, he didn't have the time to dwell on this. He had to get to the bottom of it all and move on to business as usual.

No one stole from Cabe Jordan and got away with it.

When Jenna returned to her office, Nora ran fast on her heels. "Is there anything else I can do for you, Mr. Jordan?" the older woman asked as she cleared the tray of mugs and coffee pitcher.

Cabe turned and flashed them both a smile that made Jenna's knees go weak. "As a matter of fact, you can, Nora," he replied. "Please clear Jenna's calendar for the next two hours or so and cancel her appointments."

What? Why?

To her shock and horror, he added, "I'd like to take my regional manager to lunch."

Oh, no. She had to nip this in the bud right now. She did not want to sit across a table from this man, just the two of them. She was absolutely no good at small talk. And her presentation earlier had covered all the business details she could possibly bring up. Whatever he had to tell her, he could do so right here in this office. "I'm afraid I just can't do that, Mr. Jord—"

"Cabe."

She took a steadying breath. "I can't steal away for lunch today, Cabe." She glanced at Nora, willing her to help. Instead, Nora threw her overboard.

"Nonsense. Of course she can. There's nothing pressing on her calendar this afternoon. And she hardly ever eats a real lunch. Usually a granola bar at her desk as she continues to work."

Cabe's smile dripped with satisfaction. "It's settled, then. Do you have a preference where to eat, Jenna?"

She could only shake her head.

He led her gently to the door. “How about Nawlin’s, that sidewalk café on Newbury, then? It’s a pleasant enough day to eat outside and I’ve missed their sandwiches.”

Like it mattered. As if she’d be able to taste anything. She’d be lucky if she could keep it down.

“That’s fine.” Only it wasn’t fine at all, and her stomach did another little flip to prove it.

The queasiness hadn’t subsided at all ten minutes later when Cabe pulled a chair out for her at the quaint outdoor café on one of Boston’s swankiest streets. The lunch crowd milled and bustled around them. Two food trucks parked nearby had lines several feet long. All in all, a perfect day to enjoy a leisurely meal outside. If only she could enjoy it.

Their food came out in no time. She was picking at her Caesar salad when things went from bad to catastrophic. Cabe was going to try to make small talk. And his first choice of topic: the absolute last thing in the world she wanted to get into right now.

“So, Jenna. If I recall, you have an older brother.”

She had to discuss her broken, dysfunctional family, with none other than Cabe Jordan.

“Yes. Sam. You two must have been in a few of the same classes.”

“It was just the two of you and your mom, right? How is she, by the way? Do I recall she hadn’t been feeling well for a while?”

Jenna’s blood froze in her veins and she lost her grip on her fork. It fell to her plate with a clatter so loud the sound echoed through the air. Of course he must have heard rumblings over the years. Stories about Amanda tended to get around.

Cabe stopped eating and stared at her.

She stammered for a response. There was no good way to talk about her mother. "Yes. Yes, she's doing better." Such a lie.

Cabe stopped eating. "I'm so sorry, Jenna. I hope it isn't anything too serious."

She so didn't want to go down this path. Any topic but her mother. Anything but discussing Amanda and her problems in front of this perfect man who grew up with the perfect family in his perfect home. But what choice did she have? He waited for an answer, staring at her expectantly.

"Uh…she actually is ill. In a way." She took a deep breath. "My mother's been having a hard time the past few years. Trying to kick a drug and alcohol problem."

Cabe blinked at her. Clearly, he hadn't seen that coming.

"She's trying really hard," Jenna added. Another lie.

In fact, her mother had just shown up at her door last night, asking for money for "groceries." When Jenna had insisted on taking her to the market herself, Amanda had grown violent, shattering a vase on her hardwood floor before storming out. She'd wanted groceries of the more liquid variety. It had been the last thing Jenna had needed as she'd been trying to finish up her presentation for today. Thanks to Amanda's visit, she'd been up most of the night due to the upsetting interruption.

"I'm sorry to hear that," Cabe said in a gentle and soothing voice.

"I'm sure you're a tremendous source of support for your mother," he continued. "She's lucky to have you."

Though her mother didn't see it that way. In Amanda's

eyes, Jenna always came up short. Even though if Jenna hadn't stepped in on numerous occasions, Amanda would no doubt be in jail. Or worse.

"I'm doing what I can to help her."

Cabe cleared his throat. The look he gave her was so understanding, so gentle that it made her breath catch. "It's quite admirable that you're trying to help your mother."

Oh, heavens. What could she say to that? She didn't have a choice but to help her mother. Otherwise, she and her brother would be left to deal with the cleanup.

"Thanks."

Several moments passed in awkward silence. So awkward that she wanted to give the waitress a hug when she interrupted to fill their glasses.

Jenna watched her leave before hesitantly turning her gaze back to Cabe. He gave her an unreadable look. Curiosity? Admiration?

She didn't and couldn't care. What did it matter what Cabe Jordan thought of her or her broken family? In a few days, he'd be gone from Boston and hopefully he wouldn't return for another three to four years. He would just go back to being nothing more than an electronic signature at the bottom of her office emails.

But for now, she still had to get through this godforsaken lunch with him sitting right across from her.

He'd never understand, Jenna thought as she pretended to eat. Even under the best of circumstances, she'd never be in league with people like Cabe or even his parents, who had always been so sweet to her. Cabe had probably never had to hide from a drunken tirade or had to clean up after a parent who'd barreled in at three in the morning then promptly gotten sick all over the carpet.

She and Cabe Jordan may have grown up in the same town, but they were from two different worlds.

CHAPTER TWO

CABE PUSHED HIS plate away with half his sandwich still untouched. He'd lost his appetite. Clearly, Jenna had none, either, since she did nothing more than move lettuce around her plate.

He couldn't help but wonder. Maybe Jenna indeed did have some involvement in the jewelry theft. Was her mother in that much trouble that Jenna may have needed a large supply of cash to help her? Cabe didn't want to believe the worst, but his manager of security had been adamant that Jenna may indeed know something.

Damn. That would change things. Though wrong and criminal, if Jenna was guilty, she hadn't done it for herself but for her mother. She'd practically just admitted that she would do whatever she could to help her parent.

He'd decided back at the office that he wouldn't ask her about it there. Not in front of her friends and colleagues. So he'd taken her to lunch instead.

Now he just wanted to know the truth. He wanted to tell her he could help. That in turn she could get her mother some help.

After all, he and Jenna Townsend were not that different under the surface. His life could have easily turned out as difficult as hers if not for the random hand of fate all those years ago. Pure luck so often determined the entirety of one's life. He knew how lucky he'd been.

"Listen, Jenna," he began, not sure exactly where to start. Business school didn't prepare you for every scenario. "About my visit to Boston. There's something I came here specifically to see you about."

"Yes?" Her question was barely a whisper.

"I want you to know that I can be a friend as well as your corporate CEO."

Was she trembling? "You can be straight with me," he added. "I hope you realize that."

She gave her head a quick shake. "I'm afraid I don't understand."

"You really don't have anything you might want to talk about? Regarding the store, perhaps?"

"No. Not really." She swallowed. "Have I done something wrong?"

Cabe leaned back in his chair. If she did know anything, then she had the acting skills of a Hollywood-caliber actress. "Huh. You really have no idea what I might be talking about?"

"Not a clue."

Cabe tried to regroup. Damn. This conversation was becoming way too messy. "Allow me to explain. A routine inventory check last week by security resulted in a troubling discovery."

She sucked her bottom lip, and heaven help him, he lost his focus for a split second. "Why wasn't I made aware of this? As the regional manager of that store?"

"It's our policy to keep such matters quiet until a thorough investigation."

She gave her head a quick shake. "Investigation? What exactly was this troubling discovery?"

"One of the more valuable pieces seems to be missing. A bracelet."

Cabe watched as understanding dawned. Jenna sucked in a breath and grew as pale as the white linen tablecloth. "Oh, my God. You think I took it."

Whoa. He hadn't expected her to go there quite so soon. "Jenna, wait just a second—"

Her cheeks suddenly grew cherry red. "That's why you came down here yourself. You think I stole from my own store. You think I stole from *you*!"

It came so fast he didn't have time to react. Before he knew it, he wore the rest of his sandwich on his lap and his shirt was drenched in iced tea.

As he watched her storm away, Cabe came to three distinct conclusions. One, Jenna Townsend moved as fast as a prizefighter ducking a punch. Second, judging by her confusion and the vehemence of her reaction, she was most definitely innocent.

And third, if he didn't get to the bottom of it all real soon, he was likely to lose a damn talented regional manager.

Stupid. Stupid. Stupid. She would never learn.

Jenna bypassed the elevator and ran up the three flights of stairs to get to the floor that housed her office. She didn't want to risk running into anyone. How would she explain the tears?

To think, for a while there she'd believed Cabe Jordan might actually be in town to promote her! What a laugh. Instead, he'd accused her of stealing from him.

People like her weren't promoted to corporate-level positions. They were suspected of thievery. They were the first ones investigated when valuable jewelry went missing.

People like her dumped food on others' laps.

She tried to take a deep breath. She probably shouldn't have done that. It was reckless and impulsive. Rather than calmly and reasonably defending herself, she'd let her emotions take over. She'd succumbed to the urge to lash out.

Just as her mother would have done.

And she was her mother's daughter. The apple and the tree and all that. Why did she ever think she could escape that simple truth? The rest of the world wouldn't ever let her forget that fact.

It didn't matter how hard she worked, or how many hours she put in. All the years of studying and working her butt off didn't mean a thing to people like Cabe Jordan. The only thing they saw when they looked at her was where she'd come from.

She'd been fooling herself.

Well, if Cabe hadn't intended to fire her right there on the spot, there was no doubt he would now. She'd dumped his lunch in his lap! Never mind that she'd never actually stolen anything. She wouldn't even get a chance to defend her innocence now.

She no doubt should have handled it better. But she'd been barely functioning given what little sleep she'd gotten and the stress of being prepared for Cabe's visit.

How could he have even suggested such a thing?

She didn't realize she'd asked the question out loud until a voice across the room responded.

"Trust me, it wasn't easy."

Jenna's head snapped up. Cabe stood in her office

doorway, pants stained and shirt wet. She resisted the urge to cover her mouth in horror.

She pulled her planner out of the desk drawer. "I was just leaving."

"Could you recommend a good dry cleaner first?"

He had the nerve to joke at her predicament? God help her, if the coffee tray were still here she might have very well dumped more on him.

"Jenna, listen—"

"What?" she interrupted. "What could you possibly say to me? Do you want me to confess?"

He stepped into the room and shut the door gently behind him. "I simply want to talk."

"About how I stole from you?"

"I was given the information from my head of security. About a theft at the Boston store."

She crossed her arms in front of her chest. "Right. And then you decided that if something had been stolen, it must have been that no-good Jenna Townsend. She must have had a hand in the whole mess. It only makes sense. She comes from bad stock. She's never had much to begin with and she can't be trusted."

"Jenna, stop. That's not how this all came to be."

She merely glared at him. How dare he deny it?

He walked up to where she stood and gestured to the chair. "Please sit."

"Why? Would you like to accuse me some more? Should I call an attorney?" Now that she'd said it, she had the frightening thought that she may actually need one.

Her vision grew dark. This couldn't be happening. After today she may very well have no job. And no hope of finding one if word got out that she couldn't be trusted.

Despite all the years of hard work and sacrifice, she was going to end up penniless on the street. Exactly what she'd feared all along.

To think, the cause of her nightmare would be none other than Cabe Jordan, the man of her teenage daydreams. Who would have thought?

"Jenna, let's try to talk this out."

She lifted her bag. "Perhaps you want to go through this. Maybe pat me down before you let me go."

He blinked. "Pat you down? No. Of course not. I just want to clear all this up." He leaned over with both palms on the desk between them. "About a week ago my head of security requested an urgent meeting. Apparently, someone realized that a piece of rare jewelry at the Boston store had been switched out during a routine security department inventory. The real piece had been replaced with a cheap replica that looked exactly like the original."

"And you assumed I did it. Because you know where I come from and what I might be capable of."

He held one hand up. "Hold on. That's not what happened. The management team is always considered under such circumstances. It's just routine."

At her silence, he continued. "Additionally, there's an electronic log of anyone who's used their key to access that particular case, the one with the higher-end items. Your key was the one used."

Her blood went cold. But that just couldn't be. "Who says?"

"My head of security up at headquarters. He's always been very good at his job. I had no reason to distrust him."

Of course he didn't. "But you had every reason to distrust me."

Something shifted in his eyes. "Listen, Jenna. The only reason I came here personally was because it was you. I wanted to get to the bottom of it myself, do some investigating. But there's a sudden matter that needs my attention with a store opening in the Caribbean. I have to get down there. In my haste, I handled it very badly. I see that now."

People tended to do that with her, rush to judgment. She couldn't expect to be granted the benefit of the doubt, not given where she came from. Cabe may claim objectivity by saying he came to look into the matter personally, but it hardly mattered. No, she would have to find a way to fully clear her name, in such a way that there would never be any more doubt.

"There has to be some kind of mistake," she muttered, trying to think. There had to be an explanation, a way to prove her innocence. But how? She suddenly felt deflated. How could this be happening? Pulling out her desk chair, she plopped herself into it.

A sudden, encouraging thought occurred to her. She looked up at him. "The video? There has to be video footage. We have cameras all over the store."

He gave her a sympathetic look. "The video surveillance system was conveniently disengaged for a forty-eight-hour period on the fifteenth and sixteenth of last month. We believe that's when the theft occurred."

Oh, God. His words knocked the wind right out of her. If there was no video to exonerate her, she had no other ideas. Her eyes began to sting. There was nothing she could do, no way to clear her name. She had no job. She had no real family. She'd probably end up with a criminal record. Despite everything, all the years of busting her behind to get ahead, she'd end up like her mom after all.

Cabe Jordan would always question whether she was a no-good thief.

Wait a minute.

She snapped her head up. "Wait. What date did you just say? The fifteenth of March?"

He nodded. "Yes, that's correct."

"You're certain?"

"That's what I was told."

She knew it! Hopeful relief surged in her chest. "Cabe, I wasn't even in town the week of the fifteenth. I was away at a jewelry designers' expo in San Diego."

He quirked an eyebrow. "And?"

"And my keys were safely locked up in the main vault right here in this building. Including the one that would have opened that particular case. I have proof."

He didn't want to examine why he was so relieved. For some reason, Cabe had been hopeful all along that Jenna was completely innocent. And apparently she could prove it. "Proof? You have a way to prove your key was locked up?"

She nodded triumphantly. "Yes. The security officer on call the day before I left signed off on the paperwork. All my keys were locked up in the main vault before I left. Safe and secure."

"That's the correct protocol. Where is this security officer now?"

She shrugged. "I don't know. I'm not the one in charge of hiring and managing security."

Cabe pinched the bridge of his nose. "I have a sneaking suspicion he's no longer working for us. And that he has a very valuable piece of jewelry in his possession."

Jenna stood staring at him with satisfaction, clearly enjoying the upper hand. So she was indeed innocent. Just as he'd hoped. Heaven help him, he had to resist the urge to go and hug her. Not that she would have it.

"Guess your security head isn't as thorough as you would like to think," she said.

"In his defense, he's going through a rough patch personally. Clearly, it's affected his professional duties. I'll have a word with him."

She rolled her eyes at him and muttered something under her breath. He thought he heard the words "That's rich."

"Jenna, I know an apology isn't nearly enough. But it's all I have. My only excuse is that I've been swamped with various small projects as well as a major international expansion. I rushed and acted on something that I should have taken the time to examine more closely. I'm deeply, resolutely sorry."

Her face softened, and the effect nearly knocked him off his feet. "Thank you for that," she said simply, genuinely. "And I'm sorry for…you know." She pointed to his drenched clothing.

"Nah, don't mention it. I daresay I deserved a good food toss." He was also admittedly relieved. He didn't have to fire a dedicated and competent employee after all. That left only one problem. Things were extremely awkward now with a star employee who deserved better treatment than he'd just doled out. He had a major mea culpa on his hands. As usual, he had rushed to judgment, merely to save some time. Once again, he'd acted without fully thinking through the issue. Not a good attribute in a CEO, yet another character trait he had to work on.

First thing first. Somehow, someway, he had to make this all up to Jenna.

He was getting ready to say so when her assistant knocked and entered her office.

Nora stopped in her tracks when she saw the state of Cabe's clothing. "I'm sorry," she began. "Am I interrupting?"

"That's okay, Nora. What is it?" Jenna behaved like the consummate professional, addressing her admin as if nothing was wrong.

"The Wellesley store just called. They're panicked about their staffing shortage," Nora told her, her gaze still leveled at Cabe.

"I made two very strong offers this morning," Jenna said. "I have no doubt both candidates will take the job. Is that all?"

"One more thing," Nora continued. "The store manager at the Burlington site called again complaining about the lack of shelf space."

Jenna nodded. "Real Estate just called this morning about the sewing shop next door. It's finally shutting down, so we can take the space over. We'll sign the lease within the week."

Cabe watched in admiration. *Damn.* She really was good. Given her background and her hardships growing up, she couldn't have gotten this far in life without being smart and disciplined. Would he have fared as well? He had to wonder. If fate hadn't stepped in and turned his life in a different direction, would he have figured out a way to pull himself up the way Jenna Townsend had? All on his own, like her? Or would he have ended up on the streets? Or locked up in a cell somewhere? Or worse.

Jordan's Fine Jewelry absolutely could not lose someone like Jenna. Not for any reason, the least of which being his stupidity. If only he had someone like her in charge of the Caribbean project.

There it was.

The idea made perfect sense. Before this whole theft fiasco, Jenna's name had come up several times whenever a high-level position opened up at Corporate. She was already due for a promotion.

Perhaps he had a way to salvage the mess he'd made of this whole visit. And possibly even help himself in the process. He was about to make a very strong offer, too. One he hoped Jenna could not refuse. First, he had to get her to listen to him. And forget about what he'd almost just accused her of.

As soon as Nora left, Jenna stood and glared at him. "Well, now what, Mr. Jordan. Am I still under investigation?"

He reached out to gently take her by the arm. "Absolutely not. On the contrary, I need to show you how sorry I am."

She looked down at his hand, then back with clearly puzzled eyes. "Show me?"

"I assumed my security head knew what he was doing, Jenna. Please understand."

She stood silent, clearly not ready to cut him any slack. And why should she? He deserved her derision. How could he have let this happen? He hated looking misinformed. Or worse, appearing incompetent. Mistakes were a luxury he wouldn't allow himself in his position.

"You're one of the best regional managers we have at Jordan's Fine Jewelry," he continued. "I should have handled this differently. And I don't want to lose you over some…misunderstanding."

She visibly bristled. He really wasn't very good at saying sorry, not having had much experience. She had no idea how hard he was trying.

"This was more than a mere misunderstanding."

He nodded. "I realize that. I think I can make it up to you."

She pulled her arm free. But she was clearly listening. "How?"

"I could use the services of a competent and experienced regional manager to help me with a project."

Her chin lifted. "What kind of project?"

"I'm sure you know we're trying to expand internationally, starting with the opening of a new store in the Caribbean."

"Yes, I know."

"You should also know that so far it hasn't gone at all smoothly. In fact, I need to be there within two days to put out the latest fire."

She narrowed her gaze on him. "What does that have to do with me?"

"Come with me, Jenna."

It took a moment to process Cabe's words. "Are you offering me another job?"

He nodded. "One that comes with a higher title. And the adequate adjustment in pay, obviously."

Jenna's head spun. Within the span of a few minutes, she'd gone from decrying the loss of her next paycheck to being offered a promotion. If she examined the matter too closely, Cabe's offer might very well be construed as a bribe.

But it was also an opportunity of a lifetime. A very tempting one.

Cabe motioned to her desk chair. "Please have a seat. Let's discuss this."

Her pride pushed her to turn her back and walk away, slam the door on her way out. Her business-school-trained brain had other ideas.

Begrudgingly, she pulled out her chair and sat down. "What exactly did you have in mind?"

The look of relief on his face sent an odd shiver down her spine. She didn't dare read too much into it.

"I'm tired of trying to get this new site up and running by myself. I've been meaning to hire someone. You're perfect for the job."

"Cabe, you can't just expect me to forget that you were ready to believe I may be capable of theft."

"But that's exactly what I'm asking you to do," he said with the confidence of a successful tycoon who's used to getting his own way. "Rather than spend inordinate time on an extensive talent search, I'd like to offer you the position. You've been considered for several corporate positions recently, but none seemed to be the right fit for you. Until now."

"This is not how I imagined being promoted."

"That makes two of us. This is definitely not how I imagined doing the promoting. One way to look at it would be to say that we're going to start fresh," he added.

Maybe he had a point. But she wasn't about to let him know that. Why let him off easy? Clearly, Cabe Jordan was used to having things handed to him merely because he asked. Unlike someone such as her who'd had to work hard all her life for every accomplishment.

A small part of her nagged that resisting might indeed be a mistake. She still needed this job, pride or not. What if he called her bluff? Her pride won out. "You have to understand, Cabe. I'm no longer sure how I feel about working for you. Given our past history as friends, and that you've known me for decades, I would have appreciated it if you'd come to me right from the start." Oh, heavens. She nearly choked on the words. For all her bravado, she had to acknowledge that he'd genuinely and wholly hurt her. She'd been foolish to expect any more from the Jordan CEO, regardless of past friendship.

But then Cabe held both hands up in surrender and she had a split second of panic. For all her bravado, she really would prefer to be gainfully employed as she looked for another position. Her breath held while he spoke.

"Let's compromise. You just help me on this one overseas project. We'll start from there."

"And then what?"

"Then we revisit the situation and the matter of your employment."

She gave her head a small shake. "You're going to have to be more specific."

"I just mean that I don't think you should make any lasting decisions right now, in the heat of the moment."

Jenna's phone rang but she ignored it, unable to tear her eyes away from Cabe's intense, steel-blue gaze. "We don't want to be impulsive."

She decided to give in just a little. "Perhaps we don't."

Cabe pounced, assuming success. "Do you have a

valid passport? If not, we can request rush processing and you can meet me there once it arrives."

She raised an eyebrow. "Cabe?"

"Yes?"

"Do you actually know the definition of *impulsive*?"

Her question gave him pause, and then he laughed. "I see your point. Nevertheless."

"I have a current passport."

"Great. It's settled, then."

She stood, met him eye to eye. "Not so fast, Cabe."

Was that a smile still on his lips? He couldn't be enjoying this. "Before I say yes, I have a stipulation."

"What's that?"

"Once the new site is opened, upon completion of this project, I want a glowing recommendation from you. In case I decide to look for a position elsewhere."

"I hardly think that will be ne—"

She cut him off. "It's nonnegotiable. I want your word that you will assist me if I decide to leave Jordan's Fine Jewelry." It was the least he could do. After all the long hours of blood, sweat and tears that she'd put into this company. After the way he'd just treated her. And for all the work she was about to put in on this project. He owed her at least that much.

He merely nodded. "If, at the end, a recommendation is still what you want then I will give you one."

"It will be."

He crossed his arms in front of his chest and gave her a wide smile, the kind of smile that would have had her swooning if they were still in high school. Even now, her knees grew weak.

"Not if I change your mind."

CHAPTER THREE

JENNA TOWNSEND HAD clearly never been on a private jet before. Cabe guided her into the cabin and tried not to react to *her* reaction, though he had a comical urge to gently nudge her mouth closed. Instead, he patiently waited as she took small, hesitant steps up the stairs and into the aisle.

Unfortunately, there remained an awkward tension between them. In the interest of business, he chose to ignore it. She thought she might be looking for another job after the Caribbean project when it was completed. He had other ideas.

Well, he'd deal with that scenario if it happened. He'd been watching Jenna in action since he'd arrived in Boston and he had very different plans for her. He was not about to let her go anytime soon.

Now she stood in front of him, taking in her surroundings as they entered the aircraft. Cabe let her take her time.

As far as private planes went, his wasn't terribly extravagant. Pretty much standard issue. Leather seats, a mahogany table so that he could get some work done. In fact, his only indulgence had been the fully stocked bar.

"Jenna, please, have a seat." Cabe gently guided her

toward one of the leather chairs and waited until she was seated before sitting down himself.

She immediately clicked on her seat belt and tightened it. She appeared to be more than merely awed. She seemed apprehensive, downright uncomfortable.

"Are you okay with flying, Jenna?" He knew she'd been on business trips before. So what was making her so jittery now?

The smile she gave him was strained, almost shy. "Mostly. I have to admit, flying is a bit of a new experience for me. We didn't travel much when I was a child." She glanced around at her surroundings. "And as far as flying in something like this..."

"It's just more convenient than flying commercial, that's all."

She let out a small laugh. "Right. Convenient."

Something he couldn't name tingled inside him. In so many ways, Jenna's reaction to his aircraft was refreshing. How many countless women had flown with him privately over the years? None of them had even seemed to notice the lavishness around them. Every one of them had taken for granted that they'd be arriving at their destination in the lap of luxury.

Ironically, rather than making him feel smug, her genuine awed reaction made him feel petty. Hadn't he been taking it all for granted himself? But he knew better than anyone that money couldn't fix everything.

He cleared his throat somewhat awkwardly as they both settled into their seats.

The flight attendant appeared momentarily. Cabe almost groaned out loud. This particular one could be quite the flirt. Normally, he let it slide and tolerated her suggestive comments. For some reason, he really wasn't in the mood to deal with it today. Not with Jenna here.

"Mr. Jordan. So nice to see you again," she said, her smile wide and inviting. She barely spared a glance at Jenna. He couldn't quite remember, but thought she had been the one to slip him her personal phone number after one flight.

Why did it bother him that she would flirt again this time? What was happening to him?

He had to remind himself this was nothing more than an ordinary business trip. He was way too focused on the woman—rather, the employee—accompanying him. That would have to change. And soon.

"Is there anything I can get for you, Mr. Jordan? Anything at all?" the woman asked, her emphasis on the repeated word impossible to miss.

He turned to find Jenna staring out the window, her cheeks stained slightly pink. Dressed in a smart navy pantsuit, her hair up in another impossibly tight style. Not one tendril drifting anywhere near her face. How in the world did she get all that hair to behave? He had a crazy image of unclipping the pin that held it all together, running his fingers through her long, thick tresses. He shook it off.

"Jenna? Is there something you'd like? Some wine, perhaps?"

Jenna shook her head. "No, thank you. I don't dare drink wine. I'll fall asleep."

"Are you sure?" He glanced at his watch. "We'll be in flight for a while. You definitely have time to take a nap."

Her eyes grew wide. You'd think he'd just suggested that she fall asleep on the job. Which in a way, he guessed he had. He laughed at her shock. “Jenna, it’s all right. You’ll be much more productive if you’re well rested.”

“Why do I get the feeling that’s like the pot calling the kettle black?”

He laughed and dismissed the attendant with a polite nod. The woman hesitated, clearly disappointed, before finally stepping away.

“We’ll even have some time to enjoy the sights while we’re out there,” he added.

She gave him a small smile that sent an inexplicable surge of pleasure through his chest. “That would be nice. I’ve never been to the Caribbean.”

“Do you like the beach?”

“Yes, of course.”

“What about fireworks?”

Her eyebrows drew together. “I love fireworks. What do the two have to do with each other?”

“The resort where we’re staying, the one I’m trying to establish the retail store on, has a beach party every Thursday night. Live band, plenty of food and drinks. And fireworks.”

“Sounds like quite a fete.”

“Today’s Thursday. We should go tonight. It would be a good way to introduce you to the island’s characteristic atmosphere.”

She chewed her bottom lip. He watched it swell and redden and redden. *Focus.* “Cabe, I’m not sure that’s such a good idea.”

“Why not?”

“I feel that it would just be better if we solely stuck to the business at hand.”

Cabe shifted in the chair. Jenna appeared so tense, so anxious. He wanted to help her loosen up somehow.

But he was her boss. He had to tread carefully. Given her upbringing, it was no wonder Jenna seemed unable to relax and just enjoy life once in a while.

He couldn't blame her. Maybe he was the flip side of the same coin.

He wanted to tell her there was no reason to be so uptight around him. He wanted to show her how to relax. His motives were pure and simple. Perhaps that would make her rethink her decision to eventually leave the company. She didn't have to constantly toil to get ahead. He wanted her to see that.

Work hard. Play hard. She definitely seemed to have the first part down. He knew for a fact she'd stayed very late at the office last night finishing up last-minute details she didn't want to delegate before leaving.

"I get the sense you don't take many vacations."

"Well, I told you about that jewelry designers' conference in San Diego."

"That was a business trip, Jenna. On behalf of the company."

She shrugged. "Sure. But I made time to visit the zoo one afternoon."

So maybe there was hope for her yet. She was a tough cookie, tougher to crack than any woman he'd ever dealt with. He couldn't help but think how pleasurable it would be to see her enjoy herself. She was one of those rare people who truly deserved it. Though she clearly didn't believe so. He found himself both curious and intrigued. What kind of personality would this highly accomplished, intelligent woman have developed if she'd had even the simplest of breaks in life? How much more dynamic and spirited would she be?

"I'm afraid you will have to do some social mingling while we're there," he told her.

She pursed her lips. Clearly she didn't like that concept. "How so?"

"Opening a new site requires much more than pushing paper around in an office. Much of it requires networking. The resort employees are very friendly and outgoing people; you'll be working with most of them. You don't want to appear to be the standoffish stiff suit from Corporate."

Sure, it was a bit of an exaggeration, but not exactly a lie. It *would* help to have her get to know the resort employees and the regular guests. Though pushing the matter could be very dangerous ground he was treading. He couldn't seem to help himself.

"Like going to this island party, you mean?"

"Parties are considered by most people to be fun, Jenna."

"I've never had much time for them." She tilted her head in his direction: her implication was clear. *Unlike yourself.*

He was quite aware how well-documented his social life was. "Believe it or not, most of those galas I'm photographed at have some type of business angle. Nine times out of ten, I'm not there because I want to be." And lately, each party had been more tiresome than the last. It was becoming harder and harder every time to feign a level of interest he simply didn't feel.

She raised an eyebrow. "Yes, you looked downright pained in that latest photo. The one on the yacht where you're popping open the bottle of champagne, surrounded by bikini-clad socialites. How do you stand it?" Her tone held such mock seriousness he couldn't help but laugh. Surprisingly, his laughter earned a small chuckle from her as well.

"Those photos aren't always what they seem," he responded.

Her mouth tightened into a thin line. "Well, most of the parties I've attended, I wasn't there to enjoy myself. I was there to work, serving or to clean up afterward."

"Is that how you helped pay for your education? Working at social events?" he asked. No wonder she didn't associate social events with anything remotely pleasurable. And no doubt she'd watched her mother cross the line far too many times with all sorts of partying. Jenna Townsend had never been afforded the opportunity to simply have fun and enjoy life, not even as a child.

She nodded. "One of the ways. I did all sorts of odd jobs. Mostly waitressing. The catered parties paid better than, say, waitressing at the diner." She turned back to him as the aircraft began to taxi down the runway. "Your parents were particularly generous. I worked some of those swanky backyard barbecues your mom and dad were known for. I think you were off at college by then."

Had she? She'd never been at any of the ones he'd been present at. He wouldn't have missed her.

"I would have noticed if you were there," she said, surprising him.

"You would?"

The red stain of her cheeks grew deeper. "Of course. You were a minor celebrity in school. Big man on campus."

"I guess I was a bit driven, even back then."

"That's an understatement."

"Yeah, well. It's not like I was doing it for me."

She studied him with interest. "Who else?"

Cabe shrugged. "My parents were very busy people. I figured out at a very young age that I could either get their attention by rebelling and getting into trouble. Or I could try and excel at everything. I chose the latter."

Funny, he'd never admitted that to anyone before. But he wanted Jenna to understand that what outsiders saw of his life as a teen wasn't the complete picture.

"Did you so much as ever get detention?" she asked with a sly smile.

"I think once. It wasn't my fault. I was merely at the wrong place at the wrong time."

"That happened to me a lot," she responded.

"Getting detention?"

She shook her head. "No, being at the wrong place at the wrong time."

Cabe was about to ask her to explain, but Jenna turned and looked out the window as if she'd prefer the conversation to be over.

Perhaps she was right—sometimes the past was better off left to stay there. Though he remembered those years well—all the parties his parents held that Jenna had referred to. Including memories of the first corporate outdoor luncheon he was allowed to attend. He must have been around age fifteen or so. He'd been so nervous, making sure to say all the right things and behave in all the right ways.

The Jordan Golden Boy.

He'd acquired the moniker right around that time as well, due to his stellar grades and lightning-fast skills on the basketball and tennis courts. Accomplishments he worked his behind off to achieve. All to make himself worthy of the Jordan family.

When he'd first found out that he was a Jordan in name only.

What had she gotten herself into?

Mistake. This whole trip had been a mistake. She'd been a fool to take on this assignment. She'd been a fool to think she could play in Cabe Jordan's league on her own terms.

She was only going on this trip and working on this project in order to get the achievement on her résumé. Not for some kind of working vacation. Cabe had to realize she wasn't the type to do island-wide parties.

As if traveling in his private jet weren't enough, she might have to accompany him to a lavish tropical extravaganza. With fireworks! How was she supposed to act distant and unaffected? How was she supposed to avoid falling under Cabe Jordan's spell? He was charming enough under the most innocuous of circumstances.

By the time their jet landed, Jenna still hadn't figured it out.

Cabe stood and offered her his hand. "Ready?"

Of course not. But she simply nodded and let him guide her out of the aircraft, his hand placed gently at the small of her back. She knew he was just being courteous. But his touch wreaked havoc on her senses. The man had absolutely no idea of the effect of his presence. Didn't he see how women around him practically swooned at his feet? The flight attendant being a perfect example.

Yet somehow she was supposed to ignore the way his hand on her back sent a tingle clear down to her toes. Or how he so casually vowed to "show her a good time" while here.

She nearly tripped over the last step as they disembarked.

"Are you all right?" Cabe said behind her.

"Yes, I'm fine. It's just much hotter than I'd anticipated." That was no exaggeration. A wall of heat and humidity enveloped her as they walked toward the small stucco building that housed the island's airport. Her smart, fitted suit jacket instantly clung to her skin.

"It'll get better," Cabe assured her. "The airport is always ten to fifteen degrees hotter. You'll feel more comfortable once we're closer to the beach with an ocean breeze to temper the heat."

And what was going to temper her reaction to Cabe Jordan? She'd said too much on the flight over, drifting dangerously close to "pity me" territory—something she'd sworn never to do over the years. She wasn't about to start now. Not even if Cabe's significant charm had her tongue loosening.

And what was his story? All those things he said about having to prove himself growing up. His accomplishments had seemed to come so easy to him when they were kids. Maybe that had all been an illusion. Not that it was really any of her business. Cabe was her boss.

A sleek town car awaited them outside once they were through with customs. The driver was a pleasant tall man with skin the color of mocha coffee. He kept up a steady stream of conversation with Cabe as he maneuvered the busy streets. Based on the familiarity, Jenna guessed he was Cabe's regular driver on the island.

Jenna found herself too distracted by the scenery outside to focus on their conversation. Among lush, green mountains and the majestic sight of the ocean, the roadside sat peppered with run-down, decrepit shacks. Such poverty among such beauty. On a much smaller scale, it reminded her of the way she'd grown up—the days when they weren't sure they'd be able to eat while just a few miles away stood the glamorous, ritzy grandeur of downtown Boston. Well, she'd fought tooth and nail to climb out of that bleak existence. And she was proud of it. She'd done it on her own, through hard work and discipline. Unlike her mother, who still to this day waited for the right man to come along and save her—a rich, powerful man. Well, that idea hadn't really worked out for any of them. Jenna knew better than to fall for such fantasy.

Within forty-five minutes they arrived at the resort. After the striking displays of poverty on the roads they'd just passed through, it was like entering a different world.

A guard outside a tall, metal gate pushed a button to let them through.

"You have a few minutes to freshen up," Cabe told her. "Then I'd like to show you around, particularly the shopping center attached to the resort. You can see where the new store is to be built."

"I won't need that much time," she answered, grabbing her things off the seat. "I'd like to get started as soon as we can."

He lifted his head and stared at her, as if studying some unfamiliar object. "I know we're in a bit of a time crunch but there's no need to be quite so rushed, Jenna."

She shrugged. "I'm just anxious to get going, that's all."

"Well, we're on island time now. Things always move slower down here. You may as well relax."

As if that was possible, Jenna thought, watching him remove his jacket as the car came to a stop outside the entrance. His shoulders strained against his well-fitting tailored silk shirt. Deft fingers removed his cuff links and he rolled up his sleeves to reveal toned, tanned arms. His days on the Caribbean had certainly given him a good dose of color.

She tore her gaze away. None of this was at all conducive to relaxing in any way. The driver helped her out of the car and she emerged to the light sounds of steel-drum music in the air. The aroma of exotic flowers hit her as she stepped out. They were surrounded by lush plants and thick greenery. And large colorful flowers like she'd never before seen. She wanted to run up and inhale the scent of every single one.

A tall, statuesque woman with a thick braid down her back approached them. "Mr. Jordan. So nice to have you back," she said to Cabe with a glowing smile.

"Glad to be back, Seema," he answered. "Though I wish it were for a more pleasant reason."

Her smile wavered. "More snags?"

"I'm afraid so." He gestured toward Jenna to join them. "But this time I have some help. Meet Jenna."

Jenna put her hand out to greet the woman but she had other ideas. Jenna found herself gripped in a tight hug.

"Welcome to the Paraiso Resort. So glad to have you here, Miss Jenna."

"Please. It's just Jenna. And I'm very glad to be here." It surprised her how much she meant it. The woman's friendly warmth magnetically drew her in.

"May I show you to your rooms?" she asked them both while a bellman grabbed their bags.

"We're right behind you," Cabe said.

Jenna tried to take in her surroundings as they were led away. Paradise. She had entered paradise. A piece of pure heaven. She could hear the gentle waves in the distance. The clear crisp air refreshed her despite the muggy heat. She loved her hometown city of Boston but this was an entirely different world.

A world full of beauty. To think, she'd almost turned down the opportunity to come.

She had to admit it to herself. Cabe was right to bring her here.

Cabe let himself fall slightly behind as they walked through the resort to the hotel room area. Seema was giving Jenna a raving summary of all the resort's amenities and attractions while Jenna listened carefully. He took a deep breath, finally allowing himself to relax. The scent of the ocean, the crystal-blue sky and the characteristic local friendliness worked their usual magic and he felt the tightness in his shoulders give way little by little.

He could hear the gentle crashing of waves and the sounds of laughter coming from the beach. A small salamander darted out and ran in front of them on the path. Jenna shrieked and jumped back, clutching her chest. In the process, she barreled right into Cabe. Realizing the intruder was a small lizard, her panicked expression turned to one of amusement. She laughed out loud, prompting him to laugh with her.

Instinctively, his arms went protectively around her

middle. “Close call,” he said against her ear. “But you’re safe.”

“You didn’t tell me I might be ambushed by small green creatures on this island,” she admonished with a chuckle.

“I was just hoping for a chance to rescue you.”

“I hardly needed rescuing,” she countered. “I was just startled, that’s all.”

He smiled at her. “Right.”

Seema gave them a curious look. With hesitation, he finally let Jenna go and they continued walking.

Life could be so simple in the Caribbean.

They were finally here. After his colossal mistake in Boston, he wasn’t so sure he could pull it off. Getting Jenna here was one thing. Now he had to get the project off the ground with her help, all the while trying to convince her to stay in his employ afterward. Employees like Jenna were hard to come by. And if she left, he’d have no one but himself to blame.

She couldn’t leave the company. He didn’t want to have to explain her loss to his parents.

His mom and dad put a lot of faith in him, their only child. So far, he liked to think he’d done well by them and made them proud. What he’d told Jenna on the flight here was the truth. He’d had two choices as an adolescent growing up. He could gain attention through rebellion or through accomplishment. Otherwise, his parents barely seemed to know he existed. Their grief had been encompassing and powerful, as it still was to this day. He chose to be an achiever because he realized at a young age just how lucky he was.

In his position, mistakes were out of the question. He couldn’t afford the luxury of making any.

He watched as Jenna rubbed the back of her neck and nodded at something Seema told her, her face squinted in concentration. Even from this distance, Cabe could tell she was processing all the information about the resort, making mental notes. She really was one of a kind.

No matter what it took, he wasn't about to lose Jenna Townsend.

CHAPTER FOUR

"WOULD YOU LIKE to walk the rest of the way along the beach?" Seema asked her with a pleasant smile.

Jenna turned to Cabe, who gave a small shrug. "It's up to you. Though you should know, your shoes will definitely get sandy," he said, pointing to her smart navy pumps.

As if she cared. Right now, Jenna could think of nothing better than to feel soft, Caribbean sand between her toes.

"Why not?"

They took a right and the pathway led them through a network of buildings, bungalow-style structures with wooden steps spiraling up to tall doorways. The sounds of the ocean grew gradually louder and soon she could see the gentle lapping of the crystal-blue water and the golden silky sand that framed it.

She felt like she was in a travel catalog, each page a new and wondrous scene of bright, colorful images. Why had she never traveled here before? Money was always tight and her student loans were the top priority, but surely she could have scrounged and scraped and somehow over time pulled it off. How had she allowed herself to miss this part of the world for her whole adult life?

Without a cloud in the sky, the sea gleamed like liquid jewelry. She wanted so badly to run in and dive under the water, fully clothed. The image made her smile. She dared a glance at Cabe. Dear Lord, he'd undone a couple of his top shirt buttons and it took all her will to look away and not stare at the revealed patch of tanned golden skin.

Seema suddenly stopped, forcing Jenna to look around her at the reason. A procession of well-dressed men and women followed a small girl in a white lace smock toward an elaborately decorated archway on the beach.

A wedding. The scene took Jenna's breath away. A small band played reggae music next to rows of wooden chairs. Four bridesmaids dressed in calf-length, silky maroon gowns made their way down the path in front of them. Instead of shoes, their feet were adorned with golden chains and sparkly gemstone jewelry. The effect was both exotic and bohemian.

Jenna couldn't help but let a small "ooh" escape her lips. The women were all so lovely.

"Would you like to stay a moment and watch?" Seema asked her.

As much as she wanted to maintain the air of the unaffected professional, she couldn't tear herself away from the scene. She glanced at Cabe, who gave her a small nod.

"Yes, please."

Right behind them came a line of four handsome, strapping young men dressed in light gray suits. Hands clasped in front of them, they walked over to the bridesmaids' sides. The band switched to a rhythmic, reggae version of "Here Comes the Bride."

Jenna's breath caught when the bride emerged from a canopy off to the side. She was downright stunning. In a long silky white dress, she moved like a surreal vision. A tiara of colorful flowers sat on the crown of her head. A collective sigh sounded from the bridal party and those in attendance as she walked down the aisle, escorted by an older gentleman with gleaming silver hair. He looked both teary-eyed and happy.

Jenna found her eyes had moistened as well. How silly of her. Why in the world was she so moved by a beachfront wedding?

It made no sense whatsoever. None.

"Jenna? Are you all right?" Cabe materialized in her line of vision. Great. Just great. She was a sniffling fool who couldn't handle the sentimentality of watching two strangers get married.

"I'm fine." She thought about lying, claiming that sand had blown in her eyes and irritated them. But something told her he would see through that. Though they'd barely known each other growing up and though he'd only been a signature at the bottom of her memos for the past few years, Cabe Jordan seemed to be able to read her very well.

"It's just that she's so beautiful. And the scene is so touching," she admitted instead. "You wouldn't understand," she added. How could he? He'd grown up with the best that life had to offer. Two parents who were still together and who took good care of him.

He looked away. "You'd be surprised."

Jenna studied him. What could that possibly mean? Why did she want so badly to find out?

Seema patted her arm. “We have a well-earned reputation for planning the most romantic and unforgettable weddings.”

“They seem so in love,” Jenna said, staring at the laughing couple. “So lucky to have found each other.”

“Luck is a mysterious thing,” she heard Cabe say.

“Do you have something against weddings?” she asked him, then felt foolish for doing so. What a nonsense question to ask your boss.

“I don’t really give them a whole lot of thought” was his reply as he turned back to them. “But they’re certainly good for business. The resort caters to families as well as couples,” he told her. “I’ve heard stories of couples traveling here to get engaged. Then returning for their wedding. And several years later, coming back with their toddlers in tow.” She detected a hint of sadness in his voice. But that was silly. Surely she’d imagined it.

“And don’t forget,” Seema added. “When they marry here, the honeymoon immediately follows.”

That was the most wonderful thing Jenna had ever heard.

“That’s what this place is all about,” Cabe said. “Love and family.” His tone held an unmistakable tinge of something she couldn’t place. Longing, perhaps? Again, just a silly thought. Cabe Jordan surely couldn’t have wanted for much in his full and privileged life.

Boisterous applause from the wedding party suddenly erupted and she turned to see the bride and groom kiss each other in front of a smiling clergyman.

A profound sense of sadness overcame her as she watched the couple embrace. Everyone cheered them on. Friends, family. They were all so happy for these two people.

She could never hope to have such a happy ceremony in her own future, even if she met someone. She had no real family—only her brother, who was struggling just to get by as she was. She'd long ago given up on the hope that her mother might one day clean herself up and become the kind of woman who'd be able to help her daughter plan a wedding. That was a downright laughable thought.

She had no father figure to walk her down the aisle and tear up as he gave her away.

What did it matter? She had her life planned out. She had only herself and her brother. And that was fine. Her goals were set and clear. None of those goals included finding a mate and settling down. She'd be perfectly content with a fulfilling job and financial security. Even if she never met Mr. Right.

Her gaze traveled in Cabe's direction and she had to snap herself back. Thinking about Cabe in such a way was a slippery slope she did not want to find herself tumbling down.

Not that he was ever likely to see *her* in any kind of romantic light. She was no supermodel or high-profile actress, his usual type.

She shook off the useless thoughts. Nothing would be gained from them. She was here to do a job, not fantasize.

Still, it was hard not to imagine herself standing in front of a crystal clear ocean, under the bright blue sky, as the love of her life looked her in the eyes. Once more, an unbidden image of Cabe standing before her popped into her head and she nearly gasped out loud.

Now she had passed the boundary from fantasy into foolishness. As if.

On top of everything else, the man was a notorious womanizer.

She took a steadying breath and turned to Seema, avoiding Cabe's eyes at all costs. "That was lovely. You certainly know what you're doing in the wedding planning department."

"Thank you. We pay attention to details and try to make sure everything is perfect."

It certainly appeared that way to her. "I'd love to see the rooms. Something tells me those will not disappoint either."

Seema tilted her head and gestured with her hand for them to follow her. "We always reserve the best rooms for Mr. Jordan and any of his guests."

And how many "guests" had he previously traveled here with? Again, a wayward thought that didn't matter.

Jenna turned to catch one last glimpse of the fairy-tale wedding. The dancing had begun, right on the beach, in the sand. The flower girl seemed to be particularly enjoying the music. She and an older woman were happily dancing in the water as waves splashed at their feet.

Jenna made herself look away. She was happy for the unknown couple. She really was. They truly did appear to be an example of the lucky few who were fortunate enough to find their soul mate. But one never knew for sure. How often had her mother been convinced she'd found "the one," only to have the whole thing fall apart and send her into another downward spiral? Too often to keep track of. Each of Amanda's relapses being usually much worse than the last.

The sounds of bottle corks popping and joyful laughter followed them as they left.

Cabe watched Jenna as they opened the door to their suite. She inhaled sharply upon stepping inside.

The resort had provided his regular suite—he'd made certain of it. Jenna would be in the adjoining room and they'd share the center living area where they could work and go over the planning and budgeting of the new store.

Seema showed Jenna to her room as Cabe took the time to sign onto the Wi-Fi and check his messages. It was clear from the snippets of conversation he could hear that the two women were becoming fast friends. He wasn't surprised. Jenna seemed to be one of those rare authentic and open people who drew others in. She didn't even realize she was doing it.

When Seema bade them both goodbye several minutes later, Jenna wasted no time in getting to work. She hadn't even slipped off her shoes.

"Do you want to go over the project plan?" she asked.

"Why don't you freshen up first? Can I pour you a glass of wine? Then maybe we can grab a bite. The Hibachi restaurant on the premises is world-renowned."

She seemed perplexed by the question. He really had to figure out a way to get her to loosen up. People so often accused him of being a workaholic. Jenna Townsend could give him a run for his money any day.

He really wanted to change that. But he really didn't want to examine why.

"Wine? Now? With you?"

From the look on her face and the incredulous voice, you'd think he'd asked her to go streaking through Boston Common in the middle of a Saturday afternoon. "Or we could have soda. Or some juice."

She shook her head. "I'm not thirsty."

"Jenna, that's a lie. How can you not be thirsty? Or hungry? We've been traveling all day."

She swallowed. "If it's all the same to you, I'd rather just go over some of the to-do items for this trip and then call it a day."

Disappointment washed over him. The soft, affected woman who'd gone teary-eyed watching the beach wedding was nowhere in sight now. He couldn't help but feel it had something to do with him. Jenna Townsend turned into the stony, consummate professional whenever they were alone.

He pointed to the clock above the mantel. "It's five-thirty. We gained an hour due to the time change. There's still hours of daylight left. You'll be miserable if you don't fight through the jet lag and adjust to the new time."

Silence.

He sighed. "Jenna, look. It's been a tiring day. I don't know how productive we're going to be on an empty stomach after such a long trip. Sure, we can go over some paperwork. I think that's a great idea. But I'm going to have a glass of the resort's house Cabernet while we do so. I'd highly recommend it—it's spicy yet smooth with a hint of citrus. But of course, you can drink whatever you'd like. After which, I'd like to grab a bite of dinner, preferably at the Hibachi restaurant. I'd love for you to join me."

"It hardly sounds productive."

"You can't be productive if you're starving."

She pursed her lips. Most things with her seemed to

require a fight but he couldn't help but admire her tenacity. "This is no different than a working dinner that we may have had back in Boston. How about after dinner, we tour the mall where the new store is supposed to go. It's in an adjacent building to the restaurant. Everything is connected here."

She lifted her chin. "I suppose that makes sense. But…"

At least she was giving it some thought. Cabe realized he was holding his breath. He'd been on this resort countless times, both with and without companionship. Carmen had joined him just last month, lounging by the pool or on the beach during the day and then joining him for an evening meal and entertainment afterward.

But he'd also dined alone here on numerous occasions. The friendly staff being so accommodating and social, eating by himself had never bothered him.

Yet he found he really didn't want a solitary meal tonight. He wanted Jenna's company. He wanted to ask her how hard it had been to go to business school given all her responsibilities and lack of support. He wanted to talk to her about why she was so hesitant to let her guard down. He wanted to ask her about her brother. How hard had it been to put herself through school? He wanted to learn so much more about her. It would probably be the most interesting conversation he'd had with someone in ages.

Maybe it was all those years growing up that he'd had to eat his dinners alone, his parents either too busy or preferring to eat an "adult meal" by themselves. Maybe it was all catching up with him for some reason.

"But you have a different idea, I'm guessing," he said.

She lifted an eyebrow. "As a matter of fact, I do."

He waited.

"We go over the files while I have a cup of tea. And then we visit the mall. Before dinner. So that while we eat you can familiarize me with the logistics and the details."

He groaned and rubbed his stomach with mock exaggeration. She visibly fought hard to control it but an amused smile touched her lips. "As much as my hungry stomach protests…" He stood and extended his hand. "Deal."

Her smile turned to one of satisfaction and she reached for his hand to shake it. Her hand felt small in his, her skin soft. Cabe found himself not wanting to let go, silly as the notion was. Was her skin that soft, that smooth all over?

"Great. You grab a tea bag while I pour myself some wine," he said, finally dropping her hand. What in the world had come over him?

She turned to do so. Her smart, sensible pumps clicking on the tile.

Three hours later, after a tour of the mall and a very entertaining dinner, they made their way back toward their suite by way of the beach. The picnic tables were already filling up for the evening's festivities. Buffet tables lined with desserts, fruit and beverages framed the sitting area. All of it faced a makeshift dance floor with large speakers on either side.

"This is the big party?" Jenna asked, slowing her stride.

Cabe nodded. "Takes them a while to set up. I can drop you off back at the room and come back once it's in full swing."

Though the thought of coming back alone didn't exactly appeal to him. The last one of these he'd attended, Carmen had accompanied him. His feet hurt just thinking about it. The woman had an insatiable desire to dance the night away; no amount of partying seemed to be enough. He'd barely gotten a chance to sit all evening.

He wanted to experience the party through Jenna's fresh eyes. No doubt she'd be impressed if she just gave it a chance.

He was debating the wisdom of asking her again when they were interrupted by the sound of feminine laughter. Seema ran up to them, flashing a delighted smile.

"Jenna! I'm so glad you've come to our grand gala," she exclaimed and gave Jenna's shoulders a squeeze.

"Oh, I'm not—" The woman didn't give Jenna a chance to complete the protest. She took her by the elbow and guided her toward the middle of the action, closer to the speakers and dance floor. Jenna had changed into a flowing summery dress that clung to her in all the right places. But with her hair still up in that tight ponytail, she hadn't lost the look of the serious professional. Though at the moment she looked quite uncertain.

Cabe gave her an apologetic shrug when she glanced back at him.

By the time he reached the two women, Jenna was tapping her toe in tune with the music, swaying slightly with the beat. Midway through the song, Seema excused herself when a young gentleman asked her to dance.

Jenna laughed out loud when the young man twirled Seema onto the dance floor.

"Can I dare to say that you might be finding this enjoyable?" Cabe asked.

Jenna ducked her head but not before he caught the small smile. "It does seem very festive. And the music is very catchy."

He lifted a fresh coconut speared with a straw off one of the tables and reached it out to her.

She shook her head and put a hand on her midsection. "No way. I'm still full from dinner."

He handed her the drink. "Just one sip. You've never tasted coconut water unless you've had it straight from the fruit."

She scanned his face then finally leaned over to take a sip while he held the fruit out to her.

When she lifted her head, a tiny drop glistened at the bottom of her lip. For an insane moment, he wanted to reach out and wipe it away with his finger. Sanity won out and his hand tightened into a fist at his side. He pointed at her mouth instead.

"You just have a little…"

"Oh!" she exclaimed and wiped it away with the back of her hand.

"Well? What do you think? Better than the supermarket bottled kind?"

"It's heavenly. I wish I hadn't eaten so much."

"We'll make sure you get one tomorrow."

He went to take his own sip and her eyes grew wide. He'd shocked her, using the same straw she'd just had her lips on. Surprisingly, he hadn't even thought about it. A boss and his employee could drink from the same straw, couldn't they? Though he'd be hard-pressed to think of any other employee he'd ever done such a thing with. Plus, he had to admit, anyone watching them right now might get a different idea about who exactly they were to each other.

A look around suggested as much. The usual staffers he'd come to know gave them curious glances. He should have announced more widely that he'd be bringing a colleague with him this time around. The last thing he or Jenna needed was a swell of gossip as they were trying to get this project off the ground. If things went as planned, Jenna would spend a lot of time here working with these very people. He didn't want to impact their impression of her before they'd even had a chance to form one.

And he certainly didn't need her to be viewed as the boss's toy.

He was straddling a fine line here. He had to be careful not to step over the edge.

"All right. You win," she said with a small sigh.

"Win?"

"I have to admit, this is quite a party. I'm glad I didn't miss it."

He felt a surge of pleasure clear to his toes. How juvenile, but he was ridiculously happy that she was enjoying herself. Finally. To the point where she felt compelled to admit it.

"I would say I told you so…"

She laughed out loud, a mesmerizing, melodic sound that made him chuckle in return. Something about the sound of her laughter made him want to join in her merriment. "And you essentially just have," she told him.

"Do I appear smug?"

She pinched the fingers of her right hand. "Just a smidge."

"Well, forgive me. But do you know what it took to

get you out here? Worse than negotiating a store lease agreement. It was quite a challenge, I must say."

Her smile widened. "Yet another one that you've met and conquered."

"Was that a compliment? Or a dig? Somewhat hard to tell."

She shrugged, watched as a gaggle of dancing teenagers pranced by them. "Merely a statement."

He took another sip of the coconut drink. "Pity. I was hoping for the former."

"Fishing for compliments, are you?"

"My ego is a fragile thing." He held his hand to his chest with mock melodrama.

That laugh again—he could easily get used to it. "Something tells me you come by compliments quite often," she said.

He took a moment to respond, deciding to throw caution to the wind. "Some compliments mean more than others, given the source."

She sucked in a breath. He wanted to suck the words back as soon as they'd left his lips. Jenna wasn't some new acquaintance; he knew better than to sound even remotely flirtatious. Where had that statement even come from?

They stood side by side now, the party growing ever larger around them, the crowd gradually becoming louder. Cabe waited apprehensively for her response. When she finally did, it wasn't at all what he was expecting.

"I'm sorry," she said.

"Whatever for?"

"My comment was a bit personal. Inappropriately so, I'm afraid."

A jarring sense of disappointment settled in his gut.

Jenna was pulling the curtain of propriety between them. She was right to do so, of course. He was the one being foolish enough to let it bother him.

He turned to face her, though she remained in place and continued to look straight ahead. Definitely uncomfortable. “No need to apologize, Jenna. We’ll be working very closely for quite a while. You can ask me anything. Personal or not. What would you like to know?” Now he’d definitely thrown down the gauntlet. He’d never said those words to anyone else before. What was it about this woman? She was like the smoothest Caribbean rum. Or truth serum.

“What makes you think I have questions about you?”

“There’s nothing you’d like to know?”

Why was he doing this? Why did he want so badly to get her to probe? But he knew the answer. For some bothersome reason he couldn’t explain, he wanted Jenna Townsend to see through his outer demeanor. He wanted her to see the real man beneath the business titles and web articles. For the first time in his life, he wanted a woman to look inside the shell that was Cabe Jordan.

He wanted her to know the truth: that he was nothing more than a fraud.

CHAPTER FIVE

HOW IN THE world had she gotten here?

Never mind the trip itself. What was she doing here at this boisterous beach party? While Cabe hand-fed her drinks, no less. Of course, she was having fun. But that was hardly the problem.

No, the problem was her reaction to the man here with her. How aware of him she was. They way her heart had pounded in her chest when he'd taken a sip off the same straw she'd used just an instant before.

Now he stood inches from her side, goading her to ask him the questions that had been tumbling around in her head. Right. Like she could ever come out and admit just how curious she was about him. Had he sensed her curiosity? Or was he just used to people being inquisitive about him?

She could swear she felt electricity crackle between them as he waited for her response. Did he feel something also?

She was a fool. Of course he didn't. He was a worldly businessman; conversations like this one certainly amounted to nothing more than small talk for someone like him. And here she was with her heart hammering, falling for his charm.

She shook her head. "I can't think of anything I'd like to ask," she lied.

He looked away but not before she caught the clear flash of disappointment in his eyes. Her heart plunged at his expression and she sucked in a deep breath. She'd clearly let him down with her response.

That was it. She couldn't stay. A few more minutes and she was out of here. She turned to tell him so just as a tall man in a silk maroon shirt and well-fitting white pants smacked a hand on Cabe's shoulder.

"So I see you're back, my friend."

Cabe turned to greet him and the two men shook hands. Cabe's smile didn't quite reach his eyes. Animosity etched his features. She had to wonder if the use of the word "friend" was a bit of a stretch, at least as far as Cabe was concerned.

The man turned to flash her a megawatt smile. "I see you have the most beautiful woman on the island at your side."

Jenna resisted the urge to mock-fan herself. Wow. What a charmer. Cabe's fake smile turned into an all-out frown.

He introduced her while the man lifted her hand and brushed his lips across her knuckles.

"Jenna, this is Maxim Rolff. He's in charge of the on-site casino."

"A true delight to meet you," Maxim said.

Maxim was elegant—tall with dark chestnut hair and a thin mustache that would look silly on most men. On him it looked regal and distinguished. She could easily see him charming vacationers to bet significant amounts of their hard-earned money, particularly the women.

"Nice to meet you," she said with a polite smile.

"Jenna is working on the store opening with me," Cabe told him.

Maxim winked. "Works with you, does she? Glad to hear it."

What was that supposed to mean?

"I hope I can assume that you'll be spending a lot of time on our little island," Maxim said.

"It looks that way."

"Superb. I'd love to show you around the gaming tables while you're here."

Cabe jammed his hands in his pockets. "She'll be pretty busy, Maxim. We have a lot to do."

"Pity. Still, she does need to get to know the resort. And the casino is no small part of it."

"I'd love to check it out sometime," she said and stole a glance at Cabe. His frown had definitely grown. She didn't think he was even trying to hide it. "If timing allows," she added.

Maxim took her hand once more, held it. "We'll make sure of it. Won't we, Cabe?"

"Like I said, we both have a lot to do."

Maxim hadn't torn his gaze off her. "Don't let him work you too hard, my dear. It would be a shame to waste such beauty without fully appreciating it."

Cabe actually snorted. "Are we still talking about the island?" His question had Jenna gasping with surprise.

Maxim laughed. "Maybe. Maybe not. So what is it exactly that you do for Cabe?"

"I'm just assisting him with the opening of the new store."

Cabe stepped closer to her side, their shoulders almost touching. If Jenna didn't know better, she'd think he was trying to slightly push her farther away from Maxim. "Modest to a fault. She's going to be my right hand on this project. By title, she's my regional manager for the New England area."

Maxim lifted an eyebrow in appraisal. "Impressive."

She could feel the heat of Cabe's skin brushing against her shoulder. "Yes, she is."

"You're lucky to have found her," Maxim added.

Jenna stiffened in shock as Cabe threw an arm around her shoulder. "Jenna and I have known each other since we were kids. We grew up in the same town."

Maxim's brows lifted. "Ah, so friends as well as colleagues."

She couldn't come up with anything to say. Cabe's stance was definitely a possessive one. All she could summon was a tight smile.

"I look forward to seeing more of you, Jenna," Maxim said. "And please, if you can steal away from your overdemanding boss, stop by my office. I'll give you the grand tour of all the gaming attractions." He lifted her hand for another kiss before turning to leave.

"Well, that was interesting," she commented as they watched Maxim walk away. Cabe kept his arm on her shoulder for another beat, then dropped it to his side.

"*Interesting* is one word for him."

She had to laugh. "Do I dare ask what other ones you have for him?"

"Sure. Cunning. Sly. He's one to keep an eye on."

"Why do you say that?"

Cabe accepted a bubbling glass of some kind of fizzy punch from a passing waiter. He offered it to her but she shook her head to decline. Taking a swig, he threw another stare at the retreating man's back.

"He's a notorious flirt. As you just witnessed."

"Some people might call that friendly," Jenna countered. "After all, the Caribbean is known for its hospitality. You said so yourself."

"That wasn't friendly. That was shameless. The way he was flirting with you so blatantly. He would have tried to sweep you off your feet if I wasn't here with you."

A silly jolt of pleasure shot through her core. If she didn't know better, she might say Cabe was acting protective. Maybe even jealous.

But that was a ridiculous notion. He clearly simply disliked the man. And he probably didn't want her distracted when she had so much to do.

That was all.

"Come on. Let's go," Cabe said, setting down his drink on a nearby table.

Finally. She was oh, so ready to retire. Her head was spinning. Between jet lag, exhaustion and Cabe's mere proximity, her senses revved on overdrive. Plus, the party had suddenly crowded with dozens of revelers who had somehow shown up all at once when she wasn't paying attention.

But instead of leading her toward their building, Cabe took her by the arm and led her to the middle of the beach. Right toward the dance floor.

"What are you—?"

Her words were cut off when he grabbed her by the waist and pulled her into the crowd. Right into the middle of a conga line. Her knees grew wobbly. She'd never been much of a dancer.

This was a new experience, Jenna thought as she fought to get her bearings. She might have fallen forward on her face if Cabe wasn't holding her. Without any choice, she reached out and held on to the waist of the woman in front of her and tried not to grip too tight. Then she just made her feet move.

"You're not kicking," Cabe said loudly into her ear from behind.

Was he serious? It was all she could do not to stumble into the conga dancer in front of her. With Cabe's fingers splayed across her midsection, holding her. She felt the strength in his hands, his touch warming her flesh through her dress where he held her above her hips. Even in the middle of this large and noisy crowd, his touch felt intimate, private.

Oh, Lord. She had enough trouble keeping her wits around him under the best of circumstances. Now she had to ignore his touch and try to dance at the same time.

"It's one-two-three kick and kick," he told her, shouting above the noise.

This was so not the time for a dance lesson. "I've never done this before," she yelled back over her shoulder.

"It's easy," he said, then laughed when she stumbled yet again. "You can do better than that. You're just not letting yourself."

"I'm trying not to let myself be trampled."

He laughed and she felt his warm breath against the back of her neck. "Don't think too hard. Just relax and let go."

Hysterical laughter bubbled up inside her. Relax, he said. Right.

"I won't let you fall, Jenna."

She believed him. And surprisingly, as soon as he

said the words, some of the tension left her body. Her legs started moving easier, more fluidly. She moved much smoother in the line, not disrupting it nearly as often.

Now that she was no longer horrified, she had to concede that she was actually having fun.

Her respite was short-lived. Just as she was finally synchronized with the other dancers, the music changed. The beat slowed drastically to a smooth, rhythmic reggae tune. Definitely not a conga. Almost everyone around them stopped to find a partner and began to slow-dance.

Jenna's pulse hammered. Sure enough, she turned to find Cabe watching her expectantly. She wanted to turn away, to run from him. But when he lifted his arms and beckoned, she found herself stepping into his embrace instead. He gently wrapped his arms around her, clasping his hands against her lower back.

Then Jenna promptly stepped on his foot. To his credit, Cabe didn't so much as wince. At her mortified gasp, he dipped his head toward hers. "Don't worry. You'll quickly get the hang of this, too. You're a natural."

Jenna's mind barely registered his words. He was so close, she could smell the now familiar sent of sandalwood combined with the sea salt air. The heat from his hands warmed the skin at the small of her back as he swayed with her to the music.

She should pull away, Jenna thought. Thank him politely and then just make her way off the dance floor. She really wasn't being terribly professional at the moment.

As if reading her thoughts, Cabe's hold on her tightened ever so slightly.

"Just relax. You can't dance to a slow song when you're tense," he coaxed.

She wanted to say something, anything. But her mouth had gone dry.

Surprisingly, once again her body reacted to Cabe's words. She felt some of the tension leave her muscles, and the tightness in her shoulders lessened. She leaned into him, let her head rest on his hard chest. She heard his heart beating against her ear, the steady rhythm soothing her down to her soul. She was beyond comfortable in Cabe Jordan's arms. It wasn't that preposterous. She knew Cabe. She'd known him most of her life. They'd grown up within a few short miles of each other, had roamed the same school hallways. And right now, she felt completely safe and secure in his arms.

What was happening to her? Who was this girl, dancing on a silky beach with a wildly handsome, enigmatic man she had no business being attracted to? She'd never behave in such a manner if they were back in Boston.

Or anywhere else on the planet, for that matter.

This wasn't her. Some type of island magic had turned her into someone else. The song ended and Jenna awkwardly stepped out of Cabe's embrace. A foreboding expression shuttered his face, a tic working along his jaw. Her pulse was hammering as well. Before she could think of anything appropriate to say, a beaming Seema ran up to them, holding something out to her.

"Congratulations, Jenna. You won!" Jenna looked down at the object the other woman handed her, three small gold statuettes mounted on a marble base—dancers in a conga line.

A trophy. Jenna had never been rewarded a trophy before.

"You were selected as the best conga dancer at the party," Seema exclaimed, her smile beaming.

Clearly, a sympathy win. Still, Jenna found herself inexplicably pleased.

"Wow. Thanks." She couldn't help the wayward smile that sneaked to her lips. "I've never won anything like this before. And especially not for dancing."

Seema gave her a hug before walking away.

"Nice job," Cabe told her. "Your first time and you get a trophy."

"No doubt it's for *most improved*. Still, this will look great in my office."

He studied her. "You're really excited about it, aren't you?"

She felt the flush creep into her cheeks. "You wouldn't understand. You most certainly have cases and cases full of all the trophies you've won over the years. All the athletic competitions you won."

"There were a few first-place math-club ribbons as well."

Jenna rolled her eyes with amusement. "None for modesty, I'm guessing." She rubbed her finger over one of the small statues. How silly of her to feel so touched—it was just a cheap trophy. One she didn't even really do anything to win. But she was proud of it just the same. "Like I said, you wouldn't understand."

"I'm glad it means something to you, Jenna."

"You're laughing at me. You must be, given all the real awards you've won over the years."

He shook his head. "No, I promise I'm not laughing at you. Trust me, my trophies never meant much. Not to anyone."

Something in the tone of his voice gave Jenna pause.

Cabe took a swig of his drink. "No one ever really saw me win them, after all."

"What are you talking about? The whole school witnessed you win or place most every contest." But as she said the words, an odd thought struck her—Cabe's parents had been noticeably absent at all those events. In fact, now that she really thought about it, she'd be hard-pressed to recall ever seeing James or Tricia at a single school game or play.

Despite the fact that their son had been the star at most of them.

The cursed insomnia plagued him again. Cabe tossed with annoyance onto his side in the king-size bed and noted the time on the bright digital clock. Twelve-thirty. He hadn't slept at all. Nothing unusual about that. But this was the first time it had happened in the Caribbean. Usually the combination of the heat, the long travel time and a packed agenda had him falling asleep before his head hit the pillow.

Not so this time.

Cabe knew the reason. He couldn't help but replay the events of earlier this evening repeatedly in his head: Jenna by his side as he led her through the beach party. The way she swayed to the music. Her delight at the colorful night sky as it burst in fireworks. The way she'd felt in his arms.

He'd behaved utterly unprofessionally.

Especially once Maxim had shown up and expressed a clear interest in her. He'd never been a fan of the overbearing man. But this was the first time he'd actually felt a desire to do him physical harm. And it showed.

Cabe hadn't tried hard enough to hide his animosity. Then he'd really lost his mind. He'd taken her to the dance floor. And he hadn't let her go when the music slowed.

It was unacceptable and he couldn't let it happen again. He was treading on thin ice as it was when it came to Jenna Townsend. He couldn't seem to stop acting erratically where she was concerned. He sighed and rubbed a hand down his face.

Outside, the party was still going strong. The band, contracted for up until an hour ago, continued to play. Island time was fluid. They would quit when they felt like it. And people would dance up until they did. The night was muggy and the air conditioner wasn't quite keeping up, none of which helped his insomnia. Shirtless, with just his pajama bottoms on, he reluctantly got out of bed.

He may as well go out onto the balcony for some fresh air. Maybe it would help.

Pulling the screen door open, he stepped into the moonlit night and watched the glitter of the ocean.

Jenna's light was on next door.

Her screen door sat adjacent to his on the same balcony. Though her blinds were shut, it was obvious she was still awake. He could hear her shuffling about. Either she was a night owl or she was having trouble sleeping also.

Well, he wasn't about to ask.

He'd been careless enough with her today. The last thing he wanted to do was knock on her door in the middle of the night.

He heard more muted sounds coming from behind her screen door. What was she doing in there?

Without warning, her screen door flew open and

she stepped outside with a huff. She did a double take when she saw him.

"You're awake," she observed, her eyes wide.

"And so are you."

He leaned over the banister, his arms resting on the railing. He didn't want to think too much about the formfitting tank top she wore or how it offered a tantalizing view of her shoulders, nor the thigh-length boy shorts she had on. Or how they sat low on her hips. Hips he'd had his hands on just a few short hours ago. His fingers tingled at the thought and he shook it off.

"What's keeping you up? The music? The sounds of laughter and partying?"

"None of the above," she answered. "Sorry. You probably wanted some time alone. I'll just go back in."

Damn it. He wanted her to be more comfortable around him. She didn't have to feel like she had to dash inside just because he was out here, too.

"Jenna. We are obviously both having trouble falling asleep. I'm out here to get some fresh air. So are you. There's plenty of it for both of us. We can share our insomnia."

She halted on the threshold and pivoted back. "Okay, then. But I don't have insomnia."

"No? You could have fooled me."

"I can't sleep because I can't stop scratching. My legs in particular are in bad shape."

He glanced down. "Sand fleas."

"Is that what caused the coin-sized itchy welts all over my calves?"

He bit his lip to keep from smiling. It really wasn't funny. "I'm sorry. I should have warned you. Some people are more susceptible to them than others."

"Oh, I appear to be one of the lucky ones."

"Is it bad?"

"I'm ready to scratch my skin off."

He approached her. "Can I take a look?"

Even in the dim lighting of the half-moon, he could see her cheeks redden. "I'm sure it'll be fine. I'll just go soak in the tub or something."

She turned to step away but stopped when he leaned down to her feet. He studied her legs, trying not to notice the toned shapely flesh of her thighs and how they led up to feminine, rounded hips.

Yep, she had several angry-looking bites.

"Soaking won't help," he informed her. "The hot water might actually make it worse."

"Great. Just great."

"But you're in luck."

She gave him a look of disbelief. "Um. How so?"

"Last time I was here I had a couple of bites. Seema gave me something for them. Seemed to work really well."

"Two whole bites, huh? And I'm the lucky one?"

He laughed and motioned for her to come inside his room. "Follow me."

She hesitated. "That's okay, Cabe. I don't want to interrupt your night any longer."

There she went again. Why was she so damn timid around him? Did she think he would bite her, too? Not that the thought hadn't crossed his mind.

"There's no reason to suffer, Jenna. I'll just go get you the stuff."

Without waiting for a response, he turned and walked inside and to his bathroom. She was still waiting outside on the balcony when he returned with a tube of ointment.

He handed it to her. “This works wonders. Put a dime-sized amount on each bite. Here, I’ll help you.”

She looked mortified at the thought. “I can do it.”

“Fine.”

Taking the tube, she went to work on the numerous spots, some already on the verge of breaking open.

“It stings at first,” he warned just as she let out a cry of “Ow!”

“Sorry.”

Several moments later, she handed the tube back to him. “Thanks again.”

He sensed her hesitation. “Is there something else?”

She looked away, off to the side. “No. Good night.”

He reached out and took her by the arm to stop her as she turned on her heel.

“Jenna, what is it?”

She closed her eyes and let out a deep breath. “I feel one just below my shoulder blade. It’s very itchy.”

“I see. You can’t reach it.”

She sighed. “I’ve been trying to scratch it all night.”

“To no avail?”

“I wouldn’t ask but—”

“It’s okay.” He gently turned her around and lifted her ponytail up. Apparently she even slept with her hair in a cursed bow. He fought the urge to untie the ribbon and release her thick curls.

Focus. Sure enough, right above her tank’s line, she had a nasty-looking bite immediately to the bottom of her left shoulder blade.

“That one’s a mosquito bite,” he told her. “It appears all sorts of things are attracted to you.”

Damn. Why in the world had he said that? An awkward silence fell between them before she finally broke it.

"I can't even reach it to scratch it."

"That's because you're not double-jointed." He laughed but she didn't respond. "I can't see how you're going to locate that one let alone reach it. Here, let me."

Before she could argue, he uncapped the tube and began to apply the ointment.

His breath caught as he touched her. Her skin felt warm beneath his fingers. He found himself leaning in closer. The aroma of her hair teased him, a hint of strawberries and a subtle feminine scent that was distinctly her own.

"Jenna." He whispered behind her ear, unable to help himself. His arm moved of its own accord to reach around her middle. She stiffened for the briefest of moments but then went totally lax against him. Her back against his bare chest. She felt like heaven and he knew he shouldn't be doing this. Shouldn't be holding her like this or touching her even. Hadn't he just vowed as much? But he couldn't seem to let her go. All he could do was repeat her name.

As if on cue, the clouds shifted and erased the faint moonlight they'd been bathed in. Only the dim artificial beams from the party lights in the distance afforded them any hint of respite from the dark.

"You were lying earlier, weren't you?" he found himself asking foolishly. "When you said you weren't curious about me. That you had no questions to ask."

He felt her exhale a long, deep breath. Several moments passed before she replied. "Yes," she finally admitted on a whisper.

She turned her head and his gaze fell to her lips.

What would she taste like? He wanted desperately to find out.

"So do it now. Just ask me."

"I don't know, Cabe. It feels too much like gossip."

"It's okay, Jenna. We're having a conversation. That's very different."

He felt her shrug. "I can't help but see it that way. Your family has always been a source of gossip. So elevated, so unattainable."

He'd help her. "And you want to know if any of the rumors are true?"

She exhaled under his arms. "There were too many rumors to keep track of. It was more the general sense of the villagers talking as they stared at the castle."

He let out an ironic chuckle, though he felt anything but amused at the moment.

She made no effort to turn around and face him. Thankfully. Talking was so much easier this way, with her in his arms, both of them staring off at the dark shadow of the ocean in the distance.

"It was far from a castle."

His words had some kind of impact on her. She stiffened as he said it, suddenly tried to pull away. He instinctively held on to her, didn't let her leave his arms. "What?" he asked, taken aback at her reaction.

"Says the crown prince."

He'd offended her. How could he explain it to her? Did he even want to? That what she grew up seeing was a facade. A well-crafted, expertly framed image of the perfect family. The reality had been so very different.

"It wasn't quite a fairy tale, Jenna. Please believe that." At her silence, he added, "You don't, do you?"

"You said on the beach that your trophies never

meant anything. Are you trying to tell me your life was anything less than idyllic? How so? You're going to have to explain it to me. Because it sure looked that way to me and anyone else in that town."

The skepticism in her voice rang clear and loud. He swallowed, tried to gather the words.

"You know what?" Jenna said. "Never mind. Forget I asked. I only did because you told me to."

"I know. And I meant it. I'm trying to answer in as truthful a way as possible." He took a deep breath. It was true. Something about her, maybe her strength or her openness, made him want to confide in her in a way he hadn't done with anyone else. Maybe it was the way she'd looked at him after they'd danced together on the beach. He wanted to open up more of him for her to see.

"We were supposed to appear that way," he began. "It's what we wanted everyone to see when they looked at us. Do you understand?"

She shook her head slowly, her soft silky hair skimming the stubble on his chin. "I'm afraid I don't."

"From the outside, we projected the image of the perfect little family."

"But inside the castle walls?" she prompted.

Cold. It was the first word that came to mind. Followed by *distant* and *unfeeling.* "It's hard to explain."

Her spine stiffened slightly. "Cabe, are you saying that Tricia and James were…?" She paused to take a deep breath. "That they didn't treat you well?"

Damn. She'd just jumped to the absolute wrong conclusion, that he'd been abused somehow. Physically or emotionally. That was also far from the truth. The truth sat somewhere in between.

He was really making a mess of this whole conversation. First he'd come off as the clichéd poor little rich boy. Now he'd led her to believe he'd been harmed by his very own parents. He should end this. He should just drop the whole thing and bid her a hasty good-night. But having her in his arms felt like some sort of balm. It felt right, her pressed up against him, numbing his senses. Dulling the pain.

If he stopped now, if he let her go and walked away, he'd never make his way back.

Not with Jenna. Not with anyone.

He'd never again find a way to open up about the darkness that hung over his perfect life like a heavy curtain, casting all sorts of shadows.

So he took a deep breath and just let it go. "I'm not a real Jordan, Jenna. I'm not really James and Tricia's son." The words hung thick in the air between them. Another layer pulled away from the fantasy.

What he didn't say was that his very existence was a result of his parents' greatest tragedy.

Jenna stilled. Trying to absorb what he'd just told her, no doubt. He couldn't blame her. He knew no one at school ever suspected. James and Tricia were that good at hiding the reality. And so was he.

He finally turned her around to face him, grateful for the darkness that hid what his expression must have held. "I was adopted by James and Tricia as an infant."

She lifted a shaking hand toward his chin. He resisted the urge to turn into it. "I didn't know," she offered.

"You weren't supposed to know. No one is. We moved into town when I was a preschooler. Started the business right after."

"It doesn't make you any less their son."

How many times had he heard that over the years from James and Tricia themselves? Just words. He'd always seen the truth in their eyes. The harsh reality: if they hadn't tragically lost their real son, they wouldn't have even known Cabe existed.

"Thank you for that. But it does."

She sighed, hesitated before she spoke again. "Did it bother you so terribly? Because you never showed it."

He shrugged. "The fact that I was adopted? No, that's not what bothered me."

"Other things?"

"Like I said. It's hard to explain."

"I know your father has always been very proud of you. Everyone in town knows that."

"I worked hard and made sure of it," he said. He'd tried so hard to earn their affection. He'd studied longer, played harder. Everything in his teenage power to make himself what he thought they wanted in a son. None of it was ever enough. "Still, there were those ever so rare times when I caught him staring at me," he told her.

"Staring how?"

"It's not important."

"Please tell me."

He let out a small laugh. "I don't know. He just had this look on his face, you know. A look that made me wonder and think about the reality." He'd spent his whole life trying to erase that look off his father's face. But no amount of achievement had done it so far. Nor had any of it erased the chronic, haunting sadness in his mother's eyes.

"What reality?"

The one that had shaped him since that fateful day when he'd turned fifteen, Cabe thought. That was the day the mystery fell into place just as the whole world around him crumbled. He wanted the knowledge of it off his chest, once and for all. His very heart told him that this was the moment, the chance he thought he'd never get. The woman in his arms was the key to lightening the burden. They'd grown up in such different ways but she'd be the one to understand somehow. Jenna would know what he meant when he told her that he'd been given everything he could have wanted as a child and teen. Except for one minor omission: genuine, honest parental affection.

He sucked in a breath and choked out the words. "That I would never have been their son if they'd had the choice."

"Oh, Cabe. But they did choose you," she said, her voice gentle and soothing. The situation was almost surreal, the way he was opening up to Jenna Townsend on a dark balcony in the middle of the night. Finally having the words out in the open combined with the heady way she said his name sent a surge of pure longing through him. Instinctively, he pulled her closer against him. She let out a soft moan and his gaze fell to her lips. What would they taste like? He dipped his head to find out. A mere brush of his lips against hers. Hardly a kiss at all. But it was enough to rock him straight through to his core. She sighed against his mouth and he wanted more, needed to taste her fully. He pulled her closer so that he could plunge into those lips deeper.

The band outside suddenly stopped playing and a loud cheer erupted, shattering the moment in a fast instant. The effect was like a splash of cold water. Cabe reflexively dropped his arms and for a moment they both stood frozen.

What in heaven's name was he doing?

He ran a hand through his hair. "Jenna, I shouldn't—"

Her sharp gasp cut him off. She stepped away as if struck by lightning. He almost reached for her but some small speck of sanity stopped him.

Without a word, she turned on her heel then fled into her room. He could only watch as she closed the screen door and pulled the curtain closed. In more ways than one. Her light went out an instant later.

Leaving Cabe in the dark shaking with need. And wondering what the hell he'd been thinking.

What in the world had she been thinking? She should have just turned right around and gone back into her room the second she saw Cabe out on that balcony. She'd tried but not hard enough. But then she'd never have known.

Jenna lay in bed and listened to the chirping of the birds outside as the darkness of dawn slowly evolved into a bright sunny morning.

She hadn't slept a wink.

In a couple of short hours, she was supposed to meet Cabe for a working breakfast meeting. Calmly and professionally. She had no idea how she would pull it off. They had to address what had happened between them and everything he'd revealed.

He'd certainly dropped a bombshell on her. Cabe was not the Jordans' biological son. And he seemed very affected by it.

There had to be more to the story. For instance, why had the three of them kept the truth so under wraps? And for that matter, Cabe may have been adopted but he still seemed to have led a charmed life. But the man she'd encountered last night seemed very different than the impression she'd always had of him as the high-achieving, handsome playboy.

His words echoed in her head. *It was supposed to look idyllic from the outside.*

He'd been drinking last night. It wasn't any kind of excuse but it was more than what she'd had. She'd been stone-cold sober while practically melting into his arms. Oh, Lord. He'd kissed her. Well, almost. He'd touched his lips to hers and would have gone further before Jenna had found some semblance of sanity. The memory of it quickened her pulse and that just made her madder at herself.

The kiss didn't mean anything. It couldn't have. She would blame this magical location, being so far from home in such an enchanting place. So far removed from reality.

Even if Cabe was attracted to her, which he seemed to be last night, it wasn't anything to dwell on. She wasn't the type of woman Cabe Jordan was ever going to be interested in long term. They belonged on two different spheres.

Still, what he'd revealed about himself last night led her to the age-old saying: appearances could be deceiving. There was clearly more to her boss than the image she'd held for all these years. As much as Jenna had wanted to pry and get to the bottom of it all, she'd resisted. It clearly cost him to reveal as much as he had. Cabe would tell her the rest when he was ready. She would be there, available for him when he needed her.

But he pushed you away at the end.

There was that. She tossed aside the covers and got out of bed.

She was contemplating it all still two hours later after showering and getting dressed when she heard Cabe's knock.

She took a deep, fortifying breath before opening the door to greet him.

"Good morning." He didn't mean it. He looked miserable and he clearly had slept about as much as she had. Still, even with the dark circles he was utterly, heart-shatteringly handsome in his stone-gray suit and crystal-blue tie. Her mind automatically shifted to the way he'd felt last night, hard and firm against her back. She could still smell the hint of his sandalwood scent, could still feel the way his breath had felt against her cheek. The firmness of his lips as they'd touched hers.

Stop it.

She stepped aside to let him in. He didn't move though, which surprised her. Then she saw the look on his face. Regret. He thought the whole balcony encounter was a big fiasco. A mistake. He'd probably been kicking himself all night for divulging his lifelong secret. To someone like her, no less.

"Are you ready to go?" he asked.

Jenna blinked. That was all he was going to say to her?

No hint of the gentle, open man from last night could be detected this morning. The one who'd bared his soul to her. Well, what had she expected? That he'd sweep her in his arms the moment he saw her, overwhelmed at the sight of her and all that they'd shared in the darkness?

"Do you need another minute?" he asked, glancing at his watch.

Jenna gave her head a shake. "Um, no. Let me just grab my things."

She forced a smile upon returning to the doorway. "I'm ready."

He silently turned and made his way down the stairs. Jenna stared in stunned silence before following. Now what? Did she dare say something? The awkward silence was downright unbearable. Cabe seemed in no hurry to break it. Perhaps she'd only imagined last night. Maybe it had only been a crazy dream.

No.

It had been real. She had the bug bites to prove it.

Blasted bugs. They were the reason all this was happening. If only she'd taken a moment to peer outside last night before she'd jumped out on the balcony. She would have never gone out if she'd known Cabe was there. Her legs had been itchy and stinging but no amount of balm was worth the discomfort and awkwardness of this moment.

Instinctively, she reached down and rubbed the biggest bite on the top of her thigh.

"Did the ointment not work for you?" Cabe asked, his tone brusque.

"It did. It worked great. Thank you."

"Don't mention it."

The double meaning was clear. Cabe wasn't going to bring up anything that had happened on that balcony. Nor did he want her to. The tight set of his jaw left no question about it.

Also no question that he deeply regretted it all. A brick settled in Jenna's chest. Such foolishness on her part not to see this coming. Cabe had succumbed to a moment of weakness last night. Nothing more. She'd just conveniently been there. He'd been tired, probably missing the companionship he usually had on these trips.

"I'll get you some more of it later. We have a lot to do today. We can't have you distracted. Not by itchy bites, not by anything."

Her composure almost faltered and she gritted her teeth. Subtle, he wasn't.

"I hardly feel them," she threw out. Two could play at this game.

He didn't bother to look at her. "Good."

Her eyes stung. She tried to convince herself that it was the bright early-morning sun. It was easier than facing the truth.

Just as well they'd be busy all day. The busier the better. The less time she had to think and dwell on senseless emotion, the better off she would be.

She just had to hope her highly honed focusing skills didn't let her down. It wouldn't be easy given that she'd be spending the day side by side with Cabe. After a night where she'd done nothing but toss and turn and think about him and what they'd shared.

All of which Cabe was telling her to forget.

CHAPTER SIX

CABE WANTED TO hit something. An hour spent in the resort's gym at the break of dawn followed by a two-mile jog along the beach had done nothing to ebb his agitation or his anger at himself.

Jenna knew the truth. There was no turning back on that now. At some point he had to acknowledge it. Just not now.

Of all the asinine, idiotic—

"Is something wrong?" Jenna asked him as they reached the podium where the maître d' greeted them with a smile.

He realized he'd cursed out loud. "I was just saying, this is the main dining area of the resort. Vacationers can eat here at any time of day."

She studied him with clear doubt. "Oh, really? Is that what you were saying?"

He didn't respond as they were seated. Their table sat poolside and faced the beach, affording them a perfect view of a clear and sunny horizon. A waiter immediately greeted them and poured steaming hot coffee into two porcelain cups. A moment later, he brought out a tray of assorted pastries and platters of eggs and crispy potatoes.

They went to work right away, going over the numerous to-dos that would lead to the opening of the new store. Jenna impressed him repeatedly with her knowledge and insight. Not to mention her ability to offer solutions to matters that would have taken him twice as long to figure out by himself. Though he had numerous people working on the endeavor both in New York and on the island, he found it invaluable to have another mind just to help him with the sheer volume of details involved. He couldn't have chosen better than Jenna.

They made quite a team.

A team he couldn't risk jeopardizing again by doing anything foolish or reckless. The way he had last night. What had he done? How impulsive of him, how uncharacteristic. An unbidden image of her leaning back against him invaded his mind. He shoved it out of his head.

An hour and a half later, when the dishes had been cleared and the coffee carafe was empty, Cabe felt more in control about the opening than he had in weeks. They both had clear agendas—with phone calls to make and emails to send out.

To her credit, Jenna was staying mum about last night and giving him time to bring up the matter himself if he chose to. She apparently could tell that he was in no mood to deal with the fallout of his revelations. Once Jenna took her last sip of coffee, he stood and pulled out her chair. "Follow me. We can head to the business center and get some work done there before our meeting with the resort's retail manager this afternoon."

She had her hair up again this morning, this time in some kind of tight bun. But it was no match for the Caribbean's morning heat and humidity. A few tendrils had escaped their confines, forming wispy curls around her temples. The few short hours of daylight she'd spent here yesterday had somehow already resulted in a hint of red color across her cheeks and on the bridge of her nose. The effect was a subtle beauty that no amount of store-bought makeup could have achieved.

He stopped short. Not this again. What the devil was he doing? He had no business noticing the added color on her cheeks. Or anything about her looks, for that matter.

He couldn't even blame it on punch this time.

"Do you need to stop at your room for anything?" he asked. "It's on the way."

"No. I have everything I need."

Several children frolicked in the pool while their moms relaxed on lounge chairs reading magazines or the latest bestseller. A squealing wet toddler darted past them toward the kiddie sprinklers with his father fast on his heels. The man caught the child in a hug and carried him the rest of the way, despite the toddler's squirmy efforts to be let down.

They reached the concrete path where the resort grounds met the sandy beach. They hadn't gone far when Cabe realized Jenna had stopped. He turned to find her staring off to the side, her hand cupped over her face to shield her eyes from the blare of the sun.

"Jenna?"

He followed her line of vision to where a young local girl sat, a variety of handcrafted items set up on display on a folding table in front of her. The resort was pretty accommodating about locals who tried to sell various wares on the property. This one had gotten here relatively early.

"Do you know what she's selling?" Jenna asked.

"Looks mostly like beaded jewelry of some sort. Maybe some leather items."

"She looks very young."

He had to agree. The girl couldn't be more than thirteen or so.

"Shouldn't she be in school?" Jenna asked.

"They're pretty relaxed about school here sometimes." She hadn't torn her gaze away from the girl. "Fridays are a good day to set up shop on the beach. A lot of tourists are either coming or going. Those arriving have their wallets still conveniently in their pockets. And the ones departing are often looking to buy last-minute souvenirs."

"I see."

"She probably had to choose between going to school or helping to feed her family for the week."

Jenna seemed torn and took a hesitant step in the girl's direction. Cabe doubted she even realized having done so. "I know we have a lot to do…" she began.

"Would you like to go take a look at the items?" he asked, unnecessarily as the answer was obvious.

He led the way without waiting for a response. "Let's go." She was fast on his heels.

The young girl's eyes lit up as they approached. Two well-dressed interested tourists was always a welcome sight.

"May I take a look?" Jenna asked.

She trailed her hand along the items and picked one up, some kind of leather necklace with colorful beads.

"This one would look so pretty with your hair color," the girl stated with a Creole accent.

"It's beautiful."

Not wasting a second, she came around the table and hung the necklace around Jenna's neck, then held up a mirror.

She turned to Cabe. "You should buy it. For your lady."

Jenna corrected her right away. "Oh, no. He's not… He won't be buying it."

The girl's face fell but she wasn't ready to quit. "You look amazing wearing it, miss." She held the mirror up higher. "See how pretty."

"I know," Jenna blurted out then blushed. "I mean, I like it. I will buy it myself."

She glanced down at the table. "Actually, I think I'll buy everything on this tray."

The girl's eyes grew wide. "Did you just say you want all of this?"

Jenna nodded and smiled. "Yes, please. I'll take that tray, everything on it."

Cabe looked down. The tray consisted of at least twenty items. Mostly necklaces made of beads. A few bracelets made of braided rubber bands. Was one of those a dog leash? Jenna didn't even care what she was buying.

That was probably more than the girl typically sold in a month. Maybe even six months.

"And a couple of those slippers," Jenna added, pointing to a pile of rubber flip-flops under the table. She hadn't even asked the price. Or size.

The girl still hadn't recovered. She stood staring at them both with a stunned expression. "You are joking? Yes?"

Jenna vehemently shook her head. "No. No joking.

I'll come right back with my wallet." She turned to him. "Cabe, will you wait here? I'll be right back."

Before she could turn around, Cabe stopped her with a hand on her arm. "Stay here." He pulled out his wallet, yanked out several bills and handed them to the girl. "We'll take the whole table."

The girl audibly gasped, hesitantly taking the bills, as if Cabe might change his mind any second. Then she sprang toward Jenna, wrapping her in a big, tight hug. "Thank you. Thank you both. So very much."

She pocketed the bills and pulled out several large plastic bags, filling them with the items off her table.

Jenna turned to him with her mouth agape. "What? Why? I could have paid for the things I wanted."

"Consider it a business expense."

"How in the world would such purchases be considered a business expense?"

"Well, for one thing, they're handcrafted jewelry pieces. We're in the jewelry business. Who knows? Maybe it will give us ideas about trends and designs." Not bad for an off-the-cuff response. He was pretty impressed with himself for coming up with that one on the spot.

She pursed her lips. "You didn't need to do that. It was totally unnecessary."

He took the bags the still-grinning girl handed to them and motioned for Jenna to go forward. He could hear the young girl humming a happy Marley tune as she folded up her empty table.

"It wasn't as if you actually *wanted* any of it," he argued. "You were just trying to help the child. You can't deny that."

She lifted her chin. "As a matter of fact, I was buying souvenirs for the personnel in the Boston regional office."

"Is that so? You were going to buy the whole tray."

"My staff works hard. They deserve to be rewarded for it."

"Well, now you can reward the whole building."

"Be that as it may, you didn't have to step in and cover it all for me."

He didn't break his stride. The truth of it was, he could tell Jenna was moved by the girl's plight. And he'd merely reacted to the look in Jenna's eyes when she'd looked at the girl. Then he'd actually felt a sense of shame about all the times he'd seen that very same child set up on the beach and never thought to help her out by buying anything. When he compared that to Jenna's reaction, what did that say about him?

He'd been brought up better than that.

"Are you angry?" he asked Jenna when she'd stayed silent for several steps.

She took a deep breath. "I don't know."

Her honesty gave him pause. The females in his life usually decided right away when they were cross with him and they made sure to let him know.

He sighed. "Don't be. All that matters is we made that girl's life just a little easier. You can't argue with that."

She rubbed a hand over her eyes. "I guess not. I guess I should be thanking you instead. What you did was very generous."

"She has you to thank."

"You purchased her entire table!"

"You're the only reason we went over to her table in the first place."

Jenna looked away with a small shrug. "I wish I could do more for her. She so reminds me of—" She caught herself before she went any further with the statement. He knew what she'd been about to say. The girl reminded Jenna of herself. The Townsend kids hadn't exactly had an easy time growing up, a fact the whole town had been aware of. He wondered how many times during their adolescence Jenna and her brother had struggled to get by. How often had Jenna spent her paycheck on groceries rather than the frivolous knick-knacks most teenage girls spent their money on?

They'd reached a somewhat empty area of the beachfront. Only a handful of suntanning tourists dotted the sand and a couple of kids building a simple yet muddy sandcastle. He'd deliberately taken her this route, hoping it would settle her thoughts.

She'd had quite the forty-eight hours.

"Who knows?" he added. "Maybe once the store is opened, we'll have her or other vendors set up a booth or something inside. We'll do the high-end stuff while displaying the local ware."

She suddenly stopped in her tracks and turned to him, forcing him to stop as well. "You would do that?"

"Why not? Don't you think it's a good idea?"

She smiled up at him then. A true smile unlike he'd seen from her before. And a strange feeling unfolded in his chest, one he couldn't name.

"I think it's the most wonderful idea."

"We could establish a whole program around it. Local craft jewelry being sold along our expensive deluxe pieces." Wow, he was getting really good at coming up with all sorts of ideas right on the spot, completely off the top of his head. He had no one but Jenna to thank for it.

She touched his forearm, clearly pleased. "Oh, Cabe. I think that could really work."

"Of course it will work. And it will please the local authorities. It's a win-win." He stopped to face her. "As a matter of fact, I think you may have helped with our zoning issues. The local brass always appreciate when any new business expands community ties."

Her eyes grew wide. "But I didn't do anything. You came up with the idea yourself. You're the one who can implement it."

None of it would have even occurred to him if she hadn't been by his side. "Not so. My project manager can also implement it. I might put her in charge of the program entirely. If she's interested."

The mild touch on his arm turned to an all-out grip. "Of course I'd be interested. I know firsthand how opportunities like that can make a monumental impact on someone's life." She literally bit down on her lip after she'd said the words.

"Is that right, Jenna?"

She looked off at the horizon, her eyes growing distant and pensive. Several moments passed in silence and Cabe didn't think she would answer. Finally, she took a deep breath. "When you said she was probably out there so that she could feed her family..."

"Yes?"

She clearly struggled to find the right words. "There were plenty of nights when my brother and I didn't eat," she confessed. "Especially during the summers when there was no school lunch to fall back on. I felt responsible when he was hungry."

So unfair, Cabe thought. Jenna had been forced to parent not only herself but also her older brother. "You were just a kid yourself."

"But he was the confused teenage boy. He looked to me for answers. Who else was there? Things got better as I grew older. Once I could start working, I made sure we both had at least one square meal a day. The elderly store owner on the corner of Falmouth and Main, down the street from our apartment, he offered me my first job. He knew I needed it. I never forgot that. Or his kindness. That man made all the difference in our lives."

"What about your mother?"

Her lips formed a grim smile. "My mother wasn't around much."

"Still. She must have had some source of income."

Jenna didn't tear her gaze off the horizon. "She mostly lived off her boyfriends. In between men, she had odd jobs. Waitressing on and off. Cleaning offices here and there. Nothing really stuck. And she had other ideas about what to do with the little income she did earn."

"Others must have helped you along the way." He sincerely hoped so. Or what did that say about the town he'd grown up in?

"Of course they did. But once I started to earn it, then it wasn't charity. It was accomplishment."

He felt the breath leave his lungs in a whoosh. Even at such a young age, Jenna Townsend had valued her pride. While he'd been out pursuing tennis trophies and merit ribbons to prove himself to his parents, she'd been fighting for survival. And she hadn't even done it for selfish reasons. She'd done it for her brother. To make sure they ate.

He didn't know what to say to her. His own struggles in life seemed to pale in comparison. Cabe had never wanted for anything. Not for anything materialistic, anyway. Sure, he'd spent most of his hours alone, his parents completely absent or completely disconnected if they were around. But the thought of going hungry was an absolute foreign concept.

"You've achieved a lot, Jenna. You're a successful, accomplished businesswoman."

A false and bitter laugh escaped her lips. "I had no choice. I had to work harder and be smarter than everyone else. I promised myself I would never be like her."

No wonder she was so driven, so rigid. Like that young vendor, Jenna had been carrying around a heavy burden since she was barely a teen. It all made sense now. Her inability to relax, her workaholic tendencies. All to outrun a legacy she'd already left so far behind. Yet somehow, it still chased her.

He and Jenna Townsend had a lot in common.

Jenna swiveled around in a large leather chair in one of the cubicles in the business center where she and Cabe had been working for the past two hours. Well, she'd been trying to work, anyway. She hadn't really gotten as much done as she would have liked. The scene from this morning kept playing over and over in her head.

Cabe hadn't even thought twice about offering that lovely girl whatever he'd had in his wallet. Sure, he could afford it. But not every wealthy man would have done the same thing. And his idea to have crafters set up in the store, that would be a true way to give back to this wonderful community she'd already grown so fond of in her short time here. Not only had he helped the girl with her immediate concern, he'd figured out a way to help her long term. All in all, a very monumental gesture.

So why did she feel so unsettled? She'd been tense and uneasy since the whole encounter. Something about the way Cabe had stepped in, taken charge of the situation, and gone above and beyond what she had intended.

It had impressed her. His kind gesture had impressed her.

And she didn't like it.

She didn't need any kind of white-knight hero to take over for her in such a situation. Hadn't that been exactly the kind of thing that would have impressed someone like her mother? Amanda loved it when the men she was with took care of things for her. Especially if the gesture involved a display of wealth.

But Cabe's actions had been all about kindness. Then he'd gone further to come up with an idea about how to continue the kindness on a broader scale.

It would be utterly selfish of Jenna to be cross with him. After all, it wasn't the use of his money that had impressed her, it was the use of his heart, his generosity. He had helped that girl more than Jenna would have been able to. So now she was an annoying bundle of frustration, anxiety and anger. Not to mention confused.

She'd spent her life ensuring that she could stand on her own two feet, that she didn't need any kind of assistance or guidance from a man the way her mom did. Cabe's take-charge personality was now blurring that previously solid image of herself she'd worked so hard to achieve.

Yep. Cabe Jordan was totally, overwhelmingly confusing her. The man was a complete enigma, impossible to comprehend. He'd opened up to her about a monumental part of his life—that he'd been adopted. But then he'd refused to even mention it again the next day. Then just when she thought she'd imagined his openness and vulnerability, he'd gone ahead and made the wishes of a needy girl come true right before Jenna's very eyes.

Basically, he'd walked into her office a few short days ago and completely scrambled her senses. She had no idea how to handle him. Nor could she imagine what her life was going to feel like when she went back to it without him in it. Once Cabe returned to Manhattan and she was back in Boston, her life would never be the same again.

But she'd have to accompany him back here to the resort at least once or twice more before the project was completed. Wouldn't she? Not only was she his project manager for the store opening, she'd just been recruited for the local vendor outreach idea.

The thought of returning both excited and terrified her. Her psyche might not be able to handle another trip like this one.

She could not fall for Cabe Jordan. He was absolutely wrong for her. Look how much he'd disrupted her life in the few short days since he'd stepped into it. Who was she kidding, anyway? As if he would even entertain the thought of the two of them in any kind of serious relationship. Haughty models and bright-eyed actresses were far more his style. Technically, he was dating one now.

As if her thoughts had conjured him, he materialized in front of her. His shirtsleeves were rolled up to reveal tan, muscular forearms. The man looked like he'd stepped right out of a male trends magazine. Though that was the kind of thing she did not need to be noticing.

"Late-morning doldrums?" he asked, holding out a sweaty plastic cup of iced tea. "Freshly brewed. Thought you might need a break."

Well, his timing was certainly a point in his favor. She inhaled the scent of the aromatic, lemony brew and felt her senses sharpen before she even took a sip. "Hmm, perfect. Thank you."

"You're welcome. Can't be too long a break though."

"Wow, and you said you weren't a harsh boss."

"Demanding versus harsh. Big difference. We have that meeting with the retail manager."

She turned to check the small bar on top of her laptop screen that read the date and time. "It's not for another two hours. You said we're meeting him right here on-site."

"True, but you might want to change first."

"Change? Why?"

"I meant to mention, Sonny likes to hold his meetings in an open cabana on the beach. You'll be way too warm in that pantsuit."

A business meeting in a beachside cabana. She could really get used to this lifestyle. It did pose a problem, however. All she'd really packed were other suits. Well, except for her tankini in case she had time for a swim in the ocean. That would hardly be appropriate for a meeting, even in this environment.

"Oh, dear." She looked down at her outfit.

"What's wrong?"

"I didn't really pack anything much different than what I'm wearing."

He narrowed his eyes in disbelief. "Really? All you packed are business suits and one sundress?"

He remembered her dress? He didn't seem the type to make note of such things.

She nodded, an embarrassed flush warming up her cheeks. How foolish of her. She didn't even know how to pack for a business trip. "And a swimsuit."

He seemed to think for a minute then turned abruptly. "Okay, let's go."

She knew he was a man used to being in charge and having others jump to fulfill his every demand, but these sudden turns were a bit tough to get used to. "Where exactly are we going? Two hours before our meeting?"

"The adjacent shopping center. I can check the status of the new paneling they're to start putting in today."

"Okay. What will I be doing?"

"You're going to visit the ladies' boutique. There's got to be a couple of outfits you can pick out that are more suitable for an outdoor conference."

She hadn't seen that coming. "You want me to go shopping? Now?" She gestured to the piles of paperwork on the desk and her laptop blinking with several new emails. "I don't have to remind you about all the work that needs to get done. Oh, and we have a meeting very soon."

"Well, I'm not saying you should take all day. Just go pick out a couple of things." He seemed to contemplate her, looked her up and down. "You don't strike me as one of those women who takes forever and tries on a hundred outfits."

She huffed out an exasperated sigh. "No. Of course not." She was never indecisive about clothes. She just couldn't usually afford to buy anything that wasn't marked down and finding adequate, comfortable items on sale took a bit more time. She couldn't be one of those women who shopped indiscriminately.

"Then I don't see a problem. But we're wasting time. Let's go."

"I need to get my purse from the suite."

"Why?"

Was he being deliberately obtuse? "Because you're making me shop."

"Just have them put it on my account."

Jenna halted. Oh, no. Not again. He was oh, so ready to buy things for her. The thought sent an irritated bristle up her spine. After all, this was no way comparable to the way he'd helped that girl on the beach. This was totally different. She wouldn't have it.

"You are not buying me clothes, Cabe."

"No. I'm not."

She was about to breathe a sigh of relief when she paused. Way too easy.

She was right. "I'm ensuring my project assistant has what she needs to be productive and useful at a very important meeting," Cabe said.

Productive and useful! She lifted her chin. "It doesn't take clothes to do that."

Cabe pinched the bridge of his nose and let out a deep sigh. "Why are we arguing about this? You need something to wear. The solution is simple."

"But why do you want to pay for it? I can purchase the outfits myself. You do pay me well." The second half of her statement was true. As far as the first part, well, she was on shaky ground there. She had no idea how expensive this boutique would be. And though she'd rather die than admit it to Cabe, she had to live on a strict budget and justify the spending of every dime. Or she'd never have anything left over for a rainy day after paying off her monthly school loan dues and taking care of all the other responsibilities.

"That's not the point. The point is, I'm asking you to purchase the items. It's not something that you have asked for or even want apparently. Anyway, it's my fault you're unprepared. I should have warned you about needing some casual beach clothes."

Irritation flooded through her. Why did he have to make sense? But his argument did hold some truth. It wasn't like this was her idea. She would have no intention of buying more clothes if he wasn't asking her to.

Cabe obviously saw her softening. He moved quickly to further rally his point. "It's just another asset."

That was also true. If she needed a different laptop or a new tablet, she wouldn't be expected to pay for it herself.

Besides, she had to admit the utter foolishness of walking into a luxury boutique on her budget and expecting to be able to find something. She doubted a place like that would have a sales rack.

Cabe broke through her thoughts. "If it makes you feel better, consider it a loan."

She worked hard not to grit her teeth. "Oh? How so? Will you be wearing the clothes after I'm done with the meeting?"

His mouth twitched. "An interesting solution. But I was thinking more along the lines of donating the items in the company's name to the women's shelter back in Boston."

That gave her pause. Of course, Cabe immediately sensed her hesitation and pounced.

"You know I'm making sense." He drove the point home.

That may be, Jenna thought, but the fear that she was

tumbling down a dangerous slippery slope sent an icy trickle between her shoulder blades.

He stood staring at her, waiting for her response. She forced herself not to look away from his intense stare. His eyes had grown dark. Due to utter irritation, she'd bet. Cabe probably wasn't used to women turning him down when it came to such offers. Or anything else, for that matter.

The dress would go to good use. It wasn't as if she'd be keeping it. A serpent of doubt crawled into her brain. Was she merely justifying the concept? Giving her head a quick shake, Jenna made herself take a mental step back. She hadn't even seen the dress yet and she was already fretting about having to return it. Cabe continued to stare at her.

She folded her arms across her middle. "Fine. I'll go take a look. If, and only if, I find something that I think may work, then I'll put it on your account. And I will guarantee a donation receipt upon our return from the charity."

"I have no doubt you will."

"Fine."

"Fine," he repeated. "Well, that required more of a battle than it should have. You know, most women would jump at the chance of a shopping spree on the house."

"I am not most women."

He let out an exasperated sigh. "Oh, I'll give you that."

"What is that supposed to mean?" she demanded, ready to do battle yet again for some reason.

He held up his arms in surrender. "I'm agreeing with

you. You are definitely not like most of the women I know. Not in the least."

She noticed the slight upward turn of his lips. He was teasing her! And she was falling for it.

She pushed her chair in and stepped away from the desk. "I'm going to take that as a compliment."

He winked at her and her insides quivered like pudding. Not good. Not good at all. A professional, serious Cabe she could handle. She couldn't say the same about this playful one. Or the generous one she'd witnessed on the beach. Or the concerned one who helped put ointment on her bites. Then held her against him as he told her the pressure he'd felt his whole life to be perfect.

Those Cabes were dangerous indeed.

"Go right ahead," he said. "It was meant as one."

As she moved to the door, Jenna had to remind herself that she was irritated.

Cabe reread the same email for the seventh time and found he'd be hard-pressed to recall exactly what it said. He couldn't focus. His mind insisted on wandering to Jenna. No little wonder with her scent still clinging to the air. Things certainly weren't dull when she was around him. This morning alone, she'd managed to have him buy a tableful of island souvenirs and then she'd sparred with him over the simple purchase of a meeting-suitable dress. He hadn't realized how uneventful these trips had been until this time. This trip had so far been one unexpected adventure after another because of her.

Had she found a dress she liked? Was she trying it on even at this moment?

Those thoughts had him wanting to kick himself. Surely, he had better things to do than contemplate the shopping status of a woman who was merely here to help him with a large venture.

He had to admit, however, that he'd be more than a little disappointed if, after all the back and forth about it, she came back empty-handed. It had not been easy to convince Jenna Townsend to accept something he'd offered to purchase for her. He'd done it twice in one morning.

She would have never accepted if it hadn't been presented as a loan. Pledging the dress to charity had finally trumped it for her. Or so he hoped. He couldn't really be certain of anything when it came to her. Why in the world did he find that so enticing?

He understood. Or thought he did. Jenna had fought fiercely her whole life to become and stay independent. He admired her for it. Who would blame her, growing up as she had? Rather than taking even the slightest risk of becoming like her mother, Jenna had worked hard and sacrificed to make a success of herself. And what a tremendous job she'd done.

His email folder dinged at him again, signaling the arrival of ten more urgent messages in his mailbox. He leaned back in his chair and decided it wasn't even worth his effort to open any of them. His attention was too scattered, a first for him, he admitted with a jolt of surprise. Even more surprisingly, he wasn't going to try to fight it. None of his to-dos were going to get done at this rate anyway. He may as well take a walk over to the shopping center.

Something told him yet another adventure awaited over in that part of the isle.

"Will this be on Mr. Jordan's company account or his personal one?"

Jenna paused at the question.

Cabe had a personal account here? At a women's boutique? The answer dawned on Jenna as she handed her purchases to the impeccably dressed saleslady who'd been helping her.

Cabe had traveled here with other women. Apparently, he had treated them to expensive clothing.

Well, she was not like them. Her situation was completely different. She was here to do a job and work hard to make Cabe's life easier as the CEO of Jordan's Fine Jewelry. Big difference. She did not need to depend on a man to buy her things. She was not like her mother. In fact, the outfit she'd found was quite sensible and quite a bit less costly than many of the other items in the store. Though it was still higher than what she could actually afford herself. But she had managed to find a pair of butter-soft leather sandals that had been drastically marked down. Those were going to be her one and only splurge on this trip as a way to treat herself.

"Definitely the corporate account, please."

The woman began to ring her up and Jenna couldn't help but let her eye travel to the gown sitting on display behind the register. A piece of art—that was the only way to describe it. A shimmery gold color that reminded her of the sand on the beach when the sun hit it just so. Draped over the mannequin like someone had sculptured it into place. The straps holding it up appeared impossibly thin and fragile. She imagined that was an optical illusion. Nothing about this dress appeared to have been left to chance.

She made herself look away. It probably cost more than she made in a year. The saleslady noticed.

"Would you like to try it on?"

Jenna blinked. The thought would have never occurred to her. "Oh, no. That's okay."

"You should. It would look so exotic on someone with your coloring."

Jenna shook her head and took a deep breath. "I'm afraid I'm not in the market for something so glamorous." Especially considering the price would make a nice down payment on a small house.

She smiled. "You're just trying it on. Come, I'd like to see it on you." She moved over to the mannequin and gently began removing the dress. "You'll be doing it for me."

Jenna gave her head a shake. "How so?"

"It will help break up the day and make my shift go a little quicker."

Jenna's heart did a little jump in her chest. Did she dare?

Why not? When would she ever get an opportunity to have an haute couture item actually on her body? She'd probably never even get a chance to set eyes on such a lavish garment again. What could be the harm in indulging in a little fantasy just this once?

And just like that, Jenna found herself in the dressing room, the dress hanging like a golden waterfall off a small garment hook. Her fingers trembled as she handled the silky, delicate material. Light as air and smooth, as though she were somehow holding liquid within her hands. Carefully, she put the gown over her head and gently tugged it down over her shoulders. She closed her eyes as it fell into place.

For several moments, she simply allowed herself to revel in the smooth texture of the material against her skin. Soft and airy, it must have been made from the finest silk.

When she dared a look in the mirror, her breath caught. It was like looking at a different person. A Jenna Townsend she hardly recognized stared back at her. One who belonged in a whole other universe. More magical.

She ran a hand down her midsection and couldn't resist doing a small little spin. The dress twirled around her like a light, airy cloud. Reaching up, she released the complicated clip that held her hair in place and shook out her curls. Giddiness wasn't usually a part of her personality but she felt that way now. She looked good. Better than good. If she had to say so herself, Cinderella had nothing over her in this dress.

She could have been a picture straight out of the pages of an international fashion magazine. Maybe even on the cover. Puckering her lips, she struck a pose in the mirror. Just like those haughty, glamorous runway models. The ones Cabe was always being linked to and seen with. The idea made her smile. It was silly, she knew, but her heart thudded in her chest at the vision staring back at her from the glass. Who would have thought that a girl from the fringes of South Boston could have pulled off a garment like the one she had on? It was such a far cry from the last formal gown she'd worn. The one she'd scraped and saved for close to a year in order to purchase secondhand for her high school prom. The one she'd stood out like a sore thumb in because it was clearly out of style and clearly used.

If only her former classmates could see her now. Suddenly she wished it with all her heart. Memories of the snickering and sideways glances she'd endured that night came crashing down upon her. No one had said anything, but their knowing, condescending stares communicated it all. She wouldn't let those memories mar this moment.

They wouldn't believe their eyes if they caught a look at her now. She hardly believed her own. Maybe a sneaky invisible little fairy had sprinkled some pixie dust her way and she had entered some kind of delicious alternate universe. And maybe, just maybe, she actually belonged there.

"Are you going to come out so that we may see it?" the saleslady asked from behind the fitting room door, pulling her out of her fanciful thoughts.

"Just one moment." Jenna inhaled deep and straightened to her full length. Such a dress demanded the utmost proper posture. Lifting her chin, she yanked aside the curtain and stepped out of the dressing room then executed a flamboyant, exaggerated bow.

And nearly dropped to the floor when she realized the saleslady hadn't been talking about a figurative "we."

Cabe stood less than three feet away.

CHAPTER SEVEN

CABE FOUND HE could do nothing but stare. He couldn't recall any moment in his life when he'd felt so completely frozen. No words came to his head, no thoughts he could formulate.

His mind zeroed in on one thing and one thing only: Jenna Townsend sheathed in a dress that hugged her so well, all he could do was imagine taking it off her.

She was something out of a portrait. An unearthly goddess who could command an army of men to live or die for her. At the moment, he himself would do anything she bade. The unusual color of the dress matched the golden specks in her hazel eyes. The effect was mesmerizing. He had to remind himself to breathe.

"Cabe." She spoke his name on a whisper. It sounded like a verbal caress beckoning him. How would it sound if she were to cry it out in pleasure?

His jaw clenched tight. He couldn't think of a thing to say. Here he was, the CEO of a highly successful private company who had to make multimillion-dollar decisions every day. And he'd been struck dumb by a woman in a dress.

She subconsciously ran a hand over her hair. Heaven help him. Her hair. A heavy cascade of dark, flowing curls curtained over her shoulders. He'd feared he'd never see it down. He'd tried to picture the way she would look if she ever saw fit to release it in his presence. But his imagination hadn't nearly done the image justice. Heat raced along his skin. He had to fist his hands at his sides in order to keep from reaching out and running his fingers through the lush, silky strands. His mind may have gone numb but his body knew exactly what it wanted to do.

He swallowed, clenched and unclenched his hands in a strained effort to keep from reaching for her.

She was saying something. He had to force himself to focus. "…just for fun. I obviously had no intention of trying to buy this."

"A shame." The words came out hoarse, strained even to his own ears.

She narrowed her eyes, and an expression of confusion settled over her features. What didn't she understand? Couldn't she see the effect she was having on him? Not just right at this moment but ever since he'd first laid eyes on her in Boston. He'd never behaved so irrationally. She'd dumped food on him and instead of firing her on the spot he'd promoted her! She teared up watching strangers get married. She attempted to buy a tray full of baubles she didn't need, pretending she wanted every piece. She had an amazing head for business.

And looking at her now took his breath away.

Damn. This was bad. This was very, very bad. He had lost all control. It was totally unacceptable. He didn't have time for this. His vast experience with women consisted of taking them to a few social gatherings followed by explosive breakups due to his lack of willingness to move things along to the next level. It had suited him just fine. Until now. Now he found himself thinking all sorts of thoughts about the future that he had no business entertaining.

Well, he had to grasp at some kind of sanity. He had too much to do.

Everything in his life was planned out, controlled. That was the only way to avoid regrets and mistakes. He wouldn't allow himself either of those luxuries. He didn't deserve to.

None of his plans included the kind of complications that would result from any kind of fling with a woman like Jenna Townsend.

He knew the best course of action would be to pivot on his heel right now and just hustle right back out of the store.

He couldn't be what she deserved.

Cabe didn't have time for any kind of a real relationship. He had to spend his time and every ounce of his energy proving himself worthy of the Jordan name. What kind of mate or partner would that make him? A lousy one.

The lady standing before him deserved so much more than he could give.

It was settled. He'd made his decision. From now on, he would make sure the relationship between the two of them remained strictly professional. He would keep her at arm's length during the day, and he would make sure to stay off the cursed balcony at night. No more mistakes. He had to promise himself that. He had to guarantee it. All he had to do right now was turn around and leave.

So the next words out of his mouth surprised him indeed. "Come here, Jenna."

* * *

Oh, boy.

Jenna took a hesitant step forward. The look on Cabe's face was impossible to read. Was he cross with her? All she'd done was try a dress on. She'd tried to explain she didn't actually intend to buy it.

That idea was preposterous.

He couldn't think she would buy such an extravagant item on the company's account. So what was with the look he currently had on his face? His jaw was tight, his eyes hard, his brows furrowed close together. She couldn't venture a guess what he was thinking. Then again, she'd be hard-pressed to guess what Cabe thought at any given moment.

"I said, come here."

She'd tried to ignore that command, hoping she hadn't heard him right. Her breath caught in her throat, and her limbs didn't seem to want to move. She'd never really seen him angry. Maybe he was about to chew her out and didn't want to do it too loudly. The other woman had made herself scarce. That couldn't be a good sign.

She took a hesitant step forward. "The salesclerk said she wanted to see it on me. I honestly wouldn't even consider actually…"

The words died on her lips as he moved with sudden swiftness, breaching the distance between them. His hand reached out and for one insane moment she thought she might reach for him as well. A bolt of electricity shot through her chest. The room seemed to shrink, to just the small patch of space where the two of them stood.

She felt a rough yet gentle finger trail along her shoulder, up toward her collarbone. There was no way to even try to hide the shudder his touch elicited. Cabe leaned closer, his lips a mere hair's width away from her ear.

She read clear, utter desire on his face.

When he spoke, his breath felt like a subtle caress over the skin on her neck. Her stomach did a flip, the feeling one got when just about to fall but caught herself just in time. Or someone else caught her.

"You need to take this off." Barely a whisper, his command sent a shiver of excitement down her spine.

This couldn't really be happening. She'd obviously fallen down some kind of rabbit hole. Cabe Jordan was not standing in the middle of a chic dress shop with her, telling her to undress.

She swallowed the hard lump that had formed in her throat and licked her suddenly dry lips. "Like I said, it was just in fun."

"Jenna?"

"Yes?"

"We have to go."

"Go?"

Every inch of him was tense, his jaw clenched, his hands fisted at his sides. He looked like he wanted to throw her over his shoulder. The thought had her cheeks burning. She thought of the way he'd almost kissed her and wondered if he would do it again. Heaven help her, she wanted him to. Very much.

"We have to go," he repeated through gritted teeth. "Or we'll be late for our meeting."

If Jenna thought their walk this morning to breakfast had been awkward, their stroll after leaving the shopping center was downright torturous. The fierce blare of the late-afternoon sun didn't help. They passed a lazy-strung hammock slung between palm trees and all Jenna wanted to do was collapse in it for a while. And try not to replay the scene in the dress shop over and over in her head. The way the touch of Cabe's finger had sent a tingling rush over every inch of her skin. She couldn't think about any of that. Instead, she had to somehow focus on a business meeting.

Next to her, Cabe cleared his throat. "That was a smart choice."

She had no idea what he could be referring to. Her brain seemed to have ceased functioning.

"The dress," Cabe added.

What? Was he seriously going to bring it up?

"I mean, you know, the one you have on. Right now. Not that other one." He pointed at her. "This one."

Oh. She could only nod in his direction.

"I don't mean to say that other gown wasn't flattering." He rubbed a hand over his forehead and cursed under his breath.

"It's okay, Cabe. I know what you mean."

He let out a long sigh, his frustration palpable. She fully understood. Life, and this trip, would be so much easier if they had a smooth, uncomplicated relationship. "That makes one of us."

"You're saying this dress I'm wearing now works well for an important meeting that's being held in a casual, outdoor atmosphere."

"Yes. That's exactly what I'm saying. The light color works well in this heat."

"Thank you."

"You're welcome." He hesitated. "I like your shoes, too," he said after a beat, somewhat wryly.

Jenna glanced down at the strappy, low-heel leather

sandals she had on. She'd bought them somewhat impulsively, using her own money, of course. Her navy, thick pumps were not handling well in all this sand. Despite the awkwardness between them, she felt downright giddy that Cabe had noticed.

How schoolgirlish of her.

He suddenly stopped and turned to her. "Jenna, listen—"

Oh, no. No way. He was not going to do this to her. He was not going to try to discuss the dress shop fiasco. Did he want to totally scramble her brain before this meeting?

She didn't break her stride, forcing him to resume walking and catch up.

"So tell me about Sonny," she asked, before he could finish his sentence. Cabe got the hint and followed the change of topic.

Thank heavens for small blessings.

"Sonny is in charge of the retail establishments in the resort's shopping center. He can help us with the latest zoning issue." They turned a corner on the path and Cabe pointed to the distance. "There he is now."

Jenna looked up to see a stout, thick man sitting at a picnic table at a cabana, pounding away at a laptop. Introductions were made when they approached and the three of them wasted no time before getting to the business at hand.

Jenna even managed to focus on taking notes rather than the magnetic pull of the man sitting next to her. No small miracle after this morning and last night.

At the conclusion of the meeting two hours later, she was actually pretty impressed with herself. She'd held her own and even made some useful suggestions.

Now she just had to get through the rest of the day.

After Sonny left, she looked up to find Cabe staring at her. Like a specimen he couldn't understand. She suddenly felt a nervous hitch in the middle of her chest. Perhaps her performance in front of the retail manager hadn't gone as well as she'd thought. Had she done or said something wrong?

"Sonny seems very efficient," she commented, by way of fishing.

"You impressed him." Cabe's answer surprised her. The other man had shown no outward signs of any such thing. In fact, he'd been very matter-of-fact throughout the whole two hours.

"Why do you say that?"

"I've dealt with him quite a bit over the past several months. Trust me, you impressed him."

Jenna swallowed. "I was just trying to get all the details covered."

"You did well."

Her heart thudded at his words. It was one thing to impress Sonny, but to hear Cabe was pleased with her performance sent a lightning bolt of pleasure through her core.

"You're truly one of a kind, Jenna Townsend."

She looked up at him then and realized instantly that this was one of those moments she would never recover from. She was lost—lost in Cabe's steady blue gaze, transfixed by the silky smooth sound of his voice. She'd never find her way again.

She grasped for some kind of response but none would come to her lips. Several seconds went by—she couldn't guess how long. Suddenly, the unmistakable sound of a camera shutter snapped her out of her daze and broke the spell.

"A quick photo, Mr. Jordan." She hadn't even noticed the photographer approach them, holding a large camera to his face and wearing a colorful shirt with the resort logo.

Cabe held his hand up to hold off any further picture taking. "Maybe later." Gently taking Jenna by the elbow, he led her away from the cabana.

Jenna had to remind herself to breathe as they walked away.

"Damn it," Cabe bit out, sparing a glance behind him.

"You don't like your picture taken?"

"Not particularly."

"He's just doing his job."

"Let's hope so," Cabe bit out.

"What do you mean? Isn't he just one of the resort photographers?"

Cabe kept walking, apparently trying to gain as much distance between them and the camera. "Yes, but sometimes my photo doesn't merely end up in a souvenir frame for me to purchase."

"Where does it end up?"

"Too often it ends up in a tabloid or some tawdry website."

It took a moment but his meaning slowly dawned on her. He wasn't merely upset that his picture had been taken. Cabe was upset that it had been taken *with her.*

"Will Carmen be cross with you?" she blurted out without thinking.

Cabe paused then, just long enough to give her a

confused look. "Carmen? No. I mean, I guess not. I honestly don't know."

She merely nodded as they resumed walking.

"You're not worried about her potential reaction to the photo, then?"

"The thought hadn't even crossed my mind."

That was interesting. Then again, Carmen was probably one of those women so secure with her beauty and attractiveness she probably wouldn't have cared if Cabe had taken a hundred pictures with someone like her. The likes of Jenna Townsend were certainly not enough to elicit any kind of jealous reaction from an international supermodel.

"I thought maybe that's why you wanted to avoid the camera."

His answer was notably matter-of-fact. "Carmen and I broke up. Just before I left Boston."

Jenna nearly stumbled before she recovered her step. She had no business feeling giddy at that bit of news. "I'm sorry to hear that."

Cabe shrugged. "Don't be. It was bound to happen."

"I see."

"Carmen's been pursuing a movie career for as long as I've known her. She finally got her big break this past month. She'll be filming a horror piece. In the Amazon. She asked me to visit her. I said I didn't have that kind of time."

"Oh." Jenna took a deep breath. If Cabe was shaken over the breakup, he certainly had shown no signs of heartbreak. Not that she'd ever expect a man like Cabe Jordan to wear his heart on his sleeve when it came to women. Still, Jenna didn't detect any sense of loss or regret. Well, she had no business speculating on that.

Or hoping the notion to be true. "Then, if you don't mind my asking..."

Cabe finally stopped, took her by the arm and gently turned her to face him. "Spit it out, Jenna."

"Why are you so agitated about the photographer, then?"

She knew she shouldn't have asked. And wanted to kick herself when he answered.

"I really don't want a picture of the two of us plastered all over the gossip sites."

Jenna felt the lump form in her throat and made herself swallow it down. She understood, she really did. She knew whatever was happening between them right now on this resort wasn't reality. Once they were back in the States, they would go back to living their regular lives. She'd return to her boring, repetitive existence back in Boston. And Cabe would return to his exciting life in Manhattan. Why would he want to answer anyone's questions about public photos with his project manager?

He took a different way through the center of the island in order to ensure they'd ditched the photographer. And besides, this route held something Cabe wanted Jenna to see.

He had to catch her as she stepped on the wooden hanging bridge. Or else Jenna was headed for a dramatic face-plant. Cabe didn't realize how fast he'd been walking or how Jenna had made sure to keep up with him. Unfortunately, she'd miscalculated the steadiness of the wobbly bridge and was about to fall over. "Here. I've got you," Cabe said, taking her by the arm and gently pulling her up.

She gave him a look of surprise and gratitude, and

then her gaze fell to the hand that held her arm. Her skin felt smooth and warm under his touch.

She gently pulled her arm free and took hold of the thick rope railing.

"Thanks. Guess I'm still breaking into these new sandals."

"You can always take them off. Feel free to go barefoot, now that our business day is over."

She gave him a small smile that didn't really reach her eyes. "Can we slow down now? I think we lost our tail."

"Sorry. I didn't realize how fast I was walking. Not like the photographer was actually following us."

"Well, we couldn't have risked that now, could we?" Her voice held a hint of annoyance.

He didn't want to be the reason Jenna's picture was pasted all over the internet. He'd grown used to the lack of privacy over the years. But for someone as inexperienced with it as Jenna was, the intrusion could be daunting and upsetting. She'd done nothing to deserve that. Not to mention what his parents would say.

"Like I said, I'd rather not give the tabloids any fodder."

"Got it," Jenna replied. "I am clearly not an ideal photo op."

Her tone was sharp. "Something wrong?" he asked.

She let out a deep sigh. "No. Nothing at all."

He waited a beat but she didn't go on. "Doesn't sound like it's nothing. Is there something you'd like to say?"

Her cheeks suddenly turned pink with annoyance. Maybe even anger.

Which made no sense. All he'd done was try to spare

her the unwanted scrutiny an international photograph would garner. But Jenna remained frustratingly silent.

"You have no idea what kind of attention one lousy picture can elicit," he told her. "I was trying to protect you."

She blinked and her expression softened. "Is that the only reason? That was all for me?"

What in the devil's name was she talking about? Of course it was. "You are clearly a very private person, Jenna. I didn't think you'd appreciate such an intrusion."

He waited as she let that sink in.

"I guess you're right," she said, looking up and finally noticing their surroundings. They had reached the majestic waterfalls at the center of the resort. Surrounded by lush greenery and gray rocks, three high waterfalls dropped close to a hundred feet into a crystal-blue river. A series of rustic wooden bridges like the one they currently stood on webbed throughout the area.

Jenna's expression held wonder and awe, as he knew it would. Their swift jaunt just now had brought a rosy hue to her cheeks, and her lips remained parted. "Wow, this is beautiful."

Breathtaking, Cabe thought. But he wasn't thinking of the scenery. Jenna's skin glistened with the thin sheen of mist that drifted in the air. She looked like a heavenly angel ascended from paradise.

"Why did it bother you so much, Jenna? That I had us run from the photographer?" he prompted. The situation had triggered something in her, something he wanted to get to the bottom of. This was a perfect spot to do it.

Her eyes narrowed on his face. "You were saying how clearly guarded I am."

"Yes?"

She blew out a deep breath, went back to studying the scenery. "I didn't exactly have an ideal upbringing, Cabe. As you very well know."

"I know you didn't have it easy. And I know how much you've overcome to get to where you are."

She sniffed. "I'm Amanda Townsend's daughter. The town drunk, the desperate single mom who flirted with everyone's husband."

"None of that was your fault, Jenna."

"I know. But it was certainly my responsibility. It fell on me to take care of her when she drank so much she was sick for days. It fell on me to find a way to feed and care for my brother when there was no food or money to be found."

He ached to hold her, to erase her past and pain somehow. She deserved so much better than what she'd been handed in life. Unlike himself. "You were the caregiver, even though your brother was older."

She smiled, with genuine affection clear on her face. "We split responsibilities. He's protected me in myriad ways, too, over the years. A girl tends to get picked on when she's known as the trashy daughter of the town's trashy drunk."

"You and Sam are lucky to have each other."

He heard her inhale deeply, slowly let the breath out. He'd do anything to bear some of the weight on her shoulders, if only he could.

"I suppose we are. I can't imagine dealing with Amanda over the years without him. Though sometimes I wish he didn't have to deal with it at all. That I was a single child, for his sake." A small laugh escaped her lips. "I used to daydream that someone rich would show up one day and adopt—" She stopped suddenly and cupped her hand over her mouth, as if she could pull back the half-spoken word that hung in the air.

"It's not all it's cracked up to be," he said.

"I'm so sorry," Jenna whispered. "I should have known better than to say something like that."

"It's okay, Jenna. It's a common fantasy among children. Funny thing is, I had the opposite daydream."

"What do you mean?"

"After I found out, I kept having these visions of my real parents appearing at the door one day. To tell me how sorry they were that they ever gave me up. Then they would beg me to forgive them, ask if they could take me back." He grew somber as the memory further surfaced. "Then I would feel terrible. Guilty for hoping to leave James and Tricia when they were so sad." What a silly kid he'd been. Worrying himself sick over a fantasy that had no basis in reality.

"You've been trying to prove yourself for as long as you can remember, haven't you?" she asked in a soft voice.

"I guess I have. It's hard to live up to a ghost."

"A ghost?"

"James and Tricia adopted me after losing their biological son. Unlike you, I may not have had an actual living, breathing sibling. But his presence was always there. Right down to the room my parents never altered after he died." A room he was never allowed to so much as enter.

"They never emptied his room?" Jenna asked, her voice breaking.

"No, never."

"Cabe, there was no way you could have reached them. Nothing you could have done. They were broken and shattered over their loss."

"It's tough for a child to see through all that."

She leaned closer. "You never stopped trying, did you? To make them happy?" She was close enough that he could read her eyes even in the dim light. They held no pity. If anything, she appeared to be looking at him with something resembling admiration. "Cabe, you deserve to be happy."

Her words hammered into his soul. In one simple sentence she'd cut to the very core of him, through to all his childhood insecurities and disappointments.

"Jenna, you amaze me," he told her. He'd never made a truer statement. He thought back to that first day in Boston. It horrified him how insensitive he'd been. He should have realized someone like Jenna, who'd had a lifetime of trying to escape the shadow of her mother's reputation, would take questions about the theft personally.

And just now, with the photographer. She'd thought he was ashamed to be seen with her for the very same reason. Jenna's whole life had been about others judging her based on the actions of her mother. He could be such a careless, thoughtless lout at times.

"This conversation is getting pretty deep," Jenna said quietly in a tone that broke his heart. "Too deep to be having with my boss." She let out a small laugh, clearly forced.

If only she could really see him, not just as a boss, but as a man. A man who wanted to unearth the many layers that were Jenna Townsend. "Do me a favor," Cabe began. "Take a good look around this place. A really good look."

She did as he asked, although not before giving him a confused frown. "It's wondrous. I didn't realize places like this actually existed." Jenna ducked her head shyly, as if embarrassed by what she'd just revealed.

"It's all an illusion."

"What do you mean?"

"That large waterfall in the middle, that was in the original landscape. The other two smaller ones on either side, those were formed by manipulating the cliff side. Just like everything else in this place, it's been painstakingly planned and created. None of it is genuine or the real thing. Just like me," he added, meeting her eyes.

The lines on her forehead deepened. "Cabe, why would you think that?" Maybe she did see the real him after all.

Before he could answer, a strong gust of wind shook the bridge they stood on. Without giving it a thought, Cabe reached to grab her around her middle and pulled her closer, both feeling and hearing her sharp intake of breath. "Sorry, these bridges aren't really meant to stand around on for extended periods of time." He spoke low against her ear.

"Right. They're more for appearances as well."

"It would seem." It was safe to let go now, but he continued to hold her anyway. For some reason, he couldn't seem to stop touching Jenna. He would enjoy it while he could. For now, he was simply happy that she made no attempt to step out of his embrace.

"Why was it me?" he blurted out. Her eyes searched his even as her touch soothed him, comforted him. So he went on. "I wonder about it every day. The mere randomness of it."

"Oh, Cabe." She reached for him then and he felt as if time had stopped. Her soft, delicate fingers found his face then ran gently along his jaw. He reflexively dipped his head into her touch.

"I'm also a made product, Jenna. As artificial and fake as these waterfalls. I'm not an original. I'm not any kind of rarity. I was merely randomly selected, treated and polished to transform into someone else entirely. A lie. A falsehood I've lived every day of my life. It's hard not to feel like a fraud. My parents lost their real son. Their one and only precious child. And somehow I was chosen by some mysterious twist of fate to step in and take the life he was meant to lead."

To his shock, she stepped farther into his embrace. A shiver ran through him at her closeness. He knew one of them should pull away. But, heaven help him, it wasn't going to be him.

Her eyes glistened and it tore at his heart. She remained silent, giving him time to continue if he desired. Apparently, he did. "I have everything. And he's gone. How can my mother and father not resent me for that? They tried so hard not to show it. But I could tell by their indifference. I could see. How in the world would I blame them?"

"You worked hard for all that you have, Cabe," she said. "Everyone knows how much you've done for Jordan's Fine Jewelry. The way it grew once you took over."

"Maybe so. But so much of it was handed to me."

She gave her head a small shake. "You aren't giving yourself any credit. I can't even imagine the company being run by anyone else. You're really good."

"I had to be good." He tightened his grip around her waist, pulled her closer. And she felt so right up against him. "Don't you see?"

"See what?"

"The reality is, I can't squander it. It has to mean something that it was me." He took a deep breath, inhaled the scent of her shampoo. "After all, I'm the Jordan Golden Boy."

She shook her head slowly. "I know who you are. You're Cabe Jordan. A talented and accomplished CEO. You've done so much for your employees. And you're a credit to your parents. Just today you changed the life of a young girl you just happened to see selling cheap jewelry on the beach. You're the kind of man any woman with a pulse would fall head over heels—"

The roaring in his ears kept him from hearing any more. He didn't need to. What he needed was to taste her, to feel her up against him. Inside his very soul. Pulling her even closer, he took her mouth and plunged in. She tasted like heaven, like redemption, like everything he could have hoped for.

He'd never be able to let her go.

This was a fairy tale. She was convinced now. Or it was a sweet, unimaginable dream. Jenna hoped never to wake up. Cabe held her tight against him, his mouth devouring hers. She wrapped her arms around his neck and shifted her hips closer against his, felt the strength of his desire for her. The knowledge made her skin burn. This dazzling, enigmatic man wanted her. She'd seen the longing on his face, and now could feel it in the power of his kiss and in the reaction of his body.

"Jenna," he whispered against her mouth, his voice full of longing. A heady shiver of need ran up her spine. "Tell me. I have to know."

She couldn't think, couldn't seem to breathe. What

was he asking for? She'd give him anything. Her soul, her heart. Anything. So she simply answered yes.

His hands moved down her rib cage, down farther along her hips. Then she felt herself suddenly hoisted off the ground. He lifted her completely off her feet and started to carry her, steady and balanced despite the crooked and wobbly bridge. She couldn't tear her gaze off Cabe's face. His eyes reminded her of the ocean during a violent storm—dark and shadowed. The sound of the crashing water grew fainter and fainter behind them. She couldn't guess where they were going, but would let him take her anywhere. As long as he never stopped holding her.

She wanted so much more. She wanted all of him.

She'd wanted him since the moment he walked into her office. No, she'd wanted him since she'd known him, practically her whole life.

Cabe was the star of her daydreams, her girlhood crush. He'd transformed her life since walking back into it. He'd transformed *her.* She didn't recognize this reckless, careless woman she'd become. Was she really kissing her boss outside in the open, where anyone could walk by? This wasn't like her—this was downright wanton. But she didn't care. All she cared about was having Cabe completely.

He carried her out of the maze of bridges. The sounds of the waterfalls echoed soothingly behind them. An unseen bird chirped a melody in one of the trees above. He clearly knew the island well. The path he took her on was completely deserted. Before she realized, they were somehow in the hallway outside his suite. Cabe managed to unlock the door and bring her into his room, still holding her tight in his embrace. Slowly, he set her down on the thick, plush comforter on the bed.

She was in Cabe Jordan's hotel room as he kissed her and caressed her. The ocean view outside the balcony window looked like a painting created by a master painter. Her desire-fogged mind told her this all had to be some separate fantasy away from the rest of the universe.

And she would pretend it was. She would make believe she was in a universe where Jenna Townsend for once in her life got what she wanted. One where she succumbed to her desires. Just this one time, with this one man. Gently, slowly, he lowered himself to balance on his elbows just above her.

"Jenna?" He said her name as a question, touchingly making sure this was what she wanted.

It was, more than anything. She answered him by slowly undoing the top of her dress. She didn't get a chance to unbutton the rest. Covering her mouth with his once again, Cabe took over, making quick work of the remaining buttons.

There was no doubt in her mind. She wanted him. It was the only thing that mattered in this moment. Jenna knew this was what paradise would feel like.

Cabe confirmed it by taking her straight there.

She'd fallen asleep in his arms.

Cabe ran his fingers through Jenna's soft, thick hair. He sat cradling her with her back against his chest. Outside his window, the ocean shone like a rare glittering jewel in the distance.

Let her sleep, he thought. This moment would be over all too soon. Once they stepped out of this room, reality would set in. Then he would have to examine what had just happened. But not now.

Now he was just going to enjoy the feel of Jenna's languid body against his, savor the sensation of what it had felt like to hold her and love her.

He stroked her hair, breathed in the scent of her tropical shampoo mingled with the salty sea air. Jenna was not like anyone he'd ever known. That she was still helping her mother, even as an adult, didn't surprise him. This amazing, dynamic woman in his arms was the type of person who'd never turn away from anyone who needed her. Didn't she realize how special that made her?

Thinking of what she must have endured as a child made him want to throw something. Or punch the headrest behind him. She really was extraordinary. Jenna had prospered and shone into adulthood despite the genetic cards she'd been dealt. She'd worked hard and earned it all. Unlike those who'd had everything handed to them. Unlike him.

Suddenly, he felt lacking, inadequate. Jenna had accomplished so much in her life despite being given so little. Compared to her struggles, he'd had it so easy. All he had to do was take advantage of all the ample opportunities he'd been awarded.

The memory of the first day of his Boston visit flashed through his mind's eye. Her anger had been vibrant and strong. He'd deserved her ire then. He'd been an utter ass. When he thought about what that must have felt like for her, to have the boss come to town and practically accuse her of being a thief.

He was her boss, the CEO. Someone who had a direct say on her career, her very future.

And he'd just made love to her.

A bubble of acid churned in his gut. Damn his impulsiveness.

Jenna wasn't the type to have a meaningless office fling. She had substance, character. With all that she'd been through, she had every right to a bright and fulfilling future. Complete with the rewarding career and a caring steady man who would always be there for the woman in his life.

She deserved the kind of future Cabe would never be able to give her.

For one hazy moment upon awakening, Jenna thought perhaps she had dreamed it all. There wasn't any kind of way the fates would have really allowed it to happen. She had *not* just been intimate with Cabe Jordan.

"Hey there, Sleeping Beauty." His rich baritone served to pull her out of that fallacy very quick. As did the weightlessness in her muscles. Not to mention the warm body she was snuggled against.

Dear heavens. What had she done? How could she have just made love with her *boss*?

Scrambling to gain some sense, she removed herself out of his embrace and stood up off the bed with the top sheet wrapped around her. Cabe sat up at the edge of the mattress and rammed a hand through his hair.

A glance at the window showed the sky had turned a deep, rich purple. The hour had to be approaching early evening. They'd apparently been there awhile. What time was it? She never wore a watch but where was her phone? She had no idea. If she had dropped it on the bridge, she hadn't even done a backup since arriving.

How utterly unprofessional—she didn't even know

where her phone was. But then again, so was sleeping with someone she worked with. Correct that—Cabe was the man she worked *for*. The blood left her brain. She dared a glance in his direction. He was clearly avoiding looking at her.

Cabe cleared his throat. “We should probably go get cleaned up.”

“Um, I seem to have misplaced my phone.” Great. On top of everything else, she had to admit to misplacing company property.

They both saw it at the same time, resting on the carpet near the leg of the bed. Disastrously, they both bent to reach for it, bumping heads.

This had to be the most awkward moment of her life. She had no idea how to process it. There were no excuses but she’d just felt so off balance on the bridge by the waterfall, literally and figuratively. Cabe’s anguished face coupled with the way he’d opened up to her. And the location. It was all a perfect storm of overstimulation and she’d just snapped. She’d given in to her aching desire to be close to him. In every way.

Straightening, she took a deep breath. “Cabe, I—”

He held a hand up to stop her. “Let’s just both get cleaned up. I, for one, could use a long hot shower before dressing for dinner.”

Jenna winced. He’d effectively just dismissed her. There had to be a large sinkhole or underground cave on this island she could go crawl in. Or better yet, she could run into the ocean and dive into a large wave, just swim out into the open sea. It couldn’t be any worse. She already felt like she was drowning.

“Probably a good idea.” She forced out her agreement and grabbed her phone off the floor.

And her blood went cold again. Her screen was lit up with text messages. Most of them from home. Her mother. She could think of no good reason for Amanda to be trying to reach her here. The messages could only mean one thing: Amanda was in some kind of trouble.

CHAPTER EIGHT

CABE JORDAN HAD made love to her—there was no way to focus on anything else.

Jenna lathered up the rich mango gel soap and let the soothing water of the shower wash over her still-tingling skin.

She could still feel his touch. Every word he'd whispered in her ear still echoed in her head. Every second of what they'd shared would be ingrained in her memory for the rest of her life. She'd never forget the way he'd felt, the things he'd said to her. It would all torture her for the rest of her life. Stifling a sob, Jenna turned off the water and grabbed the thick Turkish robe hanging from the shower door, wrapping it around herself and stepping out of the stall. Cabe had said he would wait for her in his room while she got cleaned up. She had no idea what she would say to him. He couldn't possibly know how torn she felt right now.

How in the world could she have let things get so far between them? And what in heaven's name was she to do now?

The beeping of her cell phone interrupted her thoughts again. Two more texts came in, and several missed calls registered.

Not now…not just yet.

She just couldn't tackle any of it now, not on top of everything else she had to grapple with. Call her a coward, but despite knowing that she should just answer the phone and find out what was happening back in Boston, her nerves just couldn't handle anything else at the moment. First she had to gain back some of her equilibrium before she faced Cabe. She would deal with Amanda's newest crisis when she regained some semblance of sanity and strength. A couple of hours more when she was half a world away certainly couldn't make any sort of difference anyway.

With shaky hands, Jenna gripped the phone and pressed the reset button until her finger hurt. When the device finally powered off, she sank down onto the love seat against the wall of her room. Her knees had suddenly gone weak.

What a fool she'd been. Forgetting about her reality for even a few moments of guilty pleasure. Pretending she could escape who she truly was. Her truth had even found her here, on this beautiful island paradise.

She could never be anything to someone like Cabe Jordan.

She had too much baggage, too much of a responsibility, the likes of which he'd never be able to relate to. An alcoholic mother who was repeatedly in and out of jail. Dear God, Amanda may even need bailing out right at this very moment. Or perhaps she'd been evicted again and couldn't get ahold of Jenna's brother nor find the spare key to her apartment that Jenna had given her.

Cabe was worried about a reporter simply posting a picture of the two of them. She shuddered to think how he would feel about being tied to a woman whose mother had such a sordid past. The press would have a field day with Amanda's history.

Well, there was nothing Jenna could do about it now, being hundreds of miles away on a Caribbean island.

Jenna took a deep breath and forced herself up. First thing first, Cabe awaited her. She had to shake off the self-pity and get dressed. They planned to get an early dinner at a seaside tavern and then head over to the casino. As far as she knew, none of those plans had changed.

How was she going to face him? Just a couple of short hours ago they'd been as close and as intimate as any two people could be. But next time she faced him, things had to be different. She had no one but herself to blame. She'd let her guard down, let herself forget who she was and where she belonged on the hierarchy of life.

Somehow, she had to rectify all that. What had happened between them this afternoon could never happen again. She had to make sure of it, even though it was breaking her heart into a million jagged pieces.

Pieces that would never be put back together no matter how hard she tried.

Jenna refused to meet him in the eye.

For the life of him, Cabe couldn't figure out what to say to break the ice. Should he apologize? Or would that just make things even more awkward? One thing was certain—the silence was becoming unbearable.

He cleared his throat, decided to go with something mundane, just to start. "I hope you're hungry. This place has quite an extensive buffet. Everything from seafood to the finest Kobe steak."

Again, she didn't face him, barely turned her head. "Sounds good."

Cabe stifled a groan of irritation. He deserved this; he'd done it to himself. Jenna clearly wanted to take back what had happened between them. He could guess why. They were completely wrong for each other. He'd never be able to give her the kind of things she deserved from a man.

Jenna needed someone with substance, a man who could give her a future. She'd grown up with enough instability. She didn't need any in her adulthood.

Between his nonstop workdays and his lifestyle, Cabe couldn't pretend to be that man. Hell, he barely stayed in the same city for more than two weeks at a time. She was smart enough to see that. A future with him wouldn't be much of a future at all. Not for someone who had as much going for her as Jenna did.

He should never have touched her, never so much as let himself stroke a hair on her head.

He had no excuse, only the fact that once again he'd proved what a weak person he was. His resistance had completely crumbled when she'd cupped his face and uttered soothing words no one had ever said to him before, her voice full of concern.

He would have to find a way to apologize. If not with words, then with some kind of way that would make all this up to her.

The soft music of a steel-drum band started up behind them on the beach as the maître d' greeted them. It took all of Cabe's will not to touch her as they were being led to their table. He wanted so badly to place his hand at the small of her back, feel the heat of her skin beneath his touch.

He cursed under his breath. To anyone in the dining area, they appeared to be the perfect picture of a well-suited couple enjoying each other's company while on vacation.

He would never have that. Not with Jenna. Not with anyone. How silly of him to believe that even for a moment he could. He'd long lost his appetite. Jenna hardly looked interested in food either. But it appeared they were both willing to go through the pretense.

But she surprised him when the waiter appeared. Instead of her usual water or iced tea, she asked for a glass of wine. He lifted an eyebrow in question after the man had left. "Looking for something a bit stronger this evening?"

She ducked her head when answering. "I'm afraid there isn't anything strong enough."

Cabe indulged in a deep sigh. Enough was enough. "Jenna, I think it's time we faced this head-on. Something happened between us. Something major."

She ducked her head. "I know that."

Unable to help himself, he reached for her hand across the table. At her flinch, he hastily pulled it back.

He just didn't learn, did he? Always taking too much, offering too little in return.

The tension between them hung thick and palpable.

"Maybe we should just cancel the visit to the casino," Cabe suggested, pulling his hand back. In an act of self-preservation, Jenna had jumped when he'd reached for her. As much as she might long for it, she lost all her resolve when he touched her. "I don't think either of us is really in the right frame of mind," he added. "Maxim will have to understand."

Great. Another work obligation that was being impacted because of her. She shook her head. "It's okay. That won't be necessary."

Try as she might, Cabe saw through her attempt to act professional. He rammed his fingers through his hair. "Jenna, please. Just say something. Tell me what's going on in your head."

Her eyes stung. There was really no good way to begin. "Oh, Cabe. We both know there's really only one thing to say."

He lifted an eyebrow. "And that is?"

"It's all wrong, what's happened between us."

He sucked in a breath, looked away. "Trust me when I say I didn't see it coming, either, the way I suddenly feel about you."

She shook her head, held her hands up. The lump in her throat made it hard to speak but she pushed through it. "That's what I mean. You can't do that."

"Do what?"

"I can't hear about how you feel about me. Nor think about how I feel about you. I can't do this, any of this. This project is too important to me. My job is too important. I can't believe I jeopardized everything by sleeping with my boss." A deep shudder shook her through her core. Her heart felt like it was splitting down the middle. And there was nothing she could do.

"Who says you jeopardized anything?"

"It's the truth. My reputation means everything to me."

"And it's still intact."

She shook her head. "Maybe for now. But everything I've worked for, none of it will matter if people find out I was intimate with the boss on a business trip!"

"It's not as scandalous as it sounds."

How she wished he was right, that things could be different between them. That she could somehow actually be sitting here and enjoying a moonlit dinner by the ocean with the man she— She gave her head a shake. That word kept popping up. And she had to stop even thinking it. Imagine, she'd practically said it out loud to Cabe at the waterfall earlier. What did it matter if she knew she was in love with him, that perhaps she'd always been in love with him? The cold slap of reality was all that mattered now.

"Jenna, I never meant to put you in such a position. It just kind of happened. I'm not sure what I can do to make it up to you, but I promise you I will. I'll think of some way."

The blood left her brain. "Oh, my God. You're not suggesting that I get some kind of reward because of what happened between us! Like some kind of—"

He jolted in his seat. "No! Of course not. I just mean— I don't know what I meant. Just that I hate what's happening, what you're feeling right now."

Suddenly it was too much. The events of the afternoon, the mystery texts and phone calls. This whole conversation. She just had to get away. Without a thought as to how it would look, she rose from her seat and dropped her napkin onto the table. "Excuse me."

Cabe stood as well. "Jenna, wait."

She didn't. The waiter gave them both a curious look but Jenna didn't care. She needed to get away. Cabe was fast on her heels. Part of her wished he would stop chasing her. But another foolish part would be crushed if he let her just run off into the night.

He kept on. She heard him calling her name behind her, felt a sharp pang of guilt for ignoring him. But she couldn't bring herself to stop, couldn't let Cabe see the tears in her eyes, the anguish that had to be written all over her face.

Her nerves couldn't handle the conversation that would ensue if he caught up to her. She'd fallen for him. Cabe was a known playboy who had a new woman on his arm more often than the moon changed phases. She knew she could never be anything more than a flippant affair for him. And yet she'd still gone and risked her professional career.

For a few moments of pleasure, she'd risked everything.

She figured it would just be a matter of time before he found her, and she was right. When he did, she was sitting on a large boulder on the edge of the beach, her toes submerged in the sand. She didn't look up at him as he approached.

"Hey there," he ventured.

"Hey."

"Mind if I sit?"

She didn't respond but shifted slightly to make room for him on the big rock. And instantly regretted it. Hardly a hair separated them, and his warmth seeped through her skin. And brought back unwanted memories of this afternoon, the absolute last thing she needed to be thinking about.

"I keep saying the wrong thing to you," he told her, looking straight ahead. She'd inadvertently run toward the casino. They could see its bright and colorful lights in the distance across the water.

"It's not you," she answered.

He grunted. "I beg to differ."

"We both seem to be stumbling here." She was just so embarrassed. And downright disappointed in herself.

"So…maybe we just move forward, acknowledge that even the best of us make mistakes?"

The word made her cringe, but he was right. "I guess we don't have much choice."

They sat in awkward silence, for how long Jenna couldn't guess. Cabe's sigh finally broke through it. "Well. There it is. That's the grand Paraiso Casino," he said, nodding his head in its direction.

She followed his gaze across the water. Even from this distance she could tell she had no business there. The place was completely out of her league. A steady stream of sports cars and luxury sedans pulled up the circular driveway. Those cars cost more than she'd hope to make in several years. Much more.

The people emerging out of those cars looked elegant and regal. Men in tuxedos and women in gowns. She looked down at her simple outfit. She'd been resourceful, finding a fitted black blouse in the boutique this afternoon to match one of her slim business suit skirts. At the time, she'd felt great pride for coming up with the idea and making it work. Now she felt like a lowly pauper who'd thought she could sneak into the prince's ball.

Which was exactly who she was.

"I've never been to a casino before," she admitted.

"Really? There are quite a few in New England. You haven't even been to any of those?"

She shrugged. "I'm not much of a gambler."

"Well, if you'd like, I could show you how to play some of the tables."

"No, thanks. Gambling's not really a habit I want to

pick up." She wouldn't bother to explain that her aversion to gambling was due to another one of her mother's failings. How many times had Amanda skirted her parental duties to go spend time on the slots? How many times had she gambled away money they could have desperately used for food or rent?

"I understand," Cabe told her. And somehow, she knew he did, that he grasped exactly what she was referring to. That was part of the problem. She felt as if Cabe understood her better than anyone else ever had. It was one of the reasons she'd forsaken all sanity earlier and let herself become intimate with him.

"Well, you get to tour one right now," he said and clapped his hands in mock excitement. "I guess I better get you over there before Maxim sends out a search party for us. We're already late."

Great. So now she could add tardiness to her list of professional missteps on this trip. She suppressed a groan of irony. In the overall scheme of things, being late to meet her casino tour guide was relatively trivial.

"We'll be taking a boat there," Cabe added.

"A boat?"

He nodded in the building's direction. "The casino is on its own little island, across the water. I'll drop you off."

"You won't be joining us?"

He shrugged. "He only mentioned you specifically."

"He did?"

"Uh-huh. And I guess you shouldn't keep him waiting."

She should be relieved, Jenna thought. But instead a dull disappointment settled in her chest. She didn't want to spend the evening with Maxim. She wanted to spend it with the man right next to her. Laughing with him, enjoying the warm tropical air. But this was for the best. It would give her some time to sort out her thoughts, settle her nerves. Things she had no hope of doing with Cabe anywhere nearby. It made sense. So why did she want to cry? To beg him to stay by her side? She bit her lip to stop herself from doing so.

They made it to a dock where a small open-air boat waited. A smiling captain took her hand and helped her on board. It appeared no other passengers were embarking for this go-around.

At her quizzical look Cabe responded, “All the avid gamblers are already at the tables. We’re a little late to the party.”

Only it wasn’t going to be a party at all. Not if Cabe wasn’t going to be there with her. The boat revved up and started a steady path across the water. The breeze suddenly picked up and made her shiver. Without a word, Cabe slipped off his suit jacket and draped it over her shoulders. The warmth of his body against the fabric cocooned her skin. She resisted the urge to snuggle deeply into it. “Thank you.”

“It can get chilly on the water. I should have warned you.”

Her heart ached as she thought of the picture they must have made. Alone on a boat on their way to a glamorous casino, his jacket draped over her shoulders to keep her warm. She wanted so much to make believe the idyllic picture could be reality.

But how could it given who she was and where she came from? How soon would someone like Cabe start noticing similarities between herself and the woman who at this very moment was still texting her? Because that needy woman would always text. Amanda would never be out of her life. And Cabe didn't need that kind of lowbrow drama in his.

Jenna knew better. Some things were simply not meant to be.

Maxim stood waiting for them as they disembarked. He greeted her with a warm smile and a barely-there nod to Cabe. Cabe offered a small grunt in response. Any other time, she might have found the competitive aura between the two men humorous and maybe even flattering. But not right now. She had too much on her mind. Too much to deal with. Her pocketbook buzzed yet again with another message on her phone.

Maxim stood staring at her. Cabe looked at her expectantly. One of them had obviously just asked her a question.

Jenna forced a smile and nodded, hoping it was an adequate response to whatever may have just been posed to her. Cabe's eyes grew wide. And clouded with something else she couldn't name. Hurt? By contrast, Maxim's grin had grown twofold. Oh, dear, what had she just agreed to?

"I guess I'll leave you two to yourselves, then," Cabe said then turned away. Her heart plummeted. Apparently, she'd just agreed to being alone with Maxim, essentially sending Cabe away. The exact opposite of what she really wanted. For one insane moment, Jenna wanted to yell at him to stop, to run after him and just explain everything. That she was oh, so wrong for him. That she had too much baggage. She'd never be the type of woman Cabe Jordan needed to have on his arm at his swanky social functions and his family gatherings.

She wanted to tell him all that. And then beg him to want her anyway.

But Maxim was speaking to her. She'd better listen this time. Who knew what she would agree to next without meaning to? Besides, Cabe had already walked several feet away. How foolish would it look to chase after him like a silly twit?

"Let's go find you a drink, my dear," Maxim offered. "Then we'll get the tour started." Dear heavens. The last thing she needed tonight was another drink.

What she needed, down to her soul, was to have Cabe back by her side. He was her anchor, a tether in this alien world full of riches and excess. Maxim was nice enough, every inch the attentive gentleman. Any single woman with a pulse would be thrilled to have him as her very own personal guide for the evening. Just not Jenna.

To top it off, she might have just hurt Cabe. She'd certainly be hurt if he'd dismissed her the same way. To spend time with another man, no less. Professional or not.

Meanwhile, her phone kept buzzing, buzzing, buzzing… Jenna cursed Amanda under her breath. She'd been cursing her all night. What did her mother want? Maybe ignoring her hadn't been the wisest decision, because now she could hardly think of anything else. What fresh hell had Amanda created for them all this time?

They'd made it to the entrance of the grand casino when Maxim turned to her. "Are you all right, dear?" he asked, concern etched in his face. "You look a little pale."

Jenna gave her head a shake and placed her hand on her midsection. "I'm afraid something I've eaten doesn't seem to be agreeing with me." It wasn't exactly a lie. "I'm not used to such rich food, as delicious as everything is."

Maxim gave her a sympathetic nod and pointed behind her. "The ladies' restroom is down that hallway. Take your time."

She gave him a grateful smile and turned on her heel. When she got there, the restroom was blessedly empty. Taking a breath to steady her nerves, she fished her phone out of her small purse. Without giving herself a chance to change her mind, she pulled up her brother's contact file and clicked on it.

It was time to face the piper. And the harsh reality that was her life.

He answered on the first ring. "Hey, sis."

"Sam, what's going on back in Boston? Amanda's calling and texting me relentlessly."

Sam sighed deeply before he spoke. "It's bad, Jen. You should probably sit down."

Oh, no. Jenna leaned back against the tiled wall. "Just tell me."

By the time he finished, Jenna really was going to be sick. According to Sam, the person who'd robbed Jordan's Fine Jewelry, committing the crime that had started Jenna on this whole journey, had been discovered.

That person was her mother.

She'd barely said three words to him last night as he walked her back to her hotel room. Cabe shuffled the papers on the table in the conference room and glanced at the door for the umpteenth time. Jenna hadn't made her way in yet. They'd agreed to meet here in the morning and get some work done. She still had a few minutes but he couldn't help but be impatient. There were things he needed to say to her. Questions he needed to ask.

He hadn't played his cards right yesterday. When Maxim had asked her if she needed Cabe to come along with them, he should have interjected right then and there. He should have said something along the lines of *Of course I'm going with her.* It just hadn't occurred to him that she might actually decline his company on Maxim's silly little tour.

He pinched the bridge of his nose and reclined in the plush leather chair. He stared at the door again, willing it to open and for Jenna to walk in. He checked his phone again. No messages from her. It wasn't that she was late, just that she was usually early to every meeting.

He wanted to see her, first to make sure she was all right. And secondly to finally clear the air between them. They had to start behaving like adults about what had happened between them. They were attracted to each other and they'd acted on it. He wanted to reassure her that it wouldn't happen again. She didn't need to be so skittish around him. He couldn't wait to explain that to her. In fact, if she didn't come in within the next couple of minutes, he would walk back to their villa and go knock on her door.

But then she did walk in, and with one look at her face his resolve faded like a punctured balloon. Her eyes were red-rimmed and puffy, the tip of her nose crimson. Her cheeks held a light sheen. There was no question in his mind—Jenna Townsend had been crying, probably for most of the night.

Maxim. That son of a bitch! But they'd left Maxim

at the casino last night and walked back to their suite together. So what had happened?

He watched as she pulled out her laptop and took a seat across from him, a tight smile plastered on her face. “Good morning. Where would you like to start?”

Was she serious? Did she honestly think they were going to simply get to work like it was a typical morning?

She blinked when he didn’t answer. “If we could get started, there’s something I need to tell you as soon as we’re finished.”

Yeah, no kidding. He leaned toward her over the table. “Maybe you should just tell me now.”

She shook her head. “No. It can wait. We should get some work done first.”

Right. As if that was even a possibility in the state she was in. Not to mention his own. “Jenna. I insist.”

She looked down, picked at her fingernail. Several beats passed in silence. As much as he wanted to, he couldn’t push her. She clearly struggled to blurt out whatever her news was.

When she looked back up at him, the fake smile was back in place. “Please, Cabe. We need to get through these to-dos.”

He nodded once. “We have plenty of time.”

“That’s just it—” She took a deep breath, but apparently couldn’t make herself continue.

“What?” he prodded.

Her mouth opened. Then shut again. He waited for her to say something, anything. Nothing but more silence.

That was it. He’d had it. A man could only muster so much patience in the face of so much left unsaid. Cabe pushed out of his seat, slamming his pen on the table in frustration. The action startled her and she clamped a hand to her mouth.

"Jenna, I'm trying to understand what's happening here. Can you help me do that?"

To his horror, her eyes filled. What had he said to cause that?

"Are you crying?" he asked, his tone harsher than it probably should have been. He was just at such a loss about what to say or do. His arms ached to hold her, to tell her everything would be all right. But he had no doubt in his mind that any such gesture of comfort or physical closeness would be shunned.

Suddenly, she stood. "I'm leaving in a couple of hours, Cabe."

He couldn't have heard her right. Surely, whatever was upsetting her couldn't be that pressing. "You're leaving? Why in the world are you leaving? Our jet doesn't even return for another two days."

"I understand that," she told him. "I've booked a seat on a commercial flight."

"Why would you do that?"

"Because I'm dropping this project. I can no longer work on it. In fact, I can no longer work for *you*."

He couldn't have heard her right. Was she that regretful about their relationship? "Listen, Jenna. What happened between us will not happen again."

She shook her head, her cheeks growing a fiery red. "That's only part of it, Cabe."

"I get that I crossed a line."

Anguish flooded her eyes. "No. It's just—there's something you should know."

"I'm listening."

She sucked in a breath before answering. "You're going to get a call soon from your security personnel. Or maybe it will be Boston PD who notifies you first."

Cabe blinked. "Come again?"

Whatever he'd been expecting, it hadn't been anything along these lines. And then he remembered. "Does this have anything to do with the stolen bracelet?"

She nodded, swallowed hard. "I'm afraid so."

"Jenna, what's going on?"

Her face visibly crumbled and she held a hand to her midsection. In that instant, Cabe wanted nothing more than to hold her and find a way to alleviate her anguish. Clearly, Jenna thought she was at fault somehow for whatever had happened. Maybe she'd left the jewelry case unlocked and the thief had gotten to the jewelry that way. That certainly wouldn't be grounds for her dismissal. She had to know he didn't care. Everyone made mistakes. No bracelet, no matter how costly or valuable, was worth the pain she was clearly burdening herself with right now.

But he kept himself in check, stood firm where he was. It wouldn't do either of them any good to interrupt her. She had to continue. Had to get this over with. "See, there was a reason your security head suspected me."

He could have sworn the room spun around him. "What exactly are you saying? Did you have something to do with the theft after all? Just tell me, Jenna." Could she really have been that cunning? Kept it from him all this time?

He just needed her to come clean. He needed her to be straight with him.

"Cabe, I'm so sorry. I didn't know. It was my mother."

"Your mother? I don't understand. I thought they

were investigating the security guard on duty that night?"

She pursed her lips, her eyes full of tears. "They are. He stole it with her help. Apparently, she'd been studying my routine. Knew where I kept my keys and told him everything. She gave him hints about what my passcode might be. She also told him to strike while I was away at that conference." She took another steadying breath. "He pretended to be interested in her in order to get her help."

His mouth had gone dry, which didn't matter. He couldn't seem to find any words anyway. Questions pummeled at him like a jackhammer in his brain.

"You have to believe I didn't know," she continued, her lip quivering. "I only just found out last night."

"Of course I believe you. I know you're not capable of being that duplicitous."

Jenna's shoulders visibly relaxed. "Thank you."

"I wish you'd just told me, instead of all the dramatics." He sighed, eyed the manila folder on his desk. All that would have to wait now. "I guess we should wrap up here. Then we can fly back together and deal with all this. I'll call the jet back today. We'll meet with Corporate Security as soon as we land."

Her eyes grew wide at his words. "Didn't you hear anything I said? My very own mother stole from you."

"I heard every word."

"She used me to do it."

"That's right. She used you. Am I missing something?"

"You said it yourself, Cabe. I didn't even know what she was up to."

"And none of that has anything to do with your competence. Or how valuable you are to this company." *To me*, he added silently.

"Nevertheless..." She looked away before adding, "There's no way I can continue to work for Jordan's Fine Jewelry as if none of this ever happened."

"You're not thinking this through, Jenna."

"I can't stay, Cabe." Her voice was low, pleading.

"What you really mean is that you *won't* stay," he corrected her. "The choice is yours to make. Yours alone."

She held up her hands. "That's what you're saying now. But this is just going to get uglier. You're going to end up regretting the day you hired me, that you had anything to do with Amanda Townsend's daughter."

He studied her, decided to call her bluff. "That's not what any of this is about."

"What does that mean?"

"It means that the real issue here is that you're blaming yourself. You're covering for Amanda. And as far as I can tell, you've been doing that your whole life."

She lifted her chin. "All that may be true. But it doesn't change anything."

"And that's the sad part. It doesn't change a thing. How long are you going to let Amanda's shortcomings impact your life?"

Suddenly, her eyes grew darker. She stepped closer to him, jabbed a finger in the air toward his chest. "You don't get to lecture me about this. You don't have any kind of cred when it comes to family dynamics."

The air crackled around them, the words hovering menacingly in the air. Jenna sucked in a breath, seemingly surprised by what she'd said.

He could only respond with silence. What was there

to say? She wasn't wrong. He certainly couldn't confront her about the real reason he was so frustrated and angry about her decision. There was so much more at play here than Jenna's response to Amanda's crime.

The harsh reality was that she was running. From him. Here he was, offering to stand by her. To help her through this. And her response was to slam the door in his face, to totally shut him down.

It didn't even occur to her to turn to him, to trust him.

What did that say about him?

The silence prevailed until Jenna finally turned on her heel. "Goodbye, Cabe. I'll contact you in Boston via an attorney."

Well, that had gone well. Jenna adjusted her seat belt and tried to settle into the too-tight space. Just her luck, she had been seated between a heavyset gentleman and an overpacked older lady with a purse larger than she was. But when had luck ever been on her side?

The tears threatened to flow again and she fought them back. What good had crying ever done? She had to gather her wits about her and figure out what to do. First she needed an attorney. One who would no doubt take all her life savings. But she couldn't risk any less—her life depended on it.

Bad enough Amanda had devised the theft, but in true maddening form, she was now bragging about it. All over town. So much so that word had eventually gotten back to her brother, who was trying to convince Amanda to turn herself in. Before the authorities figured it all out and she had the book thrown at her. That was why Amanda had been trying to get hold of her so desperately. She wanted to get Jenna to try to convince her brother to back off.

The man next to her started to snore. A baby wailed from somewhere in the back. This was a far cry from the private jet she'd arrived on. That was another lifetime ago. Back when she was still a professional with a career. She'd still had a future, maybe even a shot at happiness. Someone the likes of no other than Cabe Jordan had actually been attracted to. Jenna closed her eyes and tried to pretend that none of it had ever happened. That she was back to that first day on the jet with Cabe.

She remembered the look of shocked disappointment on his face when she'd told him about her leaving.

Snap out of it. She had to get that image out of her mind. She also had to forget about how he had looked at her that day near the waterfall. Like she was the only one who could have brought that smile to his face. Like she was the only woman for him.

There was no doubt that the next time he saw her, he would have nothing but disdain in his eyes. Jenna's stomach churned and it had nothing to do with the plane taking off. The things she'd said to him. Why couldn't she learn to control her mouth? He'd only been trying to help.

But she'd had to show him that he couldn't help her. There would be no white-knight scenario for Jenna Townsend. Cabe had his own demons. She wouldn't burden him with her own. He didn't know it now, but she was doing him a favor. Soon, he would realize it.

The sooner the better. For his sake.

Jenna surveyed the mess that was her mom's apartment. Take-out containers littered the floor, and empty beer bottles sat turned sideways on every flat surface. Various puddles of unknown liquids spotted the ground. And what in heaven's name was that smell?

She certainly wasn't in paradise any longer. In fact, Jenna would be hard-pressed to prove she hadn't imagined the whole Paraiso Resort and her time on it.

No, this was more like the depths of Hades. And she had her mother to thank for it.

She walked down the hall to the bedroom. Hard to believe, but there was an even bigger mess in here. An empty pizza box sat at her feet. Half-eaten bags of chips and candy cluttered most every surface. And of course, more assorted bottles lay strewn about the floor. She'd only been out of town a few days.

Looking for a priceless bracelet in this mess would be like looking for the proverbial needle in a haystack. Not that it was likely to be here. But she had to make sure.

Jenna felt the tears burn her eyes and a welt form in her throat. Why had she thought she could escape this? This was her life—this depressing, dirty town house and the woman who lived here, the burden of whose care fell solely on Jenna's shoulders. How could she have let herself forget that? How could she have let herself get close to anyone? Let alone someone like Cabe.

Her lips tingled as she remembered their kiss in the conference room. Such a mistake, she should have never let it happen. She thought she could let herself indulge, just one last time before he found out who Jenna Townsend really was. But then again, he'd always known. Everyone did.

Suddenly it was all too much. Her legs grew weak and she perched herself on the edge of Amanda's bed.

Several moments passed as she just sat there. Jenna felt nothing but shame. Even her anger had left her. All she held in her soul was a gnawing, hollow sense of shame.

"Hey, thought I might find you here." Her brother's voice startled her; she hadn't heard him come in.

She hurriedly wiped the moisture off her cheeks then turned and stepped over the garbage piles to give him a hug. "I just got here. Thought I'd look for the bracelet. Just in case."

Her brother let out a low whistle. "I doubt it's here, sis."

"It couldn't hurt to look, right?"

"Guess not."

But hours later, they were both ready to admit defeat. Despite having turned the mess in the apartment upside down, they couldn't find the bracelet anywhere. In fact, the place held nothing of value whatsoever. At least her mother's thievery had been a one-and-done affair.

Sam gave her shoulder a reassuring squeeze. "We'll fix this, Jen. I swear I won't let you fall because of her latest stunt."

She managed a weak smile. "I'm not so sure this time's going to be fixable, Sam. Even if people believe I had no part in the theft, my reputation is ruined. What retail establishment is ever going to hire me again? I'm too much of a risk."

She choked as she said the last word. She was no longer employed with her dream company. She'd never be with Cabe again, not in any way. Reaching behind her, she found the edge of the bed once more. Her legs just weren't going to hold her up.

"Don't say that," Sam insisted. "We'll make them believe you. We'll make her." He pointed an accusatory finger at the empty bed, as if Amanda were still in it. "She'll explain what she did. Tell them that you had nothing to do with it."

"Who do you think is going to take her word for it?"

"Jen, we'll make them see the truth."

As usual, her mother had wreaked complete havoc in her children's lives.

"I have to go," she told her brother.

"Where are you going?"

"To find Amanda. I have to try to make at least part of this right." She turned on her heel and walked out the door before Sam could see the fresh round of tears.

Not that she really could make any of it right in any way. Not with the Jordans. And certainly not with Cabe. An anguished cry tore from her throat and she dropped down to sit on Amanda's cold stone stoop.

She thought about the way Cabe had smiled at her at the beach party as he'd sipped from the straw that she'd just used. The way his eyes had traveled over her that day in the boutique when she'd worn the designer gown. Now she wished she'd never gone to that party with him. She should have never set foot in that boutique.

Because it was all a fairy tale that she'd been living these past few days. One she now had to give up. It would have been so much easier on her heart never to have lived it at all.

CHAPTER NINE

SO SHE WANTED to see him.

Cabe set his office phone back down on the top of the mahogany desk, resisting the urge to listen to Jenna's message once more just to hear her voice. She'd left it at two o'clock in the morning. Apparently, neither of them had gotten much sleep last night. Hell, he hadn't gotten much sleep at all since he'd seen her last. He'd barely been able to think straight. Now she was requesting "time on his schedule" the same day he'd arrived back in Boston. That was exactly how she'd phrased it. So formal. So straightforward. As if nothing had ever happened between them. It would serve her right if he ignored her. Make her come to him.

He sighed. Of course he wouldn't do that. Instead, he typed out a text to her cell phone.

I have time right now. My office.

It took less than five minutes before he heard her knock on his door. He fixed his cuff links and stood. Maybe he'd finally get some answers. She opened the door and he motioned for her to come in. He lost his breath when she did.

So beautiful. The severe ponytail was back, as tight as he'd ever seen it. Her navy pin-striped suit—all business. Dark circles smudged her eyes. She looked utterly beat. And still, she was the most beautiful woman he'd ever laid eyes on. Insanity nearly took over his better judgment and he almost went to her. All he wanted to do right now was pull her into his arms, absorb her warmth, kiss those beckoning lips that so haunted his dreams. He wanted to tell her that everything would be all right, that he would see to it.

Instead, he tightened his fists at his sides.

She stopped in her tracks several feet away from him then took a deep breath. Definitely hesitant. Cabe perched himself on the edge of his desk, motioned to the chair opposite him. "Can I get you anything?" he asked, just to get some kind of conversation going before sitting down.

She shook her head. "No, thank you. And I'd rather do this standing, if you don't mind."

Well, now he felt awkward as he'd already sat. But standing again would look silly. Wouldn't it? Damn it, she was the only woman in the world who could get him so riled. He made million-dollar decisions on a daily basis. But around her he didn't even know whether to sit or stand, for heaven's sake.

"It won't take long," she added.

He simply nodded for her to continue.

"I just wanted to return this." She stepped over and dropped something shiny and bright onto the desk in front of him.

The bracelet.

"How?"

"We found the thief, Sam and I. Convinced him to

hand it over. The authorities are on their way to arrest him now." She pointed to the object that had caused so much havoc in their lives. "I assure you, it's the real piece."

Cabe could only stare. "I don't understand."

"It's simple. I made my mother tell me where your sneaky security guard could be found. Then Sam and I had a heart-to-heart with him."

He didn't like the sound of this, not at all. "Let me get this straight. You and your brother searched out and approached a known thug. Just to retrieve a stolen bracelet. Putting your very life at risk in the process."

She narrowed her eyes on him. "Hardly. We just convinced him it was only a matter of time before the cops came for him. He was almost relieved to dispose of it. Couldn't even fence the thing on the street. Too valuable. He didn't have those kinds of connections. Lord knows Amanda doesn't."

Cabe's heart pounded with anger. To think she had jeopardized her personal safety. For some bauble he honestly couldn't have cared less about.

"At least Jordan's has the piece back," Jenna said.

How could she be so flippant about this? "Look. You didn't need to risk your safety by retrieving it. We had the matter under control." That was a lie. Cabe hadn't even thought about the cursed bracelet since the day Jenna had left his office. He'd done absolutely nothing about its theft. Not even so much as to call Jordan's Security and give them an update. That bracelet had only caused one headache after another. But she didn't need to know that. When he thought of the danger she put herself in, he wanted to grab her by the shoulders and shake her.

Then he wanted to kiss her until she finally started to see some sense.

"I know it doesn't really solve anything," she said, apologetically.

No, it didn't. Not at all. Which made it all the worse. "What the hell are you trying to prove here, Jenna?"

Ire flashed in her eyes. "I wasn't trying to prove anything. Merely rectifying a mistake I made."

Cabe wanted to throw something. "There you go again. *You* didn't make a mistake. You did nothing wrong. *Amanda*, your mother, stole from the store." He emphasized the name, hoping it would drive his point home.

No such luck. Her back stiffened before she spoke. "My mother was targeted by a charming con artist because of where I worked."

"Are you apologizing for where you chose to be employed?"

She actually stomped her foot. "I'm not apologizing at all. Not for getting the bracelet back. I'm merely returning it."

"Which you did by risking your own safety, going after a known thief. Can you not even see the danger you put yourself in?"

"I've been dealing with people like that thief since I can remember. My mother didn't exactly have high standards when it came to her boyfriends."

"How long are you going to let her run your life, Jenna? You quit your job because of her, you foolishly went and got the bracelet back to make up for her mistake. When are you going to realize that you have your own worth? Beyond the stain of your mother's reputation?"

She gasped. “I made my own decisions.”

He actually laughed. “Do you really think that? You just keep trying to prove yourself.”

Her jaw dropped. “Did you just accuse me of trying to prove myself to atone for who my mother is?”

“Don’t you?”

She snorted a small laugh. “You have no idea how hypocritical that is.”

The one word struck like a dart in his brain. “Hypocritical?”

“You really don’t see it, do you? You’ve done nothing but reach for and achieve goal after goal, just to prove yourself worthy of the Jordan name. The whole world can see you’re a credit to your parents. Everyone except you!” She threw her hands in the air. “It’s almost as if… Oh, never mind!”

Cabe crossed his arms over his chest. “No, please. Continue. I’d really like to hear this.”

“It’s as if you have to ensure James and Tricia don’t ever regret adopting you. Like you have to continually find ways to earn their love, only to come up short time and time again.”

The room grew dark around him; he felt the muscles in his neck tighten to the point of pain. Jenna had no idea what she was talking about. Why in the world had he ever thought she might be someone who could understand? He’d been a fool to ever confide in her about his parentage.

“Thank you for bringing back the bracelet. Now, if you don’t mind, I have a lot of work to do. On top of my regular workload, I no longer have any assistance with the Caribbean expansion.”

Jenna flinched, his words finding their target. So be it. "That's it?" she asked incredulously.

"Yes. It is. I believe we've both said all there is to say to each other."

She shook her head and turned to the door, slamming it hard on her way out.

Cabe paced the length of the room and tried to get his pulse in check. It didn't help. All the confusion and frustration of the past two days formed into a barreling rage inside his chest. He turned with a vicious curse and landed a swift, hard kick to the parlor table in the center of his office. It landed with a thud so loud it must have resonated to the floor below. But he barely heard the noise over the roaring in his ears.

Cabe's administrative assistant knocked on his door again. This was probably the fourth or fifth time this morning. She'd been doing that, checking in on him, ever since the incident a few days back when he'd kicked the table over and caused such a loud ruckus. Apparently she wasn't buying Cabe's story that he'd tripped and toppled it accidentally. The interruptions were getting annoying. Not that he'd actually been focusing enough to get anything done. He hadn't been able to focus on anything since Jenna had left his office three days ago.

"Betty. I really am fine," he began. "You don't have to—" He stopped when he realized there was someone in the reception area behind her.

"Actually, Mr. Jordan. Your father is here to see you."

Cabe put down the spreadsheet he held in his hand. James was here? Now what? Then it occurred to him—

his parents had no doubt heard about Jenna leaving their employ.

Cabe had some explaining to do.

Standing, he nodded at her. "Show him in."

James entered wearing jeans and a blue checked shirt, no tie. His father had a sharp head for business, but had never been interested in dressing the part.

"Father. I've been meaning to set up a time to talk to you. And Tricia."

"I figured I'd come by while you were in town. I probably should have called first."

Did he always have to sound so overly polite with him? "It's technically your company."

His father pulled out the chair opposite the desk and sat. "You run it. Although that's what I came to talk to you about. I hear we may be losing a valuable member of the Jordan team."

He should have seen this coming, Cabe thought. Very little happened within the business that James wasn't swiftly made aware of. He made it a point to know everything that went on with the company he started, regardless of who actually ran it.

"Jenna Townsend was on location to help me with the Caribbean expansion when things got a little… complicated."

"So I gathered. Was there more than one complication? In addition to the missing jewelry?"

At Cabe's puzzled expression, James continued. "Your reputation as a ladies' man somewhat precedes you, son. Jenna's a very attractive woman."

Cabe grunted. Despite ditching the photographer back at the island, it looked like the gossip mill still churned out its story.

"I'll squelch the rumors. This isn't a long-term concern."

James held up a hand. "That's not why I'm asking, not because of the business."

"It's not?"

James shook his head. "Your mom and I, we've known Jenna since she was a little girl. She hasn't had the easiest life."

Cabe barely suppressed a groan. "Don't I know it?"

His father's eyebrows lifted. "She confided in you?"

He hadn't really thought about it that way, but now that his father mentioned it… "I guess she did."

"That's surprising. She tends to keep that stuff about her family close to her chest."

"We had a few opportunities to talk." He looked his father square in the eye. "I sort of confided in her, too. I know we don't normally talk about it with anyone, but I told her the truth."

"The truth?"

"That I'm not really your son."

His father sucked in a breath. "Is that how you put it? When you told her?"

"More or less."

"That's how you see yourself, then. As not really my son."

How in the world had this conversation veered in this direction? They were supposed to be talking about Jenna and what it would mean to their business if she left the company.

"It's not like I don't realize how lucky I am. I owe everything to you and Tricia."

James nodded slowly. "You're not really my son and you owe us for bringing you up."

Well, when he phrased it that way… But, as off-putting as it sounded, it was essentially the truth.

"As parents, you did everything you could," Cabe reassured him.

"If that's the impression you have of us, we clearly needed to do more." He looked off to the side, summoning the words. "Listen, Cabe, your mother and I probably should have waited before adopting another baby. Tricia couldn't handle her grief, and I wasn't strong enough to help her. I was barely containing my own. But that doesn't mean you weren't wanted. Or loved."

James may as well have sucker punched him. A lump formed at the base of Cabe's throat. "Thank you for saying that."

"I should have said it years ago. And more." He swallowed visibly. "But I never found the right times. And frankly, I never found the courage. Until now. Better late than never, right?" James chuckled, thought it sounded false and the smile didn't reach his eyes.

"Truth be told," his father went on, "not only have you earned our respect repeatedly over the years, you've been a constant source of both joy and love in our lives, more so than we could have hoped that first day we brought you home. And I'm ashamed to admit that I didn't tell you that or show you nearly as often as I should have."

Or at all, Cabe thought. James's words were beyond unexpected. He'd never so much as uttered an affectionate word to him over the years.

The James Jordan sitting opposite him right now bore little resemblance to the distant and distracted man Cabe had grown up with.

Was Cabe mistaken or were his father's eyes actually shimmering with moisture? James was the strongest man he had ever known. Never once in his life had he seen him so much as shed a tear. He'd just appeared perpetually sad.

When James spoke again, his voice was thick. "You are and have always been my son."

Cabe had to remind himself to breathe.

The words hung powerfully in the air. Both men stared uncomfortably at each other for several moments. For the life of him, Cabe couldn't come up with a single thing to say.

Finally, James cleared his throat. "Now, where exactly do we stand with Jenna?"

Cabe blinked at the sudden question. His father was clearly ready to change the subject. Pushing his hair off his forehead, Cabe searched for a way to answer. How to describe where he stood with Jenna? "She's unlike anyone I've ever met. She's got an incomparable business sense, yet she's sensitive and so aware of the needs of others. She can be infuriatingly stubborn but somehow knows when to compromise. She can make me angry as a hornet one minute, and then make me laugh the next. I've never been with anyone like her."

"I see." James studied the carpet, didn't look up when he asked the next question. "Does she know?"

"Know what?"

His father looked at him as if he should be wearing a dunce cap. Maybe he was right. But he was still trying to process the overwhelming conversation of a few minutes ago. "I mean, did you ever actually come out and tell her any of this?"

"Uh. No."

James shifted in his chair, uncomfortable again.

"Listen, Cabe. Your mother and I haven't exactly been the most open or, God forgive me, the most willing, when it came to demonstrating affection. I've known that in my gut. But I guess what we just talked about drove it all home."

Another shocking admission. His father was making all sorts of confessions here.

"Maybe we're not the best examples to follow."

Cabe hadn't realized that he'd been following anyone's example. But he had to acknowledge James's point. In his last few conversations with Jenna, he'd been totally focused on her complete willingness to set aside her own needs for the sake of her family. He'd been trying to point out to her how wrong that was.

It was Cabe who was wrong; James had just shown him that. No, that wasn't correct. Jenna had been the one to show him. James had merely just confirmed her point.

Up until today, Cabe had been too blind to see what was so clear all along. He'd always had the love of his parents. They really did value and cherish him. They just had no idea how to show it.

At least Jenna had the courage to accept the family she had and to love them anyway. She was right to call him a hypocrite.

"What I'm trying to say is," James continued, "you've been a fighter your whole life. This is something worth fighting for. Jenna's not the type of woman you want to lose once you have her."

Clearly, James was no longer referring to the company.

CHAPTER TEN

JENNA TENSED WHEN her doorbell rang. She just couldn't bring herself to entertain the possibility that it might be the police. She had no clue what she would say to them if they were already here for her. Though it would have to count for something that the bracelet had been returned. Taking a fortifying breath, she yanked open her door. Then did a double take when she saw who her visitor was.

"Cabe? I thought you would have returned to Manhattan by now."

"Not yet. I had some agenda items to finish."

Her heart plummeted. He was here on some kind of business.

"I wanted to come by and tell you that you can relax. No one's going to press charges against your mother."

Could she have heard that right? "I don't understand."

"Roger, my head of security, is former Boston PD. He's still got a lot of connections. He'll make sure the authorities know you had nothing to do with the robbery. And he can put in a word on your mom's behalf, make sure she gets a break. They'll be easier to convince now that the item is back in its rightful place. And because she's seeking help for her addictions."

Jenna's relief almost had her knees buckling beneath her. That was an unexpected turn. She didn't want to look a gift horse in the mouth but the development begged a question. "But why would your security head do that?"

"Because I asked him to."

He had? Her mouth fell open. "I don't know what to say. Except that I can't thank you enough. Really, Cabe, that was above and beyond. You don't know how much I appreciate it."

But it still didn't explain why he was here, at her door. He could have called with the info. Or had his secretary do it even.

He surprised her further by asking, "Can I come in?"

Stepping aside, she motioned him inside and shut the door. His eyes grew wide when he saw her packed airline bag against the wall.

"Are you going somewhere?"

She nodded. "I have some interviews lined up. Out of state."

His lips thinned into a slim line. "I apologize. I should have called first."

Suddenly he was serious, matter-of-fact. His mouth didn't hold a hint of a smile. Still, all she could think about was how good it was to see him, just to have him in the same room. It didn't seem possible that fate had given her a chance to see him one more time. Taking a moment to study his face, she thought how haggard he looked now. Dark circles framed his weary bloodshot eyes. He clearly had not bothered to shave this morning.

"It's okay," she assured him. "I have some time." Though the truth was she'd actually be cutting it really close if she delayed any longer, barely giving herself enough time to get to the airport and check in. But she couldn't bear to send him away just yet. She missed him! She'd been walking around zombielike these past few days, barely able to function, the features of Cabe's face etched in her mind. The feel of his touch imprinted onto her skin. "Can I get you anything? Coffee?"

"Sure, that'd be great."

Jenna went to the still-warm coffeepot, half full. She was glad she hadn't had a chance to empty and rinse the carafe. When she returned, Cabe was sitting on her sofa, with her sketchbook lying open on the coffee table in front of him. He pointed to the page she'd been working on. "These are really good. Did you do them?"

She ducked her head at the compliment. "I try some designing in my spare time. Mostly necklaces."

He picked up the book and studied it. "I had no idea you designed jewelry."

Jenna set the coffee cup down, hoping he didn't notice the trembling in her hands. This conversation was so awkward. All she wanted to do was wrap her arms around his neck and feel his lips on hers. Instead, she was racking her brain trying to come up with what to say next.

"I don't know if it's any good," she replied with genuine doubt. No one had ever actually seen any of her sketches until now.

"You're full of surprises, Jenna."

Another awkward pause settled between them.

He inhaled a deep breath. "Jenna, you're unlike any

woman I've ever met. You design jewelry. You have an amazing head for business. You charm everyone you meet. And you've done an amazing job of managing your severely troubled parent while raising yourself and a brother." He stood to face her, ran a finger down her cheek. A hot tingle ran up her spine at his touch, and the smell of his aftershave teased her senses. "You're one of the bravest people I know, man or woman."

Whoa. Jenna gave her head a shake. "Brave? How in the world am I brave in any way?"

"You really don't see it, do you? The way you put your mom first, despite what it's cost you. That takes the kind of rare courage few people possess. You actually confronted a known criminal to rectify what she'd done." He visibly shuddered. "Please don't do anything like that ever again, by the way."

She sniffled on a laugh. "I won't—I promise."

He motioned toward her suitcase. "I know I have no right—but cancel those interviews. Say you'll stay, Jenna."

"You want me to stay at Jordan's Fine Jewelry?"

Cabe shook his head. "Not exactly."

She swallowed down the hope that had blossomed in her chest. How foolish of her. Of course she'd misunderstood him. Until she heard his next words.

"I want more than that. I want you to stay with *me*."

He grasped her hand in his. Jenna couldn't seem to make her brain work. Thoughts scrambled around in her head like fallen leaves during a windstorm. It was hard enough to wrap her mind around the fact that he was here, in her home. She couldn't process what he was telling her. It was simply too good to be true. "Cabe, what are you saying?"

"I'm saying that watching you walk out of my office that day nearly broke me. I haven't been able to sleep. I keep thinking about the way you felt in my arms, the way we were together on the island. I can't lose that, Jenna." He inhaled deeply. "I know I have a lot to work on. To make myself the kind of man you deserve. I just need you to be patient."

That settled it. She'd obviously awoken to some alternate reality. The world had turned upside down. Cabe Jordan was pleading with her to be patient with him. Asking her to understand that he would work hard to become the right man for her.

"I know it's a lot to ask," Cabe continued. "You've obviously had the patience of a saint over the years. You've raised yourself and your brother on your own, made sure your mother didn't completely self-destruct. It's unfair to ask you to extend yourself any more for my sake."

Tears sprang into her eyes. She reached for him, clasped his unshaven chin in her hand. "As far as courage goes, you have it in spades, Cabe Jordan."

It was his turn to look shocked. So she explained, "You've done your utter best all your life to try and make your parents happy. Even knowing that it may never be enough. That's the definition of loyalty. Of bravery. You're everything anyone could ever hope for in a son."

He turned his face in her cupped palm, exactly as he had that day at the waterfall. "Then why? Why did you feel the need to leave at first?"

She choked down on a sob. "How can you ask that? I could barely face you. By then you meant so much to me. How was I supposed to ask you to accept the fact that my own mother had stolen from you?"

"You beautiful, silly fool. You have no idea how you impressed me."

She was definitely hearing things. "Impressed you?"

He nodded. "You could have surrendered Amanda to the authorities. Then gone back to your job and lived your life. No one would have blamed you for doing so. Instead, you quit the job you loved and hired an attorney for her. You might not realize what kind of a person that makes you, but I do."

"Is that really how you see me?"

"It's exactly how I see you. I just didn't know how to tell you any of that."

Just those simple words, and somehow the steel bands around her heart snapped open. Cabe didn't judge her on who her mother was or where she came from. He saw her strengths and judged her on her actions. He saw Jenna for who she was.

Maybe he could help her see it, too.

He pulled her to him then, kissing her deeply and holding her tight against his frame. "Besides, by then I'd already fallen in love with you. You could have asked me anything."

Her heart had not only just sprung free but Jenna was certain it would burst any moment now. "You love me?" she stammered, her mind on the verge of going numb.

He didn't need to use any words when he answered her.

"You look beautiful, Jenna."

Jenna turned away from the boutique mirror to face

the two ladies helping her get ready. "Do you really think so, Seema?"

Seema beamed back at her. "Yes. That dress may as well have been made for you." She walked over to give Jenna a tight squeeze around the shoulders. Martine, the saleswoman who had encouraged her to fatefully try on this very dress all those weeks ago, gave her a conspiratorial wink.

A low rumble of thunder sounded through the walls from outside. The forecast this morning called for a major storm far off the coast. No doubt she and Cabe would be saying their vows under a cloudy sky with sprinkles of rain. None of it mattered or could make so much as a dent in her joy. She could weather any storm with Cabe by her side.

As she turned back to her reflection in the mirror, Jenna's heart did a little jump at the sight. Was that really her staring back from the glass? Jenna had known the moment Cabe asked her to marry him that this would be her bridal gown.

She also knew there was no other place on earth she'd rather have her wedding than here, at the Paraiso Resort.

And no other man she wanted to spend the rest of her life with.

Cabe was in the process of admiring his bride and marveling at his luck when his father surprised him by standing up. His parents were seated at the closest table to the wedding dais, along with Seema and Jenna's brother. Jenna's mom remained in Boston, getting the rehabilitation treatment she so desperately needed. That had been part of the deal when the Jordans agreed not to press charges.

His father picked up his wineglass and raised it, clearing his throat to get everyone's attention. A toast. The roar of chatter gradually diminished as their guests noticed.

Cabe inhaled and braced himself. He honestly had no idea what his father might say; it hadn't even occurred to him to ask his father to speak. No doubt his speech would be all about the growth of Jordan Enterprises under Cabe's leadership. Or something.

He was wrong. In fact, his dad surprised him and didn't even mention business.

James took a deep breath and began. "I'm not sure if I can find the word to adequately express what I want to say. But here goes," James said and smiled in a way that didn't quite reach his eyes. He turned toward the wedding guests. "My son has managed to do so much in his life. He's been a terrific son and he's achieved more into his thirties than most men do in a lifetime. And now he's managed to snare himself a wife as accomplished and beautiful as Jenna."

Cabe heard Jenna gasp in surprise as she reached for his hand and gave it a gentle squeeze. He in turn clung to her fingers.

His father went on. "You've done so much for yourself, Cabe. All on your own. We should have been there for you more than we were. For that, I can only ask your forgiveness." James looked him straight in the eye as he said the last word.

Cabe could only stare frozen, unable to come up with anything appropriate to say or do. He stole a glance at his mother and immediately realized there'd be no help from that corner—she was definitely crying. An awkward silence ensued.

James took a deep breath, opened his mouth to presumably say more, but then suddenly shut it again. He looked to the ground, clearly struggling to find the wherewithal to continue.

Jenna's hand slowly released his. He felt the loss of her touch immediately. But then she did something so simple yet so powerful, it reaffirmed why he'd fallen head over heels in love with her in the first place. She stood and slowly started to clap. It wasn't long before the rest of their guests joined her. The look of gratitude and relief on his father's face said it all. No, not his father, Cabe corrected himself. His dad. James held the expression of a man who'd just been rescued from drowning.

And they had Cabe's new bride to thank for it.

Once the applause died down and everyone had lowered their glasses, Jenna looked up to find Cabe holding out his hand to her.

She stood and he took her by the waist, led her to the dance floor. As they swayed to the rhythmic reggae song, he leaned over to whisper in her ear. "I love you, Mrs. Jordan."

The words, coupled with the magic of the moment, brought tears of happiness to her eyes. "And I've always loved you, Mr. Jordan."

He laughed and it sent pure pleasure through her whole body, down to her toes. "If only I'd known. Think of all the time we've wasted."

"It was your fault for never asking me to prom."

He affectionately nipped at her ear. "Perhaps. But you know, *you* could have asked me."

"Hmm. You're right. We'll just have to find a way to make up for lost time," she teased.

He brushed his lips against hers. "I can't wait to start."

Jenna knew they already had.

* * * * *

“So I’d only get hurt if I got involved with you,” Cora said.

“Yes. You’d essentially be getting a locked box.”

He was being transparent, completely up-front. She was the one who’d set that tone. So it surprised him when she barked out a laugh. “You think you’re doing me a favor by staying away!”

He was trying to adhere to the decisions he’d made after that last ugly blowout with Tina. He’d been glad for the peace and balance he’d found since they’d broken up a year ago. But twelve months was a long time to go without a woman… “Essentially.”

“Well, you’re taking a lot for granted, Mr. Turner. First of all, how do you know I’m going to want you to love me?”

“Experience,” he said wryly. “I have yet to encounter the opposite problem.”

* * *

Silver Springs:
Where love changes everything!

FINDING OUR FOREVER

BY
BRENDA NOVAK

All rights reserved including the right of reproduction in whole or in part in any form. This edition is published by arrangement with Harlequin Books S.A.

This is a work of fiction. Names, characters, places, locations and incidents are purely fictional and bear no relationship to any real life individuals, living or dead, or to any actual places, business establishments, locations, events or incidents. Any resemblance is entirely coincidental.

This book is sold subject to the condition that it shall not, by way of trade or otherwise, be lent, resold, hired out or otherwise circulated without the prior consent of the publisher in any form of binding or cover other than that in which it is published and without a similar condition including this condition being imposed on the subsequent purchaser.

® and ™ are trademarks owned and used by the trademark owner and/or its licensee. Trademarks marked with ® are registered with the United Kingdom Patent Office and/or the Office for Harmonisation in the Internal Market and in other countries.

First Published in Great Britain 2017
By Mills & Boon, an imprint of HarperCollins*Publishers*
1 London Bridge Street, London, SE1 9GF

© 2017 Brenda Novak

ISBN: 978-0-263-92290-5

23-0417

Our policy is to use papers that are natural, renewable and recyclable products and made from wood grown in sustainable forests. The logging and manufacturing processes conform to the legal environmental regulations of the country of origin.

Printed and bound in Spain
by CPI, Barcelona

New York Times and *USA TODAY* bestselling author **Brenda Novak** is the author of more than fifty books. A five-time RITA® Award nominee, she has won many awards, including the National Readers' Choice Award, the Booksellers' Best Award and the Silver Bullet Award. She also runs Brenda Novak for the Cure, a charity to raise money for diabetes research (her youngest son has this disease). To date, she's raised $2.5 million. For more about Brenda, please visit www.brendanovak.com.

To all lost/hurt boys.
May you find an Aiyana Turner in your life.

Chapter One

Cora Kelly had never met her birth mother.

The records had been sealed when she was adopted as a newborn twenty-eight years ago. Her adoptive mother didn't even know her birth mother's name, so it wasn't as if Lilly Kelly had ever mentioned it. Cora had had very little to go on. Even with two different attorneys, a website designed to help families reconnect and a private investigator who'd taken her case for free since he was an adoptee himself and did what he could, in his spare time, to help others who'd been through the same thing, it'd taken six long years to glean the information she craved. But here she was, only moments away from coming face-to-face, for the first time since the day she was born, with the woman who'd brought her into this world.

Would she like her mother? Would they resemble each other more in person than in the one picture she'd seen? Would Aiyana Turner somehow recognize her for who she was?

Those questions churned in Cora's mind, making her stomach churn, as well. But one question weighed heavier than the others: Was she making a mistake?

Wiping her palms on her slacks, she told herself to calm down. As far as Aiyana knew, they were only meeting to talk about Cora's new job working as an art instructor at New Horizons Boys Ranch, a boarding school for troubled teens, ages fourteen to eighteen, ninety minutes outside LA. No way would Aiyana have any reason to suspect Cora's true identity. And Cora didn't plan to tell her who she was. Not today. Maybe not ever. That was why she'd sought this job—and accepted it. So she'd have the chance to see what she might be getting into before making that decision.

Hopefully, her mother would be someone she could admire, at least. From what she could tell, Aiyana had done a lot to help teenage boys who acted out, some who'd been orphaned as well as many who hadn't. Her work as executive administrator of the school she'd founded twenty years ago seemed to be her one true love. She'd never been married, and she'd never had any more of her own children. According to a newspaper article honoring Aiyana on the anniversary of the date the boys ranch opened, something the private detective who finally solved the mystery of Aiyana's identity had provided, Aiyana had adopted quite a few of the residents who'd come to the school through the years—eight of them, so far. The oldest, Elijah Turner, was now a man in his early thirties. He helped run New Horizons. Cora knew because he was the person who'd interviewed and then hired her. That was why she hadn't yet met Aiyana. Aiyana had been out of town when Cora came two weeks ago.

"I'm sorry it's taking a few moments. Ms. Turner is on an unexpected but important call." The receptionist, a gray-haired woman who had to be in her sixties, smiled kindly as she imparted this apology. "I can't imagine it'll be much longer."

Hauling in a deep breath, Cora smiled. "It's fine. I don't mind waiting." She *didn't* mind, except that she was beginning to fear she'd have a heart attack right there outside of Aiyana Turner's office. Somehow, she had to stem her anxiety…

"Are you too warm, dear? I can turn down the air…"

She glanced up at the receptionist again—and realized she'd been fanning herself. "Um…no. I'm okay, thanks," she said and dropped her hand.

"It's been hot this summer."

"Yes, it's particularly warm today," Cora said, but it was generally worse where she lived in Burbank. Along with Jill, her best friend, Cora rented a small condo just outside of Hollywood, where her adoptive parents still owned the lovely four-bedroom home where she'd been raised.

She felt a twinge of guilt when she thought of her parents, Brad and Lilly. They'd been good to her, treated her just like her brother, who was two years older and their biological child. They wouldn't be pleased that she'd landed this job if they knew the driving force behind it.

Don't think about that. What they don't know can't hurt them. It would be premature to drag them into this, anyway, since she had no idea where it might go. For all she knew, it wouldn't go anywhere. And maybe that was for the best. Several years ago, when she'd first mentioned that she'd like to find her birth mother, Brad and Lilly had acted shocked and disappointed. They'd taken it personally, didn't understand that they didn't do anything to cause the emptiness inside her and weren't the ones who could fix it. The hole was just there, and Cora felt it would be until she could figure out where she came from, who she was and where she belonged.

She hoped this would help. Her boyfriend—*ex*-boyfriend since she'd broken up with him last month—claimed it was her personal problems that'd destroyed their two-year relationship. He said she needed to let go of her past and move on, that she could be opening Pandora's box.

He could be right. But it was too late to change her plans. She'd already made a yearlong commitment to New Horizons. Today's meeting with Aiyana was merely a formality—an orientation, of sorts. Cora had given notice that she'd be vacating her condo at the end of the month, at which point her friend would get a new roommate and she'd move to Silver Springs, a town of only 5,000 people located slightly east of Santa Barbara.

After spending her whole life in the big city, Cora wasn't sure she'd like living in such a rural area, but if she had to pick a small town, this one wasn't bad. Known for its robust arts community, the renovation of its downtown, its clean water, green energy, recreation and quaint small businesses, there was a lot to recommend it. Life was just slower. Those who didn't grow up here came to retire, raise a family in a "safe place" or enjoy the beauty of the surrounding mountains—

"Ms. Kelly?"

Cora's heart jumped into her throat. The drone of the voice she'd heard coming from the inner office had fallen silent. This was it! The receptionist was about to tell her she could go in…

"Yes?"

"Ms. Turner will see you now."

For a moment, Cora's determination faltered. But when she didn't move, the receptionist—Betty May, according to the placard on her desk—stood expectantly. "It's right through here," she said with a puzzled expression.

Swallowing to ease her dry throat, Cora nodded. "Right. I was just…" *About to run the other way...* Letting her words fall off, since she couldn't readily lay her mind upon a good excuse, she threw back her shoulders and crossed the room to step inside an expansive office with several rows of pictures on the wall—every graduating class of New Horizons.

Those pictures melted into the background as soon as Cora's eyes landed on the diminutive woman with long black hair that fell in a braid down her back. *This* was where she'd gotten the golden color of her skin, Cora thought as she stared. That detail hadn't been quite so apparent in the grainy picture she'd seen with that newspa-

•er article, but her mother appeared to be part Mexican, outh American or maybe Native American.

Wasn't that something she should've had a right to know ,ithout having to go to all the trouble and expense she did?

Cora had always been conscious of the difference in er skin tone compared to the Kellys. Lilly had blond hair nd blue eyes and, like many of her friends, had indulged ı a fair amount of Botox and cosmetic surgery. Aiyana, n the other hand, didn't look as though she'd ever altered nything.

"Ms. Kelly, I'm so sorry for making you wait. That call ,as about another candidate for the school. Considering ıe mischief he's been in, I figured I should handle it as oon as possible. His poor grandmother, who's raising him, ; beside herself."

Cora blinked rapidly, battling a sudden upwelling of motion. She'd *longed* for this day. And here it was. She ,as looking at her *mother*.

But she couldn't act strange or she might give herself way. What had Aiyana just said? Something about the ,ait and the reason for it… "Of course," she managed to :spond, dragging what she'd heard out of short-term mem-ry before it could disappear into the ether. "I understand ıat the welfare of the boys has to come first."

Aiyana's smile as she gestured toward the chair on the ther side of her desk suggested she appreciated Cora's :sponse. "Please, take a seat."

Cora could hardly pull her gaze away long enough to t without missing the chair.

"Eli tells me—"

"Eli?" Cora echoed.

"Elijah," she clarified. "My son."

"Oh right." Aiyana was talking about the incredibly andsome but imposing man who'd interviewed Cora two eeks ago. If only Cora could think clearly, she would've made that connection as instantly as she should have. He'c certainly left an impression.

"He told me you graduated from the University of Sar Diego with a BA in art education six years ago."

"Yes. I love art, and I love teaching, so…putting the two together seemed like a natural for me."

"You've been working as a substitute since then?"

"That's right. When I first graduated, I was grateful fo the flexibility subbing gave me, because I was doing a bi of traveling with my parents. Since then it's been difficul to find a full-time position, given that so many school: are cutting back on their art, music and sports programs.'

"I understand. So that's why you answered our ad?"

One of the reasons—though not the most important Ironically enough, she'd been offered a full-time positio for the coming year at the school for which she'd substi tuted most often, so she'd no longer needed the opportu nity. The art teacher at Woodbridge High was retiring an had put in a good word for her. But, to her parents' conster nation, Cora had turned it down. Aiyana was *here*. Tha meant New Horizons offered something no other schoo could. "Yes."

Aiyana peered at her more closely. "Is somethin wrong?"

Tears were getting the best of her despite all her effort to suppress them. "Allergies," Cora explained. "It's tha time of year. Fortunately, they don't last long."

"Would you like me to get you a tissue?"

Cora used her finger to remove the tear that was abou to roll down her cheek. "No, I'm fine. My eyes are just. a little itchy, that's all."

"Let me know if you change your mind," she said. "I' get you something if you need it. Meanwhile, I'd like t talk to you about the importance we place on art here a the ranch. Most other schools focus on core subjects, an as an accredited high school, we certainly make that a priority here, too. But it's my feeling that our students cannot excel in those classes—in *anything*—if they're too broken to care or try. I believe in healing those who will be healed by showing them the beauty of life and giving them a healthy form of expression. I guess it would be safe to say that, around here, you aren't merely an extra, the first teacher to go when the budget gets tight. You are our most important teacher, which is why I asked to meet with you before you started in a couple of weeks."

"I admire your philosophy." Cora agreed with it, too. But hearing that *she* was the most important teacher at the ranch was intimidating, since this was her first full-time position.

"I want my boys to be educated," Aiyana continued, "but even more than that, I want them to be whole, to find peace."

"Makes sense to me."

"Good. I should warn you that most have never been introduced to drawing, painting or pottery. They think school has to be boring and hard, which is what makes it so rewarding to introduce them to the fun side of learning. Creative endeavors are one of the best tools we have to ease the pain and anger that's inside so many of them."

"Does that mean all of the students here come from a difficult background?" she asked.

"Quite a few. Some have been abandoned. Some have been abused. Some have behavioral issues that can't be blamed on any of those things."

"You mean like autism."

"We have a few autistic students but only those who are highly functioning. More often it's something else—a chemical imbalance, genetic factors. No one can say for sure. Some brains are just wired differently than others."

"Those boys must be the toughest to reach."

"Sometimes we don't reach them at all. But, that said, we're going to reach all we can."

Cora could easily imagine the rich parents of a boy who had behavioral problems being willing to pay a large sum to enroll him at the ranch. But how could orphans afford such a school? "What about the costs associated with coming here—for those who don't have parents, I mean? Does another member of the family pay for it? Or maybe the state?"

"We get some state assistance, we have private benefactors and we do two big fund-raisers a year. As much as thirty percent of our students come here without paying a dime. This year, that equates to eighty students. But as long as we can meet our monthly expenses, I'm satisfied. If we have extra, I'd much rather use it to try to save another boy."

Cora almost felt guilty that she'd be taking a salary. She nearly spoke up to say she could make do with less, but she knew that wasn't the case. In LA, she'd been able to augment her income by waiting tables on the weekends. Chances were, in such a small community, she wouldn't have the opportunity to get a second job. "That's very noble of you."

Aiyana gestured as if she wasn't interested in praise. "I only mention it so that you'll understand what's important to me. It isn't turning a profit—it's making a difference. And I'm looking to work with people who are as invested in the progress of these boys as I am."

"I understand. I'll do my best," Cora said. "But…why have you focused exclusively on helping boys? Why not girls? Or girls *and* boys? Do you have a strong gender preference or—"

"No. Not at all. I didn't want the added responsibility of mixing the two genders, knew it wouldn't be easy to keep them apart," she said with a chuckle. "The boys who come here have enough to worry about without adding that kind of temptation. This is a time for them to focus on getting their lives in order. Hopefully, as a result, they'll make better husbands and fathers later."

"You're saying it was purely a practical decision."

"Absolutely. Someday, on the opposite side of town, I'd like to open a school exclusively for girls, and do essentially the same thing. Now that I have Elijah handling so much around here, that's more of a possibility than ever before. I just haven't geared up for the push it will require."

"I'm sure you'll do equally well with girls." At least now she knew that her mother hadn't given her up because she didn't like girls. Perhaps that'd been a silly thought to begin with, but Cora couldn't help searching for The Reason. Maybe that was all she really needed to know in order to be satisfied…

"We'll see. Now, I've been told you'll be moving into the housing on campus. But have you seen where you'll be living?"

"Not yet. Mr. Turner showed me the school and some other parts of the property, but he didn't offer me the position until after I got home, so we didn't go inside the faculty housing."

"Well, the cottages aren't big, by any stretch of the imagination, but I like being able to include them in the package we offer our teachers. I figure discounted rent might tempt them into staying for a while." She grinned. "Longer than a year."

This comment revealed that Aiyana was well aware of her arrangement with Elijah. "It's a nice benefit."

"You'll find we're more like a family here than what you've most likely experienced in the past," she said with a wink.

A family… Those two words nearly caused Cora to

burst into tears. Aiyana had no idea how literal their connection was.

As Cora followed Aiyana out of the building, she couldn't help thinking back, over all the different ways she'd imagined her mother while growing up. As a drug addict who didn't care about anything except her next hit. As a prostitute eager to rid herself of the child from an unwanted pregnancy. As "the other woman," abandoned by her lover after telling him she was going to have his child. As a businesswoman who refused to allow motherhood to get in the way of her ambition. There were more, but each scenario provided a ready excuse for adoption. She'd never pictured Aiyana like she was—soft-spoken, seemingly wise, well educated, accomplished, stable, kind, loving and devoted to a cause.

Cora had expected that just by meeting her mother so many of her questions would be answered. But she was more baffled than ever. What happened twenty-eight years ago? Why would someone like Aiyana Turner put her only child up for adoption?

Chapter Two

"So...do you like the woman you'll be working for?"

Cora was packing up the kitchen of her condo in Burbank with Lilly when Lilly asked this question. For a second, Cora froze, fearing her adoptive mother had figured out the reason she was moving to Silver Springs. But when Lilly kept wrapping glasses in newspaper and putting them into the box she was filling, it became apparent she was merely making conversation. She *didn't* know—not yet, thank goodness.

"I do." She forced a smile despite the discomfort her deception caused. "She seems really nice." Although Cora had been home for a week, getting ready for her big move, she hadn't been able to quit thinking about Aiyana. She'd spent nearly every extra minute on the internet, doing searches on all of the teachers and many of the students who'd graduated from New Horizons—whatever names she could cull from their website, including a graduate who had turned into a professional football player, one who'd just recently been accused of killing the couple who adopted him when he came to the ranch at fifteen and Elijah Turner, who'd hired her. Only one article had come up on him, but it told a lot. When he was ten years old, he'd been kept in a cage like some animal in the basement of his parents' house, and starved until he was only sixty pounds.

Imagining what he'd been through turned Cora's stomach. What kind of people could do that to one of their own children? And where were those people now? Did he know?

Considering what he'd been through, it was no wonder the man was so guarded, so aloof—and so devoted to Aiyana and New Horizons.

"I can't believe you'll be staying right there on the property," Lilly said.

"The school is about ten miles outside of town, so it'll save me from the daily drive."

"What drive? Ten miles is nothing," Lilly scoffed. "The people in Silver Springs must have no idea how long it takes to go two blocks in LA when the traffic is bad."

"Or they *do* know, and that's why they live there." Cora held up her blender. She made a lot of smoothies and "green" drinks, but her machine was nearly worn-out. Was it worth taking with her—or was it time to get a new one?

Newspaper crinkled as Lilly continued to wrap. "Traffic or no, I could never leave the city."

Brad's office was only a few blocks from their house. He'd been so successful managing other people's money that he could set his own hours. And Lilly did charity work, mostly on nights and weekends. "You two are in the kind of situation that makes it easy to stay. Traffic isn't a huge part of the equation for you."

"Our lives haven't always been so perfect," she said.

Reluctantly, Cora put her blender in the pile for Goodwill. "No. You've worked hard for what you have," she agreed and meant it.

Her mother stopped packing long enough to squeeze her shoulder. "You'll build something, too, honey."

"I hope so." Right now it felt as if Ashton, her brother, was going to be the one to make them proud. Although Lilly and Brad hadn't been too pleased when he left law school to become a movie producer, he already had an indie film out that'd garnered several awards, so they were less critical of his decision than they once were. "From this vantage point, it looks like I have a long way to go."

"It all comes with time."

Cora checked the clock on the wall. Jill, an assistant to a film editor at Universal, would be getting off work any minute. Cora had been hoping to be done by then, so they could meet some other friends for drinks, but there was a lot yet to pack. "Is Ashton going to be able to make it to my goodbye dinner on Sunday?"

"I'm sure he will. Your brother adores you."

"Slightly less than he adores all of the women he's dating," she grumbled.

"That's not true!"

It wasn't *entirely* true, but Cora had been feeling a little neglected by her brother since he'd turned into such a big shot and become so busy.

The packing tape screeched as her mother closed and sealed the box she'd filled. "Does Aiyana Turner offer discounted housing to *all* the teachers at the ranch?"

The scent of the marker Lilly used to label the box "Kitchen—Fragile" rose to Cora's nostrils. "She can't. There's not enough for everyone—just a handful of small cottages on the far side of the property, away from the school and the boys' dorms."

"So who looks after the boys at night?"

"Each floor has a live-in monitor they call a 'big brother' who makes sure the boys go to bed at lights-out, get up for school, study during study time and clean their rooms."

"Are they teachers, too?"

"No. Most work in town during the day. I was told that some even drive to Santa Barbara. It's merely a way to acquire free lodging, kind of like managing an apartment building."

"How does—what's her name, Aiyana Turner?—decide who gets the other housing?"

"Every teacher has the option to add their name to the

waiting list and move in if one becomes available. I just happened to hire on at the right time. The teacher who quit left earlier than planned, and my unit wasn't spoken for—probably because it's so small. It wouldn't be big enough for anyone with kids."

"So where do the other teachers live? In town?"

"I'm assuming they do. Although I suppose some might live in Santa Barbara. It's only about twenty minutes away, not a long commute by our standards."

The packing tape screamed again as her mother built a new box. "But will there be enough of a social life for you in Silver Springs? I mean…if you're living on campus, will you ever get out? How will you meet people?"

"I'll meet the other teachers."

"Who will most likely be older or married."

"I really won't know until I get there."

Lilly straightened and rested her hands on her hips. "There's more to life than work, honey. A year might not sound long right now, but, trust me, it'll seem long if you have no one to do anything with that whole time."

"I can always drive home, visit you guys, Jill, my other friends."

"I hope you come home often. But…what about the man who hired you? Maybe you can get something going with him. Jill told me you said he was hot."

Thank you, Jill. "He *is* hot, but…"

"What does he look like?"

Cora pictured the dark-headed, rather intimidating man who'd shown her around the ranch. He didn't say too much, certainly didn't waste words. But those blue eyes were laser-sharp. They didn't miss a thing. Truth be told, he made her uncomfortable. "Sort of like…a pirate."

Her mother opened another cupboard and started packing the plates. "A pirate? That's a positive association?"

"In this case it is." Mostly… When it came to his physical appearance, anyway.

"How tall is he?"

Cora put her salsa maker, which she'd barely used, in one of the boxes she planned to take with her. If she was going to live in the country, she was going to attend a farmer's market occasionally and make homemade salsa. "*Really* tall. And built."

"He sounds perfect."

"Not perfect exactly." That was what she found most compelling about him—that he was a little rough around the edges. "He's got a fairly big scar on his face." She indicated the line of her jaw. "Right here."

"What's that from?"

"I didn't ask." And now that she'd read the article chronicling some of the abuse he'd suffered, she wouldn't. "As far as I know, he's already married."

"Did you see a ring?"

"I didn't look," she said, but that was a lie. She had looked—and seen no ring. She'd been curious about Elijah from the first moment they met. But she'd also been apprehensive about the fact that she'd had an ulterior motive for applying at New Horizons, had known he probably wouldn't appreciate that she wasn't being fully transparent.

Her mother grinned at her. "You should have."

"Matt and I barely broke up, Mom. I'm not ready to start dating again, especially in a place where I don't plan to stay." Besides, she wasn't sure she'd be capable of taking on a man as complex as Elijah. There was no telling what kind of scars his upbringing had created, and she wasn't referring to the one on his face, although that could easily be part of the legacy his parents had left him.

"So you're only staying there a year?" her mother said.

"That's right."

"I can't tell you how happy I am to hear it's temporary." Lilly bent to give her a hug. "I love you, you know."

Cora *did* know. And she was grateful. She could easily have gone to a family who weren't so kind and accepting—a family like Elijah had known. "I love you, too," she said and tried to ignore how selfish she felt for doing what she was doing in spite of the fact it would hurt Lilly if—or when—she found out.

Elijah Turner was brushing down his horse when Aiyana found him. At the sound of her footsteps, he didn't need to turn in order to see who it was. If he didn't come for dinner when she invited him, she tracked him down. She always acted as if she had some official reason, some business question to ask him, but he knew she was simply assuring herself that he was okay. Whenever he complained that he was too old for that kind of coddling, she'd say it didn't matter, that he'd always be her boy.

"How was your ride?" she asked.

He lifted Atsila's foot and used a pick to gently clean his horse's front left hoof. "Relaxing."

"Cora Kelly arrives tomorrow."

"I know."

"Is the cottage ready?"

He moved on to the other front hoof. "Of course."

"Are you ever going to explain that decision to me?"

"What decision?" he said, but he knew what she was going to say before she explained.

"To hire Cora Kelly. You knew, as well as I did, that Gary Seton, from right here in Silver Springs, was waiting for that job to open up."

"I interviewed Gary, too—gave him a chance."

"And…"

"I thought Ms. Kelly was better suited for the position."

"She's pretty."

"That had nothing to do with it."

"Let's say that's true—you're not worried that she might be a distraction to the boys?"

"You're saying I should've discriminated against her because she's attractive?"

She gave his shoulder a little shove. "Stop it."

"You were talking about her looks!"

"Because I wanted to see if you agreed with me."

"That she's pretty? I'd have to be blind not to see that."

"So…do I surmise a bit of interest on your part?"

"None. I'm not the marrying type. You should know that by now."

"I'd like grandkids at some point."

"You have plenty of other sons to give you grandkids."

She sighed as if he was being purposely stubborn. "Fine. Obviously, you don't like talking about this subject."

He didn't argue. There were moments he wondered if he truly wanted to be alone for the rest of his life. But he also saw nothing to be gained from allowing his happiness to hang on the love or will of another person.

"You missed dinner tonight," his mother said.

"You said to come by if I was hungry."

"You should've been hungry. It's nearly eight."

"We've talked about this before," he responded. "I'm too old for you to worry about."

"You'll *never* be too old for me to worry about. And you know why? It's called caring."

His problem was that he had the tendency to care too much, to be *too* intense. "I'm fine." He started on Atsila's fourth and final hoof. "I'll grab a bite while I'm in town tonight."

She leaned against the fence post. "Whoa, don't tell me you're leaving the ranch for a social outing. You don't do that very often."

He gave her a look that let her know he didn't appreciate the sarcasm.

Unperturbed, she smiled. "Your dark looks don't frighten me the way they do everyone else."

"They should."

"Why? I know you love me, even if you rarely say it."

"What good are words?" His parents used to claim they loved him, but they only loved themselves and the twisted joy they received from tormenting him. "Words are empty, meaningless."

"Hopefully, someday, you'll regain your trust."

He winked at her. "Don't hold your breath. But… I am very grateful for everything you've done for me. I hope you know that."

"Stop!" She started to walk away.

"What?" he called after her.

"That wasn't a leading statement. I'm not looking for your gratitude."

She wasn't comfortable with it, either. "You want me to fall in love."

"I want you to be *able* to fall in love. I want to see you lose your heart—and not be afraid to let it go. Then I can rest easy, knowing you're completely fulfilled."

"*You* never married," he pointed out, but she offered the usual lame excuse.

"Because I'm married to this place."

Knowing that was all he'd ever get out of her on the subject, he studied her retreating figure. "Yeah, well, so am I."

Chapter Three

Cora was using her Bluetooth to talk to Jill when she passed through the wrought iron arch at the opening of the school, her car packed full of her belongings. "I'm here," she announced as she wound slowly around to where she'd be living.

"That didn't take long. What time did you leave again?"

She'd gone in to hug her friend goodbye, but Jill, dead asleep, had mumbled something about missing Cora, promised to call and dropped back onto the pillows. "Six."

"That's not even two hours ago."

"See? I'm not that far away." Although…it almost seemed as if she'd moved to another planet; Silver Springs was nothing like LA.

"I should've come with you," Jill said.

"How?" Cora asked. "You have to be to work in an hour."

"I could've called in sick. You need someone to be there to help you unpack."

"No, I don't. My mother would've been hurt if she found out I let you come, since I told her I preferred to organize everything on my own." Cora had definitely not wanted Lilly on the ranch. She knew Lilly had never met Aiyana, that the whole adoption had been handled through an agency. According to the documents her private investigator had uncovered, Aiyana had demanded absolute secrecy. But that didn't change Cora's need to keep the two women apart. "I can handle this. The cottage is furnished. And everything I'm bringing fits into my car. It's not as if I'm towing a trailer."

"Still, I'm curious."

"About..."

"The ranch, for one thing. What does it look like?"

"Your basic high school, but with horses and cattle—and some dorms and a machine shop. You'll see it when you come visit me."

"I've been to Ojai but never Silver Springs. How does it compare?"

"The towns are similar, which makes sense. Silver Springs is located in the same valley, has some of the same mission-style architecture. Only they've added a few murals in Silver Springs, like they've done in Exeter."

"Where's Exeter?"

"Central part of the state." Cora pulled into the drive that would be *her* drive for the next year and cut the engine. "My mom took me there once to show me the murals, thought I'd be interested because of my art degree."

"I'm not that big on murals," Jill said. "I've seen some pretty bad ones."

"I've seen a lot that are worse than the ones they have here. The man who painted the one downtown interviewed for my job. I'm still surprised they didn't hire him instead."

"They told you who you were up against?"

"Aiyana and Elijah didn't. When Aiyana showed me the house, she got a call on her cell, leaving me to speak with a neighbor. He said Gary Seton was a friend of his and was really disappointed."

"Why *didn't* they hire him?" Jill asked.

Cora gazed at her bungalow, trying to imagine calling this place home for the next twelve months. "I'm not sure. I would've guessed they'd prefer a local."

"Could it be that Elijah wanted *you* to come to town?"

"No. I didn't get those vibes at all."

"So you think he's married?"

"Not married." There was too much sexual energy surounding him for him to be in a committed relationship. She could tell he found her attractive—couldn't help finding him attractive, too. A woman would have to be dead not to feel a *little* sizzle when a man like Elijah Turner came around. "Just completely closed off."

"I've seen you approach guys before. You've never been afraid of a challenge."

In this situation, she was. She had a lot to cope with already, didn't need to add a romantic relationship into the mix. Even if she could manage to gain Elijah's attention, she doubted she'd be able to keep it for long. He was too remote. "I'm only here for a year."

"That could prove to be a very *long* year if you plan to remain celibate the whole time," she joked.

"I'll survive." Although…she was already missing certain aspects of her relationship with Matt and, if she was being honest, sex was one of them. "It'd be kind of odd to hit up the man my mother adopted."

"Why? You're not related by blood. You didn't even grow up together. For all intents and purposes, you're part of a different family. You're a Kelly."

Cora dug through her purse, searching for the house key Aiyana had provided her. "On paper."

"More than on paper! You've spent your whole life with the Kellys."

"I was talking from a strictly literal perspective. But that reaction right there is part of my problem."

"What do you mean?"

"Am I being ungrateful simply by wanting to know my birth mother? That tears me up inside, because I *am* grateful. I love my parents dearly."

"It's the same with regular parents. All kids should be grateful and aware of their parents' sacrifice."

"No, it's not the same. There's a sense of entitlement with children who've been kept and raised by their biological parents that doesn't extend to me. Anyway, let's not get caught up in all of that. Bottom line, people would look askance at Elijah and me if we ever admitted to having the same mother."

"You wouldn't admit that, because you don't have the same mother."

Cora groaned to show her frustration. "It's murky. You have to give me that. Regardless, Elijah makes me jealous." So did the other boys Aiyana had accepted into her life. That Aiyana would give Cora away and then take in eight other children left Cora feeling hurt, baffled. "He holds such a prominent place in Aiyana's heart that it makes me wonder why she wanted him and not me."

"We've talked about this."

She climbed out of the vehicle and circled around to grab the suitcase that held her essentials. "You believe she feels the need to fix things—fix people."

"You told me he had a rough childhood. The other boys probably did, too."

Other than her ex-boyfriend, Jill was the only person she'd confided in about her search for her biological mother, her true purpose in coming to Silver Springs, and the background of the man who'd hired her. "No doubt Elijah's defies imagination. Which only makes me feel worse. When I think of what he's been through, I can't even be jealous without an avalanche of guilt. Considering the emotions he dredges up, I doubt he and I should even be friends."

Jill ignored her uncomfortable laugh. "There were a number of years between the time Aiyana gave you up and adopted him. Her situation must've changed, that's all."

Since both hands were full, Cora used her hip to close the car door. "Maybe that's it."

"You can't always assume the worst."

"It's hard not to. Especially now that I see how func

tional she is. I mean…if she were a down-on-her-luck prostitute, I could point to that and say, *Makes sense*."

"The fact that she isn't a down-on-her-luck prostitute is why you're interested in getting to know her. There's promise there. You believe she might be someone you'd like to have in your life. That's what scares you. You're afraid she'll reject you a second time."

Cora had to set her suitcase down to let herself into the house. "Do you have to be so frank?"

"It's important to know when fear's doing the talking—to keep things straight in your head."

"It could be a while before *anything*'s straight in my head—another reason I'd be crazy to get involved with Elijah, even if he were open to a relationship, which I can tell he's not."

"Fine. You won't listen to me, anyway. You're too busy throwing up roadblocks."

Cora wasn't sure she felt any better now that Jill had conceded. She sort of liked it when Jill was arguing the other side. Maybe that was because she *did* find it hard not to think about Elijah. Even though she'd been almost completely focused on the fact that she'd just found her birth mother when she had that interview with him, she couldn't help wondering what was going on behind those inscrutable eyes… "You were never given up for adoption. You grew up in a big, boisterous, happy family. You can't relate."

"I've tried to be understanding," Jill said.

"I'm sorry," Cora responded. "I don't know where that came from. It was uncalled for."

"You're angry. That's where it comes from. And I can see why. But I'm on *your* side."

Cora opened her mouth to say she believed that, but before she could formulate the words, she heard a car engine and turned. What she saw wasn't a car; it was a silver truck. And Elijah was behind the wheel. As he parked in front of her house and jumped out, she felt her pulse leap. "I've got to go," she told Jill.

"Why? What's up?"

She ducked her head so she could speak without being overheard. *"He's here,"* she whispered and clicked the button on her Bluetooth that would disconnect them.

Cora was wearing a silky orange tank with a pair of white linen shorts that showed off her long, tan legs. As Elijah approached with the orientation materials he'd brought, he found those legs to be distracting. But she was a teacher at New Horizons. That meant he couldn't get involved with her, even on a casual basis. Contrary to what his mother seemed to believe—and probably everyone else who was surprised he hadn't hired Gary—he hadn't offered her the position because he had any romantic interest in her. He'd been impressed with her portfolio. Each piece—a sculpture, a painting, a photograph and a piece of pottery—moved him in some way. He liked that she could make *him*, someone who knew very little about art, feel something. Gary Seton's work simply hadn't been the same.

One piece that Cora had brought, the conceptual sculpture of a mother cradling a child, affected him deeply. When she'd unveiled it during their interview, it'd been hard for him not to stop and stare. He'd wanted to keep it—not because he felt *he* needed that kind of love. No one would ever be able to hurt him again. He wanted the boys here at the ranch to experience the safety and security that piece inspired, and he wanted to give them a teacher who could not only depict that emotion but understand it, *feel* it.

Because he knew Gary was disappointed, he hoped he'd made the right choice. Fortunately, the sensitivity he saw in the large brown eyes staring up at him as he drew closer reassured him. She'd wanted the job even worse than

Gary. He wasn't sure why—if she'd needed to get out of whatever situation she was in or was on her last dollar—but he'd been able to feel her eagerness during their interview and he'd responded to that. Maybe this woman would never be able to teach the boys how to create a decent picture or vase, but she should be able to entice them to see the beauty of the world. She *was* part of the beauty of the world. And she seemed open and vulnerable to the point that he almost felt he should warn her to be careful or life would chew her up and spit her out. After what *he'd* experienced, that she could get so far without learning that lesson was a bit of a shock to him.

"Hello," she said.

"I see you made it safely."

"Yes."

He motioned toward the older BMW X3 sitting in the drive. "Can I give you a hand with anything?"

"No, it's okay. I was careful when I packed—didn't make the boxes too heavy. I can grab it."

"Are you sure?"

She nodded, so he handed her the orientation manual he'd brought over. "I doubt you'll care to read *all* of this. Watching paint dry would be more interesting. But there's a table of contents. I figured you could glance through, check out any topics you're curious about and become familiar with how we do things around here."

"I'll take a look at it." When she hugged it to her ample chest, he decided her body was partly what he found so attractive about her. She wasn't as skinny as some of the girls he'd dated. She was curvy—looked soft, comfortable, sexy.

He searched his pocket for the more important part of what he'd come to give her. "Here's a key to the high school, as well as one to the art and ceramics rooms. With school starting next week, you'll be eager to set those up."

"Definitely. Thank you."

"You bet. You received the group email about the staff meeting tonight?"

"I did. That's why I came a few days earlier than I would have otherwise."

"Great. I'll see you there." He started back toward his truck. "Everyone is eager to meet you."

"Mr. Turner?"

"Call me Eli," he said as he turned.

"Okay, Eli it is. Where, exactly, is the meeting tonight? You showed me the library when we toured campus the day I interviewed, but I'm a little turned around at the moment."

He went back and flipped past the syllabus he'd given her to the campus map on the next page. "You're here," he said, and drew a line from her house to the library so she could easily find her way.

"Thank you."

"Sure," he said. But instead of leaving, he went over to her SUV and began unloading the boxes. He just couldn't leave a woman to do that alone, not when it would be so much easier for him.

"Whoa, I can get those," she said, hurrying out to him. "Really."

"There's no need for you to carry all of this stuff by yourself. Just point to where it should go. It'll only take me fifteen minutes."

As promised, in a short time, he had her vehicle completely unloaded.

"Thank you," she said as he put down the last box.

"See you later." His conscience appeased, he started toward his truck.

"Eli?"

He stopped again. "Yes?"

"I—I have a boyfriend. Sort of."

He felt his eyebrows slide up. Then he almost laughed. She was assuming he had an ulterior motive for helping her. "I'm sorry if I gave you the wrong impression," he said. "I was only trying to make your move a little easier."

Her cheeks bloomed red. "Right. Of course you were. I'm sorry."

Cora's face burned as she watched Eli drive off. "What's wrong with you?" she muttered to herself. "Of course he was just trying to help. It's not as if he asked for your number."

That blunder actually said more about her than it did him, she realized. *He* hadn't been anything but circumspect. *She* was the one who'd had a difficult time keeping her eyes off him. She was so aware of him on a sexual level that it was hard to act as if she wasn't, which was odd. She couldn't remember having such a strong reaction to any other man. That was the reason she'd suddenly tried to throw up a barrier. She'd been hoping to give him a reason to look at her differently—or stay away entirely—and wound up making a fool of herself instead.

"I *told* you I didn't need your help," she grumbled to him even though he was gone, and cringed at the prospect of having to face him at the staff meeting in a few hours.

"You had to do that on your first day here, Cora?" she said as she started to unpack.

Her phone dinged to let her know she'd received a text, and she paused to pull it out of her pocket.

Jill. What'd "dark and brooding" have to say?

Dark and brooding. How apropos. But since she was still writhing with embarrassment, Cora didn't want to talk about Eli, so she scowled at the clock. Aren't you at work?

You know I am. I was talking to you while driving here.

I don't want to get you in trouble for being on the phone. I'll call you later.

Is that a dodge?

Yes. But as long as her friend was willing to risk getting caught on a personal call at work, Cora figured she might as well break the news. He said he's not interested in me.

What? Seriously?

Seriously.

But...you just got there.

Cora shoved a hand through her hair as she recalled his startled expression. Yeah, it came up quick. Thanks to her...

How? He couldn't have come by just to let you know he's not interested.

Again Cora hesitated, but when she didn't respond her friend sent her a question mark, so she typed, I brought it up.

At that point, texting fell by the wayside. Jill called to make her explain the whole thing.

"Oh jeez," she said when Cora was done. "I should never have let you go there without me. I could tell you were rattled, nervous."

"I'll get my feet underneath me. I'm just...not myself at the moment. The prospect of rubbing elbows with my birth mother has me...floundering a bit. I was expecting *that* to be difficult, but when I started this whole thing, I was *not* expecting my mother to have adopted a son who..."

"Who..." Jill pressed.

She pictured the muscles that bulged in Eli's arms as he hefted box after box into her cottage. She really wanted to touch the smooth curve of his biceps. But it was the size of his broad chest and wide shoulders that *really* made her short of breath. "Who somehow gets under my skin!"

"To whom you feel an immediate attraction, you mean."

"He's good-looking. That's all," she said, hoping to minimize it.

"That's why you told him, out of the blue, that you have a boyfriend as if you were accusing him of hitting on you? Because he's good-looking? What were you thinking?"

"I don't know! I was merely attempting to wall off the possibility. So I wouldn't even consider it. That's not *too* weird, is it?"

"You might've gotten ahead of yourself, but… I'm guessing you succeeded. I doubt he's hoping for anything now, so you can relax."

Cora took a deep breath. Jill was right. Maybe she hadn't done it gracefully, but she'd put Elijah Turner on notice that she wasn't a romantic possibility. Even if he hadn't considered her one to begin with, establishing certain boundaries was important to *her*. She needed to focus, to keep her life simple while she was here so that she could do a good job for the kids at the ranch while getting to know Aiyana. If she decided she wanted to be part of Aiyana's life, she'd eventually have to determine if Aiyana wanted to be part of hers—and break the news. Imagine how awkward it would be if the answer to that question was no and yet she was seeing Eli!

"It's better that we covered it early."

"If you say so. How's the cottage?"

"Small but cute." She wandered over to a Mason jar filled with wildflowers that someone had left on her table. It was a thoughtful touch, one she hoped Eli wasn't responsible for…

"I can't wait to see it." Jill suddenly lowered her voice. "I've got to go. My boss is here."

Cora wasn't even sure she said goodbye when they disconnected. Her attention had switched entirely to a small card she found beside the flowers.

Welcome to New Horizons. We are so excited to have you here.

Aiyana

Bending slightly, Cora put her nose to one of the delicate yellow poppies that made up the bulk of the arrangement. "I hope you'll be just as glad once you learn who I am," she said as she exhaled.

Chapter Four

"So *you're* the new art teacher."

Cora smiled at the middle-aged man with thick glasses who sat on her right side. "Yes."

"Ah. Makes sense at last."

"What makes sense?" she asked, but he didn't get the chance to answer—or even introduce himself. Aiyana stood near the circulation desk and called the staff to order. Cora felt she knew where the man had been going with that comment, anyway. Everyone thought she'd gotten the job based on her looks. Otherwise, Gary Something-or-Other would've gotten it.

"Thank you all for coming," Aiyana said. "Although we had a few of you here during the summer, handling one program or another, classes were limited. So I hope, now that the rest of you are back, you feel refreshed, because I'm anticipating one of the best years in ranch history."

As Aiyana spoke, Cora glanced around. There were thirtysomething people in the room, an assortment of teachers and support staff, but she couldn't see anyone even close to her own age. Half the people seemed to be in their forties, the other half in their fifties. A few looked even older.

She was beginning to believe Jill and her mother were right: the next year was going to be terribly lonely...

"Before we get started, let's go over a few of the changes that have occurred in the past two and a half months. First, we will have 256 students when we start classes on the twenty-eighth, up from 223 last year. That's a significant increase, so we'll have to watch out for the newcomers and help them feel at home. We also have a new football coach—Larry Sanders, who played in the pros thirteen years ago. Larry couldn't be here tonight due to a family commitment, but he's been practicing with the boys for over a month. I believe he'll be a real asset to our sports program—at least that's what Elijah tells me. As most of you know, Elijah is our athletic director in addition to many other things—basically whatever he needs to be in order for the ranch to operate smoothly."

Cora's neighbor leaned over. "Someone with real experience, huh? Maybe we'll finally win a game," he muttered.

Cora didn't respond; she was too interested in witnessing the pride on Aiyana's face when she looked at her adopted son. They were close. That was obvious without either one of them having to say a word—but as nice as that was for Elijah, Cora found it a bit disheartening. Was there any room in Aiyana's heart for her?

Cora didn't get the impression there was, but she didn't have the chance to think about it for too long. Aiyana was moving on.

"Not only do we have a new football coach, we have a new art instructor." She stretched out her hand in invitation. "Cora, will you please stand?"

Elijah's eyes seemed to cut right through Cora as she got to her feet. Why she could feel the weight of his gaze and not anyone else's, she couldn't say, but she'd been struggling to ignore him since she walked into this meeting.

After a nod to acknowledge all the smiling faces that were turned to see the new art instructor, she sank back into her seat.

Aiyana was talking about how they were going to allow student government to run the assemblies from now on when the man next to her leaned over again. "Where have you taught before?" he asked.

After his earlier comment, Cora almost provided the name of the high school that had offered her a permanent position a few weeks ago, but a quick word with Aiyana or Elijah would too easily reveal the truth, since she'd been honest with them. "I've never had a permanent position."

"You're a *brand-new* teacher?"

"Relatively new," she admitted. "I've been subbing for six years."

"Do you have any idea how difficult some of the boys who come here can be?"

Aiyana hadn't given the bad behavior Cora was likely to encounter much emphasis. But Cora had known from the beginning that this school wasn't for the well-adjusted. "I understand that most of the boys come from a very difficult background," she replied. "But it shouldn't be *too* much of a change. You should see how some regular students treat substitutes," she joked.

The man laughed but quickly sobered. "Subbing isn't easy. Kids will get away with whatever they can. Still, for an attractive young woman of your age—"

"I'm nearly thirty," she broke in, but she had to wonder—in her hurry to get close to Aiyana, had she given what she might face here enough weight?

"Still," the man said. "It won't be easy. I hope you haven't gotten in over your head."

When Cora glanced up, she happened to catch Elijah watching her. He didn't look away, as she expected him to; he continued to measure her with those enigmatic eyes. Was he experiencing any doubts about having hired her?

Possibly. *Probably.* She hated to even consider that. But if she had to fight to find her place in the world, she'd do it. She supposed, in that respect, she wasn't much different from Elijah or the other boys who'd come through here, or were still attending.

"I'll be fine," she said—and hoped it was true.

* * *

"I see you met Sean Travers."

Cora recognized Elijah's voice even before she turned to see him standing at her elbow. Why he'd put her through the discomfort approaching her was bound to cause, however, she couldn't say.

"The guy who was sitting next to me?" she asked.

"Yes. Our science teacher—or ranch pessimist, depending on how well you know him."

She nibbled at the cookie she'd just snagged from the refreshment table. "He doesn't think I'm capable of teaching here. I guess I look too young and delicate to handle the boys who act out."

"Does that shake your confidence?"

"I admit I'm a little worried. Everyone seems to believe the job should've gone to a man named Gary..."

"Seton," he filled in as he handed her a cup of punch. "Because he's local—they know him."

"But..."

"It wasn't their decision," he said simply.

She couldn't help envying him his long, dark eyelashes. She knew she had pretty eyes—guys told her that all the time—but she felt his were prettier. "No. It was yours. So...can you tell me why?"

"Why I chose you?"

"I know it isn't what they all seem to think. You made that clear earlier."

He took a sip of his own punch. "As far as I'm concerned, your competition has no...vision."

"Am I supposed to understand what that means?"

His massive shoulders lifted in a shrug. "I wasn't impressed with his work."

"You were impressed with *mine*?"

"You're talented," he said evenly. "Perhaps more than you know."

"I'm *teaching* art, not selling it. I'm guessing he was at least proficient."

Elijah finally shifted that unnerving gaze away from her. "You have to understand certain concepts to be able to teach them."

"What concepts are you specifically referring to?" she asked, but someone else approached him at that moment, interrupting, and he turned away without answering.

Since Eli fell deep into conversation with a woman who looked sixty or so and was concerned about a particular student Cora had no way of knowing, she felt awkward standing there waiting for the chance to speak to him again. So she gave them some privacy by carrying her punch over to the corner. She was looking for an unobtrusive vantage point from which to observe her birth mother. Aiyana was mingling with the staff. But then Cora saw the science teacher who'd sat next to her approach Aiyana and knew, when they both glanced in her direction, that they were talking about her. Sean Travers was expressing his reservations.

Disgruntled that this man she'd barely met would jump to conclusions based on her age and gender, and start to advocate against her, Cora finished her punch, dropped the paper cup in the wastebasket and left the library. Her phone kept vibrating in her pocket anyway, making her feel as if someone really needed to reach her.

When she got outside and felt she could check, caller ID indicated it was her father.

Gazing up at more stars than she'd ever seen in the sky before, she wandered around the campus as she spoke to him. Most of the students were away, at home if they had a home to go to, for a quick holiday before classes started in earnest, so the campus was quiet, especially this far from the outdoor basketball courts and the dorms.

"So are you going to like it there?" her father asked.

She tried to let the energy in his voice help lift the depression that had set in. "It's definitely going to be a change."

"A positive one, though, right?"

"Sure," she said, kicking a small pebble across the sidewalk.

"Whoa. Is something wrong?"

"It's just different, that's all. I'm not used to smelling manure at night. Or seeing stars that shine so bright."

"The manure can't be pleasant, but the stars sound nice."

"They are nice. And the manure isn't all that bad, not if I stay away from the livestock pens. I guess it's more that… I'm beginning to wonder what made me think I could handle teenage boys who have significant behavioral issues." She'd mostly been thinking of her own emotional issues, not the responsibility she would feel to be a guiding light to teenage boys who'd lost their way. Was she bound to disappoint Aiyana and Elijah and let her students down?

She couldn't abide the thought of failure.

"Don't make it too complicated, babe," her father said.

"In what way?"

"Everyone responds to love."

"I have to do more than love them, Dad. I have to *teach* them. And what if they won't let me?"

"If you love them, they'll trust you. Love and trust come first. Then you'll be able to teach. I promise you."

She thought of Gary Seton. Maybe he had no "vision," whatever Elijah meant by that. But she was willing to bet he'd be firmer when it came to meting out discipline. *She* didn't want to punish anyone. "I'm not sure why these people hired me," she grumbled.

"They must've seen what your mother and I see in you."

"And that is…"

"You can do anything."

Tears filled her eyes. She was tired, which made her

emotional. But she was also experiencing a little culture shock, and she missed her family already. "Maybe I was a bit hasty making the decision to come here, Dad."

"It's only for a year, honey. Do your best. That's all anyone can ask. And come see us when you can."

She wiped her cheeks as she told him she loved him. But she felt even worse after she disconnected. She had good parents. The conversation she'd just had with her father proved it yet again. So why was she betraying them?

The moment she got back to her cottage, Cora went straight to bed. She had a lot of unpacking yet to do, but she figured that could wait. She needed sleep, knew it would help her cope with all the recent changes—as well as the uncertainty.

Fortunately, she felt a lot better when she woke up. She spent the morning unpacking the rest of her belongings and stacking the cardboard from the boxes in her SUV so she could take it to a recycling center. Then she decided to go into town to look around, have lunch and buy a few groceries. Someone—she guessed Aiyana since Aiyana had also been responsible for the flowers—had put a few essentials, like eggs, bread and milk, in her fridge, but the cupboards needed to be stocked.

Cora was halfway to town when she saw a man on horseback galloping down a dirt road off to her right. She would've thought nothing of it—she could only see the rider from the back as he wove in and out of the trees between them—but she recognized the man. It was Elijah Turner!

She pulled over and angled her head to see through the passenger window, trying to get a better look. He was something else. A puzzle. What drove him? What did he want out of life? Had he put the past behind him? How did he feel about the boys who came to the ranch? Did he see himself in each one? Where were the people who'd abused him? Did he have any contact with them? Was his work enough to fulfill him? Or was he seeing someone?

Maybe he was dating around…

Cora was also curious to learn how he'd gotten that scar on his face—but equally afraid to find out. What she'd read about him scared her. She didn't want to imagine him going through any more pain and suffering than what she'd been forced to imagine when she'd read that article about him. She wondered if other people had the same reaction—if they shied away from him for fear they might have to walk into that darkness.

Movement behind him caught her eye, and she realized that he wasn't alone. He had three boys with him. It looked as though he was taking some New Horizons students out for a ride…

She glanced into her backseat. She had her camera, had brought it to take some pictures of Silver Springs she could send to Jill and her family. She still planned to do that, but her fingers itched to take a few shots of him and those boys first. She'd never seen a man sit so comfortably in the saddle as Elijah. And she loved the way he kept looking back at the boys, like a mother hen checking her chicks.

This wasn't about admiring Aiyana's adopted son so much as it was about the symbolism she saw here, she told herself as she cut the engine. He represented a man who'd not only survived tremendous difficulty but risen above it. Someone who'd conquered his demons. And now he was helping others battle theirs. There was a great deal of artistic beauty in that, and she had to capture it.

She couldn't get a clear shot from the roadside, however. There were too many trees in between.

After hiking down the embankment, she wove through the forest to get close enough. Luckily for her, or she never would've caught up with them, Elijah and the boys had stopped and were laughing and talking while drinking from a canteen Eli passed around.

She fastened her heavy telephoto lens to the expensive camera her parents had given her for Christmas last year and clicked away, using a fast shutter speed so that the pictures wouldn't turn out blurry. In one picture, she captured Elijah laughing. She'd never seen him smile, not so easily. He was in his element out here, and he cared about the boys he was with. Those two things were readily apparent; she could see it in both his body language and his expression.

Cora was disappointed when he put the lid on the canteen, slung it over his body, where he'd been carrying it before, and charged up the next hill, making it impossible for her to get any more pictures of him.

As the boys whooped and hollered in their efforts to keep up with him, she hiked back to her car. They were having a blast. She could easily imagine any problem they had disappearing while they were out enjoying the beautiful scenery and the equally beautiful weather.

Witnessing the impact Elijah was having on the students at the ranch—by taking enough interest to guide them on a ride even during their "off" period—inspired her. He was embracing the spirit of his job. Like Aiyana, he was doing it for the right reasons. And so could she. She had a lot of love to give. Who needed it more than abused, neglected and angry teens?

How are you doing today?

Her father's text came in just before Cora started her car. Better, she wrote.

Because...

Because coming here was no longer only about her. I feel like I could make a real difference with this job.

That's the spirit!

Cora responded by sending a smiley face, put her phone down and headed into town, where she took quite a few pictures. It was a great way to investigate her new surroundings. Those were the ones she posted on Instagram and sent to family and friends who were eager to see where she'd moved. But it was the photographs of Elijah and the three boys that she downloaded onto her computer when she returned that night. She spent over an hour experimenting with different filters and other bells and whistles on Photoshop. In her favorite photograph, one where Elijah was smiling at the boy to his left, the lighting was perfect as it came through the branches of the trees.

She could win a contest with that shot…

"Hail to the conquering hero," she muttered before she set her computer aside and turned off the light so that she could get some sleep.

Chapter Five

Over the next few days, Cora put her classroom in order by making sure the large, commercial-sized kiln and sixteen throwing wheels in the pottery room were clean and in good repair. She also took stock of the clay and other supplies. The teacher before her had done a respectable job caring for the equipment and maintaining the necessary inventory, so it wasn't too overwhelming of a job. She obtained permission to order some glazes she'd been hoping to get, as well as a new set of colored pencils and paintbrushes for each student, so she'd at least have the supplies needed to start the year off right.

By the end of the week, Cora was feeling pretty encouraged about beginning school on Monday. She'd been running into more and more students as the boys returned to the ranch and was looking forward to meeting the rest. Other than texting and calling her old friends and her brother, who promised to come out and see her soon, she'd had virtually no social life since she arrived, so she figured more distraction, work and activity would help fill that gap. The neighbor opposite to Sean Travers, Doug Maggleby, a math teacher at the school, chatted with her whenever he caught her out and about. But she'd started to avoid him, where possible. The more he talked, the more uncomfortable he made her. He liked to rave about politics, and she rarely agreed with his opinion. He'd also mentioned taking her to the movies even though he was clearly too old for her. She wasn't looking forward to having to say no, but knew that was coming. So instead of visiting with him in the evenings like she had the first few nights, she'd sneak out of her bungalow and walk down to the pond to watch the sunset or stop by the horses' pen to say good-night. If Mr. Maggleby happened to be in his yard working in his fall garden, however, she'd settle for having a glass of wine in her cottage and reading a book or going over her lesson plans.

She'd seen very little of Elijah since taking those photographs of him horseback riding with the boys. Although she wasn't pleased by the fact, she'd developed a habit of looking for him whenever she was out. Occasionally, she'd spot him at a distance and couldn't help admiring what she saw. But he seemed extra busy getting the ranch ready for the fall semester, so she was fairly certain she was the last thing on *his* mind.

Aiyana had been especially busy, too. Since Betty May had handled the purchase requisition for the art supplies, Cora had had no interaction with her birth mother—not until Friday afternoon. She was in the cafeteria between lunch and dinner, nibbling on a chocolate chip cookie while she finished reading the orientation materials she'd been given, when Aiyana came in, poured herself a cup of coffee and walked over to join Cora.

"Hello." Instantly self-conscious, Cora closed the manual as her "boss" sat down.

"How are you holding up, dear?" Aiyana asked.

"Good." She cleared her throat. "Great."

"I'm relieved to hear it—and glad to find you here. This time of year is so crazy for me. I apologize that I haven't had the chance to check on you. Did you get the supplies you requested?"

"Not yet. But last I heard they've been ordered, so they should arrive soon. Thanks for giving the okay on that."

She took a drink of her coffee. "I told you how I feel about art. That isn't where I choose to skimp."

"I have to admit your attitude is refreshing. I'm not used to art being much of a priority."

"The practicalities of running a school can often get in the way of even the best intentions," she said. "Fortunately, right now, we've got some wealthy benefactors who are giving us the support we need." She winked. "Makes a difference when we have a fair number of students with rich—and sometimes famous—parents."

"Are we talking movie stars?" Cora hadn't considered that possibility, but she supposed, since they weren't far from LA, it was logical.

"A few. Others are the children of producers and movie execs, attorneys, doctors, that sort of thing."

"Are the wealthy kids ones who are typically loved, or…"

Her lips curved into a rueful smile. "Oh, they're loved, just a little more generously than would probably be best. From what I've seen, being given too much can be as difficult as being given too little."

"Doesn't that create quite a disparity? I mean…you mentioned taking in orphans who have no one to support them."

"We have some of the richest *and* some of the poorest students in the state. But we make it clear from the beginning that everyone is on an equal footing here at the ranch. There is no favoritism, no bending of the rules because of who their parents are."

"I can't imagine that goes over very well—not for people who are used to receiving preferential treatment."

"I've lost several students over that policy," she admitted. "All parents agree to it when they enroll their child—but can change their minds once they want or need special treatment." She pushed a strand of loose hair out of her face. "Regardless, I won't bend. To me it's a matter of integrity. And, if a parent will stand behind me, their son usually settles down and begins to learn the lessons they were hoping we'd teach him."

Cora swallowed another bite of her cookie. "How does that play out in a social setting—for the kids, I mean?"

Aiyana took another sip of coffee. "Depends. We take a hard line on bullying, too—watch carefully for it. Most get the message early on that the rules are firmer here, but fair to all, and life falls into a sustainable rhythm. I don't think we're too terribly different from other high schools—all schools have some behavioral problems."

"But you've taken on the behavioral problems other schools can no longer cope with. Doesn't that ever make you feel…intimidated?"

"I wouldn't want to go back and start over—I can tell you that," she said with a mirthless chuckle. "But now that we're up and running, and I've got the momentum that comes from doing this for so long, it's easier than it was. Still, I couldn't continue without the community support I've received, not to mention the devoted teachers we have here—and Elijah, who has such a knack for communicating with these boys. Even if I can't get one to behave, he usually can."

Cora pictured Aiyana's son on top of that horse. "Elijah's your secret weapon."

"Absolutely."

She studied Aiyana's face. Her mother was so pretty despite the lines that were beginning to appear around her eyes and mouth and the ribbons of gray in her hair. "I hope you don't mind me asking, but…"

"Ask me anything," she said.

"I was wondering what nationality you are."

She seemed surprised by the question—that Cora would have any interest in that—but not put off. "My mother is a Nicaraguan immigrant. My father was a white farmhand in the Central Valley."

"Are they still alive?"

"They are. But my mother is no longer with my father. He was an abusive man, so I don't have any contact with him, either. For many years now she's been with the farmer who employed them both and has been so much happier. What about you? What nationality are you?"

Cora thought it might be too coincidental if she were to say she was part Nicaraguan, but that was good to know—filled in one of the many blanks in her life. Aiyana had said her father was white; from her skin tone, Cora assumed hers was, too. "I'm a mix, I think."

"And your parents? Where are they?"

"In LA. My father's a financial planner. My mother's sort of a…socialite."

She smiled at that. "Do you have siblings?"

"An older brother who's larger than life and terribly handsome. Like a lot of people in LA, he's a movie producer. What about you?"

"I have one older brother and two younger brothers, but I don't see my younger brothers very often."

She seemed noticeably saddened by that. "They don't live close?"

"My brothers are all over California. One owns a winery in Napa. One is in banking in San Francisco. The oldest runs the farm for my mom and stepdad in Los Banos, where I grew up."

"Are they all married?"

"Yes. With kids. What about your brother?"

Suppressing her curiosity about why Aiyana had never married, Cora answered the question. "Still playing the field."

"Sounds like my sons."

"Where are they all? I mean, besides Eli, of course."

"Gavin, my second oldest, has a house in town but works here. He's a handyman, can fix anything."

"Really?" Cora had been around for five days, yet she couldn't recall ever seeing a handyman. "Was he at the meeting on Monday?"

"No. He's not someone who likes to get involved in the administration aspect of the ranch. He prefers to remain in the background, which is why he lives in town."

"How old is he?"

"Twenty-eight. I adopted him three years after I adopted Elijah. Then there's Dallas. He's twenty-five and a mountain climber, so he's usually off, traveling to remote destinations all over the world. I don't get to see him much." She seemed to regret that but moved on. "Seth is twenty-three. He recently graduated from UC Berkeley, wants to be a sculptor. That's one of the reasons I love art so much," she confided. "I'm not sure what I would've done with him if I hadn't been able to reach him in that way…"

"He has…emotional issues?"

"Anger issues, mostly. I seem to gravitate to the most damaged of the boys. I can't help trying to make them whole."

Did Aiyana always accomplish that? Or were some of her sons *too* damaged? "Let's see—Elijah, Gavin, Dallas and Seth. That's four sons, but I heard you have eight," Cora said. "What about the others?"

"Ryan and Taylor are twins. Well, they're not actually *related*, but we call them twins because they're the same age and have done just about everything together since they met here at the ranch. They're still in college. Ryan wants to be a planetary scientist, and Taylor has set his sights on becoming a theoretical physicist. They're both too brilliant for their own good," she added. "Now that they're actually applying themselves."

"Where do they go to school?"

"MIT. Then I have Liam and Bentley, who go here. Liam's a senior. Bentley's a sophomore."

"I wonder if I've seen either one of them around."

"Not yet. They've been with Dallas at Yosemite the past ten days. He's teaching them how to climb."

"That's nice of him."

"They *live* to spend time with their older brothers." She lowered her voice. "He better not let them get hurt, though."

"It's a scary sport." Cora dusted the cookie crumbs off her "boyfriend" jeans. "Would you ever consider adopting more?"

Finished with her coffee, Aiyana pushed the cup aside. "I keep telling myself I need to stop. But every couple of years, it seems as if there's at least one more I'm dying to take home with me."

"That means…maybe?"

"I guess. It'll depend on the circumstances."

So she would take in another boy if she felt he needed her that much, Cora decided. "Did you always want a big family?" she asked and then held her breath. She thought this might be the most revealing question yet, that it might give her some clue as to why Aiyana hadn't wanted *her*, but Aiyana's face grew shuttered as she shook her head.

"No. Never thought I'd have any kids."

Cora was dying to ask why, but there was something so forbidding in the sudden change in Aiyana's expression and body language that she could tell it would be too intrusive. Aiyana had essentially slammed the door shut on that subject, and she didn't stick around long enough to give Cora much of a chance to talk about anything else.

"I'd better go." She reclaimed her empty cup as she stood. "It's been wonderful having a chance to chat, but I've got a lot to do before the pizza party tonight. You're coming, right?"

Cora had found a flyer taped to her door when she got back to her cottage last night announcing a Kickoff Party for all the teachers at a place called Moonstruck Pizza in town. "I haven't made up my mind, to be honest."

"Oh, don't miss it," she said. "The entire staff gets together the Friday before school starts to celebrate the end of summer and the beginning of a new year. It's a tradition."

"And the students? They stay on campus?"

"Yes. The floor monitors keep an eye on them. So come to the party. It'll give everyone a chance to get to know you. And there'll be plenty of pizza and beer—and karaoke, if you sing."

"I sing a little," Cora said, but that was an understatement. She sang a lot. She and a handful of friends liked to compete in various local contests, enjoyed standing behind a mic. And she really needed to get out and have some fun. She just hoped Doug Maggleby wouldn't be too determined to monopolize her time. She could easily imagine spending the evening trying to dodge him.

"So you'll be there?" Aiyana seemed eager for her company.

At that point, Cora didn't feel as if she could refuse—not if it might afford her a few minutes more with her birth mother. "Sure. Why not?" she said, but as soon as she agreed, she began to wonder if Elijah would be part of the festivities. Then she chided herself for having the desire to see him. She was letting herself get quite a "thing" for Aiyana's handsome son, even though she barely knew him and he'd made it clear he wasn't interested in *her*.

He *was* there. Cora spotted Elijah as soon as she walked into the pizza parlor and hated herself for suddenly being so glad she'd come. She didn't need to get her heart broken; she was trying to mend it by moving here, to finally get over the sense of rejection her adoption had engendered.

But she figured she shouldn't be *too* hard on herself.

She didn't yet know anyone other than the staff she'd been introduced to at the school, so it wasn't all that surprising she'd fixate on the one man she'd met who was in her age bracket—especially when she factored in how darned handsome he was.

She couldn't get hurt if he never responded, anyway. His disinterest made the attraction safe. So she figured she might as well enjoy the view he provided, maybe even indulge in a few harmless fantasies. If allowing him to fuel her imagination helped pass the time and made her stint in Silver Springs more enjoyable, why not?

Feeling slightly empowered by the fact that she had no expectations, she smiled widely when he looked up. Once she found a seat and everyone went back to chatting and drinking their sodas and beer, she even winked at him, since he was still watching her.

He didn't wink in return—or even smile. But he didn't look away, either. He studied her that much more closely, as if he was trying to figure out what she was up to.

Since Doug Maggleby insisted on crowding as close to her as possible, she was glad when the pizza finally arrived. Doing her best to keep interaction with him to a minimum, she focused on the female English teacher on her other side, a recent divorcée with two kids, neither of whom was with her now because her ex had picked them up for the weekend.

Cora also kept an eye on Aiyana. She hoped to speak to her mother again—at some length, if the opportunity presented itself. She now knew that she had living grandparents and uncles and where they all lived and what they did for work! It was a revelation, considering the dearth of information she'd had until six months ago. There were a lot of other things Cora wanted to know—but Aiyana was always surrounded by an eager group of teachers or other staff.

Everyone who worked for her liked her, Cora realized. They all seemed to bask in whatever attention she gave them. Thanks to that, there was no chance for Cora to approach her while they waited for the pizza, and Aiyana left shortly after it came, before the karaoke even started.

"Are you leaving, too?" Cora asked Darci Spinoza, the English teacher she'd been chatting with most of the night, when another group from their party started to say goodbye.

"No way," she replied. "You said you were going to sing. Since I don't have a voice, and wouldn't have the nerve to perform in front of a crowd even if I did, I'm waiting to hear you."

"Me, too," Doug chimed in.

Although Cora was grateful that Darci would be staying, she wished Doug would find other friends. Her other neighbor, Sean, sat in the corner with a couple of people. Why couldn't Doug go over there? He was drinking too much, which made him feel free to touch her…

Briefly, she considered going home herself, to avoid him, but she hated to miss her chance to sing. And Elijah was still there. He stood with his back against the wall and a beer in his hand, talking to a man she'd never met. Because that man was somewhere close to their age, was part of the group from the school and seemed so comfortable around Elijah, she guessed it was Gavin, the handyman Aiyana had mentioned and Elijah's younger brother. Tall and thin, he had a beard and several tattoos on his arms. He was handsome, but not nearly as handsome as Elijah.

Once the karaoke started, Cora tried to ignore the bothersome, overbearing and balding Doug and went to the mic to sing "Jolene." On subsequent trips she performed "I Hope You Dance" and "Wrecking Ball." After that, Darci, Doug and several others kept prodding her to get up again. Some people even made requests—and a table of four men, who hadn't been part of their group but had come in later, started sending her drinks.

"Those guys are really into you," Doug said. "But of course they would be. Who wouldn't like a gorgeous woman like you?"

Cora couldn't help leaning away from his sour breath. He was getting so close when he talked it felt as if he was trying to look down her blouse.

Catching her recoil, Darci gave her a nudge. "I think it's time for Doug to go to bed, but…he can't drive in that condition."

No, he couldn't. Someone had to see that he got home safely, and Cora was the obvious choice. They lived right next door to each other, after all—and Sean had already left. "Is there any way we could call him a taxi or even an Uber?" she whispered back.

Darci laughed at the question. "Not in this small of a town. There's no such thing here. But if you'd rather not take him, I will."

Cora couldn't ask her new friend to go twenty minutes out of the way. Darci had already told her that she lived in town. "No, I'll do it. Just…help me get him to my car, okay?"

"Sure, I can do that."

They had no trouble persuading Doug that he shouldn't drive, not once he learned he'd be riding with her—and that she'd bring him back to get his car in the morning. At that point, Cora forgot about Elijah. She was too intent on stopping Doug from copping a feel as she and Darci helped him outside. She'd just unlocked her car so they could put him in the passenger seat when Elijah came out of the pizza parlor along with the man she'd guessed was Gavin.

Darci said good-night to them, so Cora looked up and said the same. She expected the brothers to go on their way, possibly to a bar if they weren't ready to go home for the night, but "Gavin" waited on the curb while Elijah came around to where they were trying to get Doug in the car.

"Here, I'll take him." Slipping Doug's arm around his neck, Eli started to cart the math teacher off.

Cora was so relieved she almost couldn't hide it. "Are you sure?"

"Why would I go home with you when I could go home with *her*?" Doug protested, his voice overloud and his expression bordering on belligerent.

"Because I'm not giving you any choice," Elijah said, and that was the end of it. Cora was fairly certain Doug knew better than to balk, that he'd be stupid to try to stand up to Elijah, because he didn't object again. "Gavin" met his brother and took hold of Doug's other arm, and Cora was left to drive home alone.

"That was nice," she said on a long exhale.

Darci smiled as if she was holding something back.

"What?" Cora asked.

"Eli could tell you weren't comfortable, that you didn't want to take Doug home."

She straightened. Of course she didn't want her drunk octopus of a neighbor in the car with her. But Darci was intimating something more than that. "What do you mean? Elijah was clear across the room. How would he know anything?"

"You're kidding, right? He's been watching you all night. Every time I glanced up, he had his eyes on you. I've known him for a year and have never seen him so focused on a woman. I think Doug got a little too close to what Eli wants himself."

"That's not true," Cora argued. "Eli was simply being a stand-up guy by putting me out of my misery—knew he was better equipped to handle Doug in his current condition than I am."

"If you say so." Her singsong voice indicated she didn't

believe that at all, but she didn't belabor the point. "It was great spending time with you," she said. "I'm glad you've come to town. What with the divorce and dealing with my ex since I moved here, it's been hard to make friends. And now it's too late to be that new girl who gets introduced around. So…I'm happy to meet someone who's starting fresh and might be open to getting to know me."

"I'm definitely open to that," Cora said.

"Even though I'm quite a bit older than you?"

Cora waved her words away. "Age doesn't matter when it comes to friendship."

"That takes care of that, then. Now maybe I'll have someone to do something with when the weekends roll around and my kids are with their dad."

"I'm sure I'll be looking for a chance to get off the campus." She waved as Darci walked down the street to her car, but her mind wasn't on her new friend. She kept mulling over what Darci had said about Elijah, and realized she was right. Elijah wasn't just being a good guy in general when he took Doug off her hands. He was looking out for her—*specifically*.

Chapter Six

Elijah found Cora leaning up against the side of his truck when he came out of Doug Maggleby's house.

"Thanks for putting my neighbor to bed for me," she said as he walked toward her. "I was not looking forward to that."

He could tell. She didn't like Doug touching her, and he hadn't liked it much, either. "No need to thank me. He's not your responsibility."

"He's not yours, either."

He shrugged. "It's not like I was going out of my way."

She tucked her long brown hair behind her ears. "So you didn't do it for me?"

He *had* done it for her, but he preferred to downplay that part. "No."

He assumed she'd let it go at that, but she gave him a skeptical once-over.

"What?" he said.

"You're so full of it."

He felt his eyebrows go up. He wasn't sure he'd ever had another woman say something like that to him before. "Excuse me?"

"You're acting like you're not interested in me, but..."

This new girl was nothing if not unpredictable, Elijah decided. She didn't play by the usual rules—at least not the old-fashioned rules he'd grown accustomed to living out here in the country. Problem was...she was right. He *was* interested in her. But he couldn't let himself act on that interest. "What makes you think so?" He rested both hands on the truck, one on either side of her. He figured if she was going to challenge him, he was going to challenge her right back.

But she didn't flounder for a response, didn't back down. She wasn't intimidated in the least, even though he had her penned between his arms and virtually towered over her.

Her gaze lowered to his mouth. "The way you look at me."

He tensed with the desire to press her up against his truck and kiss her soundly. She was baiting him, trying to see what he would do, which left him torn. Part of him felt she deserved to get a bit more than she bargained for. The other part knew better than to let things move in that direction. He'd been keeping his distance from her for a reason.

"*You're* the one who said you had a boyfriend," he said. "Maybe you've forgotten the other day. I was carrying in your boxes, you were acting all concerned, as if that might mean you owed me something, and then you said—"

"I remember," she broke in.

"So…what's up with that? Where'd your boyfriend go?"

She lifted her chin defiantly. "I broke up with him over a month ago."

"You lied?"

Still, she didn't back down. "Basically."

"Because…"

For the first time her confidence seemed to waver. "I don't know. It doesn't make sense. I… I felt something I didn't want to feel. And I panicked."

He was so astounded by her honesty he wasn't sure how to respond. So he went with the obvious—what he'd been using to warn himself off since she'd arrived in Silver Springs. "I'm your boss, Cora."

"*That's* what's holding you back? Professional integrity?"

"One of the things, yes. This school—the boys here—are important to me."

"One doesn't necessarily cancel out the other."

"I hired you because I thought you'd be the best teacher for the job." He'd also thought he'd be able to ignore how alive he felt whenever he was around her, but he'd never expected her to confront him so directly. That forced the issue out in the open, made the attraction more difficult to ignore. "I'm sure my mother wouldn't thank me for giving her new art instructor reason to quit and leave."

That brief moment of insecurity he'd noted before seemed to fall by the wayside. "You're sure dating me would go in that direction?"

His ex-girlfriend said he walled himself off, refused to give anything emotionally. And she probably had the right of it. The shrink Aiyana used to send him to said a lot of the same stuff. Dr. Anderson told him he needed to learn how to open up, which sounded good in theory but he couldn't figure out how. He'd finally refused to continue therapy. He wanted to close the door on his past and make sure it was never opened again, not rehash those painful memories.

"It's not like I've never been down this road," he said. "I've been in a number of relationships. Enough to know my limitations."

"*All* those relationships ended badly?"

He'd been taught to believe he was so terrible, so *unacceptable*, that he'd been painfully shy around girls growing up. He hadn't even started dating until he was twenty, and he'd only had three fairly serious—and fairly short—relationships since. "Let's just say…I don't have a high success ratio when it comes to women."

"You and Aiyana are *very* close."

"That's different."

"Love is love. You had to decide to trust her at some point."

"Not everyone has her patience," he said. "She was so determined to love me, I had no choice."

"And those other women?"

The scent of her perfume rose to his nostrils. He liked the way she smelled, wanted to touch all that soft-looking skin. The temptation to slide his hand up her shirt burned through him like hard liquor. "As I said, it's not the same thing."

"Because it involves physical intimacy? What, exactly, are your 'limitations'? Are you saying you can't have sex?"

He was pretty sure she was goading him. At least, he hoped she was, that she didn't really believe he was incapable. Either way, he was eager to put the question to rest. "My body works fine. It's my inability to make you feel loved and 'validated.' I think that was the word."

"So I'd only get hurt if I got involved with you."

"Yes. You'd essentially be getting a locked box."

He was being transparent, completely up front. She was the one who'd set that tone. So it surprised him when she barked out a laugh. "You think you're doing me a favor by staying away!"

He was trying to adhere to the decisions he'd made after that last ugly blowout with Tina. He'd been glad for the peace and balance he'd found since they broke up a year ago. But twelve months was a long time to go without a woman… "Essentially."

"Well, you're taking a lot for granted, Mr. Turner. First of all, how do you know I'm going to want you to love me?"

"Experience," he said wryly. "I have yet to encounter the opposite problem."

"You're in such high demand that you've grown arrogant?"

"Failure hardly makes me arrogant. It does, however, make me want to avoid running into the same brick wall."

"I see. Well, you don't have to look out for me. I'm a big girl."

"Which, of course, you'll say until our relationship doesn't progress. Then you'll quit your job and go back to LA."

She rolled her eyes. "I'm only here for one year. No matter what happens, I'm not going to quit my job."

Was she as resilient as she pretended? He couldn't help getting his hopes up. He was already starting to imagine her on her back, her hair falling across his pillow… "Then you have a decision to make."

"What kind of decision?"

"Are you up for a strictly physical relationship? Because if that's all you're after, I'd be happy to accommodate you. I have no doubt I could satisfy you there."

She studied him. "That's all *you're* interested in?"

"Yes. I'm sorry." He wasn't about to go down the same road he'd been down before. But he wasn't sure why he was apologizing, since she sounded almost…relieved by this news.

"You're *sure*? *I* could never hurt *you*?"

"No. I'm too good at keeping my gloves up." He'd been trained from a young age…

She nodded slowly. "Okay. I'll think about it."

That didn't sound as though she'd make up her mind as quickly as he was hoping. "Any chance you could think fast?"

He wanted to kiss her so badly; the way she chewed on her bottom lip made him sort of light-headed. "We should probably give it a few weeks. See how we feel," she replied.

"*Weeks?* Does it have to take that long? Because I've already made up my mind."

She seemed uncertain. "There is something I should probably tell you…"

"And that is…"

More lip nibbling. "I've never had a strictly physical relationship."

He shifted his gaze from her lips to her eyes. "Not even a one-night stand?"

"No."

"*What?* You're from LA!"

Her expression changed to one of outrage—until she realized he was joking. "Don't even start with those stereotypes," she grumbled. "Or I'll go for the country bumpkin stuff."

Somehow, he'd underestimated her. She wasn't making it easy for him to ignore the attraction he felt. He liked her spunk. "Can you at least tell me what my chances are?" he asked, leaning a little closer.

"*I'm* the one who approached *you*, so…I'd say they're pretty decent."

"What made you approach me?" he asked, because that was a game changer. Otherwise, he would've continued to skirt around her indefinitely.

"There's just something about you."

All the things he could say to coax her, to convince her she wouldn't regret spending the night with him rose to his lips. But he knew it wouldn't be fair to put any pressure on her. She could *easily* regret the arrangement he proposed. And he didn't want that.

Taking her hand, he held it to his chest so that she could feel how hard his heart was beating. Maybe he couldn't promise her forever, but she wanted him. She'd just said so. And he wanted her.

Her hand moved slowly over his pectoral muscles in a curious caress that made him hard as a rock. He almost kissed her, was tempted to use his body to convince her if he couldn't allow himself to use his voice. But as soon as he dipped his head, she seemed to understand they were only seconds away from "too late." Once they crossed that line there would be no going back. One spark could cause them both to go up in flames.

"Like I said, I'll think about it." Pulling away, she started up the drive.

Disappointment bit deep. He stood there without reacting for several seconds, trying to overcome the letdown. Then he said, "Wait."

She didn't come back to him, but she turned, so he walked over and held out his hand. "Where's your phone?"

When she pulled it from her pocket and handed it to him, he put in his number and gave it back to her. "In case the answer is yes. Maybe it won't take as long as you think."

Cora stared at Elijah's number for at least an hour after he left. She switched between the contact information he'd put in her phone and the picture she'd taken of him out on that ride. She loved that picture so much. And yet…they'd never really spent any time together. It was ridiculous that she'd feel so compelled to call him.

She was just lonely, she told herself. She'd made a big change, was out of her element. She needed to forget about him and concentrate on what she'd come here to do, which was to teach and get to know Aiyana. She was part Nicaraguan. She had grandparents. She had uncles. These were the things she'd hoped to seek out. Her plans didn't include Elijah.

But she couldn't have anything serious with Elijah, anyway. Not without telling him that she was Aiyana's biological daughter. And she wasn't ready to do that. So he'd offered her the perfect solution: the chance to fulfill the desire he evoked without expectation.

After another ten minutes spent pacing around her small cottage, she decided to walk over to the pond. She thought sitting on the dock with the moon shining down on the water might help calm her mind. But even there, she was restless—too restless to remain on the jetty. Eventually, she made her way over to the horses' pen where she hoped, with the animals, she wouldn't feel quite so alone.

"There you are, big boy," she crooned, petting the nose of Elijah's giant horse when it ambled over to see her. "Looks like you're not getting much sleep tonight, either."

"You okay?"

Startled by the sound of Elijah's voice, Cora turned to see a dark figure sitting on the fence of the llama pen not far away, in the shadow of the nearby barn.

She pressed a hand to her chest to compensate for the shock he'd given her. "How long have you been there?"

"Since before you came out."

"You saw me, and you didn't say anything?"

"I was considering it."

"It took you a while to decide!"

"I wasn't sure you wanted to be disturbed."

Somehow it seemed like fate that they would run into each other again tonight. Or maybe she'd been subconsciously hoping for that, hoping for another opportunity, without actually having to call him. Although she'd never seen his house, she knew he lived on this part of the ranch, near the animals. She was hesitant to admit it, but, deep down, she was fairly certain that was why she'd come over here so often already. She'd been hoping to see him all along. "What are *you* doing out here?" she asked.

"Same thing you are, I suppose."

"You can't sleep."

"I have something on my mind."

"And that is…"

"You."

Cora squinted across the distance between them, trying to make out his expression. He was lonely, too, she realized. As much as he tried to pretend otherwise, he had to be. He was so aloof, so careful to warn most everyone away. She was no psychologist, but after what he'd been through, that had to be a defense mechanism. And what he'd said about Aiyana seemed to prove it. By his own admission, Aiyana had only busted through his reserve because she wouldn't take no for an answer.

Maybe that was what getting close to him required—the ability to love without expectation, without measuring or demanding anything in return. Cora could understand why that might be the case. He was tired of disappointing the women he dated, tired of feeling inadequate when they became disappointed. She'd sensed that in what he'd had to say earlier. There'd been a degree of fatalism, as if he'd given up.

His previous girlfriends had probably wanted to establish a regular relationship, one that escalated toward marriage. So they had an agenda, of sorts. Cora, on the other hand, had no agenda. She wasn't looking for a long-term relationship, couldn't have one with him, anyway, not without a very honest conversation she wasn't willing to have.

So…what if she just gave him someone to be with while she was here, some meaningful intimacy that was warm and supportive without pushing him for anything more?

"Sounds like you could use a massage," she said.

There was a moment of silence. Then he said, "Are you offering to give me one?"

She could tell he wasn't really asking about a massage, just as she knew he understood her answer wouldn't be strictly limited to one. "Sure."

"Tonight—or do I have to wait a few weeks?"

She chuckled. "Don't push your luck."

The darkness made it difficult to tell for sure, but she was fairly certain she'd gotten a smile out of him.

"You wouldn't be out here if you weren't as taken with the idea as I am," he said.

"You have a point, I suppose."

"You're not going to pretend otherwise?"

"No. Should we go to your place—or mine?"

He hopped off the fence and came toward her. "Mine."

"Any particular reason?"

"I don't have neighbors."

"Mr. Maggleby does tend to keep tabs on me."

"Mr. Maggleby is probably down for the count, but my house would still be better."

Cora drew a steadying breath as he advanced. She'd be spending the night with him. She'd just made the commitment, wouldn't feel good about backing out now.

Fortunately, she didn't want to. But her motives weren't *entirely* altruistic. She'd been craving the opportunity to touch him since the first day she'd met him.

And now she was going to have her chance.

Chapter Seven

Elijah's small A-frame was the most isolated house on the ranch and the hardest to reach, which suited him well, Cora thought as he showed her inside and closed the door behind them. He had plenty of privacy here. She got the impression that few people were ever invited inside, and that included the students he cared so much about. This was his place of retreat where he could put some distance between him and other people, since people were what he probably considered to be the biggest challenge life had to offer. Everything else seemed to come easy for him.

"Would you like a drink?" he asked.

Cora shook her head. "No. I'm good."

"Are you sure? Maybe a glass of wine?" Now that he had her inside, he was treating her as if she might bolt if he wasn't careful or courteous enough. That was another thing that made her wonder if he wasn't quite comfortable with having company. She got the impression he almost didn't know what to do with her—how to get from where they were in this moment to where he hoped to go, which wasn't in keeping with how he behaved in every other circumstance she'd noted so far.

"Okay." She relented, thinking that might help. "I'll have a glass of wine."

While he opened a bottle and poured, she wandered around his living room, which was very utilitarian—so utilitarian that the walls were completely bare. She couldn't find one thing that defined him as a person, nothing that spoke of who he was or what he liked, even on the shelves or counters. She'd never seen a house stripped down to the bare essentials before. The men she'd known had a tendency to decorate sparsely, but still.

Was it just that Elijah didn't know how to make a house a home? Or was the ability to reveal even that much of himself also locked inside the "box" he'd mentioned?

"Aren't *you* going to have one?" she asked when he handed her a glass and stood back to watch her drink it.

"No."

So much for letting a drink ease them into the evening… "Why not?"

"I'm not interested."

He was too single-minded to drink right now, Cora decided. He knew what he wanted, and it wasn't wine. But he was trying to wait his turn. "So you were merely being polite by offering me one."

"I thought you might enjoy it."

He seemed to feel as if he needed to take certain steps for her sake, as if he'd memorized a set of "rules" for how to be successful in such situations—and that included putting whatever *she* wanted first.

Setting her glass aside, she stepped up to him. She could tell he was dying to touch her, saw his hands curl into fists and his muscles tense as he wrestled with his self-control. For some reason, he was trying to let her make the first move. She supposed he wanted some reassurance that she wasn't going to suddenly change her mind. Or maybe he merely wanted to be confident he wasn't pressuring her into anything. Regardless, he was far more wary now that they were alone and behind closed doors than he'd been at his truck earlier. But they'd never had any real chance of getting intimate there, so maybe that was why.

What'd happened to him in the past had influenced *everything*, even the way he approached sex, she realized. He didn't trust other people, didn't trust *her*. "How long has it been for you?" she asked.

"Since…"

"Since you've been with a woman."

"A year."

No wonder he watched her like a wolf chasing a rabbit. That was a long time to go without for a man his age—at least it would be a long time to the men she knew in LA. But Eli lived in a small town and had the reputation of the ranch to consider—and she knew the pain that hid behind that handsome face. As normal as he came off, every once in a while there was something in his eyes that reminded her of an animal that'd been beaten so often it growled or showed its teeth even when someone tried to be kind. He craved what she was offering, couldn't bring himself to skirt around her and continue on his way, as he most likely preferred. So he was waiting for the perfect moment—when he could safely snatch it away. Were he anyone else, she felt certain he would've reached for her already…

"These encounters don't come with a script," she said.

"Meaning…"

"You don't have to serve me wine, or…or check anything else off a list."

"I'm merely trying to make sure you get what you need. I may be sort of…limited in what I can offer you, but I'm not a *completely* selfish bastard. If you'll tell me what you want, what you like, I'll give it to you."

"I don't have a punch list, Eli. That's what I'm saying. But I'm pretty sure we can figure out what we *both* like." His nostrils flared when she lifted his hand to her breast. "Does this help?"

Elijah wished it was easier to go without human touch. His life would be so much simpler. But nothing else felt like a woman. He tried to hold himself in check, to remain in control. He didn't want to overwhelm or frighten Cora, had been trying to be measured and kind. But once she put her mouth on his, and he could feel the weight of her breast in his palm, something snapped. She didn't have to do anything more. He started kissing her so hungrily that he could hardly catch his breath. And, within moments, he was peeling off her clothes, so anxious to get to bare skin that it felt like he couldn't wait another second.

He thought she might be put off. On some level, he knew he was being pretty aggressive, probably *overly* aggressive. But she had her hands in his hair and clung to him as if she was just as caught up in him as he was her. So if she was put off, he couldn't tell.

He hoped it wasn't something he'd learn about in the morning. To prevent that, he promised himself he'd take their lovemaking slower as he carried her down the hall to his bedroom.

Once there, he made an honest effort to do just that, but her kisses were so hot and wet, and she was sucking on his neck and licking his nipples. She was even biting him, just not so hard that it hurt.

Although his shirt was already on the floor, he still had his jeans on as they rolled around in his bed. Since everything he touched felt so damn good, he forgot about taking it slow and gentle. If anything, he felt the compulsion to make everything go harder and faster.

Fortunately, she seemed to be perfectly happy. With a promising smile, she unzipped his pants.

He gasped as her fingers closed around him and, only moments later, he was naked, too.

To his credit, he took a moment to admire her full breasts, small waist and the appealing flare of her hips. She had no hair *anywhere*, which, coming from LA certainly didn't surprise him, but he'd never seen a woman so bare. He liked the way she looked lying beneath him in the moonlight streaming through his window. She was as beautiful and soft as he'd expected.

Dimly, he thought about all the things he could do to bring her to climax. He planned to do every single one before he took his own pleasure. He wanted to make sure she was glad she'd agreed to be with him tonight. But once he began to suckle her breasts, she arched into him as if she craved him inside her.

"Okay. Hang on. Let me…let me take care of you first," he said.

"I'm ready," she gasped when he slid his hand between her legs.

He groaned as he encountered the slickness he was hoping to find. She *felt* ready. But burying himself inside her, this soon, wouldn't be slowing down.

"Do you have a condom?" she asked.

Fortunately, he did—in the nightstand. But he barely managed to roll it on before she pulled him on top of her and wrapped her legs around his hips—an unmistakable invitation and one he couldn't refuse.

He felt shaky as he pushed inside her. She was so wet, so tight he had to hold himself still. Otherwise, he wouldn't have even half a chance of making her come. He didn't want to be the only one who was fulfilled tonight. Then he wouldn't have done *anything* right.

"God, you feel good," he murmured, running his mouth up her neck.

"So do you," she said. "I guess it's true what they say about guys with big hands and big feet."

That comment took him so much by surprise that he almost laughed, but she didn't give him time. She grabbed hold of him—to pull him deeper inside her—and encouraged him to thrust.

"Give me a minute." He could hardly recognize his own voice it sounded so hoarse. "You're going to be disappointed if you don't."

Crooking her arm around his neck to bring him closer,

she pulled his bottom lip into her mouth. "Quit *thinking*," she whispered.

He shook his head. "You don't understand. It's been a long time for me. I'm not going to make it."

"So what? Let go. Do it any way you want." Her breath, hot in his ear, was followed by her tongue.

Her words, the freedom she gave him, sent a fresh deluge of testosterone through him, which did nothing to help his control. But if she wasn't going to help him hold out, he figured he was facing a losing battle. So he closed his eyes and drove into her with an abandon he'd rarely allowed himself before, and felt the pleasure of each thrust escalate to the point that his whole body shuddered when he hit climax.

"Goose bumps," she said as she ran a hand down his arm. "That must've been a nice one."

He stared down at her while trying to catch his breath. "It was. But I know it was too fast for you. I'm sorry."

"I enjoyed watching you," she said. "I think you needed to let loose."

Suddenly, he was *so* tired. "Give me an hour or so, and I'll redeem myself. I promise," he said as he curled around her. But he fell into such a deep sleep that it was morning when he woke up, and by then she was gone.

Elijah had a hard time being selfish. That was the most significant fact Cora had learned about him while she was in his bed. As she drove to town the following morning to meet Darci for breakfast, she couldn't help chuckling as she remembered how he'd tried to rein himself in—and how guilty he'd felt when he couldn't. Of course, she'd enjoyed urging him on, had wanted to see what Elijah Turner was like when he threw off all of that restraint. Not only was it gratifying to her that she could have such an effect on him, she figured that was the best way to discover his true personality—when he wasn't closely monitoring everything he said and did. Although he came off as remote, she was beginning to understand that he was actually quite sensitive. He also seemed honest and intrinsically fair.

Her phone rang. Assuming it would be Jill, or maybe Darci, since she was running a few minutes late, she answered using her Bluetooth. "Hello?"

"Cora? It's Aiyana. How are you?"

She froze at the sound of her birth mother's voice. Had Aiyana learned that she and Elijah had spent the night together? Cora had slipped out of his place while it was still dark so that no one would see her. They were both consenting adults; she didn't think what they'd done should be a *really* big deal, at least to anyone else. They did work for the same school, however. So, of course, that would be frowned upon.

Was she about to be confronted about her behavior?

A honk from the car behind her reminded her that it was her turn to clear the intersection. "Um… I'm fine," she said as she gave her SUV some gas. "How are you?"

"Great." Aiyana covered the phone as someone spoke to her in the background. "Sorry about that," she said when she came back on the line. "We just got a new shipment of books for the library."

"From what I've seen, we already have an extensive collection."

"I won't skimp on the library, either."

What *did* she skimp on? Nothing, not when it came to the school. Cora had the impression she worked 24/7 to make sure the boys had everything they could possibly need. "Are you a big reader?"

"I am. I read more nonfiction than anything else, but I stock a lot of action-adventure, sci-fi, mysteries and thrillers for the boys. I encourage them to read by giving them books they're going to like. Feel free to take a look and borrow anything that catches your fancy."

Cora had an e-reader, which was well-stocked, but she didn't say so. She didn't want Aiyana to feel as though her offer wasn't appreciated. "I will. Thank you."

"I hope you'll be able to adjust to living here in Silver Springs," she said. "I know it might require a bit of an adjustment."

"Living out here is…different," Cora admitted. "But it's not without its attractions." She winced as those words came out of her mouth. She thought Aiyana would instantly guess that Elijah was the biggest and brightest of Silver Springs' "attractions," at least where she was concerned. But Aiyana didn't seem to clue in—thank God.

"Your supplies should be in on Monday. I checked, wanted to let you know."

Cora pulled in front of Lolita's Country Kitchen, where Darci had asked to meet for breakfast. She had to admit that it was wonderful to find ample parking—that rarely happened in LA. She wouldn't even have to pay for it. "Wow. How nice of you to follow up."

"No problem. But…that isn't the only reason I called. If you have a minute, I'd like to talk to you about something else."

Oh boy. Maybe she *did* know about Eli. Cora turned off the car but didn't release her seat belt even though she could see Darci waving at her through the window of the diner. "Sure, I've got time. What's going on?"

"One of the other teachers mentioned to me that Doug Maggleby was making you uncomfortable at the pizza parlor last night."

"It wasn't…all that bad," she hedged.

"He was drinking, which I'm sure didn't help. Anyway, I'm sorry. I'll speak to him. I definitely don't want him scaring you off."

"No, don't bother," she said. "He didn't get *too* out of line." Thanks to Eli, he didn't get much of a chance…

"Are you sure?"

"Positive."

"Well, I'll let this incident go, but only because he's had a rough few years. He lost his wife to cancer and is just now getting over it and hoping to find someone else."

"He might have better luck looking for someone closer to his own age," Cora said.

"Yes. If necessary, I'll mention that to him."

"I appreciate your support."

"Of course. That's what I'm here for." She was about to hang up when, impulsively, Cora stopped her.

"Aiyana?"

"Yes?"

"To tell you the truth…" She searched for the right words to express what she had to say and came up empty.

"Have you changed your mind about having me talk to Doug?" Aiyana asked.

"No. This is…something else."

"What is it?"

She tapped her fingers on her steering wheel. "Um… I wanted to make sure you wouldn't be…angry or—or disappointed if I ever…you know…"

"What?" Aiyana prompted.

"Showed interest in your son," she blurted out.

"Elijah?"

Cora squeezed her eyes closed. She had no idea what the heck she was doing. She just hated the feeling that she might be letting Aiyana down by going behind her back, needed to know how serious of an infraction it would be if she were to continue to see Elijah. She had no idea how *he* felt about last night, but she definitely wanted to get to know him better. "Yes. I've seen Gavin but haven't actually met him."

There was a long pause. Afraid of what Aiyana might say to discourage her, Cora hurried to fill the silence. "I realize we both work for you, at the same school, but in the high schools where I've taught, if two teachers happen to go out once in a while, it's pretty much ignored."

"I'm not so concerned about two employees dating..."

"And yet you sound hesitant."

"He bears some unique scars, Cora."

Letting her breath seep out, Cora finally opened her eyes. "I'm aware of that."

"Do you realize that what he's been through will probably always be part of him? How a background like his could affect a relationship?"

Darci was now at the door, watching her with a confused expression, so Cora lifted one finger to indicate she'd be just another minute. "Here's the thing. He's fine the way he is. I'm not asking for anything serious. I think I could be a good friend to him."

More silence. Cora didn't get the impression Aiyana was *against* her seeing Elijah—it was more that she seemed to be weighing certain reservations in her mind, trying to figure out if she should say more.

Cora bit her lip. "I shouldn't have said anything. It wouldn't be serious, like I said. I guess I just...needed to know you wouldn't be too upset if...if we ever hung out."

"I wouldn't be upset. I'm just worried that...well, because he's so hard to get to know, it may not seem as if he can be hurt—"

"Anyone can be hurt."

"*Especially* him," she said. "I guess that's my point. His heart is so big."

"Trust me—it's not like that. You have nothing to worry about."

"Well, if that's the case, no one can have too many

friends," she said, and they both laughed at her quick reversal.

"Okay. Great. Can I ask for one more favor?"

"Of course."

"Don't tell him we had this conversation?"

"Trust me—I won't. He wouldn't like the idea of me getting involved, so to be honest, I'm hoping you won't mention it, either."

"I won't. This will be our little secret. And now I'll let you go."

"Cora?"

She pulled her phone back to her ear. "Yes?"

"Relationships, even friendships, can be unpredictable at times. So protect your own heart, too."

"I will." As Cora disconnected, she felt as if a huge weight had been lifted off her shoulders. Maybe she hadn't come *totally* clean. She wasn't willing to go that far. But at least she knew she wouldn't be doing anything that would upset Aiyana if Aiyana found out about it. As attracted as Cora was to Elijah, she didn't want to kill any chance she had of being part of her biological mother's life—if she ever decided to go for that.

Chapter Eight

"Thanks for being willing to get together," Darci said.

Cora was a little self-conscious about the fact that she hadn't had a chance to shower this morning. When Darci called, she'd rolled out of bed and thrown her hair into a ponytail. She was still tired after being up until the wee hours with Elijah. "I'm glad you reached out," she told Darci.

"I almost didn't, but with school starting on Monday and my kids coming home tomorrow, I figured this would be the best time to get together."

"It's perfect. I haven't had a chance to eat in Silver Springs yet." Cora noted the number of filled tables. "This seems like a popular place."

"It's one of the best cafés in town, not that we have a lot of them," Darci added with a laugh. "Do you know if Elijah got Doug home okay last night?"

Cora took a drink of water from the glass the waitress had delivered to her a moment earlier. "He did. I saw him as he was coming out of Doug's house."

"Did he say anything to you?"

She opened her menu, pretending to be preoccupied by choosing her meal. "Not really." After what Darci had said about the way Elijah was looking at her last night, Cora didn't dare admit to anything. Her face was heating up, threatening to give her away as it was.

Fortunately, someone walked by that Darci knew, drawing her attention. "Hello, Cal!"

"Cal," a handsome, middle-aged man who wore a cowboy hat and boots, stopped, a look of pleasant surprise on his face. "Darci! I didn't even see you there. How are you?"

She got up to give him a hug. "Better. Thanks."

"That ex of yours isn't still giving you trouble, is he?"

"Things seem to have settled down for the moment." She slid back in the booth. "He's met someone else, so that helps."

He shook his head. "You've had a rough year."

"It's been a rough *twelve* years. But the divorce would've been worse without you."

"I didn't do much." He glanced at Cora. "Is this a new friend?"

As Darci introduced them, she told Cora that Cal Buchanon owned a big cattle ranch not far from town. "He supplies New Horizons with beef, gives Aiyana a heck of a deal. Actually, he helps *everyone*," she said emphatically. "Silver Springs wouldn't be what it is without him."

"Stop!" he said, obviously embarrassed. "I do my part, like everyone else. It's very nice to meet you, Cora."

"Likewise," Cora said.

He chatted with Darci for several more minutes before tipping his hat to the both of them and heading to the cashier to pay his bill.

"Cal's superrich," Darci whispered. "And he uses his money to do so much for the community. I was serious when I said Silver Springs wouldn't be the same without him."

"You seem to know him well."

"I do. He has a couple of houses on his ranch that he typically rents to his hands. He let me stay in one *for free* until I could get on my feet. Wouldn't take a dime for six months."

"Is that why you came to Silver Springs? You knew him from before, and he made you that offer, or…"

"No. I came to teach at New Horizons, like you. But the house that was supposed to open up in the faculty housing—the two-bedroom so that I'd have room for my kids—didn't, and I couldn't afford anything in town."

"So how'd you meet him?"

"Through Aiyana. She jumped in to make other arrangements when the faculty housing didn't work out for me."

"How nice of her."

"She's generous, like Cal. And, from what I've heard, Cal has been in love with Aiyana for years, almost since the day she came here. I believe he took me in for her sake. But he's been kind enough to befriend me, too."

"He's never married?"

"Not to my knowledge. He doesn't even date. He's waiting for her."

"He reminds me of Sam Elliott with that gravelly voice and weathered face. Doesn't she care for him in return?"

"I'm convinced she does. The way she looks at him… it's as if he hung the moon. But she's very private about her love life. If you ask her about Cal, she'll make some glib comment about how he's a great guy but she's too old to get married for the first time."

Aiyana was only forty-nine. Cora knew that from the documents provided by the private investigator who'd taken her on pro bono. "Do you ever see them together?"

"I run into them all the time. He supports anything her boys participate in so he comes out to the ranch a lot. And he sends her flowers or chocolates at least once a month. I wish I could find a guy as devoted to me as he is to her," she added wistfully. "My ex only cared about himself."

Cora had no business asking, but she was so curious about her birth mother that she couldn't stop herself. "Do you think they're sleeping together?" she asked, lowering her voice to a whisper.

Darci's mouth twisted as she considered the question. "Don't know, to be honest. When I lived out at his place, she never stayed over, not that I could tell. And I've never known him to sleep at New Horizons. But that doesn't mean it hasn't happened. Like I said, Aiyana's very private about that sort of thing. She'd never let on, even if they were intimate."

"There must be some reason they're not an official couple. What's missing?"

"I couldn't tell you." She made a signal to let Cora know the waitress, who'd introduced herself as Missy, was coming to take their order.

"Sorry to put such an abrupt end to the conversation," she said after she'd ordered pancakes and eggs and Cora had ordered a Spanish omelet. "I was afraid Missy might overhear us. Everyone knows everyone else around here—and even if they don't, most everyone knows Aiyana."

"No problem. I understand."

Difficult though it was, Cora let the conversation drift away from her birth mother to the school and what the coming year would entail. They also discussed some of the more troubled boys.

"How do you deal with those who won't behave?" Cora asked.

"Easy," Darci replied. "I threaten to send them to Elijah."

Cora put down her fork and took a drink of her orange juice. "Why not Aiyana?"

"Elijah tries to spare her anything difficult, anything that might upset or disappoint her. He prefers we get him involved if we need help."

"Elijah's the enforcer."

"Sort of."

"What methods does he use for discipline?"

"The threat of being sent to his office is usually enough. If they do something wrong, they don't want him to find out about it. They care about his good opinion, about getting the chance to be with him for various activities."

"Surely there have been a few who *haven't* cared enough to behave."

"Of course. He barred one boy, Ricky Peterson, from

playing sports and attending the dances and assemblies until he brought up his grades. But then he studied with Ricky for an hour a day. After a few weeks, Ricky was doing better than ever before."

Considering they were talking about a man who called himself a "locked box," Cora thought that was interesting. Apparently, he had plenty of love for the boys—but she'd already noted that when he was on the horseback ride.

She opened her mouth to ask if Darci had ever heard anything about the various women Elijah had been with but caught herself. She couldn't show that much interest, didn't want to give Darci any indication that there was something going on between them. Since they weren't serious, she preferred to keep it on the down low. So she asked about Darci's marriage and divorce, and then she tried to offer some support. But in the back of her mind she couldn't quit thinking about Elijah and the role he played on the ranch. Aiyana remained on her mind, as well. Her biological mother was such an enigma. Why wouldn't she marry Cal?

Cora had just stepped out of the shower when she heard a knock at the door. Assuming it was Doug, since he'd caught her when she got back from breakfast to say he had some fresh vegetables he planned to gather from his garden and bring over, she groaned and started to grab some clothes so that she could get dressed. Then she realized she'd have a much better excuse not to invite him in if she answered in her robe.

Prepared to thank him and quickly send him on his way, she pasted a smile on her face and cracked open the door. But it wasn't her neighbor, it was Elijah. He stood on her stoop in a pair of faded jeans, his tan, muscular arms stretching the sleeves of his red New Horizons T-shirt as he tossed his keys from hand to hand.

"Hello," she said, blinking in surprise.

His gaze lowered to her robe. "Just getting up?"

"No. I met Darci in town for breakfast and didn't have time to get ready beforehand, so I just showered." She'd also done a conditioning treatment on her hair, given herself a mani-pedi and rubbed her whole body with some vanilla-scented lotion. She told herself she wanted to look and feel her best to start her new job, that she was doing this as a matter of routine. But she knew Elijah had more to do with it than she cared to admit.

His lips curved into a devilish smile. "Then I'd say my timing is perfect."

Not only was he smiling freely, he was smiling at *her*. "For..."

"I owe you a little something, remember?"

Slightly concerned by how easily he could make her knees weak, since she was supposed to be keeping some emotional distance in this relationship, Cora drew a steadying breath. "You don't owe me anything."

He reached out and tugged on her belt to loosen it, so she stepped back to let him inside. The last thing she needed was for someone to drive by and see them. "You don't think it's too risky to come to my house during the day? If you're not careful the whole school will be talking about us."

"What do you mean? It's much safer to come during the day. Then it doesn't look like we're trying to hide anything."

That made sense, but the fact that her robe was coming open also made it difficult to think. He continued to pull on her belt—slowly so she'd have time to stop him if she wanted. But she didn't stop him, and soon the belt fell to the ground.

Suddenly nervous, she wet her lips as she stared up at him. "So now it's my turn, huh?"

"Unless you have other plans for the next hour or so..."

Cora felt she should come up with something. Put this off, at least until she could regain her perspective. She shouldn't be this excited.

On the other hand, she'd just spent two hours getting ready to see him—and here he was.

Dipping his head, he kissed her long and slow as he slid his big hands inside her robe and gripped her waist.

He wasn't holding back today. Last night had convinced him that she wasn't skittish, wasn't going to bail out too easily. "I take it you don't want to…to talk first," she said.

"No. I'm not interested in talking."

Cora found it quite erotic that she was naked while he was fully dressed. She also liked his level of focus. "So there'd be no point in putting on my clothes."

"Why make me take them off again?" He hoisted her up onto the dining table, putting her on her back.

She caught the lapels of her robe so it wouldn't fall *completely* open. The soft terry cloth was beginning to feel like a safety blanket. But he pulled the fabric out of her grasp and ran his fingers over her bare stomach and breasts.

Cora shuddered as a ripple of pleasure went through her.

"You like that?" He continued his light touch, skimming up her neck to her face, where he ran his thumb over her bottom lip. "You're so beautiful."

The compliment surprised her. He wasn't much for that sort of thing. She told herself not to take him too seriously, but at the same time she caught his hand and pulled his thumb into her mouth.

His pupils flared as her tongue moved over his skin, and he lowered his mouth to her breast.

Every nerve seemed to fire at once; she'd never been more aroused.

"Now I see how convenient a Brazilian makes everything," he said as his mouth moved down her stomach. "Easy access. I like that."

Cora couldn't even speak. His hands were on her hips, and he was pulling her toward him, spreading her legs so he could fit between her knees. "Maybe…maybe we should wait until we know each other better for this," she said, finding her voice.

"Because…"

"Because it…it makes me *really* self-conscious."

"You don't have to be self-conscious with me."

He bent his head. When she felt his tongue, she nearly jumped off the table.

"It's okay," he murmured, his breath warm. "Relax. This is going to be fun."

The next few minutes were more than fun; they were mind-blowing. Cora drew in a deep breath and closed her eyes as he used his mouth in a way she'd never experienced before. The sucking motion was so subtle, so gentle and so incredibly effective that her legs began to quiver. She felt his hand rub one of them, as if in encouragement, before that hand slid back up to her breast.

She was seconds away from the best climax of her life. Cora felt the escalation, the compulsion of her body to reach that pinnacle.

Then the doorbell rang.

Trying to force her sluggish brain to work as it usually did, she started to get up. She thought Elijah would stop so she could deal with her guest, especially because his truck was outside. They couldn't be caught doing something like this. It wouldn't look good. But he muttered a gruff, "No!" and held her that much more tightly as he continued his ministrations.

He was so insistent that she let her head fall back and reached for the sides of the table. She had to hold on to something…

"Cora, you there?"

Doug. Of course. He *would* show up at the worst possible moment.

"The door!" she whispered emphatically, but Elijah wouldn't let Doug take this away from her. She felt his beard growth on her thighs as he shook his head in refusal.

Fortunately, the climax she'd been chasing burst upon her soon after, despite the fact that Doug knocked again.

After Elijah heard her gasp and felt her body jerk, he straightened in satisfaction. He'd given her one hell of a climax. She could tell that had been his goal, but he didn't seem pleased. "Damn him," he grumbled, his voice low as he scooped her off the table, set her on her feet and bent to retrieve the belt to her robe.

"What should we do?" Her mind scrambled to decide how best to explain Elijah's presence, her disheveled appearance and their delay.

After a brief hesitation, he took charge. "She's in the shower," he called out, turning her toward the bedroom and giving her a little push.

As she hurried down the hall, he headed for the door.

"When I got here, she yelled for me to come in," she heard him say as soon as she was safely behind the closed door of her bedroom. "But I've been waiting for fifteen minutes, and she's not out yet. So you might want to leave those here or come back later. I'm going to come back myself."

Doug said something in reply. Cora couldn't make it out. His voice wasn't as strident as Elijah's. Then there was silence, and when she peeked out, they were both gone.

Smooth move, she texted to Elijah.

What I did with Doug or before? came his response.

Although she could tell he was teasing, his words let her know he was still very much fixated on what had occurred—and she couldn't blame him. She was having a hard time forgetting about it herself, and she was the one who'd at least been satisfied. Pretty proud of yourself, huh?

That felt good—even to me.

Lol. I won't lie. You could win an award with that technique.

Glad to hear it. Then maybe you'll see me again tonight.

She could only imagine how aroused he'd been when he'd had to leave. Being interrupted at that point was never fun. But she wasn't sure they should continue what they'd started. She'd been thinking of this fling in such a harmless way. She'd presented seeing Elijah to Aiyana in a harmless way. And yet…spending more time with him was beginning to feel dangerous.

Can't. Going to LA to see my folks.

Until that moment, she hadn't planned on returning home. She was essentially running away. But she knew where she'd spend the night if she didn't get out of Silver Springs, and she needed to put on the brakes, gain some perspective, rethink what they were doing. The tenderness she felt at any thought of him frightened her. This wasn't nearly as casual as she'd imagined.

When will you be back?

Tomorrow night.

Call me when you get in.

Okay, she wrote back. But she didn't return until it was late—too late to consider seeing him before school started the following morning.

Chapter Nine

Eli had never had trouble concentrating. Not since he'd overcome what he'd been through as a child and grown into an adult. He was so focused on his job and the boys he served that there were days when he almost forgot to eat. Work was what he enjoyed, what kept him going and looking forward to each new day. He was especially busy this time of year, when there was so much to do in order to get the semester started off right.

On top of that, his two youngest brothers were back, and Dallas, the middle brother who'd taken them climbing in Yosemite, was temporarily visiting. The following week, Eli spent most of his evenings with them, which he enjoyed, but he often found his mind drifting when it shouldn't. He kept remembering what it had been like to make love to Cora, felt such a strong craving to be with her again he couldn't help watching for her whenever he was on campus. She'd texted him when she left LA last Sunday night but only to let him know she'd be getting back too late to see him. With Dallas in town, Eli hadn't thought much of it. He'd told her to let him know when she'd be available, which indicated he wanted to see her again, but he hadn't heard from her in six days. He wasn't sure what she was thinking. Although she'd smile and wave if she happened to bump into him—she wasn't *un*friendly—she'd turn away right after, wouldn't really meet his eyes. And she never called him or reached out to him, even at night. Since Dallas was staying at the big house with Aiyana, Liam and Bentley, they *could've* seen each other despite Dallas's presence on the ranch, if she'd acted interested.

Eli had almost stopped by her place a dozen times. He would have at least called her, but he could tell that something was different. She'd withdrawn. He wanted to believe she was just busy. Being a new teacher, *any* teacher, the first week of school was stressful. He needed to give her time to settle in, couldn't expect to take priority over her work. From what he could tell, she was dedicated to her students and intent on getting to know them. Since he was the one who'd hired her, and he'd chosen her over a candidate most others had expected to get the job, he wanted her to excel. He'd heard from several of the boys that she was already well liked, which gave him hope. But when he saw her at their first football game last night, and she still didn't reach out to him afterward, like he'd thought she might with the weekend before them, he knew it was more than her job that was keeping her away.

She'd decided she wouldn't see him again. Why? What had made her change her mind? Had she decided a strictly physical relationship wasn't worth it? Had she gotten back with her boyfriend? Or…what?

"Hey, where are you tonight, man?"

Eli blinked and drew his attention back to Dallas and Gavin, who'd dragged him to the bar. He didn't come here often, was careful about how much he drank. Although drinking could wipe out the painful thoughts and memories that plagued him, it could also rob him of his functionality. And he was determined to show the boys he worked with how to overcome that temptation, not fall right into it.

"Sorry, what'd you say?" he asked Dallas, who'd broken into his thoughts.

Dallas finished his last swallow of beer. "You're a million miles away. I was wondering what you were thinking."

Eli lifted his own glass. "I'm thinking Freddy Nance deserves to play ahead of Jason Peachtree."

"Do you have any idea what the heck he's talking about?" Dallas looked to Gavin for an explanation.

"Cougar football," Gavin replied. "Freddy and Jason are both hoping to make first-string quarterback at New Horizons."

"Jason's so gifted," Eli said. "But Freddy's willing to work twice as hard. That counts for more, in my book."

Dallas shook his head. "I swear, big brother. You need to get off that campus a little more often. Look at the chicks here, man. Have some fun."

Dallas's childhood hadn't been any better than Elijah's. After a relatively normal life, he'd watched his father come unhinged and shoot his mother and his sister, and attempt to shoot him before he managed to run out of the house. When the police came, they found that his father had turned the gun on himself. While Eli used work to anesthetize him from his past, Dallas deadened the painful memories he carried with sex when he wasn't climbing and adrenaline when he was. Eli was fairly certain, of the three of them, Aiyana worried about him the most. Eli did, too. Although Gavin had been abandoned at six years old in a park, he seemed to cope better with life.

Or maybe he just pretended to.

"I try to leave the women alone," Eli said.

"Because..."

"Because I'll wreck their life. I should come with a warning label."

"It's only sex, man. As long as it's consensual and doesn't get too crazy, sex never hurt anybody."

"You forget," Eli said drily. "This is a small town. There's no way not to run into the same woman over and over."

"You can't do that sort of thing here," Gavin grumbled in agreement.

"Then you *both* need to get off that ranch a little more often. Drive to LA."

"If we slept with as many women as you do—" Gavin started, but Dallas cut him off.

"You'd have some fun for a change."

Eli rolled his eyes. "Or wind up with a disease."

"Not if you're careful."

"I don't get the impression you're as careful as you should be—about anything," Eli joked, but if Dallas answered, he didn't hear it. He felt his smile wilt the second he glanced up and saw Cora walk into the bar with Darci Spinoza.

She didn't notice him, not at first. But it didn't take long. Those wide, innocent eyes of hers, busy scanning the tables along the periphery of the dance floor as she looked for a place where they could sit down, stopped the second they encountered him—and recognition dawned.

To her credit, she and Darci walked over to say hello. Actually, Cora didn't really have any choice—neither one of them did. He was their boss, after all. It would've been rude to ignore him.

Fortunately, Darci didn't seem to know anything had ever happened between him and Cora. "Hey." She grinned at Dallas. "Look who's in town—trouble!"

"You know me already," Dallas responded. "It's great to see you again. You're Darci, right? The English teacher?"

They'd met at the school Christmas party. Aiyana insisted that the entire family get together for the holidays—no matter what they had going.

"Yes," Darci replied. "It's great to see you, too."

Dallas slid off his stool and stood, his gaze shifting to Cora. Eli could tell he found her attractive. "I don't believe I've ever seen *you* before."

"I noticed you at the football game last night, down on the field with Eli."

"If only I would've known *you'd* be in the stands," he said.

Darci introduced Cora, and Cora smiled politely as she

shook first with Dallas and then Gavin. "Nice to meet you both."

"You must know Eli," Dallas said.

"Yes. Eli hired me."

"I can see why." Dallas pulled over a stool and began looking for a second one. "Any chance you'd like to join us?"

Cora started to decline. She looked as though she couldn't get away fast enough. But Darci didn't seem to be paying any attention to her discomfort. She overrode Cora's response with an eager, "Sure. Why not? We were looking for some entertainment."

Gavin pulled over another chair while Dallas gave her a bow. "We're happy to provide that, aren't we, boys?"

Darci took the seat closest to Dallas, which left the stool between Eli and Gavin for Cora. She sat down, but Eli got the impression she was being careful not to touch him, even incidentally.

Darci and Cora ordered a drink. Then they all talked for an hour—about Dallas's climbing, the places he'd visited, that he'd be leaving in three days, the fact that Seth, another brother who was a sculptor, had secured a gallery showing in San Francisco, one he'd been working hard to parlay into a second and third showing in Chicago and New York, which was why he hadn't visited this summer as he'd originally intended.

Darci brought up her kids and her divorce and how much better she was feeling now that she was getting beyond it, but Cora didn't say much. She mostly listened—and focused on Dallas or Gavin, anyone but him. When Dallas asked her to dance, she agreed, but Eli had a difficult time watching. He didn't care to consider the reason.

Eventually, while they were having a second drink, she mumbled something about having to go to the bathroom and crossed to the far side of the bar, where the restrooms were located. Eli held off for a few seconds, so it wouldn't appear as if they were going together. Then he followed her and waited in the hallway until she came out.

She took one look at him and stopped.

"Have I done something to offend you?" he asked.

"Of course not."

"Then why haven't I heard from you?"

"No reason," she said. "I've been…busy. I figured you were, too."

He shoved a hand through his hair. He was so confused by her abrupt reversal. "You didn't get back with your boyfriend when you went to LA last weekend…"

She shook her head. "Didn't even see him. I went to my folks'."

"So…what is it?" he asked. "*Something*'s different."

"Nothing. Not really. I just… I think you were right."

A trickle of foreboding went through him. "About…"

"You're my boss. It isn't wise to get so intimately…*involved* when we work together."

That wasn't the reason she'd stepped back; he could tell. "So… I screwed up somehow. You don't want to see me anymore."

She rubbed her forehead. "You didn't screw up."

"I must've done something, because I thought everything went…well. Better than well. *Great.*" He lowered his voice in case someone else happened upon them. "Maybe I came too soon that first time and disappointed you, and you have every right to be frustrated that I wouldn't be more sensitive to *your* pleasure, but I hadn't been with anyone in a long time. That isn't how I usually behave. Trust me. I'll make sure it doesn't happen again."

"I'm not like that, Eli. I *wanted* you to come—to do whatever you were compelled to do. That first time has nothing to do with it."

"Then there's something else…"

She said nothing, so he stepped closer.

"I'd really appreciate it if you'd take two seconds to explain, so I don't have to keep wondering why everything was fine and then..."

After tucking her hair behind her ears, she lifted her chin to confront him. "Being with you *did* go well. *Too* well. Every night before I go to sleep, you're all I can think about—the way you touched me, the way you kissed me. Even the way you *smell*."

"So why are you stonewalling me?" he asked, stunned.

"I'm trying to do us both a favor, okay?"

He spread out his hands. "By rejecting me?"

"By adhering to our original agreement! You wanted to keep it strictly physical."

"So did you!"

"Yes, but—"

"Physical means we touch each other."

"Except I *feel* something! I know it's crazy. We just met. But you were right in the beginning. I can't do it," she said and brushed past him.

Cora wished she could go home. Sitting next to Eli, talking and laughing with his brothers, certainly didn't make her want him any less. She'd thought her admission in the hallway would scare him away, or at least make her feel so exposed *that* would douse the flames. But the way he watched her only made her crave his hands on her body more with each passing second. Sexual energy all but crackled through the air between them like electricity.

How could she become infatuated with someone so quickly? Especially when she'd only ever been lukewarm with her previous partners?

Her ex-boyfriend would've given *anything* to be able to make her feel even half as much...

Her response to Eli was a mystery—an ironic mystery. After being so cavalier with him that night when he brought Doug home, she was getting what she deserved, having to eat her words. And, to make it all worse, she couldn't slip out of the bar to escape the tension between her and the man sitting next to her. Forcing Darci to leave when she was having so much fun would be too selfish. After what Darci had been through, this was the kind of thing she needed. A night that was carefree and fun. The chance to talk and laugh and forget the difficulties of the past year. Darci was enjoying every moment and didn't seem to notice that Cora sat on pins and needles.

"Dance with me."

Dallas had danced with her twice before, but this was Eli. He hadn't danced with anyone yet, and because he'd asked in front of his brothers, she didn't feel as if she could refuse him.

"Go dance!" Darci said before she could respond, and she got up and let him lead her onto the floor.

Rihanna's "Stay" was playing as he looped his arms around her back. She tried to resist getting too close but gave up on that the moment his hands slid up her back. He was coaxing her to relax, which made it impossible to resist the temptation to melt into him.

"Why are you doing this?" she asked as they swayed to the music.

"Why am I doing what?"

His breath was warm against her ear. "Tempting fate."

"Because it's too late to back away now. We're already in this."

"It's not too late."

As he brought his head up, his lips brushed her neck. To the casual observer that move probably looked inadvertent, but *she* understood he'd done it on purpose—and felt a corresponding sizzle zip through her.

"You think we're going to be able to fight what we feel for a whole year?" he murmured.

What else could they do? He was Aiyana's son! The only reason she'd let herself go as far as she did was because she'd assumed she'd be able to remain somewhat objective. Now that she'd spent some time with him, however, she had to acknowledge that it wasn't going to be easy come, easy go.

"We can try."

"As far as I'm concerned that'll be a frustrating exercise in futility," he said. "I'm already going crazy."

She hated that she'd started something and was refusing to finish it. That didn't seem quite fair. Maybe she needed to let this play out. She'd never gotten involved in a relationship that was more physical than anything else. That meant the attraction might be explosive at first, but would eventually burn itself out, didn't it?

If so, she was worried about nothing.

"To be honest, so am I," she admitted. "So...where can we go?"

"You mean later? What's wrong with my place?"

"I mean *now*," she told him.

He pulled back to look at her. "Are you serious?"

She could already taste his kiss, had committed every detail about him to memory. "Do you have a problem with that?"

"Absolutely not," he replied. "Make your way out back. There's a side patio where smokers go that should be fairly deserted. I'll be there in a few."

Since they didn't want to be caught together, this was a risky endeavor. That she was willing to take such a gamble surprised Cora. It wasn't like her. But nothing she'd done with Elijah so far had been like her and, in this instance, the need for privacy couldn't outweigh the urgency to feel him inside her. After battling that desire for a whole week, she was more than ready to surrender.

When Eli returned to the table, Darci looked up at him in surprise. "Where's Cora?"

"She went to the bathroom."

"Again?"

He shrugged as if he hadn't asked for details, and, as soon as she was distracted by something Dallas said, he nudged Gavin. "Why don't you ask Darci to dance?" he murmured.

Gavin seemed startled by this atypical request, but Eli had spoken low and used a tone that suggested he not question it, and Gavin didn't.

As soon as Gavin and Darci walked away, Eli leaned close to Dallas. "I'm going out back," he said. "Keep Darci occupied, will ya?"

"Keep her occupied?" Dallas repeated.

"Make sure she doesn't go looking for Cora."

Dallas sat up straight. "What are you two going to be doing?"

When Eli didn't answer, his brother swore under his breath. "No way! I've been flirting with her all night, with zero results. You dance with her once, and she goes outside with you?"

"It's not like that," he said.

"Then what's it like?"

Eli lifted his beer. "None of your business. Just take care of Darci, okay?"

"Sure. What are brothers for?" he replied. "But isn't Cora your new art teacher? Is that okay? Because I'll step in for you if it isn't," he joked.

"Like hell you will," Eli grumbled and tossed back what was left in his glass before making his way to the door leading to the patio and the parking lot beyond.

Cora was waiting for him near the vine-covered trellis. Two guys were smoking on the far side of the patio, but they were so deep in conversation they weren't paying any attention. Taking Cora's hand, he quietly led her to the back of the building, which faced nothing except a wide expanse of farmland.

"On second thought, maybe this is a little reckless," she said as he pressed her up against the building.

It had taken him long enough to join her that she'd grown nervous. He could tell. "Apparently, you need a little recklessness in your life."

"Because..."

He kissed his way up her neck. "It's exciting."

"Being reckless is a good way to get burned."

Threading his fingers through hers, he held her hands above her head. "Like I said, we're in it now."

"And if someone comes out?"

"They won't."

"How do you know?"

"I told my brothers to see to it."

Her eyes widened. "You did *what*?"

"I didn't want you to worry about Darci."

"But...what must your brothers think?"

"It doesn't matter."

"It does to me!" she said. "I'm embarrassed!"

"I'm sorry. It was either that or risk having Darci come looking for you. I figured that would be *more* embarrassing, and I knew I could trust my brothers to make sure that didn't happen."

He was afraid she was going to leave. He held his breath as she stared up at him, and bit back a curse when she pulled away. But after taking a few steps, she turned back and grabbed him by the shirtfront, pulling him up against her again. "This is crazy. Look at us! We're behind a *bar*. And somehow that's not enough to stop me. What you told your brothers isn't enough to stop me, either. Because I've never wanted anyone like I want you."

He let his breath go in relief. "Hallelujah. Then I suggest you relax," he said and slid his hand up her skirt.

* * *

Cora told herself that she should care more about the fact that Dallas and Gavin knew what was going on—and that Darci could easily figure it out. But the kiss Elijah gave her was so achingly sweet that the last thing she wanted to do was walk away. This was a new side of him, one she hadn't seen before.

"I *love* the way you touch me." She'd anticipated coming together in the same heady rush they'd experienced before. They'd both felt the same chemistry on the dance floor. But tonight Eli was taking his time.

"Then you needed this reminder. Maybe it means you won't ignore me this week."

"You could've called *me*," she said as his mouth found her earlobe.

"I was getting signals that precluded that."

"I don't remember sending any signals."

"You wouldn't even look at me."

"Because I knew where it would lead."

"To this."

"Yes."

"Is that a problem?"

She sighed as he kissed her again. "It doesn't feel like one right now."

His fingers hooked the thin fabric of her thong and began sliding it down her legs. "Why hold back? Like I told you before, I'll give you whatever you ask for."

Except his heart. He'd made that clear. But, considering the situation, did it really matter? She was only here for the year. And once he found out she was Aiyana's daughter—if she ever decided to tell him—she couldn't imagine he'd be pleased that she'd allowed them to get so intimate without disclosing her true identity.

"Great. Then give me this," she said and undid his pants.

Chapter Ten

Cora had never had sex outside of a bar or any other public place. She'd heard of other women doing things like that, but she'd never dreamed *she'd* be one of them. It was humbling to learn she could be that girl, but…what'd changed? What'd made her do such a thing?

It was Eli. He had such a profound effect on her. That animal magnetism, the immediacy of what they'd done, had been potent. She'd been so aroused, so sensitive to his every touch that she'd been able to climax when he did, making the fifteen minutes they spent outside quite an experience. She'd never forget him holding her up against the building, the moon full overhead as he drove into her, the only sound she could hear above the music filtering out of the building that of their own labored breathing—and then her groan at the end, which he'd quickly smothered with another kiss.

She was having a torrid affair—with her boss. Her ex-boyfriend would be shocked. Her parents would be shocked. Heck, *she* was shocked. She and Eli hadn't even used a condom. They hadn't had one, hadn't come prepared because they hadn't expected anything to happen. They'd been forced to use the withdrawal method.

"Where've you been?" Darci asked once Cora had righted her skirt, smoothed down her hair and returned to the table.

Cora hoped it was too dark to see the blush heating her cheeks. "It's so hot in here." She slid over as Eli joined them. He'd purposely let her go in first so that they wouldn't come back at the same time. "I stepped out for some fresh air, and there were a couple of guys outside, smoking. We got into a conversation."

"Oh. You were gone so long I was about to come looking for you." She lifted her glass to catch the attention of the waitress.

Fortunately, Darci didn't seem suspicious, but Dallas wasn't about to let Cora off quite that easily. "Wasn't it every bit as hot outside?" he asked with a grin that left little question he was messing with her.

Eli shot his brother a warning glance, but there was nothing he could do or say in front of Darci, who turned to look at her in expectation of her response.

"It was…a little warm," Cora said, but the waitress Darci had called over appeared. As soon as Darci turned to speak with her, Cora leaned closer to Dallas. "Actually, after it was all over, I could've used a cigarette myself!"

Dallas burst out laughing and slapped his older brother on the back. "Damn, I like her. She's *definitely* hooking up with the wrong Turner."

"What'd you say?" Darci asked as the waitress left. "Something Turner?"

Dallas clinked his glass against Cora's. "Not Turner, *learner*. I said Cora's a fast learner."

Darci blinked in apparent confusion. "What'd you learn?" she asked Cora but Eli dragged Cora onto the dance floor to save her from answering.

Cora was fairly certain she'd never had more fun. On some level, she knew she was screwing up her life. She was so taken with Eli, too taken for it to be safe. But she could hardly feel bad about what she was doing when she was still in the middle of it. She, Darci and the Turner boys talked, laughed and danced until the bar closed. Then Eli drove them all home, since he'd had much less to drink—barely two beers. Although Cora wasn't much of a drinker herself, she'd been feeling more carefree than usual. After her stint outside with Eli, she'd quit holding back and simply cut loose. If she was going to regret this night, she figured she might as well go all the way.

Eli dropped Darci and Gavin off first, since they both lived in town. Cora would have to reclaim her SUV in the morning, but she was so happy and tired when she got home that she wasn't worried about that or anything else.

After Eli pulled into her driveway, he walked her to the door. Dallas was probably watching from the truck as he kissed her, but she didn't care about that any more than anything else tonight—and just to prove it, she pulled Eli back and kissed him a second time before letting him go. "You are *so* hot!" she said.

"And you are so drunk," he responded with a laugh.

"I'm not drunk. I mean…not *that* drunk."

"Yeah, you are."

"I'll never forget tonight."

A thoughtful expression claimed his face as his gaze moved over her. "Neither will I," he said. "But you'd better go inside if you don't want your neighbors peering out to see what you're up to."

She let him go, but once she was inside, she twirled around the living room, reliving the evening before falling onto her bed. "What a night," she said aloud. She thought Eli might come back after he took Dallas to Aiyana's. She wanted him to. But if he tried to knock, she didn't hear it. She fell asleep before she could even take off her clothes, and when she woke up, it was late morning.

Reluctant to roll out of bed, she checked her phone—and found she'd missed several calls since she'd paid any attention to that sort of thing last, which was before she'd gone to the bar. Her brother. Her mother. Jill. She'd even missed a call from Aiyana.

Expecting a nasty headache to hit as soon as she sat up,

she moved gingerly at first, but she wasn't as hungover as she'd thought she might be. She deserved worse.

With a yawn, she shoved her hair out of her face and put her phone on speaker so she could listen to her messages with minimum effort while sitting on the bed.

Her mom: "Call me when you get a chance, honey. I found the cutest dress for your birthday, but it's expensive so I'd like you to try it on before I buy it. When will you be coming home?"

Cora smiled in affection. Her birthday wasn't for six months, but her mother bought her stuff all year long.

Her brother: "Just calling to see how my baby sister's doing. I'll be in New York for a few weeks trying to line up the financing for my next film, so don't panic if you don't hear from me. I'll check in when I get back."

She hated that she'd missed his call. Ashton was always so busy these days.

Jill: "So how's Silver Springs? I was hoping to come visit you next weekend, like we talked about, but Todd's grandmother will be celebrating her ninetieth birthday in Palm Springs, and he wants me to go with him. Give me a call so we can set another date."

She'd never told Jill that she'd slept with Eli. She'd decided it didn't make sense to tell anyone since she wasn't going to be with him again.

So much for that…

Aiyana: "Hi, Cora. Sorry for the late notice, but I was wondering if you'd be able to join the boys and me for dinner tomorrow. I'd love the opportunity to get to know you better."

Cora hungered for the opportunity to get to know her better, too. But by boys, did Aiyana mean Eli and possibly Gavin and Dallas? Or was she talking strictly about the two youngest Turners—the ones living at home?

Cora sighed as she stared at her phone. She hesitated

to put Eli in an awkward situation by showing up at his family dinner, but… Aiyana was the whole reason she'd come to Silver Springs. She wanted to accept the invitation.

After mulling it over, she texted him. Your mother has invited me to dinner today. Will you be there?

His response came almost right away. Yes.

Is it okay if I accept?

Why wouldn't it be?

Because she wouldn't be attending in the capacity they thought—as merely a new teacher at the ranch. She was excited to see how Aiyana lived, felt Aiyana's house and the items in it might reveal more about who her biological mother was and what her life had been like. At a minimum, she'd probably be treated to pictures of her grandparents and uncles, maybe even some of the places Aiyana had lived in the past.

But Eli didn't know that her interest extended beyond what she'd stated in her interview.

I don't want to intrude on your time with your family.

You won't be intruding.

She thought he'd leave it at that, but he texted her again a few minutes later.

When do you want to get your car?

In an hour or so? I was about to take a shower.

No problem. I can wait.

She put her phone on the nightstand only to hear it signal another text.

This was from Eli, too: Better yet, why don't I join you?

Aiyana must've said something to Doug Maggleby, even though she'd said she wouldn't, because he'd been less intrusive the past week. Or maybe he was getting the hint. Regardless, Cora was relieved that Doug wasn't there hoping to talk to her every time she walked out her front door, but she still didn't want him to see Eli's truck sitting outside. You can't park in front. We'll have to be more careful or people are going to get the wrong idea.

You mean they might get the right idea.

She couldn't help laughing. Basically.

Well, we can't have that. I'll walk over and slip in. No one will see me.

Oh boy. She was about to sink even further into her "torrid affair." But there wasn't a darn thing she could do about it. Even if she said no now, she knew she'd say yes later.

I'll leave the back door unlocked.

"Damn, I'm glad I hired you," Eli joked as they dropped onto her bed after thirty minutes of the best shower sex she'd ever had. "But since we seem to make love in a vertical position more often than not, I'd better spend more time at the gym. My arms feel like they're about to fall off."

She leaned on one elbow so she could smile down at him. "You didn't seem to be struggling."

"Are you kidding? You weigh a ton."

The twinkle in his eye confirmed that he was teasing

her. "You said you like my body! You said it was the hottest body you've ever seen."

"Heat of the moment," he scoffed, but one finger traced her breast as if he'd meant every word.

"Fine." She knocked his hand away. "I guess I'll have to find someone who's more...appreciative of my physical appearance."

In a quick, easy motion, he rolled her onto her back, straddled her hips and pinned her arms above her head. "No way. You're mine for the entire year, remember? And I plan to make the most of it."

He'd already proved that... "Do you think we're really going to be able to pull this off?" she asked. "Without people finding out, I mean? Without it turning into a big deal that...that comes to the attention of your mother?"

He bent his head to nuzzle her neck. "No doubt there will be talk."

"You're not concerned?"

Slowly, he kissed his way up to her mouth. "Not concerned enough to stay away."

"So what do you propose we do?"

"Ignore it. As long as we're both performing at our jobs, we shouldn't have any problem."

"Maybe I should go on the pill..."

He lifted his head at her abrupt change of subject. "Would you mind? I'm willing to be responsible for birth control, but I admit I'd love to be able to come inside you."

She hated the way her heart seemed to beat in double time as she gazed up at him. She was getting in too deep. He'd told her he wasn't capable of opening up, of making her feel loved and validated.

Was she about to learn what his other girlfriends had learned?

"Cora? Would you mind?" he repeated eagerly.

She drew a bolstering breath. "No."

* * *

A bead of sweat rolled down between Cora's shoulder blades as she stood on the wraparound porch of the large, two-story ranch house that belonged to Aiyana. A gusty breeze tossed her hair around, and she'd worn a light, flowery sundress, so she wasn't overly warm; she was battling nerves.

"Relax," she muttered as she knocked. She'd seen Aiyana's home before, from a distance. Although built on the periphery of the ranch, it wasn't far from the administration building.

Aiyana answered the door. Eli's truck was already in the drive. Cora saw him the moment Aiyana showed her in, but she barely allowed her glance to skim over him as Aiyana introduced her to Dallas and Gavin, both of whom she'd met, of course, and Liam and Bentley. Cora had Liam as a student in one of her classes, so she was familiar with him, too. A tall, gangly boy with a bit of acne, he excelled in basketball, from what she'd heard. She'd only ever seen Bentley, who was African American, on the football field.

She handed the wine she'd brought to Aiyana as she said hello to everyone else.

Eli offered to pour her a drink, but she declined. After imbibing so much at the bar last night, she wasn't interested in more alcohol. She accepted a bottle of water instead while listening to Liam complain about how much trouble he was having with the self-portrait he'd been assigned in her class. After some small talk with the others, she went up to his room to help with it while Aiyana put the finishing touches on dinner.

Leaving the kitchen and dining area gave Cora a chance to see more of the house. As she would've expected, every room was clean and tastefully decorated. Aiyana had pictures of her boys all over the place—senior portraits, family portraits and candid shots from their various sports. She saw a few of Eli. Like Bentley, he'd played football. But it wasn't until after she'd helped Liam and set him to finishing the rest of the assignment on his own that she was able to look over those pictures more carefully.

She wandered down the hall, eventually winding up in the living room. She could hear Aiyana banging around in the kitchen and the boys watching TV in the great room but wasn't in any hurry to return to the group, especially when she spotted the family photograph she'd been hoping to see of Aiyana with her parents and brothers. It was framed and sitting on an old 1960s piano.

She'd just picked up that picture when she heard someone come into the room behind her.

She turned to see Eli.

"You're all finished with Liam?"

"I am. He's still upstairs working, but I figured I should make him do as much as possible." She almost put down the photograph. She felt guilty snooping around but was too curious about the people in that photograph, and her connection to them, not to take advantage of the opportunity. "These are your grandparents?" she asked, indicating the couple in the middle.

"Yeah. Hank and Consuelo."

"Your mother mentioned that Consuelo is a Nicaraguan immigrant."

"That's true. She had one son when her husband left her to come to America. He promised he'd make a better life, then send for them."

"And?"

"She never heard from him again."

Cora felt her jaw drop. "He moved on without her?"

"He was killed trying to swim across the Rio Grande to reach Texas. She came looking for him as soon as she could cobble together the money. But she couldn't find him. It was two years before she learned what happened. By then she was living in a small shack on Hank's farm with her son—German, who was six at the time—picking fruit."

"And Hank fell in love with her?"

"Eventually. Consuelo married two other guys first, Aiyana's father, who was an abusive jerk, and another man with whom she had her last two boys. That didn't work out, either. He walked out on her or something."

"Then she married Hank. So Hank's her fourth husband?"

A fond smile curved Eli's lips. "Yes. She finally got it right."

"How'd they get together?"

"He says he fell in love with her cooking first. Her third husband wouldn't pay his child support, so, to get by, she'd make homemade tortillas and tamales to sell on the weekends. Hank would come to her stand first thing Sunday morning, which was her only day off, and buy almost everything she had."

"Wow. He *must've* loved her cooking."

"That wasn't all there was to it. He couldn't have eaten that many tortillas and tamales. Once they started dating, she found he had a whole freezer full."

Cora laughed. "What a story!"

"I've never seen a man adore a woman more than Hank adores Consuelo."

His wistful expression caught Cora's attention. He loved them almost as much as Aiyana. "So…these three must be your mother's brothers." She pointed at the other men in the photograph.

"Yes." He fingered the one with the darkest skin. "None of the children actually belong to Hank, but he claims them all and loves them as if they do."

For which they should all be so grateful. Eli didn't state that, but the subtext was clear, and that subtext made it difficult for Cora not to bristle. She'd heard a lot of that type of thing herself. "Aiyana's name is unusual. Is it Nicaraguan?"

"Consuelo claims it's Native American for eternal flower. A woman who was part Cherokee came to her rescue one night when she was so hungry and tired she was ready to collapse. German was crying. Neither one of them could go a step farther. So she hid in a barn, hoping to rest before pushing on—only to be discovered by this woman whose name was Aiyana. Consuelo thought she'd be reported or turned out, but Aiyana fed them dinner and gave them a bed to sleep in. To this day, Consuelo says Aiyana was an angel sent from God, that she wasn't really human."

"That's a beautiful story, too."

"Consuelo's lived a challenging but interesting life. Fortunately, other than old age, her worries are behind her. Hank takes care of her every need. Grandma Sway, as we called her growing up, is the one who gave me my horse," he added.

"Atsila?"

"Yeah. Apparently, the Aiyana who helped her had a horse by the same name, which she gave to Consuelo so that Consuelo would have some mode of transportation, and so that German wouldn't have to walk anymore. Without that horse, Consuelo swears she and German would not have survived the next two weeks. Not long after, she had to sell it, which broke her heart, but she claims she would've starved without that money."

"How kind. What does Atsila mean?"

"I don't know. I tried looking it up once but couldn't find anything definitive—other than that it has Native American roots." He came closer and took the picture from her to look more carefully at it himself. "I figure the real meaning doesn't matter, anyway. To me, it means compassion."

"I bet the original Aiyana would be proud of her namesake," Cora said. "Your mother seems to be very generous herself."

"Yes. Not only has she helped me and my brothers, she's helped so many."

After what Eli had been subjected to, he'd deserved his own "angel." So did the others. And yet Cora couldn't help feeling rejected, jealous, left out, overlooked...*something* that felt like a knife to the heart. "Has she said why she's never had any biological children?"

"No. I've always assumed that maybe she couldn't."

Cora stood as living proof that Aiyana wasn't infertile. But, of course, she couldn't say anything to refute the assumption. "Darci told me that Cal Buchanon has been in love with her for years."

"They spend a lot of time together, more than she lets on to me or anyone else, if she can help it."

"She must care for him, too."

"I'm pretty sure she does."

"What gives?"

He scratched his neck. "She's afraid of getting hurt, or feels as if devoting herself to a relationship like that will take away from her work or something. I can't figure it out myself. And she won't talk about it." He put the picture back on the piano. "Why does this stuff seem to mean so much to *you*?"

Only then did Cora realize she was being too transparent. Straightening, she forced back the frustration and disappointment, as well as the curiosity she'd manifested so far, and conjured a polite expression. "I didn't mean to give you the impression it was overly important. I was curious, that's all."

Fortunately, he didn't get the chance to question her further. At that point, Aiyana called them to dinner.

Chapter Eleven

During the meal, Dallas tried to tease Cora about last night with a few carefully placed innuendos. But it seemed to Eli that Cora was too distracted and preoccupied to focus on Dallas or what he said, even when he made reference to what'd happened outside the bar. She'd smile or laugh where appropriate, but only Aiyana could claim her full attention. By the end of dinner, after Cora had helped Aiyana put the leftover pot roast, vegetables, mashed potatoes and cheesecake in the fridge and do the dishes, Eli was feeling a bit neglected. He got the distinct impression that she'd come to see his mother, that he had nothing to do with her desire to join them, especially when, instead of watching TV with everyone else, the two women went into the living room and talked for over an hour.

When he got up to fetch a glass of water, or he simply made an effort to listen, he could hear various bits and pieces of their conversation. Most of it was about the ranch—Aiyana's philosophy for the school, the fact that she'd chosen to place New Horizons in Silver Springs because it had wide-open spaces but wasn't too far from a major population center, why she'd adopted each one of her sons and which students she was concerned about this year.

He thought he might finally get a few crumbs of Cora's attention when they rejoined the group—even if it was only a quick, private smile. Instead, as soon as they finished visiting, Cora said she should go, that she had to get ready for her classes in the morning.

They'd made crazy, impromptu, almost animalistic love outside at the bar last night and then again in the shower this morning, but she'd hardly given him the time of day since coming to dinner.

"Thanks so much for having me," she told Aiyana. "You have a lovely home and a wonderful family."

"You're welcome. It's nice to have a little estrogen in the house," she said with a laugh. "You must join us again next Sunday. Dallas won't be here. He leaves on Tuesday. But Eli, Gavin, Liam and Bentley will."

"I'll do that, but only if you let me bring the dessert or another dish."

"I'm sure I could be persuaded," Aiyana told her.

"It was really great to meet you," Cora said to Dallas. "I'm sorry you have to leave town so soon."

"There are mountains to climb," he joked as he got up to hug her goodbye. Eli got off the couch, too, and was standing close enough to hear Dallas whisper something like, "Take good care of my brother."

Whether that was really what Dallas said or not, Cora turned and gave him a dutiful hug, one no different from the kind she'd imparted to everyone else. "Again, thank you."

"Eli, why don't you walk her out?" Aiyana piped up as Cora grabbed her purse.

Eli wasn't sure if that suggestion was as random as Aiyana pretended, but he didn't care. He was eager for a few minutes alone with Cora, so he was grateful his mother had tapped him instead of one of his brothers. "Sure."

"Dinner was wonderful," Cora said as they strolled down the drive side by side, without touching. "Now that my brother and I are adults, my mother doesn't bother to cook anymore. She's very generous about inviting us over for carryout, or taking us to a restaurant, so I'm not complaining. But a big Sunday meal from scratch? That's almost unheard of these days."

"It's not like it was a sacrifice to have you. You can come back next Sunday. You heard my mom."

"I'd like that," she said, but he didn't get the impression he was the reason she'd like it, and that bothered him.

"Are you really going home to get ready for classes?" he asked as he opened her car door for her.

"Yeah. I promised my students we'd start ceramics this week. Now that I'm more familiar with their skill level, I need to figure out the ideal project and how much time it will require on the throwing wheel."

He almost said, *And if I'd like to see you again?* but he got the distinct impression that something was causing her to distance herself from him and he'd be stupid to push.

"You look incredible in that dress," he said instead, which was the truth. Ever since she'd arrived, he'd had difficulty looking anywhere except at her.

He was glad he'd told her that when, at last, she focused on him—and smiled. "Thank you," she said, but she didn't try to set up their next meeting, didn't ask if he'd call, didn't say a word about getting together with him again. "Good night," she added, and that was his signal to close the door.

The TV played in the background as Cora curled up on her couch and thumbed through the file the private investigator had, after much searching, provided on Aiyana. There wasn't a great deal in it, just some basic background information—where and when Aiyana was born, where she grew up, a couple of articles on New Horizons. Thanks to California's adoption laws, Cora had been unable to get the records that were sealed by the court. She'd had an attorney working on that, but because of various details her adoptive mother had let slip—like where and when she was born and at which hospital—the private investigator had come through first. So she'd given up on pursuing the court order. Several states had unsealed their adoption records. She hoped California would soon follow suit. Then maybe she'd be able to find out who her father was—if his name was on her original birth certificate. Adoptees had access only to their ABC or Amended Birth Certificate, which not only facilitated the change in the name of the parents but could list a different place of birth. In some instances, agencies even altered the *day* of birth. Fortunately, Cora hadn't been given a new birthday. Otherwise, chances were she never would've found Aiyana.

Or…maybe that would've been for the best. She'd spoken to several other adoptees, online and otherwise, who'd told her to be careful what she wished for. They'd been disappointed in their birth mothers, but she was not. She respected Aiyana, admired her and wished she could be part of her life in a more significant way than merely working for her. But she couldn't see how she'd ever be able to do that if she was still sleeping with Elijah.

Regardless of Elijah, did she dare—or even have the right—to upset Aiyana's life by announcing her true identity? Would Aiyana be happy to have found her?

That would probably depend on the reason Aiyana had given her up, and there was no file, attorney or private detective who could provide that information. Perhaps her grandmother could shed some light on the matter, but even that wasn't guaranteed. It was possible Consuelo had never been made aware of the pregnancy. Aiyana had had Cora when she was twenty-one, so she'd been an adult but not a well-seasoned one. Maybe Consuelo hadn't approved of the relationship that'd left Aiyana pregnant, and that was part of the reason Aiyana had acted as she did.

After staring at the grainy picture in the newspaper clipping that'd given Cora her first glimpse of Aiyana, she put down the file and picked up her phone. She hadn't yet returned Lilly's call. She needed to do that, didn't want her adoptive mother to feel as if she was being neglected.

"There you are!" her mother exclaimed as soon as she answered. "How are you, sweetheart?"

Cora rubbed her left temple with her free hand. "I'm doing great. How are you, Mom?"

"Missing you. It's not the same without you here. I have no one to go shopping with," she said in a pouty voice that Cora knew was a joke.

"I'll go shopping with you when I visit next."

"Yes. We'll have you try on that dress I found. You're going to love it."

"I'm sure I will."

"Your father and I thought you might come home again this weekend, we're sad when we didn't see you. What'd you do?"

Cora considered mentioning that she'd had dinner at Aiyana's but decided it wasn't necessary. "I've met a new friend—another teacher here at the school named Darci. We went out last night."

"How nice. I'm so relieved you're adjusting. I was afraid you wouldn't like it, and this year would prove long and miserable. I was surprised when you decided to go there instead of accepting the position at Woodbridge. But you don't regret it?"

"No. Not at all," she said, and that was mostly true. If nothing else, the rabid curiosity that'd nearly driven her mad over the years had been appeased, to a point. As she finished talking to her mother she had to admit, however, that she had no idea if she'd regret what she was doing in the end.

Chapter Twelve

Cora knew she shouldn't have accepted when Eli texted her while she was at lunch the following day to see if he could take her horseback riding in the evening. After having dinner at Aiyana's, she was more aware than ever that she was putting them all in a difficult position. She'd decided to back away, had assumed she still had the fortitude—until she heard from him this afternoon and had thrown all of that out the window with a "one more time" excuse.

When he'd explained where to meet him, she'd guessed he was taking her to the same place he'd taken the boys—not that she intended to reveal the fact that she'd seen him here before. He'd been so carefree that day, so…unguarded. That memory was the one thing she planned to take away from this place when school let out—probably because she'd only seen Elijah like that once or twice since, when he was so caught up in their lovemaking that he dropped the aloof mask he wore otherwise. She felt like those moments were the only ones where she got to see the vulnerable heart beneath that rugged chest.

A silver truck towing a white trailer turned off the highway and parked in the clearing where she'd left her car. When she stepped out of the trees and greeted Eli, he responded with an uncharacteristically wide smile, one that suggested he was happy to see her, which made her glad she'd come. He usually kept his emotions more carefully concealed.

"Have you ever ridden before?" he asked as he pulled on a pair of leather gloves.

"Once. In Mexico. It was a four-hour-long trail ride with my family on the beach, and it was beautiful. But my horse was only allowed to walk slowly behind the horse in front."

"That's not really riding."

"After the first hour or so, it got boring," she admitted.

"You'll like this better."

She expected him to be towing two horses, but when he opened the trailer, she saw only Atsila. "We're riding together?"

"Is that okay? I figured if you're not familiar with horses, you might feel more comfortable riding double."

Since all she wanted to do was touch him—didn't care if they ever left the clearing—she had no reason to complain. "No problem."

"Great. I'll let you take the reins whenever."

He led the horse out and lifted Cora into the saddle before securing the truck and the trailer. Then he walked over and swung up behind her.

The warmth of his body made her wish she could turn and kiss him. They'd trained their bodies to expect such contact when they saw each other. She wasn't even sure what they were doing here. She liked the idea of riding, but it felt as if they were wasting what little time they could spend together.

They traveled mostly in silence. Cora got the impression Eli didn't care to talk. He'd answer if she asked a question, but only with a simple yes or no, if possible. There were a few minutes when she took the reins, but as soon as they came to a narrow pass that she wasn't confident in navigating, he took over.

"What made you ask me to go riding?" she asked as they continued to climb the mountain.

"You'll see," he replied, and that was it. Apparently, she was waiting for something. She didn't find out what until they crested the top of the mountain, where the trees thinned, revealing a stunning red-and-gold sunset.

"Wow," she murmured.

He pulled the horse to a stop. "Have you ever seen anything more beautiful?"

If she were being objective, some of the sunsets she'd seen at the beach and around the world were as spectacular. Cognitively, she knew that. But he'd brought her out here because he wanted her to enjoy this, and that made it the best darn sunset in the world. "Not with you," she said.

"What does that mean?"

"It means I'd like it even if it wasn't nearly so beautiful."

One hand came up to catch her chin as he finally kissed her. She wasn't entirely sure how everything went from there. Somehow, in a matter of minutes, they were off the horse and on the ground, their clothes open and askew, kissing and exploring and enjoying what they'd wanted from the first moment they met up.

"You can't be comfortable out here," he said with some regret, as if he hated to stop but felt too much guilt to continue. "I'll take you back down."

"No." Cora wasn't ready to leave. Not yet. When he pulled away to get up, she pressed him onto his back. Then she nibbled at his neck and his bare chest as she moved down—and heard him draw a sharp breath as she took him into her mouth.

They drove home separately, just as they'd come, as if they hadn't been together. Because Eli hadn't said anything about meeting up later, Cora assumed their ride—and what had occurred on it—was the end of their time with each other for today. She spent the next couple of hours getting ready for her classes tomorrow while trying to build up her resistance to him—so she wouldn't melt so quickly when he called or texted her the next time—only to have him surprise her by showing up at her door as she was getting ready for bed.

He didn't explain why he'd come; he didn't need to. He stepped inside as if he had every right and pulled her into his arms. Then it was like the ride earlier, when they couldn't pull each other's clothes off fast enough. She managed to remove his shirt and toss it aside before he kissed her again. Then he lifted her into his arms and she wrapped her legs around his narrow hips and let him carry her into the bedroom, where they fell onto her bed and made love.

On some level, Cora knew their affair was getting out of hand. They couldn't seem to stem the desire they felt for each other—the more he touched her, the more she craved his touch, and he seemed to be every bit as caught in the same web.

What happened to getting satisfied and moving on? she asked herself when it was all over and he was dozing beside her. That had been the original plan, but the opposite seemed to be taking place. Just watching him sleep made her feel so much tenderness it frightened her. She was losing her heart to a man who'd told her he wasn't to be trusted with it.

What am I going to do?

She reached over to push the hair off his forehead, and he opened his eyes. Since it was nearly eleven, she thought he'd get up and leave. They both had to work in the morning. Instead, he drew her into the curve of his body and, after a kiss on her bare shoulder, drifted off again.

Apparently, he didn't feel any pressure to get home at a reasonable hour. Or he was enjoying being with her too much to put an end to it. She preferred to believe the latter, but feared she was building things up in her head—a dangerous practice in its own right.

She wondered where he'd parked his truck, and guessed

that he'd left it at home and walked over. He wasn't stupid, wouldn't be that obvious.

Slowly, she allowed herself to succumb to the comfort and satisfaction of having him there next to her. She was going to be hurt; she had little doubt about that. But it wasn't going to be tonight. She'd merely take their relationship moment by moment, she decided—and the next thing she knew, her alarm was going off the following morning, and Eli was still in her bed.

Since he hadn't reacted to the alarm, she reached over to touch his shoulder. He needed to get out of the house before everyone on campus was up and moving around. But before she could even touch him, someone knocked on the front door.

That brought his head up immediately. "Doug?" he said without preamble.

She bit her lip. "It's only seven. I can't imagine he'd pop over so early."

He scrubbed a hand over his face. "Maybe he has more vegetables."

"He hasn't brought any since the last time. He's been much better about leaving me alone," she said as she got up and hurried to don a robe. She had to answer the door. Whoever it was would know she was home. Her car was in the drive. "Your mother must've spoken to him even though she told me she wouldn't."

"*She* didn't speak to him—*I* did," he said.

She paused to gawk at him. "What did you say?"

"Nothing. I just told him to keep his distance."

She laughed. Of course it would be that simple for him. No glossing over anything, no mincing words. Just the bottom line: *stop*.

"What's so funny?" he asked.

"Nothing." She pulled the belt of her robe tight. "My hair's not *too* crazy, is it?"

He grinned.

"That must be a no."

Whoever was at the door knocked again, causing her to glance toward the living room.

"You look like you've had a busy night," he said, that grin slanting to one side, "but I wouldn't want to make you self-conscious."

"Thanks for doing just that," she whispered in mock outrage but couldn't help betraying herself with a smile of her own. Maybe he wasn't capable of trusting her enough to give her his heart, but he was incredibly good in bed, especially now that they were becoming more comfortable with each other. She also liked these little moments when he revealed that he *did* have a playful side.

"It's a great look on you," he said.

She didn't take the time to answer. "Stay here. And don't make any noise," she said as she left the bedroom.

Once she reached the door, she tried to smooth her hair down one final time as she peered through the peep hole.

It wasn't Doug; it was Aiyana. Cora wanted to alert Eli to the fact that his mother was standing on the stoop, but she'd delayed too long already and couldn't call back for fear Aiyana would hear her through the panel.

Cora could only hope she hadn't come here looking for her son… "Hi," she said as she opened the door.

Aiyana's lips curved into a pleasant smile. "I'm sorry to bother you so early."

"It's no trouble," she said but couldn't help wondering why this couldn't have waited until she was in her classroom. "I was rolling out of bed, anyway."

"I figured you'd be up, what with school starting in little over an hour. There's a guy who looks like he's had a pretty rough night at the administration building, asking for you. I tried to reach you on your cell but couldn't get an answer. Apparently, he's been trying to reach you, too."

She hadn't taken her cell out of her purse last night to charge it. "The battery must be dead. Did this man say who he is?"

"He said you broke up with him when you left LA."

Matt? *Damn...* "I—I'll… Sorry about the random visit. Let me get showered and I'll be right over."

"Would you rather I send him here?"

It was going to be hard enough for Eli to get out of her house without being seen. "No. Um…have him wait there. I'll come as soon as I can."

"Okay." Her gaze shifted to something behind Cora. "Tell my son I said good morning," she added and left.

Cora pivoted to discover Elijah's shirt on the floor. Shoot! Now there would be no pretending that she and Eli were only friends.

Eli came to the doorway, wearing nothing. "What'd she say?"

Cora picked up his shirt and handed it to him. "She said to tell you hello."

To Cora's surprise, he didn't seem to be upset by that. He scratched his head and said, "I mean before that."

"My ex-boyfriend is at the office." Looking like he'd been up all night. *Why?* Cora hadn't spoken to him since moving to Silver Springs.

"What does he want?"

"I have no idea," she replied but realized her phone might provide the answer. She plugged it in and waited for it to charge while Eli dressed. She was just listening to the many messages Matt had left when Eli walked out of the bedroom again.

"You're not coming back to me? I thought we loved each other. But you must never have cared for me the way I cared for you."

Instead of heading to the door, Eli walked over to the counter and listened to Matt's next message along with her.

"You're not going to answer your phone? Seriously? I can hardly breathe now that you're gone. Whatever I did wrong, I'll fix it, okay? I'll change. Just…give me another chance."

Cora clicked away from her voice mail. She figured Eli had heard enough.

"He wants you back," he said.

"Apparently."

He raked his fingers through his hair. "How do *you* feel?"

"I feel bad that I've hurt him."

She knew that wasn't the answer Eli had been looking for, but she didn't care to address anything else. She had to shower, hurry over to see what she could do for Matt and get to class—all before eight thirty.

"You're upset he's here."

"I'm upset that your mother knows about us."

"Because…"

Because Aiyana was her birth mother, and now, if she ever decided to have that conversation, it would be even harder. She was ruining any hope she had of reuniting with Aiyana as the daughter she was! But she hadn't planned on Aiyana having an adopted son she couldn't resist. "I respect her. I don't want her to think poorly of me."

"She doesn't think poorly of you. She likes you."

For some reason, that simple statement nearly made Cora burst into tears. He'd spoken so casually, as if he was saying, "Why would you matter much to her either way?"

Aiyana was her *mother*. She wanted more than the courteous treatment other teachers received.

When she started to blink fast, trying to hold back the tears, he walked over and rested his hands on her shoulders. "I'm sorry I stayed over. If you'll still see me in the future, I'll be more careful."

"I'm not blaming you. This has nothing to do with

you." She could've asked him to go at any moment, but she hadn't—because she'd wanted him to stay right where he was. Her emotional reaction to Aiyana's appearance was about something else, something he couldn't even begin to guess because he, most likely, didn't know his mother had ever had a child of her own.

"Then it's your ex that has you upset."

She dashed a hand across her cheek. "Matt? No. It's nothing."

She could tell he wasn't sure what to say next. "I'm fine," she added.

"I'm sorry," he said again, as if he hated to see her like this, especially because he suspected he might be part of the cause.

"It's nothing, like I said."

"Okay." He had to get to school, too, and she knew it. Although he acted reluctant to walk away at this juncture, he seemed to understand there was nothing more he could do. After pressing a kiss to her forehead, he left.

Chapter Thirteen

The day seemed to last forever. Knowing that Matt was sleeping at her house, waiting for her to get out of school, made Cora glance at the clock—and grind her teeth—over and over. Time seemed to be standing still. She didn't want her ex-boyfriend in Silver Springs, couldn't believe he'd come down here.

As soon as the lunch bell sounded and the students filed out of her classroom, she considered going home. She had thirty minutes or so she could use to talk to Matt. But she preferred to wait until she could sit down with him at length and hash out whatever he felt he needed to go over. Then maybe she could send him on his way knowing that was the end, once and for all.

While she was standing at the window, watching the students who'd already finished their lunch mill about campus, Eli walked in.

"Hey."

She turned and straightened. He'd never come to her room before. "Hi."

"I didn't see you in the cafeteria so…I thought I'd bring you some lunch." He lifted a brown sack.

She'd eaten an apple from her desk drawer. She hadn't had it in her to face him or Aiyana, in case either one of them happened to be in the cafeteria. "I've had too much to do here."

The fact that she'd been staring outside, doing nothing, contradicted that statement, but he didn't point it out. He carried her lunch over to the desk. "You feeling okay?"

"Yeah."

"What happened with Matt?"

"Nothing. Yet. I had to get to my first class, and he looked like he wasn't feeling great, so I told him to sleep until I get out of school."

He rubbed a hand over his smooth-shaven chin. "You'll talk to him when you get home."

"Yes." She peered into the sack to find a turkey sandwich, some celery and carrot sticks and a big chocolate chip cookie. "This is very nice of you. Thank you."

"No problem."

He didn't seem to be in any hurry to leave.

"Did your mother say anything to you about this morning?" she asked as she broke off part of the cookie.

"We've been too busy."

"*Will* she say something?"

"I doubt it. For the most part, she's pretty good about minding her own business."

Cora wondered about his biological mother. Did he ever hear from her? Did he care about her—*could* he care? "Aiyana seems really great."

"She is." He checked his watch. "I've got to go."

"Thanks for stopping by."

He hesitated at the door. "Will you call me when Matt's gone?"

"I don't know," she admitted.

"Nothing's changed, Cora," he said.

What was he talking about? *Everything* had changed. She was falling in love with him, which was exactly what he'd warned her not to do. And Matt knew about Aiyana! If she didn't handle him carefully enough, he could tell everyone what she was *really* doing in Silver Springs. "There have to be other girls you can…be with. You might have to drive to LA once in a while, but someone like you… you'd have no problem getting laid."

He winced as if she'd slapped him. "I never said the

person I was with didn't matter—that it could be anyone. And I hope I haven't treated you that way."

He hadn't. He'd been a dream lover—as considerate and kind as she could ever expect him to be. He'd also been clear about his limitations. Despite all her big talk, *she* was the one who couldn't seem to live up to their agreement.

She opened her mouth to apologize, but it was too late. He was gone.

Cora's stomach was twisted into knots by the time school let out and she was able to hurry home. Part of her wished Matt would simply be gone—that once he'd sobered up he'd been embarrassed and eager to get out of Silver Springs. She'd said everything she wanted to say to him when they broke up. And, because of him, she felt as if she'd somehow hurt, frustrated or disappointed Eli.

But Matt wasn't gone. He called out to her from the bedroom the moment he heard her come through the door.

Since she had such a small place, and only one bed, he was in it. After having shared that same bed with Eli only the night before, seeing Matt there felt so strange. But she hadn't invited Matt to New Horizons. She was merely being kind—and cautious—by giving him a place to rest until they could discuss whatever he'd come here to discuss.

"How was school?" He propped himself up with her pillows as she walked into the room and put her purse on the dresser.

That he was just rousing indicated he'd slept since she'd been gone, which answered *that* question. She hadn't missed an opportunity to get rid of him. "Today? Tedious."

"You don't like teaching here?"

She sat on the edge of the bed. "Normally, I do. But I was on pins and needles knowing you were waiting for me. What's going on?"

"What do you mean?"

"Why did you drive down here? Show up unexpectedly—and at least partially intoxicated? You could've killed yourself or someone else, driving that way."

"I wasn't drunk!"

She suspected he'd started out that way. He was lucky he hadn't had an accident, and that he hadn't been picked up. "You were disheveled and smelling of alcohol."

"Because my mother was just diagnosed with Alzheimer's, Cora. If you'd been staying in touch at all, you'd know that."

Cora clasped her hands together. "I'm sorry. I know that you were afraid…that you suspected something was wrong, but…"

"One day last week, she forgot we broke up. Asked when you were going to come see her."

"I'm sorry," she said again. She felt terrible about what was happening to Matt's mother. Sara was a lovely woman, certainly didn't deserve something like this. But there was nothing Cora could do about his mother's condition, wasn't sure what he expected. "I'll stop by to see her next time I'm in town."

"Next time you're in town," he echoed. "You say that as if you don't really care about her."

"Of course I care. I've always liked your mother."

"Well, she *loved* you. She thought you'd become her daughter-in-law, would've offered you all the love you feel as if you've had to live without, being adopted."

"It's not that I feel as if I haven't been loved, Matt. You don't understand at all, if that's what you think. I appreciate my parents—"

"Then why are you here instead of in LA with us?" he broke in. "Can't you tell how much I'm struggling without you? You haven't called me, haven't texted me. You haven't responded to anything I've posted on social media."

She hadn't viewed his social media, had quit doing that sort of thing even before she started seeing Eli.

"I thought you'd be back once you realized we had a good thing," he went on. "There's nothing better out there, you know."

In ways, what she had with Eli was better. They didn't have a label for what they were to each other, had no commitment, but she'd never felt so love drunk in her life than when she saw him or felt his hands on her body. "I've been moving, starting a new job. That takes focus," she responded lamely.

"It can't take up every minute. You don't even know anyone down here. Aren't you lonely?"

"I've made a few friends."

"So you've kissed all your old friends goodbye."

She got up. "Not at all. I'm staying in touch. But we weren't *friends*, Matt. We were more than friends, and now we're broken up. Why would I confuse you or…or give you any reason to hope by remaining in contact? Maybe later, in a few years, when we've both had a chance to move on, we can reconnect. But it's too soon right now."

He shoved himself into a sitting position. "What are you saying?"

She threw up her hands. "What I told you before. I'm really sorry, especially about your mother. I don't want her to suffer. I don't want you to suffer, either. But I can't reciprocate what you're feeling. I don't know a nicer way of putting it, except to be honest. You're a wonderful guy, and I'll always care about you, but—"

"Who's going to treat you better?" he interrupted, his eyes snapping with challenge.

"No one! I have no complaints about the way you treated me. I said you were a great guy—"

"But you think your birth mother is somehow going to make your life better."

"Meeting Aiyana has already answered so many of

my questions," she said. "The curiosity I felt was half the problem."

When he got out of bed, she was relieved to see that he was still wearing all his clothes. "So you're glad you did it."

That would depend on what happened from here. She had to admit that things weren't looking good, not with a one-sided relationship developing between her and Eli and Aiyana showing up to find his shirt on her floor. But she couldn't say she regretted coming to Silver Springs, because she didn't. She was glad she'd met Aiyana, glad she knew where she came from and what her birth mother was like. She was also glad she'd met Eli. Otherwise, she might never have experienced the kind of passion he could evoke. Everyone deserved to encounter that magical feeling at least once in a lifetime. The fact that she hadn't been more passionate about Matt only confirmed that she'd been right to break things off with him. "I did what I needed to do."

"That doesn't answer the question."

"Then, yes, I'm glad."

His face fell. "You don't care about me anymore."

Not in the way he wanted her to. Hadn't she said that—many times? "I'd like to be friends—when you're ready," she reiterated.

Dropping his head, he rubbed his temples. "You're making a mistake, Cora. We are meant to be together."

She let her breath go in a sigh. "I can't change how I feel."

He folded his arms as he studied her. "Fine. Then…can I just ask for one last favor?"

"Of course."

"Let me stay here a few days? I need some time away from LA—to get my head around this and come to terms with my mother's diagnosis."

"I don't see how that will help."

"I'm telling you I can't go back. Not yet. You say you

care about me. Let me hang out for a while, talk things through."

She didn't want him to stay. As far as she was concerned, he couldn't hit the highway fast enough. But she did feel terrible about his mother's diagnosis. And she thought having Matt around might finally stop her from seeing Eli. So there was that, too. If Matt got his way, at least in that regard, maybe he'd believe she really *did* wish him well and would leave peaceably, without saying anything that would give her away to Aiyana or anyone else.

"I have only this one bed," she said. "You'll have to sleep on the couch. You realize that. I won't get physical with you. There's not even a remote chance."

"Fine. I understand. I'm happy just to be able to spend some time with you to sort of…grow accustomed to our new roles. I mean…if you're sincere about being friends."

"Of course I'm sincere!"

"What happened before was too abrupt."

"I got that. You can stay until Friday," she said. "But I doubt you'll really care to hang out that long. I'll be at work most of the time, and you'll be sitting around here alone, bored stiff."

"At least we can spend our evenings together. Let me stay until Saturday, though, okay? My aunt's in town to visit my mom, and I don't really want to see her. You know we butt heads. Being out of town gives me a good excuse to avoid another argument with the old curmudgeon."

"So long as it's Saturday *morning*," she said. And she hoped it would be early, before the day could really begin, so she'd have the rest of the weekend to herself. She was already looking forward to that.

"Okay," he said.

She forced herself to return his smile. She supposed, after two years together, she could give him that much. What was three or four days?

* * *

"What's wrong?"

Eli blinked and then focused on his brother Gavin. They were sitting at the bar on Friday, listening to the music and watching the people who were dancing—had gone out at his request because he'd needed the distraction. The football team had a bye this week, so he didn't even have that to think about this weekend. "Nothing, why?"

"You're not the same tonight."

He took a sip of his beer. "I don't know what you're talking about."

"You're preoccupied, quiet."

Because he couldn't help remembering what'd happened here the last time. "I'm tired."

The waitress stopped to gather Gavin's empty bottle and to see if she could get him another beer. "No, thanks," he told her. "So how's Cora?" he asked as she walked off. "Everything going okay with her?"

It wasn't going at all. Eli hadn't heard from her since he delivered her lunch on Tuesday. He'd looked for her in the cafeteria and on campus since, but if he happened to find her and catch her eye, she'd look away and leave the area soon after.

He kept telling himself he didn't care. That she'd decided to quit seeing him, which saved him from having to break things off later. Every romantic relationship he had came down to that eventually…

But this was different. She'd quit on him long before he was ready to let her go. The thought of her in that small house with her ex-boyfriend made him sick inside. He kept going over and over their time together, remembering the way she'd smile when he came toward her, the way she'd laugh if he said something funny, the way she made love without coming off so needy that she wound up making him feel cornered and desperate to get away.

And then he'd wonder what more he could've done to make her want to continue seeing him. "I guess. She's been busy."

"Meaning…what? You haven't seen her?"

He gripped his bottle that much tighter as a vision of her pressed up against the back of this very building filled his head. "Not recently."

"But you guys were so hot for each other when we were here last. I had to dance with Darci half a dozen songs in a row to keep her occupied."

Eli mustered a faint smile for Gavin's sacrifice, hoping that would finally put an end to the conversation. But Gavin went right back after it.

"Does that mean it's over?"

"Do we *have* to talk about this?" he finally snapped.

"Whoa! Okay. I see how it is."

Irritated that Gavin would even bring her up, Eli threw a few bucks on the table and stood. "Let's go. I should never have suggested we come here."

"God, you've been a bear the past couple of days," Gavin complained. "I've never seen you in such a sour mood. I'm not trying to piss you off, big brother—I'm just trying to figure out what's wrong. So cut me some slack!"

"Nothing's wrong. I don't know how many times I have to say…" The door opened, and he let his words trail away as Cora walked in with a tall, thin guy who had long, curly brown hair, a goatee and glasses. He would've finished his statement, but he could no longer remember what he'd been about to say.

This was Matt. Eli had known he was still in town. He'd walked over to Cora's a time or two and spotted the additional car in her drive.

Gavin followed his gaze. "Shit. She's with someone else now? *Who is that guy?*"

Eli couldn't make himself look away. "Her ex-boyfriend's in town."

"They're back together?"

He didn't know what the situation was. She hadn't told him, and he hadn't approached her to ask. He'd been trying to give her the space she seemed to want, had been hoping that by not pressuring her, she'd miss him the way he was missing her and come around again. "I guess."

"Ah! Finally, it all makes sense!"

"What makes sense?" Eli growled.

"You really liked her."

He said nothing.

"I've never known a woman to get under your skin before, but she's managed to do that, hasn't she?"

"You don't know anything," he grumbled.

Cora couldn't have seen his truck outside, because Gavin drove. Eli was waiting for her to realize he was there—and watched her nearly trip over her own feet the moment her eyes landed on him. She hesitated for a moment. Then she said something to Matt and they changed direction, walking around the perimeter of the bar to the other side.

"You okay?" Gavin asked while Cora and Matt found a table.

"Yeah. Sure." Eli tossed back what was left in his bottle. "Let's get out of here," he said, but he received a text while Gavin drove them home that only made his night worse.

"That her?" Gavin asked when Eli pulled out his phone to look at it. "Cora, I mean?"

Eli felt his stomach knot as he stared at the message. "No." He wished it was Cora. Maybe he wouldn't feel quite so terrible if she'd asked him to come back to the bar, or requested a few moments to talk.

Gavin gave him a funny look. "So...is it Mom?"

Not the mother Gavin meant and not the mother Eli

claimed. But that was the name by which she called herself. "It's nobody," he said. Nobody to *him*, anyway.

Determined to ignore this message like those that had come before, he slid his phone back into his pocket.

Chapter Fourteen

"Who was that guy?" Matt asked as Eli and Gavin headed for the door.

Cora's cheeks ached from clenching her jaw. She preferred to ignore that question, but she had to say *something.* The way Eli had stared them down as they came in had made an impression on Matt. She should never have brought him here. She wouldn't have, if she'd had any clue that Elijah would be here, too. She'd just been looking for some way to entertain him, to help the time pass until he left tomorrow.

"Cora?" Matt pressed when she didn't answer.

"My boss," she replied.

"He didn't look happy."

For good reason. Eli had to be wondering if she'd taken her ex-boyfriend back. She planned to talk to him; she just couldn't do it while Matt was in town. She wanted to make sure their paths never crossed.

"What do you think's wrong with him?" he asked.

"He's under a lot of pressure," she replied.

"But if you work for him, why didn't he say hello?"

"I doubt he even saw us."

"*What?* He was staring at us the whole time we were trying to find a table."

Desperate to escape this conversation, Cora came to her feet. "I like this song. Let's dance."

They danced a lot, and Matt drank a lot, which distracted him enough that he didn't ask anything else about Eli. He seemed to be having fun, but Cora was just biding her time, couldn't wait for this interminable night to end. She kept him at the bar until she thought everyone at the ranch would be settled in for the night. Then she drove him back to her place.

"What time will you be heading out in the morning?" she asked as she turned off the highway onto the narrow road that led, after another two miles, to the school.

"Tomorrow?" He acted as if this was the first he'd heard of his going.

She gripped the steering wheel that much tighter as they rolled under the high arch at the front entrance. "Yeah. I said I'd let you stay until Saturday morning."

"But you've had to work the whole time. Why don't I leave on Sunday? That way, we can do something fun tomorrow."

"Matt, you said you needed some time to pull yourself together, and I've given you that. I've even let you stay long enough to avoid your difficult aunt."

"And I appreciate it. But what's the rush?" he asked. "We've been having a great time, haven't we?"

No. She couldn't take another day. "I'm done," she blurted.

"What does that mean?"

"I'm ready for you to go home."

She was afraid this would provoke a fight, but she'd run out of patience. He thought *he* was having a difficult time; well, she was having a hard time, too. She'd felt nauseous ever since she'd seen the look on Eli's face at the bar.

Matt opened his mouth to reply but she let out an involuntary gasp that silenced him.

Eli's truck was parked in front of her house.

Eli couldn't believe he was doing this. He'd never felt the need to chase after a woman, but Cora was driving him crazy.

Matt got out of the car when she did and came around by the trunk. Eli noticed his surprised expression but refused to let the fact that Matt was there get in the way. He strode over to Cora. "Can we talk?"

He'd taken her off guard; he could tell. She paused for several seconds as if searching for the best way to respond before she said, "Um…tomorrow, okay? Tomorrow would be better for me."

She didn't understand that he was desperate or he wouldn't be here. "I don't want to wait." He needed her, needed…something with the power to divert his thoughts and ease the rage burning like acid inside him. His biological mother had been texting and calling him relentlessly since he'd left the bar, saying she was in a bad way and needed his help. But she was a psychopath and a drug addict, so she was always in a bad way. He wasn't going to let her back into his life. He wasn't the person to call even if she had straightened up, not after all the cruelty he'd suffered at her hands.

He'd finally left his phone at his place and gone out for a drive, traveled aimlessly around the valley for two hours before making the decision to allow himself to go to Cora's. He had to resolve at least *one* thing that was bothering him. Otherwise, it felt like his head would explode. Although his birth mother had contacted him once or twice before, she'd never been quite so insistent.

You know it was that damn Tim I married who treated you so bad. Wasn't me. I wasn't involved in any of that.

She'd had the nerve to send such a text—a blatant lie—as if he hadn't been fully aware of exactly what happened, and who was responsible. They'd been in it together, one feeding off the other. But it wasn't just that. He wasn't himself, wasn't in control, not since seeing Cora at the bar.

"This isn't… I mean, you're her boss," Matt said. "This isn't personal, right?"

Eli ignored him. He was wound up, on edge, afraid he'd

bash him in the face if he so much as acknowledged his presence. His birth mother triggered too many painful memories, a surfeit of emotion. Eli felt like there was a monster growing inside him that was about to bust out at any moment.

Fortunately, since Aiyana had taken him in and he'd worked through most of his issues—the ones he *could* resolve—he hadn't allowed his frustration to erupt, hadn't let it get the better of him.

But it'd been a long time since he'd been this raw.

"I asked you a question," Matt said.

Eli leveled a glare at him. "If you know what's good for you, you'll go inside."

Eyes wide, Matt stumbled back as if he'd just caught a glimpse of the rage lurking inside Eli, but before he could do anything else, Cora grabbed his arm and pulled him toward the house. "Give us a few minutes. Will you? Please?"

Unwilling to make it that easy, Matt looked from her to Eli and back again. "Don't tell me… You guys are seeing each other, aren't you!" He glared at her as if she'd cheated on him. "There's no way you'd start dating Aiyana's son! Not without—"

"Matt, if you say another word I'll never forgive you!" she broke in.

Without what? Eli had no clue and didn't get the chance to ask before she shoved her ex toward the house with more force. "Matt, please. If you value our friendship *at all*, you'll go inside this minute."

He cursed but accepted the keys she tossed him and finally did as she asked.

Once he was gone, a profound silence fell.

Suddenly, Eli was no longer sure what he'd hoped to achieve. His eyes were beginning to burn as badly as his gut, and a lump the size of a baseball rose in his throat, making it impossible for him to speak normally.

What the heck was he doing? He'd been a fool to come here. He was only making matters worse.

Without another word, he turned on his heel and opened his truck door. He intended to get in and drive off before she could realize how close he was to breaking down, but she grabbed hold of him.

"What is it, Eli?" She looked concerned as she dragged him around to face her, but that only made it harder for him to maintain his composure. He jerked away, didn't want her to see him like this. But she refused to let him go. She caught hold of him again, this time with a stronger grasp.

"*Talk* to me!"

"It's okay. I'm sorry. I shouldn't have come here." He managed to mutter that much without having his voice crack—thank God—but she didn't act like she heard him. She stared into his face, trying to read what he was feeling. Then she wrapped her arms around his waist and pressed her cheek against his chest. "What is it?" she asked, clinging tightly. "Tell me."

He lifted his hands to her shoulders. He intended to push her away, couldn't believe he'd allowed himself to need her. He should've gone home like he was about to do now. He couldn't rely on her, on anyone, no matter how tempting it was to believe otherwise. But she wouldn't let go—and the next thing he knew his arms slid around her, securing her against him instead of breaking off the embrace.

"It's okay," she said.

He knew she could probably feel how badly he was shaking, but there was nothing he could do about that now. "Where've you been?" he asked.

Her hands slipped up the back of his shirt, and he felt her press her palms against his bare skin—a move he found both satisfying and intimate. She wasn't merely offering him a light "you'll be okay" pat. She was making it clear that she cared about him and wouldn't let him down. "It doesn't matter. I'm here now."

Burying his face in her hair, he gripped her that much tighter, and they stood like that until he could overcome all the terrible feelings that had him so twisted up inside. "Come home with me," he said at length, his mouth at her ear.

When she hesitated, he feared she'd refuse. She had Matt in the house, after all. He was asking a lot for her to leave her guest, but he needed to hear her say yes, needed to know that *he* came before Matt.

And, in the end, she murmured, "Okay."

Cora promised herself she'd tell Eli. Tonight. She had to. She didn't see how she could continue sleeping in his bed without divulging her connection to Aiyana. But, despite what he'd indicated at her place, Eli wasn't interested in having a discussion. That she'd go home with him was all that seemed important at the moment.

On the drive over, when she asked him what was wrong, he said he didn't want to talk about it. So she let the conversation lapse, but the ensuing silence wasn't awkward or upsetting. It was more like everything that'd been so wrong was now right, just because they were together.

The moment they reached his house, he tugged her inside and, without so much as turning on the light, began to let her know how badly he'd missed her. He wasn't *un*willing to communicate, she realized. He just preferred to speak to her in a different way, one in which he felt more capable of expressing himself.

She did get four words out of him—"I'm glad you're back." But that was all, and she wasn't willing to push. Something significant was going on between them that he didn't seem capable of putting into words, and she didn't need him to. She could feel the difference in the way he touched her.

His thick eyelashes rested on his cheeks as he ran his

tongue across her lips. "*You're* what I need," he said, surprising her by speaking again.

What'd happened tonight? He'd been so upset at her house he'd been trembling when she slid her arms around his waist. Just the memory of it made her defensive of him. She knew simply seeing her with Matt wasn't enough to cause a reaction like that. So what was it?

Regardless, she could feel that he was doing much better. His fingers curled and locked through hers as he bent his head to kiss her.

"You can kiss like no one else," she told him, relaxing as the desire he so easily evoked began to rise inside her once again.

"It's not difficult to kiss good when the person you're kissing tastes like honey," he told her and pulled back to look at her, seemingly content just to have her back in his house.

Cora might've been embarrassed to be the subject of such close scrutiny. She couldn't hide how deeply he affected her, so there was a certain vulnerability that came with holding his gaze. The fact that she did hold it, however—that she let him see she wasn't unaffected—appeared to be what he was looking for. His lips curved into a rather boyish smile and he kissed her again, even more softly, before leading her into his bedroom.

"Will you undress for me?" he asked as he sat on the bed.

Cora was tempted to derail that request by closing the gap between them. There'd be so much less risk in what they were doing if she could accelerate their lovemaking to the point that neither one of them was thinking clearly. Doing it with such *intention*—it almost felt like this was the first time they'd ever been together.

In a way it was, she realized. He was taking her more seriously, investing more time, effort and emotion. But… dared she take this step? *Before* telling him who she was?

"Relax. It's just me." He wanted her to trust him, to act

confidently, but by not telling him who she was, she was sort of lying to him…

Although she hesitated, in the end she couldn't bring herself to ruin this moment. She'd slept with Matt for two years and never experienced what it was like to make love in such a cerebral fashion, one in which her heart and mind were as active and involved as her body. Now she understood how many times she'd merely gone through the motions, either for her own physical release or simply to be a good partner and satisfy Matt.

Eli was much deeper than the women he'd been with had given him credit for, she decided. He had a tender heart; he merely protected it well. That he would reveal his sensitive side was making her fall that much harder.

Slowly, she removed her clothes.

"Gorgeous," he said, his expression rapt. "It's been *such* a long week."

His nostrils flared as she stepped closer. "At least it's going to end well," she said and guided his head to her breast, stroking his cheek as he suckled her.

His hands slid to her waist, then moved over her hips and around to the back, at which point he lifted her easily onto the bed before removing his own clothes.

"Do we need a condom?" he asked.

She'd been on the pill for a week. "According to what I've read online, we should be safe."

His teeth flashed in another smile. "I get to come inside you," he said and, when they both reached that pinnacle, Cora couldn't help but acknowledge that she'd never enjoyed making love to anyone more.

After an experience like that she wasn't willing to have the talk they needed to have about Aiyana. That would ruin everything, destroy the memory. So she promised herself she'd tell him in the morning and faded off to sleep, her arms and legs entwined with his.

Chapter Fifteen

"What are you going to do about Matt?"

Cora pulled herself out of the last vestiges of sleep so that she could answer Eli's question. He'd begun to stir several minutes ago, but she'd been reluctant to reach full consciousness, knew she'd have to face all that awaited her when she did. "I hope he got up and left," she mumbled. "He was supposed to leave this morning."

"What's he been doing here?"

She heard the caution in Eli's tone, could tell he was prepared for an answer he didn't like. "Sleeping on the couch."

"You didn't get back together with him."

"No."

He seemed so relieved when he reached for her that she smoothed her hand over his bare chest in a comforting fashion as she rested her head on his shoulder.

"What did he want, then?" he asked.

"He wanted to reconcile, but I wasn't interested."

"So why didn't he leave?"

"He asked if he could stay—to show me what I was missing, I suppose."

Eli lifted his head. "And you let him?"

"It's complicated."

"I can't imagine it would be that complicated to me."

Because he didn't know everything. She'd let Matt stay mostly to appease him. She'd been trying to end their relationship in such a way that he wouldn't cause trouble. With what he and his mother were going through, she'd also wanted to be supportive and prove she was sincere about maintaining a friendship. "We were together for two years. He said he was having a hard time getting over me, so I figured I owed him a few days to come to terms with our new relationship."

"Wouldn't being around you only make getting over the breakup harder?"

"I told him that. He argued that he needed to get used to our new status, and I thought it might give him the closure he seemed to be missing if I didn't rush him out the door."

"He didn't know about me."

That had been apparent in Matt's reaction last night. "Of course not. I haven't told anyone."

He dropped his head back. "Even your family at home?"

She understood what that would likely indicate to him—that she wasn't taking the relationship seriously. But she wasn't supposed to be taking the relationship seriously. "No. Why would I? You told me not to expect anything."

"You've certainly taken that to heart," he said wryly.

"I don't want to get hurt any more than you do."

"And now?"

"Has that changed?"

His fingers slipped through her hair. "You can't tell?"

She could tell last night. But there were still a lot of blanks to be filled in. She leaned up on her elbow to be able to see into his face. "What is it you want from me, Eli?" she asked. "Specifically."

He thought for a moment. Then he said, "I want to be with you while you're here."

"And what would that entail? A night together every once in a while?"

"I'm asking for a little more than that."

"But more equals…what? Would we quit trying to hide the fact that we're seeing each other?"

He sat up against the headboard. "Why not? That hasn't been the best-kept secret in the first place."

She pulled the sheet with her as she came into a sitting position, too. “What about dating other people?”

“We won’t date other people.” He spoke quickly enough to suggest he knew his mind on that matter without even having to think.

“We’d be exclusive.”

“Yes, and we’ll see each other a lot. Okay?” He lifted a hand to run a thumb down her jawline. “This past week just about killed me.”

She assumed he was joking, so she chuckled, but he didn’t laugh with her. He seemed serious. “You mean that,” she said, sobering.

“I hated every minute of it.”

“So…we’ll be exclusive and see each other a lot—and then?”

“We’ll deal with that when the time comes.”

“No promises.”

His eyebrows came together. “I told you I’m not good at this. I’m hoping I’ll get better at it. But, either way, it’s too early to try and decide what might come later.”

He had a point. But she had a secret. Now that they had an understanding of sorts, would she be a fool to divulge that? What if she shared the circumstances surrounding her birth and he insisted she tell Aiyana? The deception could make Aiyana angry. Or there could be some reason Aiyana wouldn’t or couldn’t be around her. In that case, she’d lose her job, which wouldn’t be the best thing for her or the school, not midyear. She liked it here, liked being with Elijah.

So, once again, she ignored her better judgment—put what she felt now above what she’d probably be feeling at the end of the school year—and decided to wait.

Fortunately, that was made easy when Eli’s phone began to buzz, drawing their attention. He was getting a call or text. When he reached over to grab it, she thought he’d answer. But after checking the display, he cursed and tossed the phone back on the nightstand as if it had burned his hand.

"Who is it?" she asked.

Closing his eyes, he leaned his head against the wall again.

"Eli?" Whoever it was, he didn't like them—or wasn't happy they were trying to reach him. "It's not Aiyana..."

"No."

Of course not. Cora couldn't imagine he'd be unhappy to hear from one of his brothers, either. So...maybe it was an old girlfriend.

When she said nothing more, he opened his eyes and looked at her.

"What?" she said.

Instead of answering, he reclaimed his phone and showed her the text he'd received—How can you be so selfish? I only need $50.

She noted the name associated with that text. "*Maleficent's* texting you?"

"Jo Seifert. My mother."

"Maleficent's a Disney character, right? From *Sleeping Beauty*?"

"An evil character. Maleficent means doing harm."

His mother. She was tempted to touch the scar on his chin—she still didn't know how he'd gotten it—but refrained. "Seems fitting."

That he would change his mind and share this with her suggested he was making an effort to be more open, to have some semblance of a real relationship, despite what he'd termed his "limitations." She would've smiled at that but she didn't want him to think she was smiling at the fact that he was upset.

She leaned forward to peck him on the lips. "Are you going to give her the money?"

"Hell, no."

"I don't blame you." She started to get up, but he caught her arm.

"That's it?"

"What do you mean?"

"You're not going to ask me a million questions about Jo?"

God knew she wanted to. She was *so* curious about his biological family and background. But she figured he'd talk about his past when he was ready. She wouldn't try to force him to share things that were painful for him. "No."

"Because..."

"I already know the most salient points."

The old guarded expression claimed his face. "You're aware of what happened to me?"

She wished she could erase all the pain he'd suffered. She hated the people who'd hurt him, even though she'd never even met them. "I did an internet search."

"On *me*?"

"I was attracted to you from the beginning."

"My childhood is *on the internet*?" he asked with a scowl, obviously too fixated on that to react to anything else.

"You've never Googled yourself?"

"Why would I?"

"Some people do, just to see what comes up."

"I guess I've never been interested in seeing what's out there. Everyone around here knows me, so it didn't seem important until now. What'd you find?"

"An old article from when Aiyana first opened this place. They cited you and your...um...background as an example of the type of boy she hoped to help."

"Oh. Right." He relaxed a bit. "I have seen that article, now that you mention it. Although it's been a while."

"She probably needed the publicity to stay afloat."

"She tried to keep me out of it, but…there's no controlling what some reporters dig up."

"It made for a sympathetic story—a heartbreaking story—so it had to have helped with donations."

"I wouldn't know. I was just a freshman then. But…what you read about me, it didn't raise more questions?"

"It did," she admitted, "but I'm not going to pressure you for details. If you want to talk about that period of your life, I'm here. If not…let it go—if you can."

His mood lightened instantly. "Hallelujah," he said. "Let's get some breakfast."

Cora smiled to think letting him avoid that conversation would bring him so much relief. "At Lolita's Country Kitchen?"

"If you like that place."

She thought it would be a nice change to go out with him, to forget about trying to hide the fact that they were romantically involved. "Sounds good to me. But…what about Matt?"

He grimaced. "Don't tell me we have to invite him. I don't like him very much."

"No, we don't have to invite him," she said, laughing. "But I should at least go over and talk to him, tell him goodbye." And see what she could do to minimize the damage she might've caused by running out on him last night…

"Do that if you have to—then call me when you're ready," he said and tugged the sheet away to get a final look at her before rolling out of bed.

Eli's phone buzzed just as he was about to turn on the shower. He assumed it would be Jo again, but the screen showed Gavin's number, so he answered. "'Lo?"

"It's me. You on for basketball with the boys this morning?"

"Not today."

"Why not? It's Saturday. What else you got going?"

"I'm about to have breakfast with Cora."

A strained silence ensued. Then his brother said, "The same Cora who was at the bar last night with her ex-boyfriend?"

"Yeah."

"You don't find that a little strange?"

He leaned against the door to the bathroom while he talked. "They're just friends, Gav."

"I thought you were going to say *you're* just friends. That's the type of thing you normally say when I ask about a woman."

"Cora's different."

His voice changed, grew more somber. "Eli, I just passed Doug Maggleby a few minutes ago—out in his yard. He said her ex has been staying with her."

"I'm well aware of that."

"In a small house with only one bedroom…"

"Stop it. She has a couch."

"I'm just being real with you, man."

Eli started the shower so the water would get hot. "They're *friends*, like I said."

"How do you know?"

"She told me."

After another brief silence, during which he seemed to be weighing whether to continue the argument, Gavin said, "Breakfast with Cora it is, then. I guess basketball can't compete."

"You could join us."

"No. One of us needs to show up at the court. The boys will be disappointed otherwise. But…can I say one more thing?"

"I have the feeling you're going to do it regardless."

"I'll take that as a yes. Besides the fact that Cora's had

another man in her house for several days, are you sure you're doing the right thing, getting involved with one of the teachers here?"

"I'm not sure at all," he admitted.

"But you're doing it, anyway."

Eli remembered how he'd felt last night, right before she agreed to come home with him—and how having her say yes had changed everything. When he was with her he could more easily put his childhood into perspective, more easily remember the present and what his life was like now. "I can't help myself."

"That's freaking terrifying," he said.

Eli drew a deep breath. "Yeah, I know. I guess we'll see how it goes."

Matt was gone. Hallelujah! The dread in the pit of Cora's stomach eased considerably when she saw that his car was no longer in her drive. She still feared she'd find a nasty note waiting on her dresser, but at least she wasn't facing a confrontation.

After she let herself into the house, she held her breath as she wandered around. She was afraid he'd only stepped out to buy milk or something and planned to return. But everything that belonged to him was gone. And he hadn't left her a message or anything else to indicate that he was upset with her. While on the way home, she'd briefly considered the possibility that he might've dumped out her drawers, ransacked her personal belongings or thrown away her birth control…

Fortunately, all looked as she'd left it.

A ping signaled an incoming text message, so she reached into her purse to retrieve her phone.

Everything okay? Eli wanted to know.

Fine, she wrote back. She didn't think of her ex-boyfriend as particularly vengeful, but she did know he'd always been a little threatened by her search for her birth mother. He probably blamed the fact that she'd found Aiyana and was planning to move to Silver Springs as the reason she broke things off with him. It was easier to believe that than the truth—that she just wasn't fulfilled in the relationship.

Matt's not giving you any trouble? He's leaving?

He's already gone, she told Eli.

Great. Then I'm going to swing by the basketball court and play hoops for a while—until you're ready to go, okay?

The students were going to love seeing him. Okay. I'll walk over there when I'm done.

She set her phone to charge, since it was almost dead after going all night, and peeled off her clothes. Then she paused to stare at herself in the mirror.

"I hope you know what you're doing," she mumbled and turned on the water.

Chapter Sixteen

Jo tried to call three times and texted twice while he was at breakfast with Cora. Eli had believed, if he ignored her long enough, she'd simply go away. Now he wasn't so sure. His birth mother seemed determined, adamant—was desperate to get some money out of him. But she had no right to come to him in the first place.

"Have you thought about changing your number?"

The question caused him to glance up. Cora had seen him check his phone numerous times but, true to her word, she hadn't asked any intrusive questions. Although this one made it clear she knew who kept interrupting their meal, it still respected his privacy regarding the details of his past and his feelings toward his biological mother.

"I have."

"And?"

He set his phone aside. "Seems pointless to go to all that trouble."

"If hearing from her upsets you…might be worth it."

"I don't believe a new number would really get rid of her, not for any length of time. She knows where I work, could do the same thing she did before."

She drank a sip of her orange juice. "Which was…"

"She called the office, got hold of Betty May, gave a false name and claimed to be interested in making a large donation to the school. She even went so far as to claim that Aiyana Turner recommended she speak to me. After hearing Aiyana's name, Betty was so eager to make sure this 'donor' got through, she suggested Jo call my cell."

"Yikes."

"Exactly." He still hadn't had the heart to tell Betty she'd screwed up. He didn't want anyone to know that his past had come back to haunt him. He'd thought he could handle it, was determined to bear that burden alone so Aiyana wouldn't have to feel any added empathy or concern. She dealt with enough of that type of thing as it was.

"Has she ever come by—tried to see you in person?" Cora asked.

"Not yet. The last time she asked for money, she wanted me to use an app to transfer it. I doubt she has transportation."

"Where does she live?"

"I haven't even asked. I'm guessing LA, but it could be anywhere. Maybe she's out of state. I'm not sure what her situation is, to be honest. But chances are it's not good. It was never good when I was a child. I have no reason to believe that's changed, since it's obvious *she* hasn't."

He had to have raised more questions than he'd answered with the information he'd conveyed so far, but Cora simply said, "I see," and went back to eating.

"It can be so confusing," he admitted, watching her.

Her chewing slowed, and she swallowed. "What part?"

"All of it, but—" he pointed to his phone "—most especially what to do about her now."

"Parent/child relationships—even bad ones, *especially* bad ones—can be complicated," she said.

His food was getting cold, so he shoveled in a bite of his bacon-and-egg omelet. "Are you speaking from experience?"

"To a point."

"Care to elaborate?" he asked, waiting before taking another bite.

"Not really. I haven't experienced anything like what you have, which is why I hesitate to offer any advice. I don't appreciate it when people tell me what I should do or how I should feel about certain things when they've never been in the same situation."

He respected her for not being too heavy-handed with her opinions and remarks. That was what made it possible for him to talk to her even though he had so much trouble talking to most other people. He didn't have to worry that she wouldn't back off if he indicated he'd had enough. "I can appreciate that."

Cora put some jelly on her toast. "Does Aiyana know your birth mother's been trying to get in touch?"

"No. And I'd rather she not find out."

"Because..."

"Why upset her? There's nothing she can do about it, anyway."

"Do you ever hear from your father?"

"My biological father died in a motorcycle accident shortly after I was born, but he wasn't together with my mother, anyway. He probably wouldn't have been a big part of my life." Although... Eli had always wondered if it would've made a difference, had his father lived. "The man who married Jo and was there while I was growing up is in prison for sexually abusing his daughter."

She put down her toast without even taking a bite. "He had a daughter? Did she live with you?"

"No. Stayed with her mother, only came to visit once, maybe twice a year. But if she hadn't said something about me to the next-door neighbor—and that neighbor hadn't called the authorities—I might never have escaped my... situation."

"Seems more likely she would've told her mother about you. That didn't happen?"

"She was quite a bit younger than I was. Who can say how much she really understood or conveyed about what was going on at my house? The way I heard it, she said something about her father having a *boy for a dog*—as if it wasn't a big deal—which shows you right there that her understanding was limited. Anyway, Jenny's mother never did anything, even if she did know. I'm guessing she ignored what she could, felt the less she had to do with Tim and his life, the better."

"I bet she'd like to kill him now."

He turned his water cup around, making circles in the condensation. "That makes two of us."

"I don't blame you. Are you still in contact with Jenny?"

"She's married, lives in Virginia, so I don't see her often, but we've had lunch once or twice."

"And Tim?"

"Nothing from him, thank God. I wish my mother would follow suit and leave me the hell alone. I have a new life, am an entirely different person. I don't want anything to do with her."

She waited for the waitress, who'd come around with a pitcher, to fill her glass and leave. "So…what are you going to do?"

He picked up his phone. "I'm going to tell her to beat it. *Again.*" He did that, but turning her away wasn't as easy as he was leading Cora to believe. Part of him—the part that admired the mother/child sculpture Cora had brought into his office when they'd first met—still craved an apology, an explanation he could understand, some sense of closure, even a little contrition, if not a full acknowledgment of what she'd done. She owed him *something.*

Whatever that something was, however, he'd never get it. She was too narcissistic to feel the slightest bit of remorse. How could she feel bad about what she'd done when she claimed no responsibility?

As difficult as it was, he had to learn to live with the reality that she wasn't a fully functioning individual, that she never loved him and never would.

Some things just were what they were, he told himself.

"Is she or Tim responsible for the scar on your face?" Cora asked.

He fingered it, remembering. Late one night, he'd managed to get free of the cage they kept him in, but instead of running—he was too weak from lack of food—he tried to get something to eat. Tim caught him going through the pantry and slugged him so hard he'd flown across the kitchen, right into the door frame, splitting open his chin. There'd been so much blood, yet they'd never taken him to the doctor, which was why the cut had healed so badly. "Yeah."

Cora reached across the table to take his hand. "Bastards. I hope they rot in hell."

He couldn't help smiling. He'd never heard her use that kind of language before. "I like being with you," he said as if it was a revelation, because it was. Not only was she refreshing, she was *healing*, knew how to be supportive without being too overbearing. He felt like a whole new person when she was around, and that didn't happen with just anyone.

He expected her to say the same to him, but she didn't. "Who wouldn't?" she said and that enabled them to climb out of the mire of his past—to shove it all away—with a laugh.

Cora was invited back to Aiyana's for dinner on Sunday night. She'd been looking forward to it ever since she'd left Aiyana's house last week. Only this time she'd be going as Eli's girlfriend, which changed the way she'd be viewed by everyone else at the gathering. She knew Aiyana, and Eli's brothers, would be watching her in a different way. She'd also be that much more conscious of what she was hiding from them.

As it turned out, however, she didn't mind the extra attention. Gavin teased her quite a bit more and the younger brothers gave her shy smiles as if they were excited to think Eli had a romantic interest, but Aiyana treated her as kindly and politely as ever, almost as if she was determined to ignore the change. It was Eli who surprised her the most. He touched her freely and at every opportunity, despite the presence of his family. He could be so withdrawn and difficult to read, she hadn't expected him to be this demonstrative.

"How are your classes going?" Aiyana asked after they'd shooed the men from the kitchen so they could clean up without threading their way around so many big bodies.

Cora liked having this time alone with Aiyana, liked puttering around, helping with such mundane tasks. "They're going well."

Aiyana filled the sink with hot water. "You're not having any behavioral issues, are you? I remember you were worried about that."

"The new student—Zack Headerly—is giving me some trouble, but from what Darci says, he's acting out in English class, too. I think it's a general problem and not specific to me."

Aiyana lowered her voice in concern. "You know his parents were killed in a plane crash last year..."

"Yes. Eli told me. My heart breaks for him. That's why I haven't sent him to the office. I've been trying to gain a rapport with him, hoping the relationship we establish will encourage him to settle down."

"How's that going?"

Cora put plastic wrap over the cauliflower au gratin she'd made and contributed to the dinner. "It's too early to tell, but I remain hopeful."

"Let me know if you need help."

"I will. I was thinking that maybe Eli and I could take him and a friend riding this week. I feel as if some one-on-one time might help calm and reassure him. He needs to know that there are people who are still invested in him and his life."

Aiyana tossed Cora an approving smile. "That's the real secret," she said, her hands deep in suds. "I've invited him to have lunch with me tomorrow, so I'm trying to do the same thing."

Cora began loading the dirty silverware into the dishwasher. "Do you spend one-on-one time with all the boys?" That would be a daunting task, she thought, in addition to running the school and taking care of such a big family. Aiyana still had two high schoolers at home, who had homework every afternoon along with sports, but Cora supposed living on campus made a big difference.

"Just the most troubled," Aiyana replied. "I wish I had time to get to know them *all* on the same level, but the logistics are such that..."

"It's impossible," Cora finished.

"Sadly, yes." She raised a wet, soapy hand. "But enough about New Horizons and what's going on with the school. You're here to relax and have a good time. Why don't you tell me a little more about your family? I'm guessing you're missing them by now."

Cora did miss her family, although, once she got beyond that first night she'd been too caught up in adjusting to her new situation, fighting her attraction to Eli, making friends with Darci and feeling guilty for keeping her true identity a secret to get *too* homesick. "I've already been back to see them once. And I hear from them regularly."

"You're close to your parents, then?"

Cora hesitated before putting the glasses in the dishwasher along with the silverware. "Yes." Otherwise, she wouldn't feel so guilty for wanting to include her birth mother in her life.

"How's your brother doing?"

"He's been out of town. Claims he's going to come see

me when he gets back, but…he's always busy. Keeps putting it off. So we'll see. I'd love for you to meet him." In a way, that was true even though Cora knew she'd probably never introduce them—not with the way things stood now.

"I'm looking forward to that." She indicated the leftover carrot cake. "Any chance you'd like to take that home?"

Aiyana had obviously taken note of how much Cora had loved the dessert. "Sure. If you don't want it or want to keep it for the boys."

"We all get plenty of sweets as it is."

A ruckus broke out in the living room—Eli and Gavin wrestling with their younger brothers, who'd been teasing and goading them to get them to do just that. The loud noise and the rattle of dishes and other furnishings caused Aiyana to roll her eyes. "Boys."

"They seem to get along well," Cora said.

"Every family has its moments, but for the most part, they've been very good to each other. They are all wonderful people."

"They're lucky to have you."

Aiyana turned to face her wearing such an intense expression that Cora feared she'd given away too much with the longing in her voice. But when Aiyana spoke, she realized that Aiyana's thoughts were moving in a different direction. "On the phone just after you came here, you mentioned wanting to become friends with Elijah."

Cora swallowed with some difficulty. "Yes…"

"It appears the relationship has moved beyond friendship."

Feeling on the spot, Cora could barely refrain from wringing her hands. Like most all of the students and staff, she loved Aiyana, didn't want to displease her. "We are… we are dating, if that's what you mean."

"It's serious?"

"We haven't put a label on it. It's too soon."

"But you're open to getting serious with him."

When she flailed around, searching for the best answer, Aiyana dried her hands and moved closer. "I owe you an apology, Cora. This is none of my business, and Eli would be furious if he knew I was getting involved. It's just that I've never seen him like this. His eyes follow you wherever you go, and I think I indicated on the phone that as tough and unreachable as he may seem, at times, his heart is so fragile..."

After clearing her throat, Cora met her gaze. "Well, I'm just as concerned for my own heart, if that tells you anything."

Aiyana's face creased into a big smile. "For you, it wasn't quite as obvious to me, probably because I don't know you as well. So... I'm glad I asked," she said and pulled Cora into her arms for a warm embrace.

Cora breathed deeply, taking in the scent of her biological mother. She was hugging the woman who'd given her birth, a woman she was coming to love and respect more than she ever dreamed possible.

She probably hung on a little too long. When Aiyana tried to pull back, Cora couldn't quite let her go, but she didn't seem to mind. She kissed Cora's cheek—and then Eli interrupted by poking his head into the room.

"What's going on in here?" he asked.

Aiyana turned back to the dishes. "I just gave Cora the rest of the carrot cake, and she was thanking me."

"You gave her *all* of it? No way! I get half," he said, and later, once they were at his house, he decided to claim his share. But Cora didn't mind, since he ate it off her body.

"Were you really hugging my mother because she gave you the cake?" he asked as he licked a final drop of frosting off her nipple.

She caught her breath as he made sure he'd gotten it all, wondering if now might be a good time to tell him who she was. He'd just given her the perfect intro—and yet she couldn't bring herself to do it. What if their fledgling relationship couldn't withstand the shock wave?

She didn't want anything to come between them. Not only that, but Aiyana was so pleased they were together. Why risk ruining everyone's current happiness when she had all year? "Yes."

He dropped onto the bed beside her, seemingly sated and obviously tired. "Wow. You really like carrot cake."

"I really like your *mom*," she said softly.

"Doesn't everybody?" He propped his head up with his hands. "What's yours like?"

"She's…different from Aiyana. Not quite so socially conscious, but she's also a nice person. She did a great job raising me."

"You don't have any complaints about your childhood? The way you were talking at the restaurant, I thought maybe there'd been some problems."

"No big ones." Her mother's vanity could wear on her. Lilly could be a little materialistic, but Cora couldn't say anything derogatory about her. She already felt too disloyal just by being here—and getting involved in Eli's life and Aiyana's life…

"I'd like to meet her."

Cora wasn't about to invite Lilly to the ranch. She planned to keep this new world separate from the one she'd left in LA. Otherwise, she'd feel even guiltier. "She's really busy."

"Doing what?"

"She's a big philanthropist, always involved in one community event or another."

"That makes her sound caring."

Except that she sometimes gave the impression she did charity work more because she was bored and liked the positive attention it brought her. "She is caring. It's complicated, completely harmless. No one is all one way or the other, you know?"

"She doesn't have a job?"

"Doesn't need to work. But she has lots of friends she goes out with for…for brunch and movies and what have you. And she golfs," she added weakly.

"Ah, I can see she's completely buried."

Cora heard the sarcasm but pretended she hadn't. "She is."

"We're not that far from LA," he said.

"Yeah. She'll come visit. Sometime."

He lifted his head to give her a funny look. "I mean we could go there any weekend you choose."

"Maybe for Christmas," she mumbled since the holidays sounded a long way off.

He didn't say anything. He got up and went into the bathroom to turn on the shower so they could wash off the sticky residue of the frosting, and she leaned over to check her phone. She'd tried to reach Matt earlier, before going to the basketball courts to find Eli for breakfast, but he hadn't picked up. He hadn't responded to her text, asking him if he got home okay, either. She thought he was just going to write her out of his life, and was happy to have him do that. But when she took a moment to listen to the voice mail her mother had left while she was having dinner at Aiyana's, her blood ran cold. In a voice choked with emotion, Lilly asked her why she hadn't told them she'd gone to Silver Springs to meet her biological mother.

"Oh God," Cora whispered. Matt hadn't told Aiyana and Eli why she'd sought out a job at the ranch—but he had told Lilly.

Chapter Seventeen

"What did you say?" Eli poked his head out of the bathroom to see Cora grabbing her clothes off the floor and hurrying to get dressed.

"I said I have to go."

"But...you're sticky."

"I'll rinse off at home. There's been a—a family emergency."

Feeling a fissure of concern, he hooked his arms above his head using the lintel of the doorway. He would've helped gather her things, but she already had her clothes and there wasn't much he could do to help her dress. "What kind of emergency?"

"My mom...she's upset about something. I have to go home."

He turned off the shower. "Would you like me to drive you there?"

"No. It's fine. I'll go alone. I don't know when I'll be able to come back so...so you should stay here."

"Then...do you need someone to cover your classes tomorrow? If I can't get one of the other teachers to combine, I can always show them a movie or something—act as babysitter, at least."

Cora couldn't conscionably leave her students in the lurch and make him step in, not when this wasn't the type of emergency Eli assumed. No one had been hurt or killed; no one was in the hospital. This was merely the consequences of the fact that she hadn't been able to let certain things go—things that some adopted kids, maybe even a lot of them, could do with apparent ease. "No. I'll be here."

"It's already eight o'clock!"

"The drive's only two hours. I can get there and be back before morning."

"After being up all night, will you be in any condition to work?"

"I'll muddle through. School doesn't last that long."

"I'm willing to help you," he said. "Just tell me what's wrong."

When she looked up at him, she had tears in her eyes, which brought him out of the bathroom. "Cora..."

"I'm fine." She put up a hand to ward off the comfort he'd hoped to offer. "I... I need to go. I'm sorry," she said and hurried out.

Eli stared after her. Just when he felt as if he was getting close to her, closer than he'd ever been to a woman, she seemed to retreat behind some invisible wall.

For a change, it wasn't him. But that didn't mean it wouldn't turn out to be a problem.

The silence in the kitchen felt tangible—like a thousand pounds of sand bearing down on Cora's shoulders, so heavy it was hard to bear up beneath it. Both of her parents were sitting at the table across from her, but neither seemed to have much to say. Lilly had cried a lot, and Brad acted confused, as if he was still trying to piece together why she'd needed more than what they'd provided when they'd given raising her their best effort.

"It isn't anything you've done," Cora reiterated. "You've been wonderful parents, and I'm grateful for everything."

He lifted his gaze to meet her eyes. "Then...why?"

She didn't get a chance to answer before her mother broke in, "Does your brother know? Did he help you?"

"No," she replied. "I only told Matt and Jill, because they were so present in my life during the past two years."

"And we weren't present?" she said.

Her father glanced at his wife as if he wanted to comfort her but was uncertain as to how to go about it.

"Of course you were," Cora said. "That's not what I meant. I would've told you, but every time I brought it up, you acted so…resistant to the idea—as if it would be a personal betrayal."

"So you did it, anyway," her mother said, fresh tears in her eyes.

"Not because it would hurt you! I never wanted to hurt you. I love you both. Why can't you understand? I *had* to meet Aiyana. A part of me has always been insatiably curious about her."

"What about your birth father?" Brad asked. "You're not curious about him?"

"I am but… I don't have any information on him. Unless Aiyana is willing to tell me the circumstances surrounding my conception, I have no hope of ever finding him."

"Will she give you that information?" he asked.

"I don't know yet. I haven't told her who I am. No one knows down at New Horizons." When she thought of Matt, she wanted to punch him. He had no business causing this wreckage. He'd only told Brad and Lilly to strike out at her, to hurt her for breaking up with him and having the audacity to find someone else.

"So when are you going to do that?" Brad asked. "And why haven't you done so already?"

"Because… I felt I should tell you first, for one. But the timing hasn't been right. There are moments when I think I'll never tell. At least I've seen my biological mother. At least I know who she is and what she's like."

Her father scratched his head, making his hair stand up. "I understand the questions you've had must've been… difficult," he said, making an attempt to be conciliatory.

"They were! I wasn't even certain of my nationality, Dad! Such a simple thing most others take for granted. I hated being so in the dark. I have only a partial picture now, but at least it's *something*."

"It's the deception I'm struggling with." Lilly glowered at her beneath wet eyelashes, but Cora wasn't convinced her "deception" was the root of it. Fear of losing Cora's affection was the real problem, which was probably why Cora had found her birth mother in spite of Lilly's resistance. She knew Lilly had nothing to fear. There wasn't any way her adoptive mother could ever lose her affection.

"I lied because there was no way of knowing whether Aiyana would be anyone I'd be willing to associate with. If she wasn't, I was going to leave things as they are now. I didn't see any point in upsetting you if I ended up walking away."

"But you're not walking away. You adore her!" her mother said. "You talk about her like she's Mother Teresa!"

"I admit the fact that she's such a good person makes everything a bit more...complicated, but it doesn't change how much you both mean to me. *You* will always be first, Mom. You were the one who stood by me when she walked away."

Fresh tears confirmed that Cora's comments had hit the real target.

"Mom, stop," she said, getting up to hug her. "How could you question my love for you? We've always been close, haven't we?"

"*I* thought so. I did my best by you, but I'm not the kind of person Aiyana has turned out to be. I'm no champion of orphans and abused boys."

"What are you talking about? You're always working on one fund-raiser or another," she said. "You do a lot of good. Besides, that type of thing doesn't matter. You've been everything I need. I have no complaints, so don't let Matt tear us apart. That's exactly what he intended when he called you. He's angry that I'm not getting back with him, so he's hurting me by hurting you."

Lilly wiped her cheeks, smearing her mascara. "I know he wasn't trying to do any of us any favors..."

"Have you thought about Aiyana and how *she* might feel about all of this?" her father asked.

"Of course!" Cora replied. "Why do you think I haven't approached her? I'm not attempting to force myself into her life—or anyone else's. I'm just trying to figure out who I am and where I came from."

"But Matt said you went home with her son last night!" Lilly said.

"Her *adopted* son. As far as I can tell, I'm the only child she's ever had."

"So that makes it okay to date him?"

"It's not ideal, but there's nothing really wrong with it. It's not like we're truly related."

Lilly accepted the tissue Brad got for her. "Then you're not worried about how *he* will feel when he finds out you deceived him,"

"Like I said, I'm not even sure he has to find out."

"That's not realistic," Brad said. "This is all leading *somewhere*, Cora."

And there it was—what scared them all, even her.

She took her father's hand. "Can you tell me why my birth mother gave me up, Dad?"

"No. They provided us with no information, Cora. We've told you that before. We were just glad to get you."

"And we didn't mind not knowing," her mother added. "We were excited to be your parents—your *only* parents. Having that blank canvas meant...it meant we didn't have to consider the fact that you weren't actually born to us."

"But the fact that I didn't come out of your womb doesn't matter, right? You've told me before. Only love matters."

"That's true," Lilly admitted. "You'd think that would

be enough, that you wouldn't have to go searching for someone who could…who would possibly ruin our lives."

"Aiyana can't ruin our lives if we don't give her that kind of power," Cora insisted. "The woman I've come to know would never want to hurt us, anyway. She'd step out of the picture before she became a problem."

"That's how you see her now, but you never know what she may be like once she feels entitled."

Cora rubbed her tired and burning eyes. "I'm sorry. I wish I could've been satisfied with not knowing. Maybe for some people, it's easy not to look back, to only move forward. But it hasn't been like that for me. I went to a lot of time, effort and expense to find Aiyana, and I wouldn't have done all of that if I hadn't felt compelled, from when I was just a little girl, to find out who my biological parents were—and why they gave me away."

Brad shook his head. "You hardly ever said anything!"

"Because I knew it would go like this!" she said.

"We would've tried to understand," he argued.

"Then try to understand now, Dad. Please? Wherever this is going, does it *have* to be somewhere bad? Can't I satisfy my curiosity, fill in the gaps that most people don't even think about so that I can feel satisfied? At peace? Can you trust my love enough to let me navigate my way through this?"

"Do we have any choice?" her mother asked.

"I guess not, since I've already done it," she said with a sigh. "But I'm an adult now. I feel like I should have the right to these answers. You know where you came from. Why can't I?"

They didn't answer.

"Still, I'd like your blessing, because I *do* love you and care about how you feel." She stared at them both imploringly. "Please?" she said again.

"You're *my* daughter. I don't want to share you!" her

mother burst out. "Especially with some…some saint I can't compete with!"

Brad took Lilly in his arms and Cora stood so that she could hover over her mother and rub her back. "But that's just it, Mom. You won't have to compete. *No one* can threaten your place in my heart. Ever."

"You're down there with her, aren't you?" Her mother's words were muffled—they'd gone into her father's shoulder—but Cora could understand them in spite of that.

"Only for the year." She sought her father's gaze and, when their eyes met, she could tell she'd managed to convince *him*, even if she hadn't been able to completely assuage her mother's fears.

"I want you to be happy," he said. "We both do."

"Then don't be mad at me for this."

"I don't want Aiyana in our lives!" her mother insisted.

"Mom, you'd really like her—"

"That only makes it worse!"

"Give your mother some time to come to terms with this," her father said softly, indicating that Cora should back down.

"Okay." She checked the time on her phone. "It's nearly two. I have to head back."

Letting go of Brad, Lilly whipped around to face her. "You're leaving? *Now?* But you can't drive for two hours. You haven't had any sleep!"

Cora wished Matt would've at least waited until the following weekend to sabotage her relationship with her parents. That slight adjustment in timing would've made it so much easier for her to recover. "I have a job, Mom. I have to teach."

Her mother grabbed her and pulled her into a tight embrace. "Don't go. I'm afraid you'll fall asleep at the wheel and crash."

"After such an emotional conversation, I'm pretty

amped up. I'll be fine." Perhaps it would be hard to get through the day tomorrow, but she figured, with enough caffeine, she'd manage...

Her mother cupped her face. "So you really like Aiyana's son? You told me he was intimidating."

"I didn't know him very well when I said that."

"And now?"

She smiled. "I like him. I like him a lot." *Too much...*

The promise of a possible romance seemed to check some of her mother's more negative feelings. She'd been after Cora for some time to settle down and get married so they could have grandchildren, since it didn't seem as if Ashton was in any hurry to provide them. "Will I get to meet him?"

"If you can be careful not to let on to what I'd rather they not know at this point..."

"I won't say a word," she promised. "That's up to you."

Cora slung her purse over one shoulder. "Then I'll bring him home with me next time I come—if he's available."

Her mother sniffed and used the tissue in her hand to dry her face again. "Make sure he's available," she said.

Cora chuckled at her sulky words. "Okay. He'll be my peace offering."

Cora was just getting her purse to head to the cafeteria to meet Darci for lunch when Eli ducked into her room. "Hey," he said. "How are you feeling?"

"Tired," she admitted, but smiled, anyway. She loved the way he looked in the worn denim jeans and soft T-shirt he wore. Because he was so involved in the school's athletics program—as well as caring for the school's animals—unless he had a business meeting he dressed more casually than the other administrators she'd known. But he did such a good job helping Aiyana run the school, and he fit in so well with both the faculty and the students, no one questioned what he wore.

"You got back late?"

Although he'd tried calling her around one to see if she was safe, she hadn't checked her phone until she was on the drive home and by then she felt it was too late to respond. "After four."

"Then you're running on almost *no* sleep."

She covered a yawn as she checked the clock on the wall. "I'm halfway through the day. I can make it."

He didn't pull her into his arms and kiss her like she was hoping he would. When he stopped halfway to her and leaned one shoulder against the wall, she was shocked by the degree of her disappointment, which only alarmed her further.

"So…what's going on?" he asked.

She busied herself straightening her desk so that she'd have a good excuse not to look at him. "What do you mean?"

"With your family. You seemed pretty upset when you ran out of the house yesterday."

"It was nothing," she said. "Just the usual stuff."

When he made no rejoinder, she glanced up.

"Stuff that you don't care to share with me."

Cora caught her breath. Was she being unfair to continue keeping her secret? Part of her was tempted to tell him, to completely unburden herself and let it out. But she was too frightened by what could change. He meant so much to her—already. And she couldn't begin to guess how it would affect Aiyana; she had no idea why Aiyana hadn't wanted her in the first place.

Surely there would be a better time to try to explain her situation—and that "better" time always seemed to be *later*. "Matt called my mother and tried to make trouble for me."

"By telling her you went home with me."

She cleared her throat. "Yes."

"And that caused a problem?"

"Matt and I were together for two years. She cares about him."

"She's hoping you'll go back to him."

Cora stacked some self-portraits she had yet to grade in the box of stuff she took home with her at the end of each day. "Not necessarily. It's just that… I've only been here a month or so. She was concerned that I might be jeopardizing my job." Part of what she said was true, at least. Her parents were concerned about what she was doing in Silver Springs—they were just concerned for different reasons than she'd given him so far.

"By hooking up with your boss."

"Yes."

"Does the fact that you're on the rebound have anything to do with it?"

"I'm not on the rebound," she said. "I'm over Matt." Sadly, she was over him before she even broke up with him. "But we were together long enough that my mother wasn't convinced of that. She expected us to get married one day."

He pushed off the wall and came toward her. "Why didn't you marry Matt? I bet he'd pop the question in a heartbeat if that was what you wanted."

"I wasn't ready. And I didn't love him as much as I felt I should."

He picked up the blown glass paperweight that had been an end-of-the-year thank-you gift from a class she'd substituted for and tossed it from hand to hand. "So did she calm down? Is everything okay?"

"Once I promised to bring you home for dinner."

No longer interested in the paperweight, he put it down as he came around the desk to where she was standing.

"Are you still interested in visiting LA?" She arched her eyebrows in challenge as he drew close. He'd mentioned driving her home to see her folks when they were in bed together yesterday afternoon, but meeting her family said something a bit more in this context. They both understood she'd be bringing him home as "her new man."

Her skirt moved up to her thighs as he lifted her onto the desk and stood between her knees. "What do *you* think?" he asked and pressed his lips to hers in a hot, wet kiss.

His hand slid up under the silky material while his tongue mated with hers.

"Eli!" she gasped when his thumb found its way beneath her panties. "Not here!"

"Shh…it's okay," he whispered. "Give me two seconds. Everyone's at lunch. Your back's to the door, anyway. The worst anyone will think we're doing is kissing."

That was bad enough.

"Meet me at my place after school, okay?" he said as he found and stimulated her most sensitive spot.

She could hardly think straight. "You mean after dinner? You usually work until six."

He ran his nose up her neck, breathing deeply. "Coach Sanders can get football practice started without me, for a change. I've got better things to do today."

"That will be okay? He—" she moaned as a finger joined his thumb "—won't mind?"

The way his pupils dilated and his body tensed made her worry he might try to take this further, but he didn't. "He won't mind. But you're right. I'm only making this harder on both of us." Pulling his hand away, he set her back on her feet as if he had to put her out of reach while he still had the presence of mind to do so. "I'll come up with some excuse," he said. "Then I'll join him for the rest of practice and let you nap. Knowing you're naked in my bed, waiting for me, will get me through the rest of the day."

Which meant he'd also come home to her after. Whatever she'd started with Eli, it seemed to be accelerating very fast.

Chapter Eighteen

Cora enjoyed getting to know her students over the next several weeks, despite facing some difficulties when it came to Zack Headerly. With Aiyana's help, she muddled through the challenge he presented and was actually glad for the opportunity to have something important to speak to her biological mother about. Trying to turn a specific boy around was a project they could work on and feel good about together.

The passing time brought other good things, too. She admired Aiyana more and more as the days went by, and she spent every extra minute she could with Eli. When they weren't together, she looked forward to his calls, texts and lunchtime visits. He often stopped by her classroom if he could. And, true to her word, in early October she took him to meet her folks, which went over well, except they liked him enough that they grew more worried instead of less about what might happen when he found out she hadn't been entirely truthful with him.

"That man's in love with you," Lilly would warn whenever they talked on the phone. But Cora would stubbornly refute that.

"He hasn't said anything about love," she'd argue. Although she longed to hear him speak those three words—had choked them back time and again herself—she was also sort of relieved. As long as he didn't make that verbal commitment, she could justify what she was doing by pretending their relationship wasn't that serious, that they were merely enjoying each other while she was in Silver Springs.

Jill agreed with her parents. "What do you mean he doesn't love you?" she'd scoff. "Of course he does! Maybe he doesn't come right out and say it, but he shows you in so many ways."

Jill, who'd seen them together twice and heard all the details of their relationship over the phone, was right. Cora had his full attention whenever they were together. He never acted like he didn't want to see her. They spent every night together, except for when he'd go out with his brothers or do something with his mother—or she was with Darci, Jill or her big brother, who met her in LA between trips to New York. Even when they split up for various commitments, he'd check in with her often and slip into bed with her after. In addition to all of that, he took her with him to Sunday dinner at Aiyana's every week. He even invited her along when he did extracurricular activities with the students, all of whom had come to view them as a couple. Some jokingly called her Mrs. T—or warned any new student that he'd better not flirt with "Eli's girl."

It was Thanksgiving almost before she knew it, and she and Eli were trying to figure out how to split their time between both families, just like a married couple. They ended up doing Thanksgiving dinner with Aiyana, the Turner boys, Aiyana's parents and one of her brothers—who were all so wonderful to meet—on Thursday and driving to LA to have dinner with her parents on Friday, since Ashton was hung up in New York and couldn't get back until then, anyway.

"He's quiet, but I love the way he looks at you," her mother said as they finished cleaning up after the big meal. Although Eli had helped with the dishes, too, he was now in the living room, watching football with her father and brother.

"You're making more of it than it really is," she said.

"We enjoy each other. But we know it's only a short-term affair."

Her mother stopped scrubbing the big roasting pan she'd used to cook the turkey. "You're still planning on moving back at the end of the year?"

"Of course."

"What about Aiyana?"

Cora did her best to act as though she had everything under control. "I've decided not to say anything—to just… let it go. That solves everything, right?"

"Does it?" she countered. "After everything you did to find her?"

Surprised that it was Lilly who was pressing the issue, Cora nibbled at her bottom lip. This almost sounded as if Lilly would *encourage* Cora to tell Aiyana the truth, even though doing so came with the obvious risk that Aiyana would accept Cora into her life and Lilly would no longer be Cora's only mother. "She didn't want me for a reason, or she wouldn't have given me up. And she must not regret her decision because she hasn't come searching for me."

Lilly turned on the sprayer to rinse the suds from the pan. "You don't know that she hasn't tried. Do you?"

"She could've found me. I found her, didn't I? And I had a lot less resources to work with."

"Maybe she's afraid you won't be happy to see her—that she'll disrupt your life. Or that she'll be stepping on my toes."

"I was facing similar questions and concerns, and I still fought to find her."

"I know, but from what you've told me, she's pretty focused on her work. Perhaps she *will* come looking for you someday when…when she's not so busy."

"I doubt it. Let's face it, 'busy' is an excuse. If I weighed on her mind as heavily as she once weighed on mine, she would've acted by now. Instead, no one even seems to know that she ever had a child." She stood on tiptoe to return a bowl she'd dried to the cupboard. "I guess, when you put all of that together, I have my answer. She *still* doesn't want me. But…at least we're friends. At least I know her. That fills in some of the blanks and helps to… I don't know…anchor me in some way." It especially helped that they thought well of each other. That was so huge, Cora couldn't regret having gone to such great lengths to find Aiyana. Thanks to the sacrifices she'd made, she'd had the opportunity to meet her grandparents and her oldest uncle yesterday, all of whom had been so nice.

"But you haven't been able to ask her about your father," Lilly said. "Or learn why she put you up for adoption. Both of those questions were important to you."

Those questions had helped fuel her curiosity, but she only had herself to blame for her current predicament. Although, in the beginning, her plan had seemed so clever, it had turned into a far-reaching lie that she was now hesitant to expose. "I've made such a mess of everything. I guess I deserve to remain in the dark. I should've been up front—with you, Dad and Aiyana—from the start. I was trying not to hurt anyone. I wanted to test the water first, but then I met Eli, and everything just…spiraled out of control."

"Have you heard from Matt since he called us?"

"To tattle on me?" She grimaced. "Yes. But just a couple of nasty texts."

"He sent you some nasty texts?"

"Only after I called him a jerk for telling you guys," she admitted.

"What'd he say?"

"That I'm not the woman he thought I was. Blah, blah, blah. He also said I should've told you to begin with. He's right about that one."

"But if you'd handled this any differently, if you hadn't

applied for a job there, you would never have gotten to know Eli. Maybe you would never even have met him."

"That's what Matt regrets," Cora grumbled. "He's mad that I've found someone else."

Lilly, who'd wrung out the rag and started washing down the counters, turned to face her. "I think you should tell Eli, Cora."

"About Aiyana?" She shook her head. "No. I've considered that many times, but I'm fairly certain she's never told him that she ever had a baby. I don't have the right to reveal something that personal about her life, in case…in case it will somehow hurt her or what she's established." She retrieved the dish towel she'd been using before and started drying the wineglasses. "Besides, if I tell him, he'll feel like he has to share that information with Aiyana, for my sake if not hers, and I'd rather he not get involved, not be making those decisions for me." She heard a soft *ding* as she set another cup on its bell-shaped top. "So, no matter how I look at the situation, it comes down to the same thing."

"And that is…"

"I need to keep my mouth shut."

Her mother pursed her lips. "What if your relationship with Eli continues to progress? What if someday he asks you to marry him?"

"He won't," she said.

"How do you know?"

"Because he's a confirmed bachelor!"

A skeptical expression claimed her mother's face. "Surely, he'll want a family at some point."

"Why? A family isn't for everyone. He's told plenty of people that he'll never marry."

"Because he doesn't want to need anyone, doesn't want to be hurt again, right? But it's too late to protect his heart.

He needs you. And if he doesn't know that yet, he will soon."

She waved her mother's words away. "That's not true. The students at the ranch are his family. He's got his mother and brothers, too. And look at him—he could have about any woman he wanted if…if he was hungry for that sort of thing."

Her mother gripped her shoulders so that she had to look up. "I think you're underestimating him."

"You don't know what he's been through, Mom."

"Yes, I do," she said quietly. "You've mentioned a few things, so…your father and I looked him up on the internet."

Cora fell silent.

"It's tragic," her mother added in a whisper. "Does he ever hear from the people who…who were so unkind?"

"He hears from his biological mother every once in a while."

"He has a relationship with her?"

"No, he doesn't want anything to do with her. But she hits him up for money when she gets desperate." Jo hadn't called or texted him since he'd told her to leave him alone the last time, but how long would that last? She'd contact him again in the future. He said she reached out every once in a while, when she was desperate for financial support or she felt the need to justify her actions. He said she always tried to convince him that she wasn't to blame.

"How could any mother be like that?" Lilly asked.

"It's tough to imagine."

"Turned my stomach to read about it. But look how he's turned out in spite of them. I'm so proud of him."

Cora felt the same warmth pour through her she experienced whenever she saw him or thought about him. "So am I."

Her mother pulled her into a tight embrace. "I believe

you were brought together for a reason, honey. That it was meant to be."

"And Aiyana?" Cora asked.

Lilly released her. "I guess I'm finally coming to terms with the idea of sharing you."

She smiled wryly. "You just like Eli and know he wouldn't be part of our lives if I hadn't gone in search of Aiyana."

Her mother chuckled. "I admit that's part of it. Acquiring a son-in-law helps soften the idea that I might lose part of my daughter. But I've been doing some thinking—about you and me and the situation."

"And?"

"I've decided that I need to trust love," she said.

"What are you doing?"

Eli glanced up to see Gavin scowling at him for stopping so abruptly. They'd just finished breakfast, were walking down to the hardware store to pick up some parts Gavin needed to repair a sink in one of the dorms when Eli'd noticed they were passing H & G Jewelers. Sight of all the sparkling diamonds on display had caught his attention and caused him to fall out of step.

"Nothing." He pulled his gaze away from what was behind the glass so he could catch up, but turned back almost immediately. He wasn't ready to leave yet; he wanted to look some more. "I've been trying to come up with a good Christmas gift for Cora," he explained.

"You're thinking jewelry?"

"Most women like jewelry, don't they?"

"All the ones I know," Gavin agreed.

Eli gestured toward the door. "Do you mind if we stop in here for a few minutes?"

"Not at all." His brother followed him inside. "What

kind of jewelry are you looking for? A necklace? Earrings?"

It was the engagement rings that'd captured his attention. He'd begun to think about Cora in a different way. As easy and natural as their relationship had been, he'd felt the shift several weeks ago. He'd tried to fight it by giving himself all the reasons he'd be stupid to try to make it permanent. But no matter what he told himself, he couldn't seem to regain his enthusiasm for bachelorhood.

The simple truth was that he'd never cared for anyone the way he cared for her, never enjoyed someone so much. She didn't seem to mind that he couldn't verbalize his emotions or talk about his past, didn't take it personally. That helped, but there were other things about her that made her unique, too. She seemed more relaxed, more confident, more easygoing than any of the women he'd dated before. They just fit together somehow, and although she was still talking as if she planned to leave in the spring, he was beginning to dread the thought of going on without her.

"Eli?" Gavin prompted when he didn't respond.

"I don't know yet," he replied as a sales associate—a woman wearing a Santa hat—made her way over.

"Can I help you?"

"I'm looking for something special to give my girlfriend for Christmas," he told her. "Do you have anything you might suggest?"

"We have a lot of pretty things." She showed him a thick chain bracelet, a ruby heart necklace, some black onyx earrings and several other items. She had a good eye—he thought Cora would like any of the items she'd singled out. And yet his attention kept straying to that case of engagement rings he'd seen in the window.

Once he walked over there, the sales clerk quickly followed and smiled coyly when he met her eager gaze. "Or, if you really want it to be a nice Christmas, you could go for one of *these*," she said.

Gavin gestured dismissively. "Those are wedding sets."

"I know what they are," Eli said.

His brother blinked at him. "And you're still interested?"

Was he? For years he'd been adamant that he'd never tie the knot. But the four months he'd known Cora had been the best four months of his life. He'd never felt more whole or healthy in a psychological and emotional sense. The thought of presenting her with a diamond ring that showed he was not only willing but eager to spend the rest of his life with her was exciting.

It was also a little terrifying, given his past. He'd be launching out into uncharted territory. Would he be able to make her happy? Or would there come a time when things wouldn't be as easy or fun as they were now?

"Yes, I am," he told Gavin and, shaking his head at how quickly he'd fallen for her when he thought he could avoid love altogether, he pointed at a ring featuring a large round solitaire. "That one looks like her."

"Are you kidding?" Gavin cried. "That's a big diamond! It'll cost you ten thousand dollars, at least!"

The sales associate handed it to Eli, and he looked it over carefully. Unfortunately, the price was as high as Gavin had predicted, so he let his brother talk him into putting it back until he could devote some more thought to whether he really wanted to make such a purchase.

But over the next week, all he wanted to do was go back and buy that ring.

"Are you sure she'll say yes?" Gavin asked when Eli brought it up again while they were lifting weights one evening at the school gym. "Because every time I talk to her, she seems dead set on leaving Silver Springs as soon as school gets out. I mean, if she won't even stay here and teach another year..."

Eli had been a little worried about that, too. He knew she liked New Horizons and the area. She liked Aiyana, the rest of the staff, the students, too. And when she was with him? He got the feeling he meant a lot to her. Sometimes, just the way she looked at him seemed to speak volumes—especially when they were making love. But she'd never tried to commit him, never talked as if they had a future together. "I called the store this morning. The owner knows Mom, said I can surprise Cora with the ring and then return it if she says no."

"So you want to risk it."

He finished loading the barbell he was about to use. "The idea of proposing to her—of marrying her—has somehow taken hold of me, and I can't get it out of my head."

Gavin studied him closely. "You love her."

With a groan for the physical strain it cost him, Eli did eight clean and jerks before dropping the barbell. "Yeah, I do," he responded and realized that was the first time he'd ever said it out loud.

Chapter Nineteen

A week later, when Eli got up to play basketball on Saturday morning, Cora fell back asleep, so she was totally out of it when she heard a knock at the door. Eli didn't get many visitors. He gave so much to the school during the day that when he retired to his "cave," as Cora fondly called it, he demanded absolute privacy, and everyone knew it. That was what made it possible for her to stay with him so often. No one made a big deal about her almost living there because no one was privy to what he did, or who he spent his time with, after he disappeared from campus. Aiyana was about the only person who ever came over. Even Gavin and Eli's younger brothers typically called or texted him rather than showing up. So Cora wasn't surprised when she peered through the peep hole to find his adoptive mother on the stoop.

"Shoot," she whispered and waited, hoping Aiyana would realize he wasn't home and leave. Aiyana knew they'd been sleeping together, of course, but seeing Cora standing in *his* living room, wearing *his* T-shirt made it all a bit more…brazen, especially because he didn't welcome a lot of people into his house and she was becoming a regular fixture.

But Aiyana didn't leave. Another knock sounded.

Accepting the fact that she wasn't going to get out of this encounter, Cora used her fingers to comb down her hair and answered the door. "Hi," she said, squinting against the sunlight. Although Christmas was only a week away, the weather felt more like March or April.

Aiyana grinned as her eyes swept over Cora, then took in what she could see of the living room.

Nervously smoothing the wrinkles from Eli's T-shirt, Cora turned to follow her gaze. "What?"

"I've never seen this house look so…homey. My son actually has a Christmas tree—probably for the first time since he moved out of my house. And look, there're photographs of the two of you, and art you've created. Even a few plants. Wow. Who knew so much could change in such a short time."

"I tend to fill my space with the things I love," she said but flushed immediately after because this wasn't "her space."

"This place was pretty barren," she added lamely.

"So was his soul. Fortunately, that's changed, too," Aiyana said, but she didn't allow Cora any time to comment. "Can I come in?"

"Of course. Except Eli's not here. He's—"

"At the basketball court. I know. I tried calling you, but you didn't pick up so I decided to walk over."

Cora didn't get the impression she'd first tried the faculty housing. Aiyana had known right where to find her. "Are you…upset about something?" she asked as she stepped out of the way so that Aiyana could come in. Her mind raced through the past several days, searching for any incident in her classroom that might've warranted a visit from her "boss."

"Not at all. I'd like to go Christmas shopping today and was hoping you'd be interested in going with me. That's all."

Cora felt her eyes widen. "You mean…the three of us?"

"No. Just you and me. Eli's not much fun to take on an extended shopping trip. He's tolerant, if you know what you want and are just going to pick it up. But wandering around, admiring lights and decorations and such?" She shook her head. "Not particularly."

Cora laughed. She'd taken him to Rodeo Drive the last time they visited LA, since he'd never been there, and found that to be true. He was far more interested in seeking out places to eat or heading to the beach to play sand volleyball or go body surfing than shopping. "True."

"I thought maybe we could make a day of it, go to lunch, too. There's a delicious Thai place in Santa Barbara that I'd love to treat you to."

"I'd like that," Cora said.

"Great. How soon can you be ready?"

"Thirty minutes?"

"No rush. Just come over to my place when you're done."

"Sounds like fun." Cora was so excited about having the opportunity to be alone with her biological mother for hours—Christmas shopping, no less—that she grabbed Aiyana and hugged her on impulse. "I love you," she said. "You are *so* wonderful."

Although Aiyana permitted the hug, Cora could tell she was taken aback. When Cora let go, Aiyana searched Cora's face wearing a bemused expression. But then she smoothed the hair out of Cora's eyes and smiled. "I'm so glad you came to us," she said and kissed her cheek, just as she might've done had they been together when Cora was just a child.

Cora's heart was pounding when Aiyana left. She couldn't even make herself get ready. She sat on the couch, remembering every minute of that exchange. There was a moment when Aiyana was staring into her face that Cora had almost told her. She'd come *so* close…

She was still sitting on the couch in a bit of a daze when Eli walked through the door a few minutes later.

"Hey. What are you doing out here?" He used the bottom of his T-shirt to wipe the perspiration from his forehead as he spoke.

Cora summoned the energy to stand. “Nothing.”

His eyebrows came together as he dropped his shirt, which was now stretched and wrinkled as well as sweaty. “Was I gone too long? Have you been waiting for me?” He checked the clock on his phone, which he’d left on the counter. “I thought I’d wake you up when I got back. You usually sleep until nine or ten on weekends.”

“I wasn’t getting impatient. Your mother came by and woke me up.”

He crossed to the kitchen to get a glass of water. “What for?”

“To invite me to go shopping with her.”

“Does she want me to go, too?”

“No. Just me.” That was the beauty of it. Aiyana had sought *her* out. She wasn’t merely a tagalong because she was dating Eli.

“Really.” He eyed her speculatively. “Do you want to go?”

“I’d like to—if you wouldn’t mind me skipping out on whatever we might’ve done today.” They didn’t have any specific plans, but they’d started to spend all their weekends together, so she knew the expectation would be there.

“Of course I wouldn’t mind, not if you think it’d be fun.” He downed his water. “So it’s a girls’ day, huh?”

“That’s how she presented it.”

“With as much as you admire my mother, I bet you’ll enjoy that. I don’t get *any* attention when we go over there on Sundays,” he joked.

“You get plenty of attention—always.” He was almost all she could think about. If only he knew how drastically he’d impacted her in every way. “But you’re right, I’m excited to spend some time with her.”

He walked over, took her hands and straightened the

rings she wore on three different fingers so that the jeweled parts no longer slanted to the left or right. "What is it about her?"

"Nothing," she lied. "I just…like her."

"I'm glad, because she likes you, too. Anyway, I'll take some of the boys riding. I promised those who scored the highest on Mr. Travers's chemistry test that I'd take them out one day."

Cora flinched beneath the guilt she felt for continuing to keep such a secret. "Perfect time to fulfill that promise."

Being careful not to get her sweaty, he leaned in for a kiss. "I'll miss you."

"I have a few minutes," she said with a promising grin and pulled him into the bathroom so they could shower together. She needed something powerful to help her forget the confrontation she knew was coming—eventually.

The day seemed so boring without Cora. That he missed her even more than he thought he would told Eli how much he was coming to rely on her company, which made him a little nervous. Would that turn out to be a bad thing?

If she insisted on leaving Silver Springs at the end of the school year it would…

He held off contacting her until it was almost dinnertime, hoping she'd get back. But then he texted her.

How much longer are you going to be? You guys are taking forever.

We're on our way home.

Have you eaten? Should I turn on the barbecue and grill a couple of burgers? He'd been waiting to eat with her.

No. I'm bringing you sushi. We had Thai for lunch but

ended up staying so long we went to sushi for dinner. It was a great place. You're going to love it.

Did you get all of your shopping done?

Most of it.

What'd you get me? he teased.

Nothing. I already had your present, she wrote back with a winking emoji.

Where is it? I'll go take a look.

You'd better not snoop around! You'll see it at Christmas.

He imagined how surprised *she* was going to be. I've got yours, too. Picked it up today.

I have no clue what it could be.

And she'd never guess. What he didn't know was whether she'd like it.

Christmas morning dawned to dark skies and rain. Cora listened to the soft patter hitting Eli's house as she watched him sleep. She cared so much about him, had never been so in love—and that meant she had to tell him the truth. Every minute they grew closer under false pretenses was a minute she feared he might one day hold against her. Aiyana, too. She'd been sleeping with him for *four months*. That was such a long time to perpetuate a lie, so long she'd definitely struggle to explain why she didn't speak up sooner.

But when she looked back, she couldn't isolate a point in time when she could definitively say, *That's when I should've said something.* As soon as she picked a point like that, she'd realize what the truth could've cost her—Sunday dinners at Aiyana's, the nights she'd spent in Eli's arms and the days she'd spent looking forward to them, the shopping excursion she'd enjoyed with her biological mother last week, being invited to Aiyana's for Christmas Eve. If she'd told the truth from the beginning, most of that, maybe none of it, wouldn't have happened.

Choosing the path she did had enabled her to create some beautiful memories. But if she lost Eli and Aiyana, mere memories would never be enough…

Eli opened his eyes and smiled the second he realized that she was awake. "Morning."

She returned his smile. "Morning."

"Merry Christmas."

"Same to you." She tucked her hands up under her pillow as she studied him. "Would you like to open your present?"

He covered a yawn. "We're not going to wait until we have dinner at your parents'?" They'd spent Christmas Eve with Aiyana and all his brothers last night so that they could join her family today.

"I'd like to give it to you now." Because it was something she hoped would speak to, and comfort, his inner child, she didn't want him facing an audience when he opened it.

"Okay." He sat up. "Let me have it."

She slipped out of bed to grab the box she'd put under the tree after they'd returned from his mother's house last night. Until that time, she'd hidden it in a closet at her place.

"It's heavy," he said as she put it in his lap.

"I hope you'll like it." She sat nervously on the bed beside him as he tore off the paper. "I mean…it's not something the typical guy would probably like, but… I don't know. It seemed to me as if…"

His expression changed, grew less anticipatory and more reflective, as he lifted her sculpture out of the box. Although it was conceptual, she hoped he could tell that it depicted a man holding the hand of a little boy.

"Wow," he murmured. "You made this?"

"I did. I admit I'm not as good as I want to be, but I was trying to create something for you that represented the difference you are making here at New Horizons—in so many lives."

"I love it," he murmured. "I've often stared at that sculpture you created of a mother cradling her child. That piece is the reason I hired you. I've always loved it."

"I've noticed. That's why I attempted this. If you like that one better, you can have it. I just thought it was more important to focus on what *you* are giving others." And not highlight the fact that he didn't at first have the kind of mother who would nurture him as a mother should.

"I don't even know what to say, Cora. This must've taken you hours and hours. I couldn't love anything more."

He seemed so sincere that she let her breath go in relief. "I'm glad. I struggled so long with the way their hands come together. That was the hardest part. It still doesn't look right to me."

"Are you kidding? That part—all of it—is perfect." He studied her gift for several more seconds before setting it reverently to one side. "And now I have something for you."

"You're going to give me your present now, as well? You can wait until we go to dinner, if you want."

"No, I think this is the right time."

"Okay." She felt such excitement. He'd bought her plenty of things so far—lots of meals and treats and even a few clothes when they'd happened upon a blouse or something she liked. She'd bought him stuff, too. But this was their first formal exchange. She thought maybe he'd purchased some art supplies or the painting she'd fallen in love with at the boutique off the beach they'd found last time they went to LA. But what he retrieved from his drawer was far too small to be either of those things.

It was jewelry. Clearly. But what kind?

She grinned at him as she tore off the tiny bow and the pretty wrapping. Inside she found a box with a lid. Under the lid was another box, this one the velvet type. "I never would've expected you to get me jewelry," she said. "We've never even looked at it."

He said nothing, just watched as she opened the lid.

Her jaw dropped the moment she saw the ring, and she blinked several times, trying to decide what it might mean. "This is…this is stunning!" she said. "Literally. I don't know what to say. It must've been *so* expensive. And…" And it looked like an engagement ring! She searched his face, trying to figure out if it *was* an engagement ring as he took her hand.

"Will you marry me, Cora?"

Cora could hardly breathe. This was a proposal—nothing she'd expected to come from Eli. Not this soon. He'd convinced her that he would never take that step, that he couldn't trust enough to take that step. Somewhere in the back of her mind, she'd always hoped he'd find his way around that barrier. But now? She wasn't prepared! She still hadn't told him the truth!

"You keep talking about moving away after next semester," he said. "But I hate the thought of that. I hope you'll stay here, with me. You gave me that statue to symbolize what I'm trying to do here at New Horizons—"

"What you *are* doing," she broke in.

"But you're doing the same thing—making a difference in the lives of young people who need you. *I* need you, too, even though I'm not so young," he added with a grin.

Her gaze met and locked with his. "Are you saying you *love* me, Eli?"

"How can you even ask that? Nothing else could ever make me take this risk. You've changed my life, Cora. Made me whole," he added softly.

Tears filled her eyes as she stared down at the big diamond he'd bought. "This is gorgeous."

He leaned in to catch her eye. "I was hoping you'd simply say yes. Don't you love *me*?"

"I do. Without question. I just…" She wiped her cheek with the back of her hand. "I have to tell you something before I can accept this. I wasn't going to do it on Christmas—I didn't want to ruin the holidays. But… I'm afraid I've put it off too long already. And now you'll hate me, which will make this ring a moot point."

Lines of consternation appeared on his forehead. "What are you talking about?"

She shook her head. "You won't believe it. And what makes it all worse is that I don't even know if I have the right to tell you. I feel like this should come from Aiyana, since you're her son. But…but it hasn't come from her. No one seems to know about me. And once I met you, I couldn't resist you. I tried. Lord knows I tried. Anyway, here we are."

He got off the bed. "That just confused the hell out of me. What are you talking about?"

"Aiyana's my biological mother, Eli." There. She'd said it.

For a moment, she wished she could snatch those words right back. She was so terrified of what they might destroy. But she couldn't continue to live a lie. That wasn't fair to Eli, which meant she didn't really have a choice.

"That's impossible," he said.

"I assure you it's *not* impossible. It's true."

"She had a child." His words rang with disbelief.

"Yes. One she gave up for adoption twenty-eight years ago—to a couple in LA. Brad and Lilly, both of whom you've met. I'm that child."

"But…why would she give you up? Was she too young? Unable to care for you? Aiyana loves children!"

"I can't provide the reason. She was twenty-one, so not outrageously young. That's the thing. I've always wondered why she didn't want me. That's what drove me to come here—that and wondering what my biological mother might be like."

"Does *she* know who you are?"

"No."

He shoved a hand through his hair. "Holy shit."

"I'm sorry. I would've told you sooner, but…it's all been so complicated for me. Once the private investigator helped me locate Aiyana, and I saw that she ran New Horizons and was looking for an art instructor, I believed it was meant to be. What an opportunity, right? I thought I'd apply and hope to land the job so that I could get to know her a bit before…before divulging my identity. I felt if I could only learn more about her, I might understand why she gave me away and be able to determine if she might welcome me back. That's all. I wasn't trying to trick anyone, not in a harmful way. And I certainly wasn't planning on falling in love with you."

He began to pace. "That's why you wanted the job so badly."

She nodded.

"And that's why you were so set on leaving at the end of the year."

"Yes. I didn't see any other choice." She sniffed to keep her nose from running. "As I said, it was never my intent to hurt anyone. That's partly why I haven't spoken up. Once I got to know Aiyana, I realized that there must be a good reason she cut me out of her life. But I've been afraid to find out what that reason is—even while curiosity eats me alive every day. Why would someone like Aiyana walk away from her own baby? It's been nearly thirty years—why wouldn't she come looking for me? And why has she never mentioned that she once had a child—*to anyone*? No one seems to know about me, which is why I feel guilty telling you. It feels disloyal to reveal all of this, as if I'm divulging her most intimate secret—even though it's my secret, too."

His chest lifted as he drew a deep breath. "Are you going to tell her who you are?"

"I don't know. I go back and forth on that every day—another reason why I never told you. I didn't want to burden *you* with the same uncertainty, didn't want you to wonder if you were being disloyal to your own mother by not telling, if that's the way you decided to go. So… I'll ask you the same thing—are *you* going to tell her?"

He sat on the edge of the nightstand. "I feel like I should—like we should do it together."

"What if she's not happy to have me back, Eli?"

"How could she not be happy about that? Look at you! You're gorgeous and so smart and good. What mother wouldn't be proud of you?"

At that point, the emotion Cora had been struggling to hold back got the best of her. As tears began to run down her cheeks in earnest, he walked over to scoop her into his arms. "Don't cry," he murmured. "It breaks my heart to see you cry. Everything's going to be okay. We'll figure it out together."

"You don't hate me?" she asked.

He laughed as he kissed the tip of her nose. "No. If this is the worst thing we ever have to get through—I mean between us, I understand it's been very difficult for you and I'm not making light of that—we're going to be okay."

"So are we getting married?" she asked. "Do I get to keep the ring?"

He reached over to get it. "Absolutely," he said as he slid it onto her finger. "Do you like this setting, or do you want to take it back and pick another one?"

"I want this one," she replied. Somehow it meant more that he'd gone to the trouble of finding what he thought was just the right thing for her.

"I'm glad you like it." He held her chin while he kissed her. "Merry Christmas."

Chapter Twenty

Eli was so happy that he and Cora were to be married that he tried not to let the little detail of her maternity bother him. He could see why she hadn't told him that she was Aiyana's daughter, so he didn't find it hard to forgive her. Being in love for the first time made him hesitant to let *anything* destroy the excitement they were feeling. He knew how wonderful Aiyana was, couldn't imagine her reacting negatively to the news, so he figured they'd wait until the holidays were over and sit down with her and explain everything. He told Cora that Aiyana probably didn't have the support she needed, so she'd made the decision to go with adoption because she thought it would be the best alternative for Cora—and had simply been too engrossed in helping others to search for her.

But the more he mulled over the situation, the more he began to think there had to be other factors he should be taking into consideration. Cora kept saying that the woman she'd come to know would not have walked away from her child unless she felt she had to. So, why did Aiyana feel she *had* to resort to adoption? And how could they find out before dropping a bombshell that could either make her incredibly happy, or bring up a part of her past she preferred to leave buried, even if it did include a child?

He didn't dare approach his grandparents or uncles with the conundrum he and Cora faced. Like Cora had said, it felt wrong to bring *anyone* in on this, especially Aiyana's family, since they didn't have her permission. But there was one other person Eli trusted, one person who also loved Aiyana with all his heart.

"Sorry for the delay," Cal said as he walked into his wood-paneled office, where Eli had been waiting for the past ten minutes.

Eli smiled as they shook hands. He believed Cal to be one of the finest men he'd ever met—and still it felt awkward to speak to him about something so personal. Maybe it would be easier if Cal's relationship with Aiyana had been more clearly defined over the years, if Eli felt as if he could look at him as a father figure instead of just a particularly generous friend of the family. But as much as Cal loved Aiyana, and Aiyana seemed to love Cal, the relationship had never progressed—a mystery in and of itself. "Thanks for seeing me."

"You said it was important."

"It is."

"What can I do for you? Do you need food, equipment, money for the school? If so, you came to the right place."

"Thank you, but…this has nothing to do with New Horizons."

Cal's ruddy face showed concern. "Then what's it about?"

"My mother."

A frown tugged at the corners of his lips. "I should warn you that might change my position. I care about you a great deal. I hope you know that. But my first loyalties will always lie with her."

Eli let his breath go in relief. "Thank you for confirming your devotion. That's why I'm here—because I knew I could depend on that."

"I don't understand."

"You've met Cora." Eli knew he had; Cal and Cora had joined them for several of the Sunday dinners they'd had at Aiyana's over the past few months.

"Yes. A very nice woman. You chose well."

"Thank you." News of their engagement had obviously spread, but Eli wasn't here to talk about that. He scooted forward. "I'd like to ask that what I'm about to say doesn't leave this room. If anyone is going to tell Aiyana about… what I plan to reveal, it should be Cora. Can you give me your word?"

"As long as whatever you're keeping from her isn't harmful to her."

"That's what I'm hoping you can help me decide."

Cal, more somber than Eli had ever seen him, leaned back in his seat and clasped the wooden arms of his leather swivel chair. "What is it?"

As Eli explained, Cal sat motionless, listening.

"You know Aiyana as well as anyone," Eli said when he was finished. "You love her, too. Should we tell her?"

"No."

Eli blinked in surprise. Cal hadn't sounded the least uncertain when he gave that answer. At a minimum, Eli had expected a bit of deliberation. "Because…"

"I'd rather not say."

Another surprise. "You need to tell me. Otherwise, I won't know how to protect *both* of the women I love."

"I'm glad you came to me before…proceeding. I'm sorry for Cora. She must've come to Silver Springs hoping for a happy reunion with her mother, but I'm afraid it's not that simple."

"Why?" Eli lowered his voice. "Was it rape? That's where my mind keeps going. What else explains such secrecy? Was Aiyana brutally attacked? Is Cora's father some scumbag rapist who's spent time in prison?"

"I think it would be easier for Aiyana if that was the case. Maybe then she'd be able to forgive herself. As it stands—" he shook his head "—no amount of atonement seems to be enough."

Eli's heart leaped into his throat. "Forgive herself for what?"

He didn't answer, was obviously still wrestling with his reluctance to break a confidence.

"Cal, as you've no doubt heard, in June Cora will become my wife. Please help me to understand the seriousness of this situation. Trust me to guard the secret as carefully as you have."

"I would if I thought it would help Cora to know..."

"But if she doesn't have a good reason not to, she'll eventually tell Aiyana who she is! The closer they become, the safer she'll feel to do that. And, as my wife, I can only imagine they will get close. That's already happening."

Cal dropped his head into his hands. "Aiyana will never forgive me."

"She'll never know. I swear it."

"Even if she learns, I care more about her than I do myself," he said on a fatalistic sigh. "So...if this might possibly protect her, I'll do it."

Eli could feel his heart pounding in his chest. "What happened?"

"When Aiyana was just a teenager, maybe eighteen, she fell in love with her stepfather."

A sick feeling crept into the pit of Eli's stomach. This was not what he'd been expecting. "She *what*?"

"He took advantage of her youth and inexperience, touched her where he shouldn't, convinced her they were meant to be together—and, eventually, she gave in to his entreaties and ran off with him."

"You've got to be kidding."

"I wish I was. She realized almost immediately that she'd made a terrible mistake, but by then the damage was done. She felt she could never go back. She'd betrayed her mother and taken away the father of her two younger brothers, was positive Consuelo would never be able to forgive her."

"So she stayed with him?"

"She had no choice, had nowhere else to go. They rambled around from town to town, picking up odd jobs and living in motels and dumpy apartments. Before too long, she was so miserable she began to search for a way out and finally met a girlfriend who offered to help. But when she tried to leave Dutch—Dutch Pruitt was his name—he came after her, made all kinds of crazy threats against them both. Your mother was so afraid he'd act on those threats, and hurt someone besides her, that she went back to him and, for the next year or so, was treated as more of a captive than anything else."

Eli's throat had gone so dry he could scarcely swallow. "How did she eventually get away from him?"

"She got a waitressing job. The owner of the place was a retired cop by the name of 'Murph' Matheson, and he and his wife took a shine to her. They helped her get a restraining order against Dutch, let her move in with them and their children. They even insisted she start college and helped with the expenses."

"And the pregnancy?"

"Your mother realized she was going to have a baby a month after she moved in with the Mathesons. But she knew if she kept the baby, she'd never really be rid of Dutch. He'd be part of her life forever, and because she was convinced he wasn't completely sane she didn't want him around the baby. She also knew her mother would never be able to accept the child, would never be able to love it, if they ever reconciled, which was something she was beginning to hope for. So..."

"She gave it up."

"That's right."

Leaning back, Eli took a deep breath. "Did Dutch ever find out about the baby?"

"No. But he would have had she kept it. It took another three years for her to get rid of him altogether. He was a truck driver by then and took his own life by driving his semi over a cliff."

Eli sat rubbing the beard growth on his chin as he attempted to process this information. "Wow..." he said on a long exhale. Even a saint like his mother had a skeleton in her closet, and that skeleton had quite a stigma attached to it.

Cal came to his feet and circled the desk. "Eli, I hope you won't let this damage your opinion of your mother. I would feel terrible if it did. Regardless of her past, I've never met a better person. I don't think she should be defined by that one mistake."

He lifted a hand to signal that Cal had nothing to worry about. "I'm not judging her," he said. "My mother has proven who she is many times over." This just confirmed, once again, that no one was perfect.

But what did he do with the information now?

While Eli was gone, Cora cooked some Cajun pasta sauce for their dinner from a recipe she found on the internet. She was trying to stay busy, but she often found herself staring off into space, wondering if Cal might be able to answer some of the questions that'd nearly driven her mad over the years—and if Eli was getting him to talk. Would Cal know that his beloved Aiyana had had a child? And, if so, had Aiyana told him she'd put that child up for adoption?

Even if he *didn't* know, if the news came as a complete surprise, would he suggest they tell Aiyana who she was—or not?

Cora would've gone to see Cal along with Eli, so that she could take part in the discussion. She really wanted to be there. But Cal was so protective of Aiyana, she and Eli both felt that Eli had a better chance of getting him to open up without her—which left her to wait and worry.

Although Eli was gone for only a couple of hours, it felt like forever. The second Cora heard him at the door, she turned off the stove, left the Cajun sauce in the pan and hurried to meet him. "How was it?" she asked as he came in.

That Eli didn't seem to be relieved or excited made Cora's chest constrict to the point that she could barely breathe. She tried to read his thoughts and feelings as he grimaced and rubbed his forehead.

"It wasn't good," she surmised.

He pulled her over to the couch. "I think maybe you should sit down."

She did as he suggested but perched on the very edge, too nervous to relax. "Cal didn't know anything about me?"

"Actually, he did."

She wanted to feel some hope, but Eli's manner didn't warrant any. "And…"

"It's complicated—difficult to know how to proceed without hurting Aiyana as well as…others."

"Others?" she echoed in surprise.

"That's the thing. This could affect more than just you and her."

"Do you mean Lilly and Brad? Because they're okay with me telling Aiyana. They weren't at first. They felt threatened, to a degree. You know that. But they've begun to understand that I'm an adult now, and I should have the right to know where I come from. They also know it won't change how I feel about them."

"I'm not talking about Brad and Lilly, Cora."

She drew a deep breath and clasped her hands together to stop them from trembling. "Then who?"

He wore a sympathetic expression as he reached over to slide a strand of hair out of her eyes. "Remember how you had trouble telling me that you were Aiyana's child because no one knew she even had a child and you thought you might be revealing something too personal?"

Cora curled her fingernails into her palms. "Yes..."

"That's how I feel right now. What happened to Aiyana, what she did, would be hard to...to cope with. She's not completely to blame—she was so young—but she made some bad decisions that got her into a situation no one would ever ask to be in."

"She was raped?" Cora had wondered that before, many times. If Aiyana had been raped, Cora could understand why she might not care to live with the reminder, so she was surprised when he shook his head.

"No. Cal said, and I agree, that if it had been a random attack, something where she wasn't also culpable, she might've been able to get over it by now."

"You're saying she's *not* over it."

"Not from what I can see. If she was, I believe she'd be married to Cal. Instead, she's pushing him away, denying herself any hope of that kind of happiness and fulfillment."

"She's punishing herself because of *me*?"

"Not because of you. Because of guilt. Because of regret. Because she hurt someone she loves. Cal told me she doesn't believe she deserves to be happy, which is why we see her giving so much to everyone else while continually denying herself."

"*Cal* said that?"

"Not in so many words. But once he explained the situation, I understood. Aiyana's rejecting his love because she doesn't feel she deserves it."

Forcing her hands open, Cora rubbed her sweaty palms on her denim-clad thighs. "But if it wasn't rape, how bad can it be? And if it *is* that bad, why would Cal ever open up about it?"

"Trust me, he was reluctant. He just didn't have much choice, not with you living here and marrying me."

"Your mother wouldn't want me here if she knew who I was. That's the bottom line, isn't it?" She'd told herself she'd accept whatever Eli came back with, take it well. She'd been lucky enough to have Lilly and Brad. But she couldn't stem the bitter disappointment that flooded through her.

"*I* don't believe that, no. And it took some convincing, but before I left Cal agreed with me. As painful as it might be, confronting the truth is the only way you'll be able to have the relationship with Aiyana that you deserve, and then maybe she can finally heal. Sometimes things have to get worse before they can get better."

Those were harrowing words. "So what is it?" Cora asked. "You're going to tell me, right? What happened?"

Eli seemed to have trouble getting started. Whatever Aiyana had done was obviously not something he wanted to expose.

"Eli?" she prompted.

Finally, he managed to explain what'd happened nearly thirty years ago. He did so as diplomatically and kindly as possible, but what he had to say still shocked Cora.

"Wow," she said when he was finished.

"She was young, confused," he added for the second or third time. "What she did is so unlike her. There must've been some extenuating circumstances that we're not aware of."

Cora's mind raced as she tried to imagine how a situation like that could've developed and the damage it would cause. "My heart aches for her as much as it does Consuelo and her younger brothers. No wonder Aiyana doesn't have much of a relationship with those two."

"I'm guessing Consuelo has forgiven her. But I feel like those two brothers might be harboring some resentment, which is why I've hardly ever seen them."

"So what did you mean, it's time for the truth to come

out? We can't tell your mother who I am, Eli. If not for me, she'd be able to leave the past in the past, which is something she's proven she's desperate to do. I love her, too. I didn't come here to bring her misery and unhappiness."

"That's just it," he said. "Once you sit down and tell her who you are—"

"No! Aren't you listening? I don't want to serve as a constant reminder of—of all that."

Eli scooted closer. "Hear me out. Why not tell her and leave it there? I mean, just because you both know doesn't mean *everyone* else has to know."

Her mind raced as she tried to comprehend what he was getting at. But she was still processing The Terrible Secret in which she played such an integral part. "You're suggesting we tell her but not the extended family?"

"Or anyone else. Why would we have to? You'll soon be her daughter-in-law as well as her daughter. If she loves you, spends a lot of time with you, calls you her little girl, no one will think twice about it, even Consuelo or my uncles. From what Cal told me, Consuelo never knew about the pregnancy. Aiyana went through those nine months, and the delivery, alone. She made the decision to put you up for adoption alone, too. Then she did her best to move on and build something out of her life—and she did that alone, too, until she could reconcile with her family, which didn't happen until about five years after you were born."

"She didn't tell *anyone*?"

"Only Cal, and that well after she was back in touch with her family. He said she couldn't talk about those years or the adoption without breaking down. She was too ashamed. And she didn't want to hurt her mother and brothers any more than she already had by announcing the fact that she'd had a baby by her former stepfather."

Cora nibbled at her lip as she pictured what having such a discussion with Aiyana might be like but eventually shook her head. "I can't. I can't tell her if she'll only be sad that I found her. That's not why I came here."

"Cora, listen to me." He took her hands. "Imagine how she must feel when she thinks of you. She gave you up because she was convinced she had to, which means, not only did she lose her family, at least for a while, she lost her only child. That *has* to be painful. She feels she deserves the pain, which is why she's tried so hard not to look back and hasn't taken up a search for you. But if you were to come to her, and it didn't hurt her mother, her brothers or anyone else, I have to believe it might finally fill the hole in her heart. Don't you see? Finding out that her baby had a good upbringing, one in which she was treated well, and has turned into such a beautiful, fully functioning young woman would *have* to erase some of that terrible guilt. It would also make her proud. Having you back… I believe she'd feel complete—at last."

Cora's eyes began to burn with unshed tears.

"You *have* to tell her," he said. "Only you can bring her peace."

Cora almost turned around a million times. If not for Eli's words, his strong belief that she was doing the right thing, she would have. Instead, early the following Sunday, after a sleepless night she spent alone at her own house, she kept walking toward Aiyana's. At least she knew that Liam and Bentley wouldn't be there, that she and her biological mother would have the house to themselves. When Eli had called Aiyana to set up this appointment, he'd asked if the boys could spend the night with him. According to the good-luck text she'd just received from him, Liam and Bentley were still sound asleep. She knew Eli would run interference for her until he received the "all clear."

Everything was ready—except her.

"How am I going to say it?" she muttered as she trudged along, hugging herself against the early morning chill.

Fortunately, the campus was deserted. She was grateful for that, wasn't sure she'd be able to fake a smile if she happened upon a student or fellow teacher. She was close to tears, and she hadn't even arrived yet.

When she did reach Aiyana's, Aiyana answered the door immediately. Cora could tell she'd been waiting and watching for her. Aiyana knew something serious was up; the concern in her eyes proved it.

"Thanks for…thanks for allowing me to come over," Cora said.

Aiyana stood aside and waved her in. "Of course. You're welcome here anytime. I hope you know that."

"I do."

Aiyana led her into the living room where that picture of Hank, Consuelo and family graced the old piano. Cora felt a niggle of doubt when she glanced at it. Once she said what she had to say, there'd be no taking it back. But she knew she'd come too far to change her mind. For better or worse, it was time for the truth.

"Why all the secrecy?" Aiyana asked as they sat, facing each other, on the sofa. "I'd assume it was because you want to arrange a surprise for Eli, maybe for the wedding, but he's the one who asked me to set this time aside and insisted on taking the boys, so…that doesn't seem to fit."

"No, it's not that kind of surprise."

"So he knows what you're about to say."

"He does. Cal does, too. And my parents. They all felt you and I should address this at a time when we could be alone and weren't likely to get interrupted."

Her eyebrows knit above her dark, searching eyes. "*Cal*'s part of this?"

"Yes. And my parents, as I said. But it's a very small,

tight circle, and we all want what's best for you. This is no one else's business but our own."

The color drained from Aiyana's face as she stiffened. "You're giving me the impression this is bad news. You and Eli haven't changed your mind about the wedding. You're not leaving New Horizons."

"No. I love Eli more than I've ever loved anyone. I hope I'll be able to make him happy."

"I know he feels the same about you. You've taught him to trust again. I've been waiting for a woman to come along who had the power to do that. So…"

Cora couldn't help wringing her hands. "Aiyana, I… I'm…" She tapped a hand to her chest as if she could force out the rest of the words, but that was as far as she got before she choked up and couldn't speak.

Sympathetic tears filled Aiyana's eyes. "What is it, Cora?" she asked. "You can tell me anything."

"It's something I've been trying to tell you since I came here. Since the private investigator who…who helped me first find you."

With a gasp, Aiyana covered her mouth. She knew. In that moment, she knew, but Cora spoke, anyway.

"I'm the child you gave up."

"Twenty-eight years ago," she whispered, her eyes filled with nostalgia and pain. "Twenty-nine on February 21."

"Yes. I—I hope you're not upset that I went to such great lengths to find you. And that I didn't tell you from the start. I'm not here to remind you of anything that might be painful or to bring you any unhappiness. I just… I've always craved a connection. And now that I have one, I'm glad. You are everything I ever hoped you would be!"

She sprang to her feet and backed away as if Cora had slapped her. "No, you have no idea who I really am. What I…what I did."

Cora stood, too, and caught hold of her hands. "That's just it, I *do* know. And it doesn't change anything."

A tortured expression claimed her face. "But I'm so ashamed—"

"Don't be," Cora broke in. "Let it go. All the people you know love you in spite of whatever you did in the past. I want to share my life with you as the daughter I am. But as far as I'm concerned, your mother, the rest of your family, everyone else can know me as your daughter-in-law."

"I won't ask you to lie for me," Aiyana said.

"You're not asking me to lie. We'll keep this to ourselves for their sakes. Why would they need to know? Why open that old wound? They never knew I existed in the first place, so they aren't missing anything. I'm perfectly satisfied with that and would be thrilled if only...if only you could forgive yourself and let yourself love me in return."

"I *do* love you," Aiyana said. "I have never forgotten the day you were born. I can't tell you how many millions of times I've thought of you and wished...wished I could at least know where you were, if you were happy, if you had what you needed."

Which was why she'd made it her life's mission to love every orphaned child she could, why she'd adopted so many. Cora could easily see the correlation—her attempt to compensate. "The past is the past. It can't be changed. Just don't deny us a future. Please?"

"I never would." Aiyana squeezed her hands. "I can't believe I have you back, that nearly thirty years of wondering and worrying has come to an end."

Cora smiled through her tears. "Thank you."

"No, thank *you*." She pulled her into a tight embrace. "I'll never let you go again."

Epilogue

"What do you think of this?"

Cora turned to see Aiyana holding a lovely teal bridesmaid dress. Although she'd done most of her wedding shopping in LA with Lilly—who'd made it her new life's mission to throw the most spectacular wedding in the world and had dived in as if they'd given her only six weeks instead of a full six months to plan everything—they'd been unable to find the right bridesmaid dresses. Cora had been hoping to visit Santa Barbara to see if she could find anything different, so she'd invited Aiyana to drive over with her and have lunch.

"Oh my gosh! That's it!" she exclaimed. "Finally! Do you know how many shops I've visited?"

"More than ten?"

"More than twenty!"

"Lilly must've loved such an in-depth hunt."

Cora smiled at the sparkle in Aiyana's eyes. They both knew how much her adoptive mother enjoyed shopping. "She did. I'm sure she'll be slightly disappointed that we came up with this on our own."

"I'll have to tease her about that," Aiyana joked.

"It's a good thing she likes you."

"I never realized that by getting my daughter back, I'd also be getting such a good friend."

They checked the price, sent Lilly a picture and, after receiving her exuberant reply, ordered one in the appropriate size for Jill, Darci, an old childhood friend who Cora kept in touch with every few months, two other friends from high school and a teacher she'd met while substituting at Woodbridge High.

"Well, it's exciting to finally meet with success, but finding the dress so early cuts our day short," Cora said as they left the boutique. "I didn't expect to buy from the first shop we visited."

"We can start searching for something else on the list. What's left?"

"My shoes. I haven't yet found a pair that's both pretty and comfortable. But the restaurant's just down the street, so let's eat before we do any more shopping. I'm starved."

"Me, too." As Aiyana linked her arm through Cora's, Cora felt such a tremendous rush of love and admiration. Her relationship with her biological mother was every bit as good as she'd ever dreamed it could be.

"Thanks for taking the time to come with me today," she said.

"I love being included, love having you in my life. I can't wait for the wedding."

Cora covered her mother's hand as they sauntered down the sidewalk. "We could always make it a double wedding, you know."

Aiyana pulled Cora to a stop. "What are you talking about?"

"Me and Eli—you and Cal."

A blush suffused Aiyana's cheeks. "What makes you think I'd ever marry Cal? We're just friends."

"It's hilarious you'd even try to say that!" Cora said, laughing. "I know you stayed over at his place last Friday, when we had Bentley and Liam."

Her cheeks, already red, turned crimson. "I got home late, that's all."

Cora couldn't quit grinning. "Uh-huh."

"How'd you know?" her mother asked.

"Liam forgot something, so we dropped by the house. Your car wasn't there."

"Liam doesn't know I slept at Cal's, does he?" she said with a gasp.

"He didn't even seem to notice that your car was gone. He was too preoccupied with getting the video game he wanted. And Eli and I didn't talk about it until later, after the boys were asleep."

"I can't get away with anything," she grumbled.

Cora laughed again. "Which brings me back to the idea of a double wedding…"

Seemingly flustered, Aiyana waved her off. "Don't even suggest that! We would never horn in on your happiness."

"You wouldn't be 'horning in.' We'd be thrilled to share the limelight."

"You're jumping to conclusions." Aiyana started to walk away from her, picking up the pace as if she could outdistance the conversation, too. "Let's not even talk about it."

Cora hurried to catch up with her. "He loves you, you know." And the two of them had grown so much closer in the last few weeks. Eli had noticed the same thing.

"I'm too old for that sort of thing," she insisted.

"That's what you always say. But I think you should reconsider your stance—to allow yourself to be happy at last."

Aiyana stopped again and pivoted to face her. "He's mentioned it," she suddenly admitted, sobering.

Cora felt her eyebrows slide up. "And?"

"I'm not ready. But—" her lips curved into a rather shy smile "—maybe soon."

"That's wonderful!" Cora cried.

She lifted a hand. "Like I said, let's not talk about it now. Your wedding comes first. After that's over, in another year or so, I don't know. We'll see."

Aiyana had already revealed far more than Cora had

expected, so she let her retreat behind her usual curtain of privacy and they talked about other things as they walked the final block. Just before they entered the restaurant, however, Aiyana stopped Cora and, to Cora's surprise, hugged her. "Eli's so lucky to have found you."

Cora stared up at the beautiful spring sky visible over her mother's shoulder, grateful that she was finally satisfied and not still questioning, wondering and searching. "And we're both lucky to have you."

* * * * *

Don't miss the next book
in the SILVER SPRINGS *series,*
NO ONE BUT YOU
available soon in e-book

MILLS & BOON®

Cherish™

EXPERIENCE THE ULTIMATE RUSH OF FALLING IN LOVE

A sneak peek at next month's titles...

In stores from 6th April 2017:

- **His Shy Cinderella** – Kate Hardy *and* **Fortune's Surprise Engagement** – Nancy Robards Thompson
- **Conveniently Wed to the Greek** – Kandy Shepherd *and* **The Lawman's Convenient Bride** – Christine Rimmer

In stores from 4th May 2017:

- **Falling for the Rebel Princess** – Ellie Darkins *and* **The Last Single Garrett** – Brenda Harlen
- **Claimed by the Wealthy Magnate** – Nina Milne *and* **Her Kind of Doctor** – Stella Bagwell

Just can't wait?
Buy our books online before they hit the shops!
www.millsandboon.co.uk

Also available as eBooks.

0417/23

MILLS & BOON®

EXCLUSIVE EXTRACT

When Greek tycoon Alex Mikhalis
discovers Adele Hudson is pregnant
he abandons his plans to get even and
suggests a very intimate solution:
becoming his convenient wife!

Read on for a sneak preview of
CONVENIENTLY WED TO THE GREEK

'What?' The word exploded from her.

'You can't possibly be serious.'

Alex looked down into her face. Even in the slanted light from the taverna she could see the intensity in his black eyes. 'I'm very serious. I think we should get married.'

Dell had never known what it felt to have her head spin. She felt it now. Alex had to take hold of her elbow to steady her. 'I can't believe I'm hearing this,' she said. 'You said you'd never get married. I'm not pregnant to you. In fact you see my pregnancy as a barrier to kissing me, let alone marrying me. Have you been drinking too much ouzo?'

'Not a drop,' he said. 'It's my father's dying wish that I get married. He's been a good father. I haven't been a good son. Fulfilling that wish is important to me. If I have to get married, it makes sense that I marry you.'

'It doesn't make a scrap of sense to me,' she said.

'You don't get married to someone to please someone else, even if it is your father.'

Alex frowned. 'You've misunderstood me. I'm not talking about a real marriage.'

This was getting more and more surreal. 'Not a real marriage? You mean a marriage of convenience?'

'Yes. Like people do to be able to get residence in a country. In this case it would be marriage to make my father happy. He wants the peace of mind of seeing me settled.'

'You feel you owe your father?'

'I owe him so much it could never be calculated or repaid. This isn't about owing my father, it's about loving him. I love my father, Dell.'

But you'll never love me, she cried in her heart. How could he talk about marrying someone—anyone—without a word about love?

Don't miss
CONVENIENTLY WED TO THE GREEK
by Kandy Shepherd

Available May 2017
www.millsandboon.co.uk

Copyright ©2017 Kandy Shepherd

CP0417_2

Join Britain's BIGGEST Romance Book Club

- **EXCLUSIVE offers every month**
- **FREE delivery direct to your door**
- **NEVER MISS a title**
- **EARN Bonus Book points**

Call Customer Services

0844 844 1358*

or visit

millsandboon.co.uk/subscriptions

*** This call will cost you 7 pence per minute plus your phone company's price per minute access charge.**